WH
DO WITH A
DUKE

Also by Sally MacKenzie

Loving Lord Ash
Surprising Lord Jack
Bedding Lord Ned
The Naked King
The Naked Viscount
The Naked Baron
The Naked Gentleman
The Naked Earl
The Naked Marquis
The Naked Duke

Novellas
In the Spinster's Bed
The Duchess of Love
The Naked Prince
The Naked Laird

Published by Kensington Publishing Corporation

WHAT TO DO WITH A DUKE

SALLY MacKenzie

ZEBRA BOOKS
KENSINGTON PUBLISHING CORP.
http://www.kensingtonbooks.com

ZEBRA BOOKS are published by

Kensington Publishing Corp.
119 West 40th Street
New York, NY 10018

All Kensington titles, imprints, and distributed lines are available at special quantity discounts for bulk purchases for sales promotion, premiums, fundraising, educational, or institutional use.

Special book excerpts or customized printings can also be created to fit specific needs. For details, write or phone the office of the Kensington Sales Manager: Attn.: Sales Department. Kensington Publishing Corp., 119 West 40th Street, New York, NY 10018. Phone: 1-800-221-2647.

Zebra and the Z logo Reg. U.S. Pat. & TM Off.

First Printing: September 2015
ISBN-13: 978-1-4201-3712-5
ISBN-10: 1-4201-3712-3

eISBN-13: 978-1-4201-3713-2
eISBN-10: 1-4201-3713-1

10 9 8 7 6 5 4 3 2 1

Printed in the United States of America

For Poppy,
the calico cat with an attitude that
we met at the White Hart Hotel in
Moretonhampstead on our 2013 trip to England and
for the staff who made our stay so pleasant.

For Kevin,
as always,
who figures out the trains, buses, and taxis that
get us around left-driving Britain.

And with thanks to
Eve Silver
for pointing the way to Loves Bridge.

Chapter One

Loves Bridge, 1617

> *April 1—I saw the Duke of Hart at Cupid's Inn. Faith! He's so handsome. My friend Rosaline says he won't have anything to do with me—his mother won't let him—but I know better. I'm going to be the next duchess.*
>
> —from Isabelle Dorring's diary

London, May 1817

"You have compromised my daughter, Hart. I demand you offer for her." Barnabas Rathbone sniffed and raised his receding chin. "At once."

The drone of conversation in White's crowded reading room stopped abruptly. Marcus would swear all the men inhaled at the same time and held their collective breath, the better to hear every word of this delightful drama. A few went so far as to peer around their newspapers.

He ignored them. "No."

Rathbone's prominent eyes widened, his fleshy jowls trembling. "W—what do you mean, no?"

The fellow was an even better actor than his disreputable daughter.

"No, I will not marry Miss Rathbone."

Rathbone's mouth dangled open briefly. Then his brows snapped down into a scowl, but not before Marcus saw the panic in his eyes. The man had likely been staving off his creditors by telling them he'd soon be a duchess's father. Fool! Did he think he was the first to try such a trick on the Duke of Hart—or the Heartless Duke, as the wags liked to call him?

When they weren't calling him the Cursed Duke.

"How can you be so cruel? The poor girl is beside herself."

Marcus just stared at Rathbone. Sadly, he had plenty of experience dealing with conniving members of the *ton*. He was far too big a prize for them to resist. Thanks to the curse, if the woman he married had any luck at all, she'd conceive his heir on their wedding night and be a wealthy widow nine months later.

He was bloody well not going to die for Rathbone's benefit.

"You cannot mean to ruin my dear daughter's reputation!" A note of desperation had slipped into Rathbone's bluster.

The other men in White's deeply carpeted reading room leaned forward in their rich leather chairs, newspapers and books abandoned along with any pretense of ignoring the conversation. Their gaze swiveled between Marcus and Rathbone.

It focused on Marcus now.

"Since your daughter has no reputation, there is nothing to ruin, Rathbone."

A gasp burst from their audience and more than a few sniggers—some muffled, most not.

Rathbone wisely chose not to dispute that. "Her heart will be broken."

Now he was grasping at straws. The girl had no heart, either, which some would say made her the perfect match for the Heartless Duke.

Perhaps. But if he had to marry—and he did have to marry someday if he wished to ensure the succession—he'd rather choose a heartless girl with better deportment and perhaps even a little intelligence and wit to make his last days more bearable.

Rathbone opened his mouth again, but Marcus held up his hand to stop him.

"You and your daughter laid a trap, sir, which I refuse to be caught in. That is the end of the matter."

He thought he heard Rathbone's teeth grind.

"I see there is no reasoning with you, Your Grace. You are indeed as heartless as everyone says."

Marcus inclined his head. "One does wonder why you thought otherwise."

The men in the room didn't even try to muffle their sniggers this time.

"Hart has a point, Rathbone," one of them called out.

Marcus didn't look to see which fellow spoke. It could have been any of them. They were like a pack of wolves, attacking at the first scent of blood. Not that he had any sympathy for Rathbone, of course.

Rathbone glared at the man who'd spoken and then glared at Marcus. "I shall take my leave then, Your Grace, but do not think your infamy will be forgotten."

"I do not think it. But neither should you think I will change my mind. You and your daughter need to look for a more achievable way to address your pressing debts."

Rathbone stiffened and lifted his chin again, but his eyes

told the tale. He might try to make Marcus's existence unpleasant for the next few weeks, but he realized he'd wagered and lost.

"Your Grace." He jerked his head in the slightest of bows and strode from the room.

Marcus looked at the other men—they all dived back into their reading material. As he expected, none said a word to him about what they'd just witnessed, but he knew the moment the door closed behind him, they'd burst into excited whispers and then go spread the tale throughout the *ton*. Dolts! He was heartily sick of them.

The club manager came rushing up as soon as Marcus emerged from the reading room. "Your Grace, I apologize for Mr. Rathbone's behavior. If I'd known—"

"It's nothing, Montgomery. Rathbone is a member. He has as much right as the next man to be an idiot here."

Montgomery frowned. "More's the pity. Can I bring you a bottle of our best brandy, Your Grace, to take some of the sting from the encounter?"

If he dosed himself with spirits every time he had to deal with Rathbone's sort, he'd be a complete sot. "My thanks, but no. I believe I'll—"

"Marcus!"

Marcus grinned, shedding some of his ill temper. He knew that voice. He turned to see his cousin, Nate, the Marquess of Haywood, coming toward him with their friend Alex, the Earl of Evans.

"You look as if you'd like to hit something," Nate said quietly, concern coloring his words as he grasped Marcus's hand.

"Or someone." Alex grinned. "And we can guess who that someone is. We just passed Rathbone."

"He tried to pressure you to wed his daughter, did he?" Nate smiled, though the expression didn't reach his eyes. "I'm glad you sent him about his business."

"By Gad, yes. Can't imagine a worse fate than being riveted to that girl." Alex cleared his throat. "Though it *is* quite the story. What actually happened in Palmerson's garden?"

Marcus glanced around. Montgomery had stepped away when Nate and Alex came up, but he was still hovering nearby, clearly waiting to produce that brandy. And he thought he heard Uppleton's annoying voice approaching. There was little hope of having a private conversation here.

"Come along to Hart House with me and I'll tell you over a glass of brandy."

"We just came from Hart House, you know," Alex said as they started for the door. "Your butler was quite insistent that, if we found you, we should tell you that a letter arrived from Loves Bridge."

Loves Bridge? Oh, God. His stomach tightened as it always did when he heard the name of that damned village.

Nate gripped his shoulder briefly in support. "It's probably just something from your steward."

Marcus nodded. Of course Nate was right. It was just Emmett writing about some needed repair. He'd write back as he always did, telling the man to do as he saw fit.

He'd been to Loves Bridge—and his estate, Loves Castle—only once in his life, twenty years ago, when the terms of Isabelle Dorring's curse forced him to select the next Spinster House spinster. The woman who'd applied—a Miss Franklin—had been very young, the victim of some scandal that made her unmarriageable—or so Uncle Philip had said. Nate's father had conducted the interview since Marcus had been only a boy.

He took a deep breath, and the anxiety gripping his chest loosened. Yes, clearly, the letter could not be about the Spinster House. Miss Franklin should live several more decades.

Something he'd not do.

"I will say Finch seemed to be in a bit of a fidget." Nate shot him a worried look as they left White's. "Said he hadn't seen you for hours."

Alex snorted. "A bit of a fidget? The man was almost in tears."

Oh, hell.

"I don't know why he would be. He could have asked Kimball where I was."

Nate's frown deepened. "Kimball seemed quite concerned as well."

"That's ridiculous." Finch he might understand, but Kimball? His valet knew the only cure Marcus had found for his foul moods was walking. And he'd done a lot of walking recently. Miss Rathbone was the third girl to try to trap him into marriage, and the Season was barely underway. "I told Kimball I was going for a stroll. I find it clears my head."

Alex laughed. "The only thing London's smoke and stench clears is your stomach . . . into the nearest gutter."

"Oh, it's not as bad as that." Truth was, he could have walked through a midden and not noticed.

"Perhaps Finch didn't think you meant you'd be *strolling* for four hours," Nate said.

Zeus! Have I really been gone that long?

Alex clapped him on the back. "If you like walking, why don't you shake London's dirt off your boots and go to the Lake District?" For once Alex looked serious. "Finch and Kimball aren't the only ones who've noticed you haven't been yourself recently."

"Confound it! I'm perfectly fine."

Silence. No one—Marcus included—believed that.

"Rolling around in the bushes with a marriageable female isn't your normal behavior," Nate said. He sounded just like Uncle Philip had when he'd scolded them for some infraction when they were boys.

Nate meant well, but his constant fretting was driving Marcus mad. He didn't need Nate watching and hovering and—

But Nate had always done that to some degree. They were cousins, but they'd grown up as brothers, Nate being the elder by three weeks.

"*Did* you have the girl half out of her dress as Lady Dunlee has been saying?" Alex asked.

"Bloody gossips." They'd finally reached Hart House. Marcus sighed. "Come in and I'll tell you the whole sorry tale."

As they climbed the steps, the curtains on one of the windows twitched, and then the front door flew open to reveal Finch, gray hair standing on end as if he'd been combing it with his fingers.

"Oh, thank God you've found him."

For a moment Marcus was afraid the butler was going to fall on his neck and hug him to his elderly bosom, but fortunately the man caught himself in time.

"I only went for a walk, Finch," he said as he stepped over the threshold.

Kimball appeared at Finch's elbow. "But you were gone so long, Your Grace." His fingers shook slightly as he raised them to tug on his waistcoat. "We were concerned. You were not in the best of spirits when you departed."

What had these two thought he'd do—throw himself into the Thames?

Their expressions said that was precisely what they'd feared.

This just got worse and worse. "Well, as you can see, I'm perfectly fine." He forced himself to laugh. "I'm a grown man. You don't have to worry I'll get lost."

Finch looked at Kimball. Oh, Lord.

Kimball cleared his throat. "It's just that your father took to disappearing when he was your age, Your Grace."

Finch nodded. "'Twas the pressure, don't you know."

He should pension these two off. He hadn't considered it before, but Kimball was well into his sixties and Finch had passed seventy.

Kimball swallowed. "It starts the day the Duke of Hart turns thirty and gets worse as time passes. It was that way with your father, and my father said it was that way with your grandfather."

"The curse," Finch said, doom in his voice.

"The succession." Kimball looked as if he might cry. "Marriage and then. . . ."

The last bit of color drained from both men's faces.

Egad, was he doomed to have these two as well as Nate hover over him for the rest of his days? It made death look almost appealing.

"Well, since I have no plans to marry for many, many years, you needn't look so Friday-faced."

The two old men straightened.

"So you aren't going to wed Miss Rathbone, Your Grace?" Finch asked.

"Of course not. Do you think me a complete cabbage head?"

Finch let out a long breath. "Definitely not, Your Grace." He mopped his brow with his handkerchief.

"This is splendid news, Your Grace." Kimball grinned so widely his cheeks must ache.

"Yes, well, perhaps now you can get back to your duties. Oh, and Finch, have a cold collation brought up to my study, will you?"

"At once, Your Grace."

"Those two are worse than a pair of nervous nursery maids," Marcus said once he and Nate and Alex were safely ensconced in his study. "Care for some brandy?" He certainly could use a generous measure.

"It's not surprising, Marcus," Nate said, taking a glass.

"They've lived with the curse for years. They've seen it unfold."

"But it's just a story, isn't it?" Alex took his brandy and sat down in one of the wing chairs, stretching his legs toward the fire. "For God's sake, no one really believes in curses these days. The notion is laughable." He looked at Nate and Marcus and frowned. "Except neither of you is laughing."

"No." Nate took one of the other chairs. "We're not."

Marcus tossed off the rest of his brandy and poured himself some more.

"You can't mean all that drivel the *ton* whispers about Marcus dying before his heir is born is true?"

Nate scowled at Alex. "That's precisely what we mean."

Alex gawped at them. "That's ridiculous. How can you believe that? You're both intelligent men. It—"

"It started two hundred years ago." Marcus leaned against his desk. Oh, God, it *was* ridiculous, but history proved it true. "Exactly two hundred years ago in 1617 when my great-great-great-grandfather insulted Miss Isabelle Dorring, a merchant's daughter."

"He did rather more than insult her," Nate said.

Yes, he had.

"He impregnated her." Marcus took a steadying sip of brandy. "Apparently Miss Dorring thought my ancestor was going to marry her."

Alex snorted. "A duke marry a merchant's daughter? Not likely."

"It seems Miss Dorring didn't realize that." Every time he allowed himself to consider the story of the curse, he wanted to wrap his hands round the third duke's neck and strangle the blackguard. Unfortunately the fellow was already very, very dead. "The bloody man should never have bedded her without making completely certain she understood marriage was not part of their bargain."

Alex arched an eyebrow. "Perhaps she trapped him just as Miss Rathbone tried to trap you."

"Then he should not have allowed himself to be trapped."

There was no excuse for the man's behavior. None. What sort of scoundrel took advantage of a young woman that way? No, if the damned duke had had a shred of honor, he would have kept his breeches buttoned.

Just as *he* would keep *his* buttoned, no matter how many marriageable maidens tried to persuade him otherwise. Even if it killed him.

Which it might. It was getting harder and harder to resist temptation.

"Surely he offered to support the child," Alex said, "if it was indeed his. Women have been known to lie about such things."

"Miss Dorring didn't lie," Nate said. "The fact that no Duke of Hart since has lived to see his son born proves that."

Marcus drank some more brandy, trying to wash away the bad taste this tale always left in his mouth.

The entire decanter couldn't do that.

"And there's no evidence my disreputable ancestor offered his support," Marcus said. "By the time Isabelle Dorring realized her, er, problem, the duke had left on a bridal journey with his new wife."

Alex grimaced. "That wasn't well done of him."

"No, it wasn't."

"So what happened to Miss Dorring?"

"She drowned herself—and her unborn baby—in Loves Water."

"You don't know that," Nate said, as he always did. "Her body was never found."

"What else could have happened?" Nate knew the story as well as he did—Nate's parents had been the first to tell them it. He hated the thought, but he had to face facts. "You know Loves Water is very deep. It's not surprising her body wasn't discovered."

Alex was shaking his head. "It's a very sad story. Tragic, really. But that's no reason to believe in a curse."

"As Nate said, my family history proves the truth of the matter. My great-great-great-grandfather broke his neck going over a jump two weeks before his son was born. My great-great-grandfather died of the ague eight months after his wedding; his wife was delivered of a son two months later. Generation after generation, the same result."

"Your father?"

"Tripped on a loose pavement stone and cracked his head open on the marble steps of this house. I was born six weeks later."

Alex scowled at him. "That's bloody unbelievable."

"Belief isn't required. Finch told me my father scoffed at it all, and he's just as dead as the other dukes."

"So is there no way to break this, ah, curse?" Alex was looking at them as if they'd just escaped from Bedlam.

Nate tossed off the rest of his brandy. "The Duke of Hart must marry for love."

Marcus snorted. "And what is the chance of that happening? Zero." Nate's parents were the only people Marcus knew who'd made a love match. His own mother certainly hadn't.

She hadn't even loved me.

His heart clenched. Stupid.

I'm thirty years old. It doesn't matter any longer.

His mother had dropped him at his aunt and uncle's estate on her way to the Continent when he was a newborn. Last he'd heard, she'd married some Italian count and was living on a Mediterranean island. Someone must be supporting her. She hadn't touched any of her widow's benefits in the years he'd been holding the purse strings.

He wouldn't recognize her if she stepped into the library this moment.

It's a good thing she abandoned me. It gave me a family. It gave me Nate.

Laurence, one of his footmen, came in then with a tray of ham, cheese, and bread. "Mr. Finch wanted me to be sure ye got the letter from Loves Bridge, Yer Grace. It's on yer desk."

"Ah, yes, thank you, Laurence. I see it." News of a leaky roof or crumbling fence could wait.

"What *did* happen with Miss Rathbone?" Alex asked once Laurence left. "I thought you were far too wily to fall prey to her."

"I thought so, too, Marcus." Nate's voice held worry, frustration, and perhaps a touch of anger. "You know you have to be careful, especially now."

He was tempted to tell Nate he'd gone outside to get free of his bloody constant surveillance, but Nate hadn't been the only one he'd wanted to escape.

"You know how stifling a crowded ballroom can be. I just needed some fresh air."

The noise and the stink of too many people in too small a space had indeed been gagging, but he'd also wanted to get away from the Widow Chesney. He'd crossed paths with her at a few events, and she'd seemed willing to explore a more intimate acquaintance. He might be the Cursed Duke—the Heartless Duke—but he was also a man, with a man's needs.

And I'm lonely.

There, he'd admitted it. He could not hope for a long, happy marriage, but he craved a woman's touch, one that he wasn't paying for.

He took another large swallow of brandy. But it had turned out the Widow Chesney did have a price—a wedding ring.

He slammed his fist into the desk. The pain felt good.

"Rathbone must have been watching me. I played right into his hands."

"He likely just saw an opportunity and jumped on it," Alex said. "Rathbone's not the brightest of fellows."

Which made his error all the more galling. Maybe he *did* need a keeper.

Now Rathbone would spread his version of last night's affair throughout the *ton*, and yet another layer of dishonor would attach to Marcus's title.

"I can't believe I swallowed his story that his daughter had gone missing."

"At least you found her," Alex said, trying with little success to muffle a snigger.

Yes, he'd found her. She'd had her hair down her back and her bodice loosened so her breasts were almost spilling out.

His mouth went dry at the memory, blast it all.

"She was hiding behind a bush and jumped out at me. I stepped back, stumbled. . . ." He stared at his brandy glass. The situation would be ridiculous if it wasn't so blasted embarrassing. "We ended up tangled on the ground, which is when Lady Dunlee came upon us."

Alex choked back laughter.

"It is *not* amusing."

"Not when you're the one writhing in Miss Rathbone's claws," Alex said. "But when you're not . . ." He sniggered again.

"You were very lucky Miss Rathbone didn't say you raped her," Nate said.

"It would be hard for her to make that claim. When Lady Dunlee came upon us, the girl had me pinned to the ground and was kissing me."

Nate's eyebrow rose. "And you couldn't stop her?"

Fortunately the study was too dark for his flush to show—he hoped. "It was a good thing I didn't try. If I'd had my hands on her, it would have looked like I *was* forcing her."

The terrible thing—the deeply mortifying thing—was that he hadn't been that anxious to remove Miss Rathbone. He'd enjoyed the feeling of the girl's body on his.

This must be what had finally driven his ancestors into marriage, this overwhelming need for a woman's touch. It was a hunger that went beyond the physical. He'd tried to satisfy it with an assortment of creative, talented light-skirts, and while that had worked for a while, now even a thorough, passionate session with one of London's most skilled courtesans left him feeling unsatisfied.

Nate was frowning, of course. "The London Misses are shameless. You should leave Town for a while."

"Let's go to the Lake District," Alex said. "You're far more likely to encounter a sheep than a marriage-hungry female there."

"Isn't the Lake District rather cold and damp?" Though the thought of getting away from Town—and temptation— was enticing.

His gaze settled on the letter from Loves Bridge.

Hmm. That doesn't look at all like Emmett's hand.

"It's not so bad this time of year," Alex said. "What? Are you afraid of a little wetting?"

"Of course not." He picked up the letter and turned it over. He didn't recognize the seal, either.

"What does Emmett want?" Nate asked.

"This isn't from Emmett." He opened the single sheet. The handwriting was very cramped—illegible, really. At least his correspondent hadn't felt the need to cross his lines, but even so, it was going to be a trick to decipher the message.

He held it closer to the lamp. Ah, fortunately the man had printed his name under his signature.

Randolph Wilkinson, solicitor.

That sounded familiar. . . .

Oh, blast. Yes, it was familiar. Wilkinson, Wilkinson, and Wilkinson was the firm that oversaw the Spinster House. Getting a letter from Wilkinson could only mean one thing.

There was a Spinster House vacancy.

"It appears I have a destination." He let out a long breath and dropped the letter back to his desk. "I'll be leaving in the morning for Loves Bridge."

Chapter Two

*April 5, 1617—The duke smiled at me as we were
leaving church this morning. He has the* most
attractive dimples.

—from Isabelle Dorring's diary

Miss Isabelle Catherine Hutting—Cat to everyone in the
little village of Loves Bridge—wedged herself into one of
the children's desks in the vicarage's schoolroom. Prudence,
her ten-year-old sister, was curled up in the only comfortable chair, reading. Sybil, age six, sat by the window with
her watercolors, and the four-year-old twins sprawled on the
floor, building a fort for their tin soldiers.

A rare moment of peace.

She looked down at the blank sheet of paper before
her. She'd been trying to begin this book for months. The
characters whispered to her when she was helping Sybil
with her numbers or looking at ribbon in the village shop
or falling asleep in the bed she shared with her eighteen-
year-old sister, Mary, but the instant she had a quiet moment
and some paper, they went silent.

Well, she would force them to speak. She dipped her pen into the inkwell.

Vicar Walker's oldest daughter, Rebecca, smiled at the Duke of Worthing.

No, that wasn't quite right. She scratched out the words and started over.

Miss Rebecca Walker, the vicar's oldest daughter and the village beauty, smiled at the Duke of Worthing.

Oh, fiddle, that sounded stupid. Who would wish to read a novel that began with a beautiful ninny grinning at an arrogant, persnickety duke? She should—

No, she should not. How many times had Miss Franklin told her she needed to write the story before she started to pick it apart? She—

Sybil screeched, and Cat's hand jerked, spattering ink all over her paper *and* her bodice. Drat!

"What is it, Sybil?"

Not that she needed to ask. She could see what it was—or rather, who it was. Thomas and Michael had lost interest in their fort and come over to torture their sister. They'd managed to spill water all over Sybil's painting.

"Look what they've done," Sybil wailed, picking up her soaking masterpiece and flourishing it for Cat's inspection just as Cat reached her.

The wet paint joined the ink on her bodice. It was a good thing this wasn't one of her favorite dresses.

She peeled the picture off her front and inspected it. It was impossible to discern its original subject. Something blue and green and white and black judging from the paint smears.

"We just wanted to see the sheep," Thomas said, his eyes wide with innocence—until you looked more closely and noted the mischievous gleam. He was only four, but he was going to grow up to be a complete terror, worse even than fifteen-year-old Henry or thirteen-year-old Walter.

How Papa, a vicar, had managed to beget so many wild boys was one of God's many mysteries.

"Sheep?" Sybil screamed. "Those were clouds, you noddy."

Thomas put his hands on his hips and rolled his eyes in an especially annoying way—a trick he'd learned from Pru. "Paint clouds? That's m-mutton-headed." He grinned, clearly pleased with the new word he'd learned, likely from his brothers.

She should be happy he hadn't learned any worse words . . . or at least hadn't used them yet.

Sybbie's brows snapped down, and her jaw jutted out. Oh, lud. She was going to have one of her explosions, which was exactly what Thomas was trying for.

"Clouds are an excellent thing to paint," Cat said quickly, laying a supportive—and restraining—hand on Sybbie's shoulder. "Many famous artists include clouds in their work."

Michael pulled on Cat's skirt. "We just wanted Sybbie to play wif us."

Sybbie saw the perfect counterattack. She raised her nose in the air and sniffed. "I don't play with babies."

God give her strength! Cat lunged for Thomas and caught him before he could reach Sybbie.

"We're *not* babies." Thomas, his little fists clenched, struggled to free himself from Cat's grasp. "And you've made Mikey cry."

Michael was the sensitive twin. Cat wrapped her free arm around him while keeping a strong hold on Thomas. Thomas was still determined to hit Sybil, and Sybbie, of course, wasn't helping matters. She'd crossed her arms and curled her lip into a six-year-old's approximation of a sneer.

Cat looked over at Prudence for help.

Prudence turned another page in her book. She didn't even glance Cat's way.

Cat had a sudden, almost uncontrollable urge to scream as loudly as Sybbie had. *She* didn't want to play with the boys, either. She wanted to be left alone in blessed, wonderful, heavenly quiet to write. She wanted, desperately, to have a book she'd written sitting on the lending library shelves. Miss Franklin thought she had the talent. All she needed was time. Some quiet. A few moments to herself.

She might as well ask for the moon and the stars. When she'd mentioned writing a novel to Papa, thinking he might let her spend an hour or two in his study every day, he'd laughed. Neither he nor Mama saw the point in telling stories that had never happened about people who didn't exist.

"No, you're not babies, Thomas." She forced herself to smile. She must remember that while they weren't babies, they were still very little. They needed her. "Leave Sybbie alone. I'll play with you."

Michael's face lit up. "Oh, good! I'd rather play wif you than Sybbie, Cat. Sybbie fusses."

"I don't fuss."

"Sybbie." Cat gave her a warning look. There was no need for more brangling. "Why don't you get back to your painting?"

"But there's water everywhere."

Cat made herself smile again. Smiling made it difficult to shout. "Pru will help you clean things up, won't you, Pru?"

Prudence kept reading.

Cat took a deep breath and smiled harder. "Prudence, please help Sybbie clean up."

Silence.

"Pru!" All right, sometimes shouting was necessary.

Prudence finally looked over at them. "Why? I didn't make the mess."

Another deep breath. "No, but there's rather a lot of water, and Sybbie can't reach the rags." Plus Sybbie would probably leave a puddle on the floor that someone—likely Cat—would slip in. "And I'm busy with the twins."

Pru rolled her eyes, heaved a dramatic sigh, and marked her place in her book before closing it. You would have thought Cat had asked her to lap the water up with her tongue. "If I have to."

Cat kept smiling. She must set a good example. Anger was a waste of energy. Telling Pru exactly what she was thinking would only give Pru an invitation to start an argument, and arguing with Pru wouldn't get the water mopped up.

"Cat." Michael tugged on her skirt again. "You said you'd play wif us."

And pulling caps with Pru would upset Michael and get Thomas stirred up again.

She swallowed her spleen. "Thank you, Pru."

Pru grumbled, but she got the rags.

Cat allowed herself one longing look at the uncomfortable school desk and then sat down on the floor with the boys.

"You can have these," Mikey said, pushing a few soldiers—the ones with faded or chipped paint—toward her.

She lined them up. She'd played this game before. It didn't take any thought. She could spend the time planning her book. She—

"Make them attack," Mikey said.

Thomas nodded. "They have to attack so we can capture and kill them."

Boys could be so bloodthirsty.

She marched a soldier forward to meet his fate. "Look, men, a bloody Frog!"

"Thomas!"

Thomas kept his eyes on his toys. "Soldiers don't mind their language, Cat."

"Perhaps not, but you will. What would Papa say?" Well, Papa might not care very much. "What would Mama say?"

Thomas made a face and then in a very high voice said, "Oh, dear, it's a French soldier."

Thomas was going to be even more of a handful than Henry or Walter.

But he was going to be *Mama's* handful. Not Cat's. She was twenty-four years old. If she didn't find some way of getting free of her family, she would never write a paragraph, let alone an entire book. But what could she do?

If only she'd been born male. Life was so much easier for men. They could go where they pleased and do what they wanted. Just look at Henry and Walter. Mama never asked them to mind their younger siblings, but when Cat had been their ages—

Oh, all right. If Mama ever left either of those two in charge, the twins would be sure to free all the chickens in the coop and then race Farmer Linden's pigs down the village green.

Mikey erupted into shooting noises. Thomas yelled and made the sound of horse hooves charging over the ground. Cat's soldier was knocked down and dragged off to the dungeon.

"Cat."

Cat looked over her shoulder. Mama had poked her head into the schoolroom. "Yes, Mama?"

"I need you to take a basket over to Mrs. Barker. Papa said he heard her gout is bothering her." Mama smiled as her eyes drifted to a point just over Cat's head. "I thought she could do with some treats."

Right. Nasty old Mrs. Barker whose son just happened to be a prosperous, churchgoing, *unmarried* farmer.

"Can't Henry or Walter take it?"

"Of course not," Pru said, giggling. She'd finished helping Sybbie with the water and was back to her book. "*They* can't marry Mr. Barker."

Mama laughed uneasily. "Now, Pru, don't be silly. The boys are with Papa, studying their Latin."

And they would leap at the chance to get free of their lessons. Neither was an enthusiastic scholar.

"And Mary?" Cat asked. But Mary would be busy, too, of course.

"Mrs. Greeley will be here shortly to finish fitting her for her wedding dress."

Mama would love it if Mrs. Greeley could start in on Cat's dress the moment she finished Mary's.

Tory and Ruth, the two sisters right under Cat, were already wed and procreating. Mary was going to step into parson's mousetrap in less than two weeks, and then there would be no more daughters but Cat to marry off until Pru was old enough in seven or eight years.

If things were bad now, they were about to get infinitely worse.

Perhaps she *should* consider Mr. Barker. He was certainly willing. He popped the question every few months and then laughed and patted her arm when she declined, promising he'd try again—and again—until she said yes.

Which only made her want to kick him in his patronizing shins.

However, marrying Mr. Barker *would* get her out of the vicarage—

And into his house with his cross-tempered, managing mother.

Oh, no, she was not doing that. Of course not! Even if Mrs. Barker were a saint—which she most certainly was not—her son had squinty little eyes and a beaklike nose and crooked teeth. He wore the distinct, pungent scent of manure the way other men wore eau de cologne.

And he would expect children. She'd have to—

Her stomach knotted.

She wasn't that desperate to get free of the vicarage.

"Mama, surely someone else can take the basket."

"I'm afraid there really is no one else." Mama's face was set, her eyes steely.

Cat sighed and played one last, desperate card. "All right. I'll bring Michael and Thomas with me." Neither Mr. Barker nor his mother liked the twins, so their presence should keep the visit short.

"I don't want to go," Thomas said. "Mrs. Barker's mean. She has a wart on her nose just like a witch. And her cook makes nasty biscuits."

Mikey nodded. "And Mr. Barker's horse tried to bite me when I petted him."

Mama frowned at the twins, but refrained from lecturing them for criticizing their elders. "It is much too far for you boys to walk." She smiled at Cat. "You go by yourself, dear. Take your time and have a nice visit with Mrs. Barker."

"There are no nice visits with Mrs. Barker," Sybbie said.

Mama glared at Sybbie before turning back to Cat. "And then perhaps Mr. Barker will be free to give you a ride home in his gig."

Now there was a treat. Mr. Barker's sullen, plodding horse could make a fifteen-minute ride last thirty, and the man's excruciatingly boring conversation made those thirty minutes feel like an eternity. The last book he'd read—perhaps the *only* book he'd read—was *Jeramiah Johnson's Thoughts on the Methods of Raising Sheep, including a Discourse on Breeding and Shearing*.

"That will give him ample opportunity to propose." Pru sounded as if she was going to choke on her laughter. "It's almost time for him to ask again, isn't it?"

"Pru!" Mama said sharply, her patience clearly at an end. "It is unbecoming to be so pert."

"Yes, Mama." Pru sounded contrite, but the look she sent Cat rivaled Thomas's for evil glee.

Cat narrowed her eyes. . . .

No, she was twenty-four. She should not stoop to a ten-year-old's level.

Michael's small fingers crept into hers. "You won't really marry Mr. Barker, will you, Cat?"

"Now, Michael, Mr. Barker is a fine man," Mama said. "I'm sure you'll come to like him once you know him better."

"I will?"

"Well, I won't." Thomas thrust his chin forward and crossed his arms over his little chest. "I'll never like him."

Cat gave Mikey's hand a reassuring squeeze and hurried to speak before Mama could snap at Thomas. "I know Mr. Barker quite well, Mama, and I am convinced we shall not suit."

Mama frowned. "But eligible men don't grow on trees, Cat, and you are twenty-four, after all. Try to see the man's good qualities." She raised her brows, giving Cat her "significant" look. "None of us is perfect, you know. At least keep an open mind."

An open mind? Did Mama think she was suddenly going to find footrot and tapeworm and other sheep maladies fascinating?

Not bloody likely.

Cat smiled. It was that or scream. "Yes, Mama."

Why couldn't she be free of her family like Miss Franklin was? The woman had the entire Spinster House to herself. She ran the village's small lending library, but when she wasn't there, she had the freedom to do what she wanted when she wanted. She could read or write or stand on her head, and no one would interrupt or criticize her. Just the other day, she'd told Cat she'd been learning to play the harpsichord.

If only *she* could have such wonderful solitude. Then she could write any number of books.

"I only want you to be happy, Cat," Mama said.

She knew that. She just didn't agree that marriage was her path to happiness.

Drat it all, she *would* find another way.

Mama's eyes had dropped to Cat's bodice. "Good heavens, whatever happened to your dress?"

"I had a bit of an accident."

"I should say so. You'll want to change before you go to see the Barkers."

Normally she would, but Mrs. Barker hated any untidiness. Mr. Barker, too. This might be a golden opportunity to give them a disgust of her. "Oh, no. If dear Mrs. Barker is in pain, I shouldn't delay an instant."

Mama saw through her ruse, of course, but chose not to pursue the matter. "Very well. Just keep your cloak on." She frowned. "Though you may be a trifle warm."

She would be melting. Mrs. Barker always insisted on a roaring fire in her sitting room. "Yes, Mama." She gave Mikey's hand one more squeeze before she let go. "Where is the basket?"

"In the kitchen. And do give Mrs. Barker my best."

Cat stopped in her room on her way downstairs and found Mary dancing around in her shift. She was tempted again to roll her eyes like Pru.

Mary paused to stare at Cat's bodice. "What happened to you?"

"Sybbie and the twins got into a bit of a brangle." Cat grabbed her cloak.

"Aren't you going to change?"

"No."

Mary's eyes narrowed. "Where are you off to?"

"To deliver a basket to Mrs. Barker." At least once Mary wed, Cat should have a bed to herself . . . unless Mama decided to move Pru in with her. Pru often complained that Sybbie thrashed in her sleep.

"She won't like it if she sees you're not precise to a pin."

"That's what I'm hoping."

Mary laughed. "And you know she's sure to complain about it to Mr. Barker." She shook her head. "I don't know why you don't accept the man's offer. You could have been wed long ago."

"And sharing a house with Mrs. Barker."

Mary grinned. "There *is* that. I'm not sure even Mr. Barker's broad shoulders trump his mother's carping disposition."

"They don't. Nor do they trump his unattractive features, his barnyard scent, his braying laugh, or his deadly dull conversation."

"Well, no one's perfect."

"I *know* that." Did everyone think her a silly girl dreaming of a knight in shining armor? "I'm certain Mr. Barker will make a wonderful husband—for someone else." She snatched her bonnet off its hook. "I have no interest in marriage."

"You will someday, Cat. You just need to meet the right man." Mary stared dreamily at herself in the cheval glass and started dancing again. "Someone like my Theo."

Theodore Dunly was a nice enough fellow. He worked at Loves Castle as the assistant steward. He was even moderately well-read. But he'd never made Cat's heart beat faster.

A good thing, as he was head over heels in love with Mary—as Mary was with him.

"I think I'm just not the marrying kind."

She must have sounded a little wistful, because Mary's face stilled into her annoyingly serious, slightly pitying expression.

Drat it, she *wasn't* wistful. Or . . . well, maybe she was just a little, when she saw how happy her married sisters were.

"You *will* find a man to love, Cat. I'm sure of it."

But once Cat reminded herself how much Mama and Tory and Ruth had to work, all the cooking and cleaning and sewing and nursing they did, how they never had a moment to themselves—then she was very happy she had no intention of marrying.

"I doubt it. But in any event that man is *not* Mr. Barker."

Mary came over and touched her arm. "Perhaps not, but don't give up hope."

Cat snorted. "Hope? What am I to hope for? That one of the village toads suddenly turns into a prince? I've seen all the available men, Mary, and not one of them tempts me for even an instant to give up my freedom."

Mary shook her arm, impatience creeping into her voice. "But you don't want to live with Mama and Papa for the rest of your life, do you?"

"I'd rather live with them than Mr. Barker and his mother."

Mary waved that away. "All right, I'll agree Mr. Barker isn't a suitable candidate for your hand, but that doesn't mean there isn't a man out there somewhere for you." Mary grinned. "Perhaps he's riding into Loves Bridge right now."

She would *not* roll her eyes. She was not ten years old. "Don't be ridiculous. No one ever comes to Loves Bridge."

"I don't know why. We're not that far from London."

"Oh, come, Mary. You do know why. There's nothing to see or do here. We're a sleepy, little, boring village."

Boring didn't begin to describe Loves Bridge. Each day was exactly the same as the one before it. There were never any surprises. How could there be? Everyone knew every little detail about everyone else all the way back to their great-great-great-grandparents. Life was all gossip and weather and sheep. Perhaps if she lived in London, she'd have something to write about.

But she wasn't going to Town. And, truthfully, the thought of London made her nervous. She'd never been there, but she'd read about its crowds and noise and filth.

Mary put her hands on her hips. "How can you say Loves Bridge is boring? What about . . . what about our fairs?"

"What about them?" The fairs were enjoyable enough, but only the villagers attended.

"I met Theo at the one last summer."

"You didn't meet him there—you just *noticed* him there. You've known him for years." Or perhaps it was Theo who had noticed Mary. Whichever it was, the two had been inseparable ever since.

Mary stomped her foot. "Ohh, you can be so maddening, Cat."

"Yes, I can, so it's a good thing I have no plans to wed."

"But what about love?"

Cat felt herself flush. Love—the love between a man and a woman—was not something she knew much about. She'd seen Papa catch Mama around the waist from time to time and try to steal a kiss while Mama laughed and pretended to push him away. And Mama and Papa *did* have ten children. . . .

It was all exceedingly embarrassing.

Mary was blushing, too, but for other reasons. "Love is wonderful, Cat. When Theo kisses me . . ." Her eyes grew soft and dreamy.

Good God. She was going to lose her breakfast if Mary kept this up.

Frankly, kissing had never sounded the least bit appealing, not that she'd tried it. But having a man's lips mashed up against hers? Ugh. And how did one keep from bumping noses?

She did not intend to find out.

Mary was quite correct about one thing, though—she did not want to live with Mama and Papa for the rest of her life. She just needed to think of some way to avoid that fate that didn't involve yoking herself to a male. The Spinster House would be the perfect solution, but there was no vacancy. Miss Franklin would likely live there many more years.

Mary had waltzed back to the cheval glass and was

looking at herself from various angles. "You never know what fate has in store for you, Cat. Perhaps the man you'll fall in love with is standing on the vicarage steps right now."

"I thought you said he was just riding into the village. He must move very quickly. Loves Bridge is small, but it's not *that* small." Fall in love? That sounded as pleasant as falling into a dunghill.

Mary glared at her. "Must you be so literal?"

Someone should keep focused on the real world. "Pardon me. Of course, he's on the steps—right next to the king of the fairies."

"Oh, you're impossible. It would serve you right if you did go to your grave a spinster."

"It would certainly serve me well."

She left the room and started down the stairs. It should take her only half an hour—twenty minutes if she walked briskly—to get to the Barker farm. If she was lucky, Mrs. Barker would take one look at her stained dress, sniff, and send her on her way—after first grabbing the basket, of course. If she encountered Mr. Barker, a quick escape would be a bit more difficult, but she should still be able to—

There was a knock on the front door. It was probably Mrs. Greeley come to put the finishing touches on Mary's gown. She hurried down the last few steps to let the woman in.

"Mary's waiting for you—oh!"

She blinked. It wasn't stout, bespectacled Mrs. Greeley. It was a tall, athletically built man. He took his hat off to reveal thick, brown hair, bowed slightly, and smiled.

He had the most attractive dimples.

She'd always thought dimples effeminate, but these were completely masculine and strangely seductive, inviting her to come closer, daring her to do something dangerous—

She took a deep breath. What was the matter with her?

The man was clearly wondering the same thing. His right

eyebrow arched up. He'd been saying something, and she hadn't heard a word of it.

She laughed nervously, feeling very much off balance. "I'm so sorry, sir. I wasn't attending. I thought you were Mrs. Greeley. Not that you look like Mrs. Greeley, of course, but, you see, I was expecting her."

Drat it, now she was blathering like a complete ninny. She *had* to get a grip on herself.

His eyes—his very nice brown eyes with long lashes that also should seem effeminate but didn't—had widened and now gleamed with suppressed laughter.

The situation *was* rather ridiculous.

She pulled the door open wider. He was just another man.

The man she'd fall in love with . . .

Ha! He was just as likely—no, more likely—to be the king of the fairies. "Please come in. Are you here to see my father?"

"If your father is the vicar, then yes, I am." He stepped over the threshold. "And who is Mrs. Greeley, if I may ask?"

His voice, now that she was finally listening to it, was warm, educated, and as seductive as his dimples.

And she was as shatter-brained as Mary, but with less reason. With *no* reason. Mary was on the verge of marriage; Cat was on the verge of making an utter fool of herself.

She did wish she'd taken time to change her dress though. His eyes had flicked down to her disreputable bodice.

Idiot! The man wouldn't care if she was dressed in sackcloth—which this dress much resembled even without the stains. She'd never been very interested in fashion.

"Mrs. Greeley is the village dressmaker. She's coming to finish Mary—my sister's—wedding dress."

He was taller than any man she'd met before, with broader shoulders—

No, he couldn't have broader shoulders than Mr. Barker. It must be the cut of his coat.

He certainly smelled better than Mr. Barker. Not a whiff of the barnyard about him.

"I see. And you are . . . ?"

"Miss Hutting, the vicar's oldest daughter." She forced her lips into a polite smile. The sooner she deposited this fellow with Papa, the sooner she'd get her errand done and her wits back. "If you would like to put your hat on the table there and come with me, I'll take you to see my father."

"I don't mean to keep you." He gestured to her cloak and bonnet.

"My errand can wait." She hung her things on a hook by the door. "Who should I tell him is calling?"

"Hart." His eyes watched her carefully as if expecting her to say something. Odd.

She turned toward Papa's study. "Are you new to Loves Bridge, Mr. Hart?" Of course he was. A man who looked like he did couldn't put his big toe in the village without everyone talking about it.

"Er, not exactly, though I haven't been here in many years. And I'm not Mr. Hart."

She turned, her hand raised to knock on the study door. "I'm sorry. Did I mishear?" Hart was not that complicated a name, but it did seem that her wits had gone wandering this afternoon.

The right corner of his mouth tilted up in a very attractive manner, his eyes still oddly watchful. "No. You merely misunderstood. Hart is my title, not my name."

"Oh." She hadn't thought of that. Silly of her. He was clearly a London gentleman, though, in her defense, it was as she'd told Mary—no one, and certainly no member of the nobility, ever came to Loves Bridge. "My apologies, Lord Hart."

"Not Lord Hart."

He was still watching her.

Damnation, what was he about? He clearly expected her to recognize him.

"Well, why don't you just come out and tell me who you are, sir, rather than have me play this silly guessing game?" She should be horrified at speaking so sharply to a guest, but she was too annoyed—and something else—to hold her tongue. "Are you King Hart or Prince Hart or the Duke of—"

Oh.

His mouth curved into a sardonic smile. "That's right. I'm the Duke of Hart." He bowed again, but this time the movement was self-mocking. "Or, as you may know me, the Cursed Duke."

Chapter Three

April 10, 1617—I encountered the duke again this afternoon when I was out walking. He offered me his arm. Such manners! Such presence! He makes all the local men look like callow boys. (And his arm was rock hard. I venture to guess he has very impressive muscles.)

—from Isabelle Dorring's diary

"Oh, Your Grace, I didn't mean . . . That is, I'm sorry I . . . I had no idea . . ."

He watched the girl flush and stammer.

He should speak, put her at ease, tell her it meant nothing.

He couldn't force a single word past his lips. Desire's hot fingers had wrapped themselves around his throat and squeezed, robbing him of breath and thought and reason. Need beat insistently behind his forehead . . . and rather lower down on his person.

Bloody hell. This was worse than anything he'd felt before.

He could *not* feel this way for this girl. She was a vicar's daughter. She could not be had without marriage, and marriage would start the clock ticking to his death. Yes, she was pretty, but she was not worth dying for. Hell, for all he knew she was a conniving shrew, worse even than Miss Rathbone.

None of his arguments had the least effect on the lust surging through him.

Her reddish gold hair gleamed, and her wide green eyes shone with spirit and intelligence. And desire. She might not realize it, but he'd swear she'd wanted him, too, if only for a moment. The flash of heat he'd seen in her lovely eyes when she'd looked at him had been unmistakable.

Zeus, his cock was going to poke a hole through his pantaloons. He needed to get control of himself. He glanced down again at her stained bodice. See? She was a bit slovenly.

Who the hell cared about a dress? It was what was under the bodice that was of interest, and Miss Hutting looked to have a very lovely pair of—

He could *not* allow his mind to travel in that direction.

Kimball and Finch were right. The urge to wed grew stronger and stronger after a Duke of Hart turned thirty. This insane desire must be part of the curse.

He would not succumb.

He cleared his throat. "Please." He cleared it again. "Don't apologize. The fault is mine for not immediately identifying myself." Though how she could not have recognized his title was beyond comprehension. In Loves Bridge, the curse's birthplace, he should be notorious.

And with the Spinster House empty, he should be expected.

"I was only four the last time you were here." She smiled. "I still remember your shiny black traveling coach with the beautiful gray horses."

That would make her twenty-four now, more than old enough to be married. Likely she *was* a shrew.

"I'm afraid I didn't appreciate anything about that journey. I was rather sulky at having been dragged here for something I didn't understand nor care about." Oh, hell, why had he said that? It didn't matter what he'd felt.

Her eyes softened.

"You must have been very young."

"I was ten years old."

She frowned. "Only a boy. You should never have had the burden of choosing the next Spinster House spinster."

No woman had ever looked at him that way before, as if she was seeing the child he'd been. It made him feel very odd.

This entire conversation was odd.

"It was my duty as the Duke of Hart."

Her expression didn't change. "But you were so young. I can't imagine my brothers even now at thirteen and fifteen making such a decision."

"They aren't dukes." And now he sounded ghastly high in the instep. He forced himself to smile. "It wasn't so bad. There was only one candidate, and my uncle interviewed her. I just had to sit still and pretend to pay attention."

She grinned at him suddenly, and his heart twisted.

Indigestion. The cook at Loves Castle had been extremely flustered by his arrival. None of the food had tasted off when he'd eaten it, but something must have been bad. He'd check with Nate and Alex when he got back to the castle to see if they were also feeling out of curl.

Nate would never have let me come alone if he'd known the vicarage harbored this beauty.

"Well, I'm still impressed that you cooperated, as you'll understand when you meet Henry and Walter." She turned to knock on the door behind her.

Having a curse hanging over one's head tended to encourage cooperation.

"Come," a male voice said.

They stepped into a study. A man with graying red hair and spectacles—clearly Miss Hutting's father—looked up from behind a large desk. The two boys on the desk's other side grinned and leapt to their feet, obviously delighted to have their studies interrupted. One of them still had the round, soft features of a child, while the other was much closer to manhood, tall and angular, but not yet filled out. His eyes now focused on Marcus's cravat as if he was trying to memorize the knot.

God, what would it be like to see a son grow into a man?

There was no point in wondering. It was never going to happen for him.

"Your Grace, my father and my brothers Henry"—the older youth made a credible bow—"and Walter. Papa, this is the Duke of Hart."

The vicar smiled as he stood. "Thank you for coming so promptly, Your Grace."

Miss Hutting sucked in her breath sharply, and her eyes narrowed. "You were *expecting* the duke, Papa?"

"Er." The vicar looked down and rearranged some papers on his desk. "Yes."

"Why?" She leaned forward slightly, her voice and her bearing suddenly tense. Something had seriously ruffled her feathers.

Her brothers grinned and nudged each other as if they were expecting fireworks.

The vicar eyed her warily, and then inclined his head toward Marcus. "Perhaps we should have this discussion at another time, Cat."

An excellent name for the girl. She reminded him of the ginger-haired cat that had lived on his uncle's estate when he was a boy. Athena they'd called her. A warrior, she'd been fiercely independent and a bit reckless. All the male cats had been afraid of her, though she must have let one get close to her as she'd had a litter of kittens. He wondered if the poor tom had survived the mating.

Hmm. He'd like to try surviving a mating with this Cat. She'd look splendid spread naked across his bed, eyes flashing—

Good *God*. It *must* be the curse that was making him entertain such inappropriate thoughts. He glanced over at Ca—at Miss Hutting.

Her eyes were indeed flashing—with anger. Lips pressed tightly together, jaw hard, nostrils flaring. She was going to explode at any moment.

Her brothers watched with clear anticipation. The vicar seemed to brace himself.

And then she let out a slow breath, and her lips jerked up into a tight smile. "Yes. I'm sorry, Papa. Pardon me, Your Grace." She looked at him. Her green eyes were stormy, but her beautiful mouth—

No. Her ordinary, unremarkable mouth was still smiling determinedly. "I don't know where my manners have gone."

Her control was very impressive. Her father's shoulders dropped in relief, her brothers' in disappointment.

"No offense taken," he said. "I confess I'm surprised you didn't think to see me." He smiled. "I'm still required to come whenever the Spinster House is vacant."

"What?!" Miss Hutting gaped at him. "The Spinster House is vacant? How can that be? What happened to Miss Franklin? I just saw her the other day at the lending library. She looked very well—glowing almost." Her gaze flashed back to her father. "She hasn't . . . She didn't . . ." She put her hand to her forehead as if dazed. "She wasn't even forty. I don't remember her being sick a day in her life, and now this."

"She didn't die, Cat," the vicar said. "She went off with the—er, with Mr. Wattles."

"She did?" Miss Hutting sounded shocked. Or perhaps horrified.

The boys hooted.

"Really?"

"The old music teacher?"

"Huzzah! No more music lessons!" Walter did a little jig.

The vicar frowned at his sons. "Show some respect, boys. And Mr. Wattles wasn't old, Henry. He was not quite forty."

A perfect age for marriage.

Though if the man wanted children, he should have chosen a much younger woman.

"That *is* old," Henry said. "And he looked ancient in those fusty coats and breeches."

The vicar scratched his nose. "Yes, well, I'm not certain why the man dressed the way he did."

"Mama isn't going to be happy," Walter said. "Mr. Wattles was supposed to play the pianoforte at Mary's wedding."

"Oh." The vicar rubbed his forehead. "That's right. Well, perhaps Mr. Luntley's mother will finally recover and he can return in time to do the honors. If not, we shall just have to make do."

"You tell Mama that," Henry said.

The vicar's shoulders hunched a bit as if he expected a blow. "Er, yes. I will."

"You haven't told Mama this news yet?" Miss Hutting frowned. "But if His Grace is here, you must have found out"—she paused, and then her brows shot up—"at least early yesterday if not the day before."

The vicar tugged at his collar. "Mr. Wilkinson thought it best not to say anything until the duke arrived."

Miss Hutting made an odd little noise that sounded suspiciously like a growl.

The vicar turned to Marcus and managed a strained smile. "You must wonder where my manners have gone, Your Grace. Here I've kept you standing and haven't offered you the slightest bit of refreshment. If you will—"

"Oh, no, that's quite all right." He shouldn't spend any more time here, especially given his inappropriate attraction to Miss Hutting. He'd intended to make his visit to the village as brief as possible. "I stopped only to see if you might be able to direct me to Mr. Wilkinson's office. I couldn't quite make out his direction from his letter."

Miss Hutting grunted.

He looked at her, his eyebrow rising in inquiry before he could stop it.

"If you can't read the handwriting, Your Grace, that means it isn't Jane's—Miss Wilkinson's. Jane writes all her brother's correspondence since his scrawl is illegible, as you've discovered." Miss Hutting frowned again. "The fact that he penned the letter himself means he's hiding the news from Jane as well." She glared at her father. "I wonder why?"

"Perhaps Mr. Wilkinson merely thought it best not to get the ladies in a pother too soon. You know what the Boltwood sisters are like."

Miss Hutting did not look convinced by her father's explanation, but as long as the village machinations didn't involve Marcus's marital state, he didn't much care what went on. He cleared his throat to recapture their attention. "So, have you Mr. Wilkinson's direction, then?"

"Yes, yes." Mr. Hutting nodded. "But it's a little difficult to explain if you don't know the village." He smiled at his daughter. "Cat will show you the way, won't you, Cat?"

Oh, God. Is the vicar trying to foist his daughter off on me?

If so, she wasn't precisely leaping at the opportunity.

"I'm supposed to take a basket to Mrs. Barker, Papa."

Henry and Walter sniggered; Miss Hutting glared at them.

"A basket? What basket?"

"The one Mama put together when you told her *poor* Mrs. Barker was bothered by gout."

Miss Hutting's sarcasm was thick enough to taste. Her brothers' sniggers had progressed to elbowing and eyebrow waggling.

"Oh, stop it," she said. "It's not funny."

The boys clearly thought it—whatever *it* was—was hilarious.

"Walter can take the basket to Mrs. Barker," her father said. "We're done with lessons for today."

Walter stopped laughing abruptly. "Why can't Henry take it?"

"Very well. Henry—"

"I can't, Papa. I have to . . ." Henry grinned. "I have to clean my room."

Walter punched him in the arm. "No, you don't. It's my room, too, chaw-bacon. You're just going to wait until I'm gone and then go do what you want."

"Ow. That hurt. And I'm not—"

"You can *both* take it"—the vicar raised his brows—"or we can read another section of Cicero."

Henry and Walter glowered at their father.

"Perhaps *two* more sections."

The boys recognized defeat when it stared them in the face. They shrugged, made their bows, and headed for the door.

"Mama said the basket's in the kitchen," Miss Hutting told them as they passed her.

"And now," the vicar said as soon as the boys had left, "you can—" He stopped to stare at his daughter. "Whatever happened to your dress, Cat?"

Of course this made Marcus stare, too, even though he'd already examined Miss Hutting's bodice far more carefully than he should have. True, her breasts weren't exceedingly large, but then he didn't particularly like large breasts in a woman. He—

He should not be thinking about Miss Hutting's breasts. He should be on his way to Mr. Wilkinson's.

Miss Hutting flushed. "Sybbie—" She looked at Marcus. "That is my six-year-old sister, Sybil." She turned back to her father. "Sybbie had an accident with her watercolors."

"Why do I suspect the twins were involved?" her father asked, smiling.

Miss Hutting smiled back at him. "Because they were, of course."

"And the ink?"

"I was writing. Sybbie startled me."

"Hmm. Working on that silly book again, were you?"

Miss Hutting's brows slammed down. "It's not silly."

The vicar pressed his lips together, but said no more on that head. "You weren't going to change before visiting the Barkers?"

"No." Miss Hutting's jaw jutted out in a distinctly pugnacious fashion. "I was not."

Her father sighed. "I do realize nothing will come of that, but your mother has hopes."

"Please persuade her to give them up."

The vicar took out his handkerchief and wiped his brow, though the room wasn't particularly warm. "Yes, well, as to that, we shall see."

"I am *not* marrying Mr. Barker."

Ah, so that was what the boys' amusement had been about.

Mr. Hutting put his handkerchief back in his pocket. "You have made that painfully clear any number of times. Now we've detained the duke far too long." He bowed. "My sincere apologies for boring you with our family squabbles, Your Grace. I don't know what you must think of us."

He thought he'd best escape before some new domestic problem reared its delaying head. At this rate, he would have had more luck finding his destination by wandering the village with his eyes closed.

"Think nothing of it. Now if you will just tell me the way to Mr. Wilkinson's office—"

"Oh, no, Your Grace. My daughter will be happy to escort you." The vicar treated Miss Hutting to a very pointed look. "Won't you, Cat?"

The man is *throwing his daughter at my head.*

The vicar was nothing like Rathbone, at least on the surface, but he was a man with an unmarried daughter on his hands.

Miss Hutting's cheeks turned pink. "Yes, of course. I'm so sorry, Your Grace. We'll leave straightaway."

The vicar smiled. "It's not far. You'll be there in no time."

Miss Hutting looked over her shoulder as she led the way out of the study. "You'd best tell Mama about Miss Franklin at once, Papa. She will not wish to hear it from anyone else."

The vicar's expression turned slightly hunted. "Ah, yes. Quite right. I'll go find her, er, now."

"I believe she's in the schoolroom."

Miss Hutting grabbed her cloak before Marcus could assist her, but he was able to open the front door while she was putting on her bonnet.

"How many of you are there, Miss Hutting?" he asked as she stepped past him.

"Ten."

"Ten?!" Good God! Not that large families were completely unheard of. Certainly not. He'd just never had experience with one.

Well, of course *he* wouldn't have, not unless he'd had nine older sisters.

Miss Hutting strode away from him, apparently intent on delivering him to Mr. Wilkinson as quickly as possible now that she'd finally undertaken the task.

"Yes, though there are only eight—soon to be just seven—still at home. Tory and Ruth, the sisters just younger than I, are already wed, and Mary, the next one down, will be married in less than two weeks"—she paused to look back at him—"to Mr. Theodore Dunly, your assistant steward."

"Ah."

She snorted. "You don't know who he is, do you?"

"Er . . ." *Think.* There'd been a thin man hovering behind Emmett when they'd arrived. "Of course I know who he is. He has thinning hair and a prominent nose, doesn't he?" He probably shouldn't have described Dunly that way since the man was her sister's intended, but it wasn't his fault the fellow looked like a broomstick with a snout.

She shook her head as she led the way up the hill toward the graveyard. "That's Mr. Phelps, Mr. Emmett's sister's son. He's a coachman—or would be if you were ever here to ride in the castle's coach. Theo is much taller and broader and better looking. I'm certain you'll meet him shortly. Mr. Emmett depends on him." She glanced at him. "You must know that Mr. Emmett is getting along in years."

He nodded noncommittally. He *should* know. He knew such things about the stewards of his other properties, but he'd admit to being rather taken aback when he'd seen how stooped and, well, *ancient* Emmett was.

"He still has a clear, strong hand, though, unlike Mr. Wilkinson."

She snorted again. "That's Theo's writing. He took over all the estate correspondence several years ago, when Mr. Emmett got a touch of the palsy. He runs the place"—she frowned at him—"with Mr. Emmett's supervision, of course. Mr. Emmett does very well for a man of eighty."

Good God, Emmett was eighty? He hadn't seemed that old when Marcus had last seen him . . .

Twenty years ago.

"Ah. Of course."

She stopped, her expression shifting from annoyed to worried. "You're not going to pension Mr. Emmett off because of what I said, are you? You can't. He loves the castle. He knows everything about it, and he's still very shrewd. He just moves a little slowly"—her jaw hardened as did her tone—"as you would, too, if you had eighty years in your dish."

Did she really think he was going to rush back and turn the old man out?

"Yes, I'm sure I would."

"You *can't* let him go."

And who was she to tell him what he could and couldn't do? He was the Duke of Hart. He was not accustomed to such impertinence. He should give her a severe set-down.

He would if he had any confidence she would be suitably chastised. More likely she'd just snort at him once more.

"And your other brothers and sisters? What of them?"

She glared at him.

He raised his ducal brows and looked down his nose at her. Even Lady Dunlee was cowed by this expression.

As he suspected, Miss Hutting was made of sterner stuff. Her eyes narrowed, her glare becoming more pronounced.

"The others?" he asked again. He was not going to discuss Emmett and the castle.

She blew out a short breath. "Oh, very well." She started walking again. "After Mary comes Henry—he's fifteen—and Walter, thirteen, both of whom you just met. And then there's Prudence, who's ten, Sybil, who's six, and Thomas and Michael, the four-year-old twins."

He glanced back at the vicarage. It was not a large building. "It must get rather crowded."

"Indeed it does."

They'd reached the graveyard, and Miss Hutting stopped again, this time by a weathered headstone. Were they never going to reach Wilkinson's office?

She looked up at him as if she had something important to say, her wide green eyes, flecked with gold and framed by long, red-gold eyelashes—

He jerked his gaze away. There was nothing special about Miss Hutting's eyes, for God's sake.

His eyes dropped to the gray stone marker.

"Zeus!" He blinked, but he'd read the stone correctly. He ran his fingers over the worn lettering.

"What's the matter?"

"This has Isabelle Dorring's name on it. I thought she'd drowned herself and her body had never been recovered." He looked more closely.

Rest in Eternal Peace, 1593–1617.

So Isabelle had been twenty-four when she'd died. He'd thought she'd been much younger. Surely a mature woman would know better than to allow a man any liberties with her person before getting his ring on her finger. Perhaps, as Alex had suggested, she *had* meant to trap the third duke into marriage.

Her intentions were immaterial. He very much doubted the duke had been dragged kicking and screaming into her bed. He should have exercised some self-control or, failing that, discovered if his actions had had permanent consequences before marrying another woman.

"I imagine since Isabelle's father donated the funds to expand the church and paid for much of its upkeep"—she glanced at him—"the duke being a bit stingy, the vicar was easily persuaded that Isabelle must have slipped into Loves Water by accident. A wall memorial would have been more appropriate since there was indeed no body, but her family wanted the gravestone."

"Her family?" This was news. "I thought Isabelle was the last of her line."

"Oh, no." She smiled at him, and his heart lurched.

Bloody indigestion.

"Her father had an older sister who married a man in Whiting Cross about twenty miles to the south."

Ah. So Isabelle had had someone she could have turned to.

Well, no. Likely the aunt would not have welcomed a pregnant but unmarried niece.

"After Isabelle died, some of her cousins moved back to Loves Bridge, though not into the Spinster House, of course. Isabelle had already made arrangements for that." Miss Hutting gave him a significant look.

He nodded. They both knew he was well aware of Miss Dorring's arrangements.

Miss Hutting smiled. "My mother's descended from that branch."

"What?" He suddenly had an odd, disorienting feeling almost as if he'd been here before. Ridiculous. "Your mother is related to Isabelle Dorring?"

"Yes, but don't ask me to draw the family tree. There's

an Isabelle in every generation. My mother and I are both Isabelle, which is why I go by my middle name."

"Ah." And the third duke's given name had been Marcus. If he was a superstitious sort, he'd be feeling chills up and down his spine right now.

Fortunately he was not superstitious.

"Merrow."

A large black, orange, and white cat appeared from behind another headstone and picked its way carefully through the grass to Miss Hutting, glaring at him before rubbing up against Miss Hutting's legs.

"A friend of yours?"

She laughed as she bent to stroke the animal. "Sometimes. Poppy likes me better when the twins aren't around. They are a bit too exuberant for her tastes."

"Where does she live?"

"At the Spinster House."

"Does she?" He stooped and extended his hand. "I'm surprised Miss Franklin left her behind. She's a very handsome animal."

The cat ignored him.

"Oh, Poppy doesn't belong to Miss Franklin. She doesn't belong to anyone."

He chuckled. "I suppose that's true of most cats."

"Yes, but Poppy is more independent than most. No one knows where she came from. She just appeared about a year ago and made herself at home."

He kept his hand still, waiting, and finally the cat decided to acknowledge his presence, delicately sniffing his fingers. Finding nothing to disqualify him from her acquaintance, she bumped her head against his hand. He rubbed her behind her ears, eliciting a low rumbling purr.

Miss Hutting's eyebrows rose. "She doesn't usually care for men."

"Then I feel quite fortunate to have met with her approval."

He concentrated on Poppy, but he could feel Miss Hutting's gaze studying him. Oh, damnation. She wasn't going to raise the issue of Emmett again, was she?

He gave Poppy one last stroke and straightened. "Shall we proceed to Mr. Wilkinson's office? I do wish to conclude my business with him as soon as possible." He watched the cat run off, and then glanced at Miss Hutting.

Her face had hardened with resolution. Blast.

"Your Grace, I have a proposal for you."

A *proposal?* Good God, now that was something he'd not anticipated. Perhaps he should have. He must be a better catch than the despised Mr. Barker.

He held up his hand. There was no point in beating around the bush. "Miss Hutting, I am not going to marry you."

Her eyes widened, and her jaw dropped like a rock.

Perhaps that had not been the proposal she'd had in mind.

"Marry me?" She snapped her mouth shut and swallowed, grabbing on to Isabelle Dorring's headstone as if she were in danger of losing her balance—or, more likely, of popping him in the nose. "*Marry* me?"

He made a small bow being careful to keep his nose out of her reach. "My apologies. I thought—"

"You thought I wanted you to marry me!" She was shouting now.

"Er, clearly I was mistaken."

"You certainly were mistaken, you"—she jabbed her finger at him—"you—"

She balled her hand into a fist, pressing her lips firmly together. This time he'd swear the air vibrated as she struggled to control her temper.

He stepped back involuntarily. Not that he was afraid of her. Of course not. She was tall, but not as tall as he, and a woman. He had no doubt he could seduce her if necessary—

Blast it. *Subdue*. He could *subdue* her if necessary.

Her eyes were still shooting daggers at him, but her lips had turned up into the same tight smile she'd managed in her father's study. He was amazed—and a little disappointed—at her restraint. He'd like to see her lose control.

No, he wouldn't. He hated scenes.

"As it happens," she said, "marriage does figure into what I wish to say to you."

"Oh?" Now what was she up to?

"Yes." She rested her hands back on the headstone and looked him in the eye. "Your Grace, not only do I not wish to marry you, I don't wish to marry anyone."

"Perhaps not at the moment—"

"Not at any moment."

"I find that hard to believe." He'd never met a female who didn't want to drag some poor fellow up the church aisle.

Miss Hutting's eyes narrowed. "Believe it. I do not wish to be subservient to any *man*—"

She could hardly have put more disgust into that word.

"—to be at his beck and call and bear his children, one after another, year after year like my mother did."

Completely inappropriate lust slammed into his . . . chest.

Miss Hutting raised her chin. "I wish to write novels. I assure you a husband and children would be very much in the way."

Madness. This beautiful, vibrant woman wished to lock herself away with a quill and paper and live in her imagination? She was made for the bedchamber—though not *his* bedchamber, of course.

"Your Grace, I wish to be the new Spinster House spinster." She nodded at the grave marker. "Isabelle is my ancestor. I have some claim to the position."

This was insane. Ridiculous. Totally wrong-headed—

And it would get him out of Loves Bridge by this afternoon. Tomorrow at the latest.

Who was he to argue with the next great English novelist?

"Very well. If you will finally take me to Mr. Wilkinson's office, I shall make the necessary arrangements."

Chapter Four

April 15, 1617—I have made a study of the duke's habits and contrive to be where I think he might pass so I can catch a glimpse of him and perhaps walk with him. My heart leaps when I see him— literally leaps in my breast—and I have difficulty breathing.

—from Isabelle Dorring's diary

The duke was going to let her have the Spinster House. Her dream was about to come true. Cat almost skipped up through the graveyard and around to the back of the church.

"I wonder why Randolph—that is, Mr. Wilkinson— didn't say anything about the Spinster House being empty and swore my father to secrecy as well," she said as they approached the back gate.

"I believe you exaggerate. Your father merely said Wilkinson had suggested he not mention the vacancy. The man is a solicitor. He must be discreet. Allow me." The duke lifted the latch and held the gate open for her.

"I assure you Papa would not keep something from my

mother if he wasn't strongly encouraged to do so. And it is most odd that Randolph didn't tell Jane. She runs his office. Randolph wouldn't be able to function without her."

"Perhaps he did tell her and she was simply busy when the letter needed to be written."

"Perhaps." But it was highly unlikely. What would Jane be busy doing? She spent all her time working for her brother. Yes, she came to church every Sunday, and she was on the fair planning committee, but that was about it. Cat and their friend Anne, Baron Davenport's daughter, had often taken her to task for it.

But then what did Cat do but tend to her brothers and sisters? It wasn't as though she had any time for herself—which was why the Spinster House opportunity was so exciting. She hurried down the narrow, tree-shrouded path that led away from the churchyard. The sooner they reached Randolph's office, the sooner she'd have the key to the house and her independence in hand.

"I would think Wilkinson would do better to have his office closer to the village green," the duke said as he latched the gate and followed her.

She *did* like his voice. It was nothing like Mr. Barker's thin, nasally tones. It was deep, though not exceptionally so, and . . . well, she couldn't quite put her finger on what was so appealing about it, but something was. Even when she'd been arguing with him, she'd thought so.

Silly. It wasn't the duke's voice that was making it hard to keep her feet from dancing, it was his promise to let her live in the Spinster House.

She looked back over her shoulder at him. "Yes, but his office is in his house. So much more convenient for him and Jane." *Wait until I tell Jane that I'm going to be the next spinster! Jane will be so excited for me.* "And everyone in the village knows where he—oh!"

Her ankle twisted. Bloody tree roots! She threw out her

hands to catch her balance, but it was hopeless. She was going to end in a heap—

A muscled arm caught her, hauling her up against a rock-hard chest.

She pressed her cheek against the rough wool of the duke's coat and struggled to catch her breath. Her heart was pounding with . . . surprise. It must be surprise.

Mmm. He smelled of citrus and soap, linen and starch. There wasn't the slightest whiff of the barnyard about him. And his shoulders were definitely broader than Mr. Barker's, as was his chest, but then he was taller than Mr. Barker as well. She had to lean her head back to look up past his strong, clean-shaven chin and firm lips.

His brown eyes were shadowed with concern.

"Are you all right, Miss Hutting?"

And warmth? Was there warmth in his eyes, too? Warmth, turning to heat—

She pushed herself back, and he let her go at once. "Yes, yes, of course I'm all right." She lifted her dress slightly and wiggled her foot. "See? No damage done."

He was staring. . . .

Oh, God, he could see her ankle. She dropped her skirt as if it had caught fire. He must think her a complete hoyden.

"It—it was my own fault." It was suddenly hard to breathe. "I know b-better than to walk here without w-watching my step. As you can see, there are tree roots everywhere."

"Indeed there are. Take my arm."

She took a step away from him. "Oh, no. That's not necessary."

"Please. I insist. I would hate for you to fall."

She looked at his arm attired in expensive blue wool. It would be rude—and more than a little silly—to refuse his assistance. Not that she needed it, of course, but if she were to take a false step again, she would feel very foolish.

He leaned closer and whispered, "I don't bite."

There was an undercurrent of something dark and seductive in his words.

Ridiculous. She was acting like a complete widgeon. "I didn't imagine you did." She laid her hand on his sleeve.

His arm was so solid. And her head came only to his shoulder. She felt small, delicate.

There was absolutely nothing small or delicate about her. She was as tall as all the men in Loves Bridge, Papa included, except for Mr. Barker. She—

She twisted her ankle again and fell against the duke's side, but this time she was able to recover immediately. "Pardon me! I assure you I'm not usually this clumsy."

He laid his hand over hers before she could snatch it off his sleeve. "The footing *is* quite treacherous."

Yes, but *he* wasn't stumbling.

The weight of his hand on hers was doing very odd things to her breathing. She swallowed something that felt uncomfortably like panic.

"I don't need your assistance. I come this way by myself all the time." Her tone sounded rude even to her own ears.

But he didn't take offense. Instead, the right corner of his mouth turned up. "Then I apologize. It must be my presence that is causing you to stumble."

Oh, no. That wasn't it. Of course it wasn't. What? Did he think her some silly young virgin alone with a man for the first time and afraid for her virtue? Preposterous!

"I just wasn't looking where I was going. It won't happen again."

He was overwhelming—so close, so big, so . . . male. She hadn't been affected by him in the churchyard, but now they were on this secluded, shady path. . . .

He'd be horrified if he could read her thoughts. He'd run screaming back to the churchyard. No, he'd run all the way back to London.

That thought made her feel better, and she managed to smile. She only had to make it to the end of the path, which they were fast approaching. Then they would be on the lane where there were no tree roots. She could put some distance between them.

She lengthened her stride, keeping her eyes on her feet, and turned her thoughts to the business at hand.

"How soon can I move into the Spinster House?"

The duke's stride lengthened easily to match hers. "I would think immediately, but I assume Mr. Wilkinson will know."

"So you don't have a document of some sort that tells you how everything is managed?"

"No. Wilkinson has all that." His mouth tightened. "All I know is that I must be physically present when the spinster is selected, and I must sign the agreement."

"You had to do that even when you were ten years old?"

He nodded.

She'd grown up with the story of the Cursed Duke. It had been her favorite fairy tale, and the arrival of the horses and traveling carriage when she was four had only added to its appeal. Isabelle, the tragic heroine seduced and abandoned by the evil nobleman, was family, albeit a cousin many, many times removed. The curse was Isabelle's victory from the grave and a source of pride, but she'd never thought about its effect on the duke's descendants. In truth, she'd never thought of them as real people—just as fairy-tale villains.

This man was very real and didn't seem at all evil.

"What if you'd been an infant? Surely then you would have been excused. It would be impossible for a baby to fulfill those duties."

"My great-grandfather was three months old when the Spinster House became vacant. His guardian and his nurse brought him to Loves Bridge and had him in the room when the spinster was chosen. The earl signed the agreement for him, but affixed the baby's handprint as well."

Superstitious nonsense. Did grown men truly think something terrible would happen if they didn't follow the letter of this ancient document? If she'd been there—

Wait a moment . . .

"You mentioned the baby's nurse, but not his mother." Certainly an intelligent woman would have introduced some sense into the proceedings.

"Because his mother wasn't there." His mouth twisted. "The Duchesses of Hart are not known for their maternal feelings."

Oh, the poor baby! She didn't wish to be a mother herself, but she couldn't imagine a woman sending her infant off on such an errand with only a nurse and a stuffy old guardian in attendance. Mama would never have done so.

"But your mother came with you, didn't she, when you were here as a child?" Had she seen a woman that day? She didn't remember. Her attention had been all for the horses.

No, that wasn't quite true. Now that she thought more about it, she did remember a boy. Two boys, but she'd only focused on one. He'd been tall and thin and his back had been very straight and stiff. She'd thought him too serious and proud, and she'd felt a little sorry for him even though he'd got to ride in the beautiful carriage with the lovely horses. Had that been the duke?

"No, my mother did not come."

His face was as closed as his voice sounded.

She had to force herself not to squeeze his arm. He wouldn't want her sympathy.

It was bad enough for a mother to send her baby with only a nurse and a guardian, but an infant wouldn't remember who was holding him. A boy of ten? He'd remember all too well.

"Was she ill? Is that why she didn't come with you?"

"Miss Hutting, my mother left me with my aunt—my father's older sister—shortly after she gave birth to me. I have not seen her since."

He sounded very haughty, but she thought he was just putting up walls. She tried to study his expression, but the shade was too deep for her to see his eyes.

"That's terrible."

"No, it's not. I'm sure I was happier growing up with my cousin and his family." He stopped and frowned at her. "I'm surprised you don't know all this. Can it be that the villagers don't gossip about the Cursed Duke?"

"No, why would we? You're never here, and few people care about what goes on in London Society. What *is* important to us is what you do in the House of Lords, and most of the villagers approve of that. In truth, I think they're impressed you bother to take your seat instead of wasting *all* your time gambling and whoring."

His brows shot up. "You are very frank."

She grinned. "It is one of the benefits of choosing spinsterhood." They had finally reached the end of the path, so she let go of his arm. "Randolph's office is just up this way."

"Splendid."

"You know," she said, starting up the lane, "I never understood why your ancestor agreed to the Spinster House arrangement. I can't imagine a duke feeling compelled to do anything a mere merchant's daughter demanded."

He frowned at her, his voice rough with emotion. "I hope it was because the man had a modicum of honor."

Heavens, was he personally offended by the events of two hundred years ago? Perhaps that was what came from living in a house where generations of your ancestors stared down at you from every wall.

He needed to join the nineteenth century.

"The man didn't rape Isabelle, did he?" Though even if he had, it had still happened two hundred years ago.

"Good God, no!" This present duke looked ill. "Or at least not that I was ever told. As far as I know, their, er, relationship was consensual. But that doesn't excuse the fact that the duke got Miss Dorring with child and then married another." He frowned. "Her heart was broken."

Cat snorted. Yes, that was how she knew the story.

The duke's eyebrow arched up. "You don't believe in broken hearts, Miss Hutting?"

"I have no patience with such romantic twaddle. Isabelle wasn't the only woman in the history of the world to have been seduced by a wealthy, handsome fellow, and unlike many, she had money. She could have held her head up and managed somehow. It would have been better than drowning herself and her innocent baby."

He stared at her. "She was a ruined woman."

"She was a selfish idiot." Cat had never been ruined herself, of course, and never would be, since she had no intention of letting a man into her bed. But she certainly hoped that, if by some odd fate she was in such a position, she'd manage things more intelligently than Isabelle had.

She grinned. "But I can't complain. Isabelle's actions have given me what I've always dreamed of—the opportunity to live on my own." She wanted to pinch herself to be certain she wasn't actually dreaming. The sooner the duke signed the necessary papers and gave her the key to the Spinster House, the better.

"Won't you miss your family?"

Did he sound wistful?

"No. You said yourself the vicarage must be crowded. I assure you it is. I even have to share a bed with my sister Mary."

"I can see how that might be uncomfortable."

He didn't sound convinced, but then he had no idea what her life was like. He was a duke.

"Your Grace, if you had ten children, none of them

would have to share a bed or even a room. And you could retire to your study and close the door and no one would disturb you." Well, that was true for Papa, too. Men definitely had an easier life than women. "No one could *find* you if you didn't wish to be found. I've seen the castle. It's huge. But I have no doors to close, no place to be guaranteed a moment's privacy. Can you even begin to imagine what that is like?"

He just stared at her. Of course he couldn't imagine it. It was like asking an elephant to imagine life as a mouse.

She shrugged. "The vicarage is just across the road from the Spinster House. If I have a sudden need to see my parents and brothers and sisters, I can do so."

But they'd best not think they could cross the road to drop in on her whenever they liked. Oh, no. She would have to take steps to be sure they understood that *very* clearly.

Why was the duke still staring at her? "What is it?"

"Miss Hutting, surely you know I shall never share my home with ten children. I shall likely never share it with one."

Heavens, was the man impotent? But how was she to know that? Still, it was very—

Oh. She stopped walking to stare at him. "You mean . . . But the curse—it's not . . . It's just a story, isn't it?"

"No. It is not just a story."

Miss Hutting was gaping at him.

He liked the girl, but she made his head spin. She wasn't like any other woman he'd ever met. Not only did she not want to marry, she said the most outrageous things.

Could Isabelle be at all to blame for what had happened to her?

No. The fault must be laid solely at the third duke's door. Women were the weaker sex, after all.

Though there was nothing weak about Miss Hutting. Perhaps she would indeed have the courage to survive an out-of-wedlock pregnancy, though he doubted she had any idea what that experience would entail.

Lust suddenly curled low in his belly. Nor did he think she had any understanding of what must occur before a woman found herself enceinte.

He would like to show her.

She was tall, as tall as many men. She must have long legs—she certainly had a well-turned ankle. He'd like to see the calf attached to that lovely ankle and the thigh and the soft hair—

Zeus! He was losing his mind. He needed to get the Spinster House settled and get out of Loves Bridge before he did something very, very foolish.

"You mean the Dukes of Hart actually die before their heir is born?" she asked.

"Yes."

She laughed. "Gammon! Everyone knows curses are only the stuff of fairy tales."

The effrontery of the girl. His fingers twitched to grab her by the shoulders and shake her.

And pull her up against my body.

She'd felt so good in his arms when he'd held her after her stumble. Perfect. She—

He *was* losing his mind.

"I assure you, Miss Hutting, the curse is very real. Every duke, beginning with the one who treated Miss Dorring so badly, has fallen victim to it."

Her jaw dropped again, and then she shook her head. "There must be some rational explanation." She started walking again. "I assure you Isabelle was not a witch—not that I believe in witches either." She frowned at him. "I'm very surprised an educated man like you does."

He matched his step to hers. They could not get to

Wilkinson's office fast enough. He looked around, hoping to catch sight of the place, but the hedgerows stretched higher than his head on both sides of the lane.

"Miss Hutting, I don't know what your cousin was or was not. All I know is my family's history."

"You must be mistaken."

Good God, did she think he didn't know his own destiny? "I am not. Five dukes, including my father, all died before their heir was born. The curse governs our lives, Miss Hutting. It is why we put off marrying as long as we can. The moment the Duchess of Hart conceives, the duke begins to count the days he has left on this earth—unless he gets a temporary reprieve and has a daughter. Which, I should add, has only happened once in two hundred years."

Where *was* Wilkinson's office?

He picked up his pace, not caring if he left Miss Hutting behind, but she matched him step for step. Clearly she was used to walking.

Too bad she'd let go of his arm.

No. It was excellent that she'd let go. The sooner he broke this odd connection with her, the better.

"I think you should ignore the curse." She smiled at him. "Well, not the part about the Spinster House. I certainly want you to attend to that. But as for the rest of it, live your life as you like. As Isabelle's distant cousin, I release you from any further obligation to our family."

Would that she could do that. "The only way I can be freed from the curse, Miss Hutting, is if I marry for love." Gah! Such drivel. He hoped he wasn't blushing, but he was afraid he was.

She snickered. "You can't be serious."

"Unfortunately I am. Deadly serious."

Her eyebrows shot up, and then she tried—unsuccessfully—to swallow her mirth. "Well, then, you have your answer. Find some female to love. I imagine they are lining up for the honor. You just have to pick one."

She could not think it was that easy. "Oh, they are lining up, all right, but to grab my purse, not my heart."

She snorted. "I find that hard to believe. Have you looked in a mirror recently? Scores of women must be sighing over you."

Clearly Miss Hutting was not one of them.

Not that he wished the woman to be sighing over him. What a ridiculous thought.

Appealing, though—

No, it was not. He looked down the lane rather than at Miss Hutting. "Have we almost reached Wilkinson's office?"

"Yes. It's just around that curve."

Thank God.

He would not run, but he did increase his pace again—and Miss Hutting kept right with him.

"Why didn't you have Randolph come to you at the castle, Your Grace? Wouldn't that have been the more ducal way to go about things?" She grinned. "Though I will say you've done a good job of keeping up with me. I was afraid I might have to dawdle while you huffed and puffed along."

First compliments, now insults.

"Thank you, Miss Hutting. I do more than sit on my throne in London, you know."

Her eyes widened. "You have a throne?"

Zeus, she was a confusing mix of worldly-wise and naïve.

"No, of course I don't. And I'm coming to Wilkinson's because that's what I'm required to do." He shrugged. "I suppose Miss Dorring took some pleasure in compelling the dukes to dance to her tune."

"You are likely correct."

They had finally reached the end of the hedgerow. Miss Hutting turned up a walk toward a pleasant, white-walled, thatched house.

"I hope Randolph can see us at once." She looked back over her shoulder at him. "I assume he's expecting you?"

"Yes. I have forty-eight hours after I receive his letter notifying me that the Spinster House is vacant to present myself at his offices."

And once he had done that and handed the keys to the house over to Miss Hutting, he could leave Loves Bridge forever. He and Nate and Alex could head off for the Lake District. Walking the fells without a single annoying woman nearby sounded like heaven right now.

Miss Hutting's eyebrows rose. "I still wonder why Isabelle believed the duke and his descendants would follow her instructions—demands, really—since she must have thought your ancestor a complete dastard."

"True. Which is likely why she added another curse. If the duke doesn't appear within forty-eight hours, he dies."

Miss Hutting's eyebrows shot up to disappear into her hair. "He dies? As in drops dead the moment time runs out?"

"I believe so. No one has been brave enough—or careless enough—to find out for certain. And if the duke is married and his wife increasing, the child dies in the womb."

She stared at him as he reached for the door latch. "That's terrible." And then she snorted again. "And unbelievable."

It did sound ridiculous. He'd laugh at the entire farce if he weren't the lead actor.

"I'm sorry you feel you must comply with this superstitious humbug," she said—and then grinned, her green eyes sparkling. "Though I'm delighted to benefit from it."

Need slammed into him. He wanted her joy, her excitement.

Her.

She's so close. If I dip my head, I can brush my lips over her mouth. I can bring her long, lovely body up against—

Zeus!

Had he really been leaning toward her?

He jerked his head back.

The curse was turning his mind. The sooner he was out of Loves Bridge and away from Miss Hutting the better. He'd attend to the Spinster House today and flee to the lakes tomorrow.

He opened the door, and Miss Hutting hurried inside and out of his reach, thank God.

"Jane!" She was almost dancing as she crossed the room. "Do you know what has happened?"

A pleasant-looking woman with brown hair, pulled back severely from her face, and brown eyes looked up from the papers on her desk and took off her spectacles. "No." Her gaze moved from Miss Hutting to him. "May I help you, sir?"

"You *don't* know!" Miss Hutting grinned at the woman and then grinned at him. "This is the Duke of Hart, Jane. Your Grace, Miss Wilkinson."

He bowed slightly.

Miss Wilkinson smiled as she stood. "How nice to meet you, Your Grace. What brings you to—" Her face froze, then her eyes widened and her gaze darted back to Miss Hutting.

If Miss Hutting smiled any more broadly, her face would split in two.

"Yes, it's true, Jane. Can you imagine? Miss Franklin has run off with Mr. Wattles."

"Mr. Wattles?" Miss Wilkinson blinked. "The music teacher?"

"There's only one Mr. Wattles in Loves Bridge—or there *was* only one." Miss Hutting frowned. "I can't imagine what Miss Franklin was thinking, giving up her independence for Mr. Wattles"—she shrugged and grinned again—"but never mind that. Her loss is my gain."

Miss Wilkinson's brows snapped down. "What do you mean?"

"I mean the Spinster House is now empty, and I—"

An interior door flew open, and a fellow who looked like a male version of Miss Wilkinson stepped—jumped, really—into the room. "Cat! Why are you here?" He looked over at Marcus. "Ah."

"Yes. See whom I've brought you, Randolph? The Duke of Hart!"

Now why the hell did Wilkinson look guilty?

"Thank you, Cat." He shot his sister a worried glance before smiling at Marcus. "And I thank you, Your Grace, for coming so promptly."

"My pleasure." Not that he'd had any choice.

"Randolph." Miss Wilkinson's voice was rather sharp.

"Later, Jane. If you'll just come this way, Your Grace." Mr. Wilkinson gestured for Marcus to precede him into the room from which he'd just emerged.

Miss Wilkinson darted out from behind her desk to block the door. "Randolph, why didn't you have me write to the duke?"

"*Later, Jane.*" Mr. Wilkinson ran his finger under his cravat. "Now please step aside. You are impeding His Grace's way."

Miss Wilkinson didn't budge. "I wondered why you had the Spinster House documents on your desk."

Randolph stiffened. "You were poking around my office?"

"I'm your secretary. Poking around your office is part of my job." She narrowed her eyes. "Why didn't you tell me the place was vacant, Randolph?"

"But it isn't, Jane." Miss Hutting had been watching this sibling exchange, chewing on her bottom lip, but she now entered the fray. "Or it won't be. The duke has agreed to let me be the next Spinster House spinster."

Miss Wilkinson's face took on a distinctly mulish cast. "He can't do that."

Miss Hutting's eyes widened, her cheeks flushing. "Yes, he can." She looked at Marcus. "Can't you, Your Grace?"

There was danger here. Fortunately Miss Wilkinson rushed to speak before he could.

"He can't let you be the Spinster House spinster." She glared at her brother. "There are procedures that must be followed."

"Jane, not now. Please." Mr. Wilkinson tugged on his cravat as though that article of clothing was suddenly strangling him. "If you will just step into my office, Your Grace?"

"Ah, but I believe your sister has something to say, Wilkinson." Surely the man realized Miss Wilkinson was going to say her piece one way or the other. Best to get it over with immediately. And if there was some rule preventing him from giving Miss Hutting the use of the Spinster House, he wanted to know it. In this matter, not following the rules could have fatal consequences. He did not care to drop dead in Wilkinson's damned office.

"Thank you, Your Grace." Miss Wilkinson trained her gaze on her brother. "You know as well as I do, Randolph, that any opening at the Spinster House must be announced to the village."

"Er. Ah." Mr. Wilkinson's Adam's apple bobbed. "I believe that is a mere formality."

"It. Is. Not." Miss Wilkinson bit off each word. "And if there is more than one candidate, each must be given an equal chance to win the position."

Miss Hutting looked at her friend. "But, Jane, I-I'm the only confirmed spinster in Loves Bridge." Her voice wavered slightly, as if she suddenly wasn't entirely convinced of her statement.

Miss Wilkinson kept her eyes on her brother. "No, Cat, you are not, as Randolph well knows. Why do you think he's been so secretive about this?" Her nostrils flared. "He even tried to send me off on a ridiculous errand so I wouldn't be here today, but I smelled a rat and refused to go."

"Oh." Miss Hutting looked from Miss Wilkinson to her brother.

Wilkinson's face had turned beet red. "Now, Jane, don't be silly—"

"Silly? *Silly,* Randolph?" Miss Wilkinson jabbed her finger at him. "You know how sick I am of keeping house for you. I want a place of my own. I want the Spinster House."

"But, Jane, please consider . . ."

"No, *you* consider, Randolph. You look through the document. I assure you I have. There are rules. There are procedures. There are steps you must follow." She folded her hands. "So follow them."

Oh, hell. Clearly Marcus was not getting out of Loves Bridge today.

Chapter Five

April 20, 1617—Rosaline thinks I'm going to have my heart broken, and Maria agrees, but they are just jealous. I know the duke loves me. Or he will love me soon, if his mother doesn't interfere. I cannot like the woman.

—from Isabelle Dorring's diary

"Read the relevant part, Wilkinson."

They'd all—the duke, Randolph, Jane, and Cat—taken seats in Randolph's office. The duke was scowling, clearly making Randolph nervous.

Blast it all, why did Jane have to want the Spinster House, too?

"I think you'll find the paragraph on page three," Jane said.

Randolph glared at Jane, straightened his spectacles, and then shuffled his papers to find the section she'd mentioned.

Cat could see how it would be annoying to live with Randolph, but Jane had never complained before, not even when Cat and Anne had teased her about all the time she spent working for her brother. Jane was usually quiet, almost shy.

She did not look the least bit shy now. She looked like she wished to carve Randolph's heart out with a penknife and feed it to Farmer Linden's pigs.

"Ah, yes. Here it is." Randolph cleared his throat and read: "'Spinster House Vacancy. Whenever a vacancy arises, it must be announced to the entire village so that all interested spinsters may apply. If there is only one applicant, the Duke of Hart may award the tenancy to her at once. However, if there is more than one, each applicant must be given an equal chance to win the position.'"

The duke shifted in his seat. "Has there ever been more than one applicant, Wilkinson?"

Randolph glanced at Jane before he answered. "No, Your Grace, there has not." He pointed to a ledger book. "I have gone through the records very carefully."

"There is always a first time," Jane said, "and this is it."

Cat clenched her teeth tightly to keep from screaming. Jane didn't need the house as much as she did. Jane might have to live with her brother, but at least she had her own room, her own bed. And while Randolph could be irritating—*was* irritating—Jane's predicament was largely her own fault. She should have stopped being so accommodating years ago. Perhaps then Randolph would have found himself a wife.

And where would that have put Jane?

Lud! Cat blew out a short, annoyed breath. There was no point in thinking about something that had never happened. Better to focus on something that was about to happen. "So how is His Grace to decide between us, Randolph?"

The duke held up his hand. "A moment, please, Miss Hutting. Before you answer that question, Wilkinson, tell me how the Spinster House vacancy must be properly announced. I don't wish to run afoul of the rules." His lips twisted. "The consequences could be, ah, very bad for my health."

Randolph mopped his brow with his handkerchief. "Yes. Quite right, Your Grace."

Good God! Randolph was a solicitor. He dealt in facts, not fairy tales. "You don't believe that silly curse, too, do you, Randolph?"

Randolph shot her a very harassed look. "I—"

Jane didn't give him a chance to answer. "Whether the curse is real or not, the duke has to follow the provisions of the legal agreement." She glared at her brother. "As Randolph well knows."

Randolph glared back at Jane. "Yes. Indeed." He straightened his spectacles again and returned his attention to the document. "'Proper Announcement. Within seventy-two hours of discovering the Spinster House to be vacant, the duke must post notices inviting all spinsters living in Loves Bridge to apply to be the next Spinster House spinster. The notices must be posted on the Spinster House door, at Cupid's Inn, at the church, and anywhere else spinsters gather.'"

Randolph looked over at the duke. "I shall draft those up as soon as we finish here, Your Grace."

The duke nodded. "Splendid. Now that you mention it, I do remember signing papers when I was last here and going round posting them with my uncle and cousin." He smiled. "That is, I remember chasing my cousin on the green and having our game repeatedly interrupted by my uncle to post some annoying paper."

Which is exactly what Henry or Walter would have done had they been forced to dance to Isabelle's tune. The poor duke had been just a boy, dragged to Loves Bridge—

It was none of her concern. The duke was a man now, and this was her golden opportunity to get free of the crowded, chaotic vicarage so she could finally write.

"How long do we have to wait for people to apply, Randolph? Not that anyone besides Jane and I will do so." Cat looked over at Jane. "Can you think of anyone else who'd want to live in the Spinster House?"

"No. Everyone else is married."

The duke's right eyebrow arched up. "*Everyone,* Miss Wilkinson?"

Jane frowned. "Well, perhaps not everyone, Your Grace, but everyone else who isn't married wishes to be."

Cat looked at Randolph. "So how long do we need to wait?"

Randolph blew out a long breath and glanced at his sister. "Three days after the notices are posted."

Three days! And she'd thought she'd be moving in tomorrow. "And once the three days have passed?"

"Yes, Wilkinson, what happens then? As I remember, my uncle conducted a very short interview with Miss Franklin at the Spinster House. I'm not certain he asked her more than one or two questions." The duke shrugged. "Or they might simply have discussed the weather. I didn't pay attention. Do your papers include a list of qualifications I need to look for, besides an antipathy for the married state, of course?"

"N-no." Randolph scanned the document. "It says: 'When more than one spinster applies, they shall meet with the duke together—'"

"Together? Why together?" Jane scowled at her brother. "I should think the interviews should be held individually."

That *was* odd, but it wouldn't make any difference. Surely Cat would win the house. Jane might wish to escape her brother, but Cat wished to escape *four* brothers and three sisters—Mary still counted until she tied the knot and moved out. And Isabelle was Cat's distant relative. Anyone—except Jane—would agree the Spinster House should go to Cat.

"Good God, Jane," Randolph said. "I don't know. None of this makes sense."

Cat snorted. "What do you expect from something purporting to include a curse?"

"There is no purporting about the matter, Miss Hutting." The duke drummed his fingers against the chair arm, clearly eager to be done with this. "I'm sure Miss Dorring wasn't in her right mind when she wrote these instructions. She'd been very badly used by my disreputable ancestor, so she must have wished to exert as much control over my family as she could, even from the grave. I wouldn't have been surprised if she'd required the Duke of Hart to stand on his head during the proceedings."

It really was too bad that he was being put to all this trouble. His ancestor might have been a blackguard, but this duke seemed perfectly pleasant. Well, once he chose her, he'd be done with the matter and could get back to London.

"So *does* that document tell me what I'm supposed to look for in a candidate, Wilkinson?"

"No. The meeting isn't actually an interview, Your Grace."

"It's not?" Cat leaned forward, all the arguments she'd been marshalling to support her claim on the Spinster House dissolving. Surely Randolph was missing something. "Then how will the duke choose?"

"The duke doesn't choose. The spinsters draw straws—"

"Draw straws?" This was all going to come down to luck? No! That couldn't be right.

Jane leapt up to snatch the offending page from her brother. "I didn't see that when I looked."

She held the paper up—and then moved it away from her. Her arms weren't quite long enough. "Blast it, I left my spectacles on my desk."

"Let me." Cat plucked the document from Jane's fingers and found the relevant language. "'The spinster who draws the short straw,'" she read, "'shall be the one to live in the house.'" She threw the paper back on Randolph's desk; Randolph grabbed it before it went sailing onto the floor. "I can't believe it all comes down to luck. Why wouldn't Isabelle have the duke choose?"

"I have no idea, Miss Hutting," the duke said. He was standing now, too, since she and Jane were; he seemed even taller, his shoulders broader, in the confines of Randolph's office. "But I am delighted—and very relieved—she did not." The corners of his mouth turned up slightly. "It would take a braver man than I to choose between you and Miss Wilkinson."

Jane ignored the duke. "Are you certain you read that correctly, Cat?"

"Yes. The words aren't difficult, but do get your spectacles and see for yourself if you don't believe me."

"All right, I will." Jane dashed into the other room; when she came back, she snatched the paper off Randolph's desk.

Randolph's brows slammed down. "Jane, please. You're being—"

Jane jerked her eyes off the paper to glare at her brother. "Don't tell me what I'm being, Randolph."

"But His Grace—" Randolph's mouth flattened into a thin line, and he looked at the duke. "I must apologize for my sister. I—"

"Don't, Wilkinson. Apologize. Unless you wish to feel your penknife between your shoulder blades."

"What?"

The duke inclined his head toward Jane. "Miss Wilkinson looks as if she would like to skewer you."

Jane snorted. "You can see why I want to live in the Spinster House, Your Grace."

"Jane! What will His Grace think?"

"I don't care what he thinks, Randolph." Jane shook the paper in her hand. "Especially now that it appears his opinion has no bearing on who wins the Spinster House. I—"

Jane's brain finally caught up with her mouth. She flushed. "Please forgive me, Your Grace." She glared at Randolph again. "I have a hard time controlling my temper when my brother treats me like a child."

"And I must treat you like a child when you behave like one, Jane."

Did Randolph indeed have a death wish? Cat had always thought him pompous and annoying, but she'd never seen him behave this badly.

Jane's eyes widened, and she drew in a deep, slow breath, obviously preparing to tell Randolph exactly what she thought of him. Fortunately the duke spoke first.

"Your sister merely needs to assure herself that all is aboveboard, Wilkinson. I quite understand." He gestured at the paper. "Have you discovered anything else about the selection process, Miss Wilkinson?"

Jane flushed. "No. It is exactly as Cat read." She frowned as she put the paper back on Randolph's desk. "I can't understand what Isabelle could have been thinking to leave it all to chance like this."

"I don't understand what she was thinking about any of it," Randolph said. "Spinsterhood is an unnatural state for a woman, after all." He tugged on his waistcoat and looked at the duke. "Women need a man's guidance, don't they, Your Grace?"

Jane made a noise that sounded like a growl. Cat couldn't see her expression—she was looking through her own red haze of anger.

"Wilkinson," the duke said, "I believe there are two women in this room who would happily have your guts for garters."

* * *

Marcus paced the length of the castle's study. Thank God Nate and Alex were out. He might snap their heads off if they tried to talk to him now.

He'd like to tear something apart. Or throw something. He eyed the heavy inkwell on the large desk. No, too messy. Perhaps the suit of armor standing guard by the globe of the world? Kicking over that metal monstrosity would make a very satisfying clatter.

And would likely have even palsied old Emmett running to see what was amiss. No, much as he wanted to take his spleen out on such a satisfying target, he would restrain himself. But, good God, it was almost impossible. He'd thought he'd be free of this blasted village in a matter of hours, and now he was trapped here for days. And for what purpose? Wilkinson could hold the straws for the ladies as easily as he.

He made another circuit of the room and stopped in front of a full-length portrait of a man in old-fashioned garb. The fellow wore an enormous lace collar that made it look as if his head was on a platter, an elaborate doublet with ridiculously full hose, embroidered stockings, and high-heeled shoes with large black pompons. What a popinjay!

He was young, at a guess five or six years younger than Marcus, with a short beard and mustache and a rather cocky expression. He'd seen his sort in London, young lordlings who thought the world and everyone in it existed for their personal enjoyment. Who was he?

It looked as if the portrait had been painted here in the study. The curtains and rug were the same, though in the painting their colors were much brighter. The fellow must be an ancestor.

Marcus leaned closer to read the small bronze plate in the frame: MARCUS, THIRD DUKE OF HART.

The blackguard.

The London house had long ago been stripped of all paintings of the scoundrel, as if banning the fellow's image from the walls could also wipe him from the family tree. Ha. Not likely. But his own dear mother had ensured that, no matter what else happened, *he* could never forget the dastard.

Nate's parents had said his father, in his last moments of lucidity, had insisted his son be given the third duke's Christian name, though that made no sense. He was already burdened with the title and its curse. Why give him more to carry? No, he felt certain it was his mother who'd thought saddling him with the bounder's full name would be a splendid jest.

He studied the fellow's face more carefully. He didn't see evil or dissipation or cruelty in his eyes. Well, likely the painter had chosen to flatter the man. An artist knew from whose pockets his fee was coming.

"There you are," Nate said, entering the room with Alex. "You were gone longer than we expected. We finally gave up waiting and went for a ride without you." He frowned. "Everything all right?"

"Everything is, regrettably, more complicated than I had hoped." Blast it, Alex had come over to stare at the portrait.

"Marcus, this could be you, you know"—Alex grinned—"except for the facial hair and the outlandish clothes. Which relative is it?"

Bloody hell! Marcus examined the third duke's face again. There *was* an uncanny resemblance.

Alex read the inscription and let out a long, low whistle. "It's the evil duke. You're named after him."

"Yes." God, he wished he could leave this infernal place in the morning, but thanks to Isabelle Dorring, he was trapped here for several days. He went over to the liquor cabinet, poured himself a healthy dose of brandy, and took a larger swallow than he normally would. The liquid burned going down, but it created a comforting warmth when it reached his belly. He held up the decanter. "Brandy, anyone?"

"Of course." Alex looked once more at the painting before walking over. "I still don't see why you let this curse business bedevil you."

Miss Hutting had said something similar. She'd laughed, her reddish gold hair gleaming in the sun, green eyes and lovely porcelain skin—

No. The decanter clinked against the glass as he poured Alex's brandy. He should not be feeling this . . . excitement. He shouldn't be feeling anything for the woman. She had no desire to wed.

And he had no desire to die.

"I believe my family history adequately proves the curse's existence," he said, as he handed Alex his drink.

Alex shrugged. "Five deaths. Very sad, but I still think they must be merely coincidence. Or perhaps if you believe something will happen, you'll act in such a way as to make it come true. Don't you think so, Nate?"

"No." Nate scowled as he took his brandy from Marcus. "For the last two hundred years, every single time the Duchess of Hart is increasing with a male child, the duke dies before the baby is born. That is far more than coincidence. And, as Marcus said in London, his father didn't believe in the curse, yet he died, too." Nate glared down at his glass. "My mother lost her father and her brother to it. She made me promise to keep Marcus safe for as long as I could."

Blast. "Nate, you are not my keeper."

Nate transferred his glare to Marcus. "*Someone* needs to keep you from dragging women into the bushes."

"I did not drag Miss Rathbone anywhere. If anything, she dragged me."

"You two are squabbling like children," Alex said.

Marcus struggled to control his spleen. He wasn't normally so emotional.

Hell, I hope this isn't more evidence of the curse.

"We were brought up together," Nate said. "I consider Marcus my brother."

But brothers have to let each other live their lives—no matter how short that life might be.

Alex nodded. "Yes, I see that. In any event, even if there is a curse—"

"Which there is," Nate snapped.

Alex gave Nate an exasperated look, but just continued, "Didn't you say you can break it by marrying for love, Marcus?"

"Yes." Marcus sounded cynical to his own ears, but hell, it would be easier to find a unicorn at Almack's than a woman of the *ton* he could care for.

"Well, there you go," Alex said, taking a seat by the fire. "Find—I say, I think this is the most uncomfortable chair I've ever sat in."

Marcus laughed as he sat, too. The state of the castle's chairs was a much more welcome topic than the state of his heart. "I don't doubt it. My nefarious ancestor probably selected it."

"More likely his mother." Nate sat on the equally uncomfortable settee. "Family lore has it that the woman was a terror. Ruled everyone with an iron fist and put far more stock in show than in substance—or, in this case, comfort."

"And none of the subsequent duchesses chose to redecorate?" Alex looked around. "I'm certainly no expert, but my guess is everything in this room dates from the early 1600s."

"I imagine it does." The room did look old and sad, though not as sad as when Marcus had left for the village. Emmett—or Dunly—had found a small army of maids to attack the cobwebs and remove the Holland cloth covers in his absence. "Since the curse, no Duke of Hart has made his home here."

Alex's brows rose. "Even the third duke?"

"Even he." Apparently the blackguard was capable of feeling some guilt. Not that guilt—or, one would hope, contrition—would have raised Isabelle Dorring from her watery grave or saved her child, but it was slightly comforting to think his relative's heart hadn't been made completely of stone.

"But this is your primary seat."

"Yes, but the dukes and duchesses have always preferred London." In London it was possible to keep busy enough to forget the curse, at least for a while. Not that the duchesses wished to forget. They looked forward to the duke's demise so they could enjoy the wealth and prestige their hopefully brief marriages had given them without the inconvenience of a husband.

Alex frowned. "Yet they must have felt the need to see if all was well with the estate."

"They did visit occasionally." Guilt cramped Marcus's gut. Once in his thirty years hardly counted as occasionally. "And they hired good stewards to look after the place."

"Even the best steward isn't the same as the landowner," Alex said. "It seems shockingly irresponsi—" He stopped, realizing at last that what he said was rather damning of the current duke. "Er, no insult meant, of course. I'm sure you have your reasons. I just . . . with my own estates, I . . ." He cleared his throat. "But that's neither here nor there, is it?"

Marcus nodded. He couldn't dispute Alex's words. Any good landowner *would* look after his land and people personally. "No offense taken. In the normal course of events, I'd visit often. As it is, I'm fairly confident none of my tenants would recognize me if I rode past him." Yet another way Isabelle's curse had twisted his life. He shrugged.

"Knowing you're going to die before your heir is born tends to dampen your interest in your property."

Alex was frowning at him. "Only if you let it."

He felt as if he'd taken a flush hit to his stomach. "Pardon?"

"He's right, Marcus."

Marcus shifted his gaze to Nate. *Et tu, Brutus?*

At least Nate had the grace to look apologetic. "It's true that no one would recognize you. When Alex and I were out riding, people stopped to ask if one of us was the duke."

Marcus snorted. "So they could gawp at me."

Nate shook his head, his expression serious. "No. So they could see you. You're their lord, Marcus. Their well-being depends on you."

Was Nate criticizing him? Anger and hurt twisted in his chest. "Blast it, I've seen to their well-being. Weren't their homes in good repair?"

"Yes, but—"

"Did you see anything—bridges or walls or roads—that needed attention?"

"No."

"Then I've done my duty. No one has reason to complain."

"No one is complaining, Marcus," Alex said. "Everyone's just curious. They want to see the Duke of Hart."

Because of the curse. They want to stare at me as they'd stare at an animal in a menagerie.

"There's no bloody reason for them to see me or me to see them."

Alex and Nate just looked at him. They didn't understand. They couldn't.

"You both have watched your fathers manage their lands. They've taught you how to go on just as you'll teach your own sons."

Nate shifted on the settee. "Marcus, I know—"

"No, you don't, Nate. Neither of you know what my life is like." Even knowing his history—and Nate knew it better than anyone—they couldn't know what it felt like to live with the burden of the curse every single bloody day. "I never met my father. I'll never meet my son—if I ever have a son, that is."

He looked at the fire and watched the ashes rise with the heat.

The kindest thing I could do is to never marry. Then the curse will finally die.

He'd been certain at twenty he'd not wed. Even last year, he'd been determined to remain single. What did he care if the title reverted to the Crown? It would be a blessing if he were the last Cursed Duke.

But ever since his damn thirtieth birthday, the loneliness and the need had eaten away at his resolve, even though he knew any woman he married would, in the final tally, only make him lonelier. Sharing his life with someone like Miss Rathbone would cause his soul to shrivel and die long before the curse took his body. But his heart—or a far less noble organ—was no longer listening to his brain.

Perhaps I should take Isabelle's way out and drown myself.

He was a strong swimmer, but Loves Water was large and deep and cold—

No. Not to judge Isabelle Dorring's actions—he'd be the last man to do that—but he'd thought Miss Hutting correct this afternoon. Choosing suicide felt selfish and rather cowardly.

Nate finally found his voice. "How did things go in the village? Are we off to the Lake District in the morning?"

"No." Marcus rubbed the spot between his eyebrows. He could feel a headache coming on. "It appears I have to advertise the Spinster House opening, which means I have to stay here for a while. You'll have to go on without me."

Oh, hell. Nate was frowning at him, worry back in his eyes. "Then we'll stay, too. What's a few days' delay, right, Alex?"

"Right. The lakes will still be there." Alex grinned. "And if we stay here, we can help Marcus end this curse."

Marcus's stomach dropped. "How are you going to do that?"

"By finding you a nice village girl to fall in love with, of course."

God—or Isabelle Dorring—help him. Confirmed spinster Miss Hutting's face popped into his thoughts.

Chapter Six

April 25, 1617—Some of the duke's friends came down from London yesterday. I saw them with him walking and laughing on the village green. Such delightful gentlemen. They say you can tell a lot about a man from the friends he keeps.

—from Isabelle Dorring's diary

Marcus, accompanied by Nate and Alex, stepped out of Wilkinson's office with the notices Wilkinson—no, more likely Miss Wilkinson—had written.

"Miss Wilkinson is quite attractive," Alex said. "If the females of Loves Bridge are anything like her, I'm sure we can find one for you to fall in love with, Marcus."

"I do not need you to play matchmaker, Alex." If the notion weren't so ludicrous, it would be revolting. "And Miss Wilkinson is one of the two women vying to be the next Spinster House spinster."

"Is she?" Alex laughed and glanced back at the building. They all saw the curtain on the window near Miss Wilkinson's desk twitch back into place. "I'm not so certain she's committed to the single life." He adjusted the angle of his beaver hat. "Perhaps I could make your job simpler and remove her from the competition."

"Not in three days."

"What? You don't think I can enthrall the lady so quickly?" Alex said as they started down the lane.

"I know you won't try." Alex could be annoying and a bit careless, but he'd never toy with a woman's affections.

"I don't know. This place *is* called Loves Bridge. Once we find you your love, I might look for myself."

"Feel free to do so, but skip the part about looking for me." He knew Alex was kidding. The man had been jilted almost at the altar only months earlier.

"I thought you'd sworn off marriage," Nate said.

Alex shrugged. "If I can find a woman to break Marcus's curse, perhaps I can find one to mend my broken heart." He grinned. "And what about you, Nate? Shall I find you a wife as well while I'm rummaging around in Loves Bridge's collection of maidens? You're looking a little lonely."

"I am not, you lobcock."

They reached the path to the churchyard. It was too narrow to walk three abreast, so Marcus let Nate and Alex go ahead.

The moment he stepped in among the trees, the woods' quiet enveloped him, causing the tight, tense feeling in his head and neck to relax. Instead of the din of London— tradesmen hawking their wares and coach wheels rattling over cobblestones—he heard birds calling and small animals rustling through the underbrush. He took a deep breath. The air was different, too, scented with pine and soil instead of smoke and filth.

Nate and Alex must feel the special quality of the place as well. They'd dropped their voices as though they'd entered a church. It was—

Marcus tripped over a tree root, but caught his balance

before Nate or Alex noticed and teased him about it. It was not surprising Miss Hutting had stumbled here yesterday. The ground was very uneven. It had been a bit of luck he'd been able to catch her. He'd reacted on instinct and had almost gone tumbling with her.

He swallowed.

Best not to think about that. It wouldn't have been pleasant. Better to wait for a soft bed—

No! What was the matter with him? There would be no soft bed for Cat—for *Miss Hutting*—and him.

He kicked a stone and watched it bounce up the path ahead of him. It almost hit Nate's boot before veering off into the underbrush.

She had felt so good in his arms. She was precisely the right size—not too tall or too short or too thin or too plump. Perfect.

He clenched his hands into fists. She was *not* perfect. She was not anything to him except possibly the next Spinster House spinster.

He lengthened his stride to catch up to Nate and Alex as they went through the churchyard gate.

"Here, Marcus," Alex said. "Give us each some notices to post. It will get the job done faster."

It would, but he was not about to risk Isabelle Dorring's wrath. Her instructions had been quite specific. The duke was to post the notices, and so he would do so. Twenty years ago, his uncle had insisted Marcus tack each paper up, even though he was only a boy of ten. He could not think the rules had changed now that he was a man of thirty.

But he couldn't say that. Nate would understand, but Alex already thought he had one foot in Bedlam.

"Thank you, but I'd rather do it myself. There are only a few, and the places aren't far apart. Why don't you go off to Cupid's Inn and have a pint? I'll join you there when I'm done."

He smiled when what he wanted to do was give them each an encouraging shove toward the inn. "I won't be long."

"All right." Alex grinned. "I'll never say no to a pint."

Nate was harder to get rid of. He gave Marcus a long look. "Are you certain you don't want some help? I was with you last time."

"Yes, but we were children then, and you were only there because your father was my guardian." His smile this time came more naturally. "If you'll remember, we were mostly playing tag on the green. I don't think we need to treat the villagers to such a spectacle today."

Alex laughed. "Oh, God, now that I would like to see, you two chasing each other over the lawn."

Nate glared at him and then looked back at Marcus. "I don't mind bearing you company."

"Thank you, but I really don't need any help." He smiled to soften his words.

Alex slapped Nate on the back. "Leave the man to his task. We'll spend the time planning our matchmaking campaign to end this silly curse once and for all."

Damnation. He did not want Alex busying himself in his affairs, and he definitely didn't like the fact it was Miss Hutting's face—and other attributes—that sprang to mind at his words.

Nate's expression twisted into one of disgust. "Good God, I am not discussing such a vile subject."

"Oh, after a couple pints, you'll be inspired," Alex said.

He was joking, of course. That was it. Alex loved a good jest. The best thing to do would be to play along. Then Alex would lose interest—it was no fun teasing a man who didn't react.

"I rely on you to keep Alex from matching me with a hideous harridan, Nate."

Nate snorted and then shook his head. "All this jackanapes will be matching is himself to a glass of ale. Don't be long, Marcus, or we'll have to drag Alex's drunken body back to the castle."

"Hey now, you know I can hold my liquor better than you."

"Well, for God's sake, don't try to prove it here," Nate said as he and Alex moved off. "Loves Bridge has enough to gabble about without adding an inebriated earl to the mix."

"An inebriated marquess, more like!"

Marcus watched them leave and then turned toward the vicarage. He should speak to the vicar before he posted anything around the church. With luck, Miss Hutting would be away from home.

He crossed the churchyard, pausing to touch Isabelle Dorring's gravestone.

Well, technically just "stone" since the woman wasn't buried there—or anywhere.

It's the bloody curse that's making me want Miss Hutting.

He gripped the stone hard. *I won't let Isabelle control me. I'll avoid the woman from now on. How hard can that be? I'm only here three more days.*

He looked up—and his stomach sank. Miss Hutting was just closing the vicarage door behind her.

Perhaps she hasn't seen me. I'll hide behind Isabelle's non-headstone—

No, that would be cowardly—and ridiculous. In any event, it was too late. Miss Hutting *had* seen him.

Perhaps she would go on about her business.

Of course she wouldn't. She changed direction to stride purposely toward him. For just an instant, he was tempted to turn tail and run, but he quashed the cowardly impulse and held his ground.

"Good morning, Your Grace."

"Good morning, Miss Hutting."

She eyed the papers in his hand. "I assume those are the Spinster House notices?"

What else could they be? "Yes." He started to edge past her. "I was just coming to speak to your father about putting one up in the church, so if you'll excuse me?"

"Papa's away from home." She grinned, a wide smile that crinkled her eyes and showed her teeth.

London ladies never grinned. They rarely smiled, and when they did, they only bent their firmly closed lips slightly.

"That's unfortunate." He would have to do the church last. "When do you expect him back?"

"Oh, not for a while, but I can help you. I know exactly where the notice should go."

"I really can't impose. You were on your way somewhere, weren't you?" *I cannot spend time alone with her.*

But he desperately wanted to do exactly that.

"Only to Cupid's Inn. I'm meeting Jane and our friend Anne Davenport and some of the other ladies to discuss the village fair. I'm early though, so I have plenty of time to help you." She snorted. "I could see Mama was going to saddle me with the twins so I dashed out the door. The boys would have been very much in the way at the meeting. As you might imagine, it's impossible to keep an eye on those two and have anything approaching a sensible conversation."

Sadly he could not imagine it. He had no experience with children.

Miss Hutting had already started for the church. She looked back when she noticed he wasn't with her. "Are you coming?"

He felt himself weakening, but tried one last argument. "I'm not certain I should accept your help, Miss Hutting. Miss Wilkinson might object."

"Don't be ridiculous. Jane isn't such a cabbage head."

He *would* like to get rid of the notices as quickly as possible, and it would be easy enough to see if Miss Hutting tried to get him to hang the paper in a dark, out-of-the-way corner.

Surely I can control myself for the few minutes it will take to post a paper in the church.

He caught up to her. "Yes. Pardon me for dillydallying."

She laughed. "I didn't think dukes could do something so plebeian as dillydally."

London women didn't laugh, either. They tittered.

"I don't make a habit of it." Or did he? Perhaps that was all he did, dallying away his life. There was little point in doing anything else when his fate was out of his hands.

He fell into step with her. He'd noticed yesterday how easily she could keep up with him. It must be her long legs.

He should *not* be thinking of Miss Hutting's legs.

"If it's not prying, may I ask where your father has gone?"

"Off to visit Lord Davenport." She wrinkled her short, attractive nose—

Hell, it was just a nose, just a place to perch spectacles, and too short for real beauty.

But it suited her face.

"I imagine they'll spend hours talking about horses and hunting. Papa is the brother of the Earl of Penland—Papa was the fourth son—and grew up riding."

"Misses it, does he?" Everything about her appearance pleased him. He knew she wasn't classically beautiful, but she was beautiful to him. Looking at her made him happy—and other things.

He had to get the Spinster House issue settled as quickly as possible and get out of the village. His life might depend on it.

"A little. But unlike many younger sons I've heard of, he truly does enjoy being a vicar." She turned her head to look up at him. "I don't believe he went visiting to discuss the baron's stables, however. I think Mama sent him to see if Lord Davenport knows of any suitable suitors for me."

Something that felt perilously like jealousy stabbed him in the gut.

That was ridiculous. He'd just met the girl; she was determined never to marry; and to top it all off, she was distantly related to Isabelle Dorring, the authoress of all his woes.

"If the Earl of Penland is your uncle, why didn't your parents send you to London for your come out?"

She sent him a look of disgust. "What? So I could be paraded about on the Marriage Mart like a prize pig at the fair?"

He laughed. Miss Hutting's description was not so far off the mark. "Surely not a pig. A horse, perhaps. A thoroughbred."

She snorted. "Not a thoroughbred. In any event, Mama would never suggest it. Papa and the earl don't get on. Papa says the man's a pompous old stick."

"He is a bit." The earl was much older than Marcus, but his son had been at school with him. "Viscount Edgedon is worse."

Miss Hutting smiled at him with approval, which made him far too happy.

"Yes, indeed. When the earl and his family came down for Tory's wedding, nothing in Loves Bridge was good enough for them. Penland's daughter, my cousin Juliet, is the one who really vexes me, though. She's Tory's age and married to a viscount—"

"Uppleton." Another fellow Marcus didn't care for.

"Yes. Short, balding, and obnoxious. I rather pitied her being yoked to him for life, but, if you can believe it, *she* feels sorry for *me*. She told me at the wedding how terribly disheartening it must be to have a younger sister marry before me, and she *kindly* assured me that I wasn't quite, *quite* on the shelf and shouldn't despair yet because certainly *someone* would have me, though I should probably steel myself to settle for a farmer."

She took a deep breath, visibly struggling to get her temper under control.

"You are not the only one to find the woman odious," he said.

She managed a smile. "I am not surprised. Fortunately she and the rest of that family skipped Ruth's wedding, though they are expected at Mary's." She stopped at the church door and sighed. "I can stomach Juliet's annoying matrimonial talk for the brief time I have to endure her, but Mama is a different matter. I do wish she'd stop trying to marry me off."

He did not understand why Miss Hutting was so against marriage. He had a valid reason—for him, marriage was a death sentence. But for most people it was a sensible, comfortable arrangement.

"I'm sure your mother just wishes to have you taken care of," he said as he opened the church door for her.

She glared at him before entering the dark, cool space. "Yes, I'm sure she does."

His brows rose. "You sound as if you doubt marriage would be to your benefit, Miss Hutting, but, at a minimum, it would get you out of the crowded vicarage and give you your own home."

She snorted. "And at what price? I'd be saddled with a husband, a man I'd have to cook for and clean for and whose children I'd have to bear and rear and all with precious little help. I'd have no time for myself at all. No, thank you."

She pointed to a board that was covered with handbills. "You can put the Spinster House notice there."

"You don't want children?" Blast, why had he said that? He forced a tack into the board rather harder than necessary.

He wanted children. He felt a painful longing whenever he happened upon a nurse with her charges. Stupid. Unless he was very lucky and had a daughter first, he'd never *see* his child let alone hear him laugh or watch him take his first steps.

He'd even briefly considered having bastards if he could find a woman willing to carry the Cursed Duke's illegitimate offspring, but he'd rejected the thought almost immediately. Perhaps it was an odd offshoot of the curse, but the notion of saddling an innocent child with his blood and not his name and wealth felt deeply dishonorable.

"N-no." Miss Hutting sounded a bit uncertain, but then her voice strengthened. "Children are a great deal of work, you know."

"Actually, I don't know, and I never shall."

She frowned at him. "You really must not let that silly curse govern your life."

Good God! "The bloody—pardon me. The *blasted* curse governs my life whether I wish it or not."

If only the curse *was* such a simple thing that he could decide it didn't exist and go about his life as he wished. He could marry, have a family, live an ordinary existence like every other man in England. But no. He couldn't consider marriage without also considering his mortality.

Miss Hutting pressed her lips together as if she'd like to argue the matter. Fortunately she restrained herself. "Then you must take my word for it. Once a woman has children, she never again has a moment to herself. I've seen that with my mother."

They stepped back out into the warm spring air, and he squinted in the sun. "Ten *is* rather a lot."

Did she have any idea how those ten children had been conceived? She must. She lived in the country, with animals all around . . .

Though the coital act between animals was rather different than that between a man and a woman. At least the poets said so. There'd never been anything more than physical relief in his couplings.

A breeze caught a strand of her red-gold hair and fluttered it in her eyes. She batted it away.

"Yes, ten is a lot, but remember two of my sisters are married also. They only have two children apiece, yet all they can talk about is teething and crying and runny noses." She started walking down the hill toward the road. "I want to do more with my life. I want to do something important."

"Many people would say raising children *is* important, the most important thing one can do." Zeus, what he would give to be able to do something as *unimportant* as raise a child. "Children are the future."

Which he would never see. The blasted curse kept him tethered to the past. Once his son was in the womb, his own future would be counted in days, not years. How the *hell* could Miss Hutting dismiss raising children as if it was no more significant than sweeping the floor?

"*Your* future perhaps," she was saying. "I quite understand that."

"Do you really?" She had no idea.

At least she refrained from mentioning the "silly curse" again.

"Your name and title will continue after you're gone," she said, looking up at him. "But can you understand at all how fleeting a woman's existence is? We give up our lives and possessions—even our names—to our husbands. Our bodies become little more than vessels for children, to continue our husbands' lines." Her voice hardened. "I want something else. Something more. Something that's mine, with *my* name on it." She paused on the edge of the road. "Where are we going next?"

"*I'm* going to the Spinster House." There was no "we" about it. "Mr. Wilkinson gave me the key, so I'm having a look around after I post the notice on the door."

Miss Hutting appeared deaf to his implied snub. "Oh, good. Miss Franklin didn't invite people in to visit. I'm dying to see the place"—she grinned—"especially as I hope it will be my new home."

How bold the girl was. He should depress her pretentions and send her on her way.

But she wasn't encroaching, and this was the country. The rules of behavior were more relaxed here than in Town. She'd made it very clear she wasn't pursuing him.

And he didn't want to send her away.

He could control himself. He'd never forced his attentions on an unwilling woman. And if he somehow did forget his manners, he could rely on the feisty, independent Miss Hutting to remind him of them by whacking him in the head with whatever weapon came to hand.

He gave in, but whether it was to her wishes or his desires he refused to contemplate.

"Don't you mind the thought of spending your life alone?" he asked as they crossed the road. The loneliness that had been gnawing at him these last months stirred in his chest.

She laughed as they turned up the walk to the Spinster House. "I *love* the thought of being alone, Your Grace. I dream of it, especially when Mary's sharp elbow is poking me in the back at night. It would be heaven."

No, it was hell. He'd tried to escape it by living in London, surrounded by people, but he'd discovered it was possible to feel most alone in a crowd.

He affixed a notice to the Spinster House door and then fished in his pocket for the key. "But what of love, Miss Hutting?"

"Love?"

"Yes. I thought all women dreamed of love." He fitted the key into the lock and turned it.

"I love my parents and brothers and sisters." She grinned again. "But I would love them even more if I lived here, across the road from them."

Good God, how could she be so flippant? He shoved the door open more forcefully than necessary.

He shouldn't say anything more. If he opened his mouth, he was going to step—leap—over the bounds of propriety. He moved aside so Miss Hutting could precede him.

Something in the independent tilt of her head, or the angle of her shoulders—or, yes, the sway of her hips—loosened his tongue.

"But what about the love of a husband, Miss Hutting? What about the touch of a husband's hand, his lips, his—" Zeus! Need and desire had followed on the heels of annoyance and now beat insistently in his head and chest and groin.

He *had* to control himself. He forced a smile. "I hope you would not complain about a husband's sharp elbows in bed at night."

Bed.

Ah.

Perhaps that was not exactly what he should have said.

Cat had opened her mouth to answer, but some quality in the duke's voice stopped her. It was deep and dark and warm and . . .

And now she was being silly. She turned to face him— and stopped again.

He'd closed the door, shutting out the bright spring sunlight. His wide shoulders almost spanned the small entryway.

Suddenly she was very, very aware of being alone with him.

His eyes, partly obscured in the dim light, watched her, something intense and . . . male in his gaze.

Something intense and female fluttered low in her belly. It was difficult to breathe. Her chest felt tight; her cheeks, warm. Her entire body flushed, not with embarrassment but with an odd sensation she'd never experienced before and wasn't certain she wished to experience again. Not fear. True, if she'd wanted to leave, she'd have to have his cooperation, but she didn't doubt he'd give it. She wasn't in any danger—at least not from him.

"I . . ." She cleared her throat. "I am not going to have a husband, Your Grace. I don't wish to be a slave to any man."

The peculiar feeling in her stomach must be hunger. She would have a nice cup of tea and a lovely slice of seedcake when she got to Cupid's Inn. Mrs. Tweedon, the innkeeper's wife, was an excellent baker. "You know that. That's why I'm here in the Spinster House," she said more forcefully. "What are you thinking?"

"You don't want to know what I'm thinking, Miss Hutting." A hot, intense, *hungry* look gleamed in his eyes.

She stepped back and bumped into an occasional table, causing the candlestick on it to wobble. She lunged and caught it before it could topple off onto the floor.

"A woman gives herself to a man in marriage, true," he said, his eyes hooded now, "but the bond goes both ways. A man gives himself to his wife as well."

Oh! The fluttering in her belly intensified. She looked at his mouth. His lips were narrow and firm, not fat and slobbery like Mr. Barker's. How would they feel against hers?

Idiot! A duke was not about to kiss a vicar's daughter, no matter how hot and hungry his eyes.

And this vicar's daughter wanted nothing to do with a duke, beyond having this one hand over the keys to the Spinster House. He must be the most overbearing of men— he was at the non-royal pinnacle of the peerage, after all. He would expect everyone to bow and scrape to him.

Well, she wasn't going to be one of his toadies. It was just the odd intimacy of being in the house alone with him that was giving her these feelings. Sunlight would improve matters.

She moved into the sitting room and threw open the shutters.

The duke followed her. "Is your mother a slave to your father?"

She opened her mouth to say yes, but stopped. Mama's life might not be the one Cat wanted, but no one would call her a slave. Quite the contrary. Mama had a rather strong personality. Papa more often than not was guided by her wishes.

"N-no."

"And your sisters? Are they slaves to their husbands?"

"No." Her poor brothers-in-law were a trifle henpecked.

His right brow flew up as if a new thought had just occurred to him. "So is it that you prefer women? Is that why you have no interest in marriage?"

"What?" He couldn't mean . . . ?

No. She must have misunderstood him.

"That is, most of my friends are women." She forced herself to smile. "Though I can't guarantee Jane will feel very friendly toward me if—when—I take up residence here."

The duke nodded. "That would explain things."

Heavens, he *did* mean what she'd thought.

"Having female friends has nothing to do with my disinterest in marriage, Your Grace." She stepped closer to him to poke him in the chest, but thought better of it at the last minute and curled her hand into a fist instead. "You are a typical male. You cannot comprehend that a sensible female could possibly give up the *joy* of yoking herself to one of your kind. We poor, weak, helpless creatures must long for a man's guidance. We—"

She pressed her lips together and took a long, calming breath through her nose. There was no sense brangling with the duke. He wouldn't change—men never did.

And she must not forget he played some role in finding the next Spinster House tenant. While it seemed unlikely he would do anything to influence the lottery's outcome, there was no need to alienate him and risk limiting her chances.

She forced her lips into a smile. "Well, that's neither here nor there, is it? Shall we look around the house?"

He was staring at her in a most unsettling manner.

"Such passion," he murmured, brushing a finger lightly over her lips, "and such control. What would happen if you let that control slip its leash?"

She would have slapped his hand away, but it was already at his side. His touch had been so brief. Had she imagined it?

No. Her lips felt swollen and sensitive. Throbbing, tingling . . . as did another set of lips much lower on her anatomy.

Oh, God.

Chapter Seven

April 30, 1617—I will not listen to Rosaline and Maria. They say that all London gentlemen are alike, that they may flirt with country girls, but they marry London ladies. They are wrong, at least with regard to the Duke of Hart. I know it.

—from Isabelle Dorring's diary

He wanted to kiss her.

The girl stood so close, he could feel the heat of her body and smell the clean scent of lemon—and something else. Something hot and musky and feminine. Her face was flushed; her bodice rose and fell with her quickened breath. She felt it, too, this attraction, though he could tell from the confusion and uncertainty in her eyes that she didn't understand what it was she felt.

He'd like to show her. He'd like to put his hands on her shoulders and urge her up against him. Gently, carefully. No force. An invitation only. He knew that at the first sign of coercion, she'd bolt.

He wanted to taste her passion.

Her tongue peeked out to moisten her lips and need lanced through him, lodging in his most obvious organ.

He wanted to feel those lips under his. . . .

Zeus! What the bloody hell was the matter with him? He did not make a habit of lusting after prickly spinsters.

It was the curse—and the damn house. It must be haunted. Ridiculous, but that was the only explanation he could come up with for his mad desires. Well, Isabelle Dorring would not win *this* battle.

He forced himself to step back, putting a foot of space between himself and the alluring Miss Hutting. He cleared his throat. "We should look around if we are going to. I have those notices to post, you know."

"Y-yes. Of course." Miss Hutting took a few steps back as well. "I do want to see the place. Did you know Miss Franklin wasn't actually Miss Franklin?"

"Pardon?" The curse must be affecting Miss Hutting's thinking as well.

"Miss Franklin's real name is—or was—Miss Frost. Papa told Mama the whole tale when we were at Randolph's office yesterday. I imagine it is all over the village now."

She was talking rather quickly. Was she nervous here alone with him? He smiled—inwardly. If he let her see his amusement, she'd no doubt take it as male conceit and slap his face soundly.

He looked at the room instead. It had a beamed ceiling and pale yellow walls. He remembered the dark, intricately carved oak paneling around the hearth. As a child sitting through his uncle's interview with a much younger Miss Franklin—he was certain she'd gone by that name then—he'd thought he'd seen faces in its deep whorls and grooves. The mirror over the mantel reflected the room's worn red settee and armchair, which he also remembered from twenty years ago, as well as the ugly painting of a hunting dog with a dead bird dangling from its mouth. Apparently Miss Franklin had not had the interest or the funds to redecorate.

"Is there some scandal attached to the couple?" he asked. "It does seem odd that, at their rather advanced ages, they eloped in the middle of the night."

"But they didn't elope. Papa married them here in this very room! It turns out Miss Franklin—or, rather, Miss Frost—" Miss Hutting emitted a short, annoyed breath. "Oh, fiddle. She's now the Duchess of Benton, actually. Anyway, it turns out she knew Mr. Wattles—who's the Duke of Benton—when they were young."

"Ah." He'd heard the old duke had died, as well as the duke's heir and his spare. This Wattles must be the third son, he of the scandalous wife. Late wife, that is. She'd recently shuffled off this mortal coil also—as scandalously as she'd lived.

Marrying so soon after his wife's death would certainly get the gossips chattering, so it made sense the man wished to tie the knot quietly.

Miss Hutting was shaking her head. "I would never have guessed Mr. Wattles was a duke's son. He always looked like he found his clothes in someone's attic."

Odd. Whenever he'd seen the man about Town, the fellow had been dressed normally. Perhaps he'd been trying to disguise himself. Loves Bridge was not far from London. Word of his whereabouts—and his amorous exploits, apparently—would have got back to the gabble grinders if anyone here had recognized him.

Not that he completely faulted the man. His not-so-dearly departed wife had been a very dirty dish, worse even than the Duchesses of Hart—though it had always been said that, unlike the Dukes of Hart, Wattles had loved the woman when he'd married her.

"And why would he come to this little village and consent to teach reluctant music students like my brother Walter?"

Miss Hutting frowned. "You know, Miss Franklin, I mean—oh, bother. I'm just going to keep calling her that. Miss Franklin didn't breathe a word of their relationship to me, and I met with her every Wednesday afternoon."

That was hardly surprising. It wouldn't take a genius to discern that Miss Hutting would not be a supportive audience for such a discussion.

"It's a small village. They probably wished to maintain some privacy."

Miss Hutting's brows slanted into a scowl. "I still don't see how Miss Franklin could be so harebrained. She had her independence, and she threw it away. And for what?"

"A title? Wealth?" Surely Miss Hutting wasn't that naïve.

She shook her head. "No. Perhaps if she was a silly young girl, but Miss Franklin is almost forty."

"Perhaps she was lonely." He understood loneliness all too well. "Perhaps she loves him."

Love? Ha! Love has no place in the ton, *and Benton is a member of the* ton.

Miss Hutting gawped at him. "Love Mr. Wattles—I mean the Duke of Benton?"

And now he was forced to defend the notion. "Surely the unfashionableness of a man's attire doesn't make him unlovable."

"No, of course not." Miss Hutting's expression darkened. "Miss Franklin was learning to play the harpsichord."

Was Miss Hutting losing her hold on her sanity? "What has that to say to the matter? Playing the harpsichord is hardly scandalous."

"Her teacher was Mr. Wattles. He must have seduced her during her lessons." Her forehead wrinkled. "Though I really can't imagine Mr. Wattles as a rake."

"Then perhaps Miss Franklin seduced poor Mr. Wattles."

Miss Hutting's eyes almost popped out of her head.

"Believe me, Miss Hutting, I know from sad experience

that women can be the aggressor in such matters." Miss Rathbone being just one case in point.

She opened her mouth as if to argue, but then blushed furiously.

Interesting. He'd very much like to know what she was thinking—

No, he wouldn't. If she was thinking what he hoped she was, it would only lead to embarrassment or disaster.

Miss Hutting nodded. "Yes. Of course you're correct. Though it's very odd Papa didn't say anything, even to Mama. He tells Mama everything."

That didn't seem at all odd to him. "I suspect Wilkinson swore him to secrecy so as to keep the news from Miss Wilkinson. I got the distinct impression he was hoping to have a new spinster moved in here before his sister knew there was a vacancy."

She snorted. "That's probably exactly what Randolph was thinking."

He raised a brow. "And do you think your father wanted to hide the vacancy from you as well?"

She bit her lip as she considered the matter. He would like to—

No! He would not like to do anything with the girl. They had spent far too much time alone here as it was.

"I don't think so," she finally said. "I don't believe it would have occurred to Papa that I'd want to move out of the vicarage"—her lovely lip curled up into a sneer—"unless I was moving into some man's home as his wife."

Oh, for God's sake.

"Miss Hutting, you may not wish to marry, but marriage is not a curse." *Bloody hell! Did I actually say that?* "That is, it's not a curse for anyone but me."

She frowned and opened her mouth as if to argue. If she told him one more time to live his life as if Isabelle Dorring had no control over it, he'd throttle her. He spoke quickly.

"Shall we continue our tour?"

Miss Hutting led the way into the kitchen and opened the shutters. He strolled over to examine the cupboard. "These plates look like they're from Isabelle's time."

"Very likely. She must have had a complete set—her father *was* a wealthy merchant—and single women aren't very hard on dishes." She looked up at him. "How many spinsters have there been, do you know?"

"Eight. We've been fortunate. The shortest amount of time any woman lived here was fourteen years, but one spinster stayed for forty."

Miss Hutting grinned. "I expect I'll be here a long time, too. You won't have to worry about me running off like Miss Franklin."

Surely she didn't know—*really* know—what she was giving up by choosing never to marry? Had she ever felt a man's touch, his mouth on—

Stop. It is none of my concern.

"*If* you win the position," he said. "Don't forget Miss Wilkinson is also hoping to live here."

That transformed her grin into a scowl. "Yes, *if* I do."

She turned abruptly and walked toward the back of the house to a room that felt lived in. Books lined the walls. A desk sat at one end and a handsome, old harpsichord at the other. The windows looked out on a lovely, if wild, garden—and on one of the window seats sprawled an orange and black and white cat.

"Hello, Poppy." Miss Hutting went over to scratch the cat's ears.

Poppy glared at Marcus.

Another female who has no use for men. "How did the cat get in?"

"I don't know. Miss Franklin thought there must be a hole somewhere." Miss Hutting frowned. "She told me

Mr. Wattles had helped her look for it, but now I wonder if that's really what he was doing."

Silence was his best response. The fact that the woman and Benton had married in haste indicated to him that Benton had been looking for an entirely different sort of entrance. Something *he'd* like to find—

No. No, of course he wouldn't.

He wasn't a very good liar, especially to himself.

"That doesn't sound safe. I'll have Mr. Emmett send someone over to investigate. If Poppy can get in, all sorts of vermin can."

Miss Hutting and the cat both glared at him now.

"Just don't fix it so Poppy can't come and go as she pleases. She won't like that." Miss Hutting brushed off her skirts. "Let's go upstairs."

Poppy leapt off the window seat and, tail high, ran out of the room. They followed in time to see her vanish up the stairs. Miss Hutting started after her.

Marcus paused with his foot on the first step. A mix of dread and anticipation knotted in his chest. Did he really wish to see precisely where the curse had started?

Miss Hutting had already disappeared. He listened to her footsteps echo across the floor above him.

This was probably his only opportunity to see the house. As soon as the next spinster was chosen, he'd leave Loves Bridge forever.

Anticipation—and curiosity—won out over dread. He took the stairs quickly to a small landing with three doors, two open to his right and one closed on his left. He heard Miss Hutting moving around in the closest room on his right.

"So you decided to come up," she said as he joined her.

"Yes." It had been silly to have hesitated. This room was unremarkable, like bedchambers he'd seen in countless other houses, though smaller than what he was used to. The bed was made, but the room gave the impression of having been left hurriedly—on the dressing table, a small, empty scent bottle lay on its side, and several of the wardrobe drawers were partially open. "What's next door?"

"Let's see."

The next room was even smaller and appeared to have once been a study or sitting room, but was now used for storage. One of the window shutters was broken, and a red upholstered armchair, stuffing leaking from its worn seat, was shoved up against it, keeping it from falling.

A tall brass candlestick stood on a heavy, carved cabinet next to an assortment of ceramic figurines, some of which were chipped or missing a body part. The cabinet, though, appeared to be in perfect condition. He opened one of the doors to reveal a number of small, decorated drawers with keyholes. He pulled on one. Locked. "Where do you suppose the key is?"

"I don't know. It was probably lost decades ago."

He frowned. "I can't imagine why Miss Franklin never mentioned this disrepair. I'm sure if Emmett knew of it, he'd have it attended to at once."

Miss Hutting was admiring a detailed carving of a cat sitting on what appeared to be a windowsill that graced one of the drawers. "Likely Miss Franklin didn't wish to cause problems. Up until her shocking marriage, I would have said she was quite a timid person."

"Well, I shall have someone see to this and to the exterior of the building before the next spinster, whoever she shall be, moves in." He dusted off his hands. "It was an excellent notion to tour the premises. I hope the last room is not in such a state."

"It may be worse," Miss Hutting said as they crossed the landing. "The door is closed, after all. Who knows how long it's been shut away?"

Precisely. It was the thought of seeing rotting fabric and

rodent droppings, of breathing in two centuries of dust and dirt that caused his stomach to clench, nothing else. He pushed open the door.

"Ohh." Miss Hutting sounded almost awestruck. "How lovely."

The room was the size of the other two combined and looked to be in excellent shape, almost as if Isabelle had just stepped out for a moment. But that was likely only because it was in shadows. Marcus stepped over to open the shutters.

"Look! It's Isabelle."

For the space of one convulsive heartbeat, he thought Miss Hutting had seen a ghost.

Good God, he was definitely losing his grip on reality.

He turned to see that the light from the window illuminated a full-length painting of a girl dressed in the long bodice and wide skirt of the early 1600s. Her white clothes were heavily embroidered with blue and red flowers and golden vines; the bodice's low round neck offered just a glimpse of her breasts. But it was her face, framed by a lace collar and her lovely red hair, that drew him: her high, smooth forehead; her lips, turned up in a slight smile; her green eyes gazing directly at him. She looked young and beautiful and happy. Clearly the painting had been done before she'd met his disreputable ancestor.

She also looked strangely familiar. . . .

He turned to gaze down at Miss Hutting. "You are very much like her."

"Do you think so?" Miss Hutting tilted her head, examining the picture. "No. It's just the hair, and perhaps the eyes."

She was wrong. The similarity was striking, though perhaps Miss Hutting's chin was firmer and her expression more determined.

He turned back to the painting and frowned. Isabelle was quite pretty, but she wasn't that extraordinary. There must have been many pretty girls for the third duke to choose from. And while Marcus believed in the curse—he had no choice about that—he did not believe in witches or love potions or any of that other superstitious nonsense. So why the hell had his ancestor squandered his honor and brought disgrace—and the curse—to his line over this girl?

He'd probably never know.

"This room is beautiful." Miss Hutting had lost interest in the painting and was looking around. "I wonder why Miss Franklin didn't sleep here."

Perhaps Miss Franklin had felt the same odd heaviness he did. The walls were dark oak paneling lightened somewhat by a paler wood inlay, but they still made him feel gloomy. Or perhaps it was the thought that his future had been stolen from him in this room—in that bed. The huge four-poster was dark oak as well, with heavy red curtains and—

And Poppy sitting right in the middle of the bedclothes, studiously licking her private parts.

If—*when*—she lived here, Cat thought, she would make this her bedchamber. It was much larger and nicer than the other room, and it looked out over the garden.

But perhaps the bed was uncomfortable. That might be why Miss Franklin hadn't chosen it. She leaned on the mattress to test it—and Poppy gave her a nasty look.

Ah. Had Poppy claimed this room then, and Miss Franklin had been too timid to sort things out? Well, *she* was not so timid. She'd make Poppy a comfortable spot somewhere else. And if the mattress needed replacing, surely the duke would see to it. He was going to have someone deal with the house's other issues.

The duke was frowning at the painting of Isabelle Dorring again.

When the workers were here, she'd have them move that, too. It felt wrong to toss it on a bonfire, which is what she'd like to do, but at least she could see it tucked securely into the storage room. She did not care to have Isabelle staring down at her while she slept.

She studied the picture. Yes, she'd grant that there was a slight family resemblance. "I think she looks a bit spoiled, if you must know."

The duke's eyes snapped down to hers, a deep line between them. "Spoiled? What do you mean?"

"It wouldn't be so surprising. She was the only child of a rich merchant. She was likely used to getting whatever she wanted, and she wanted your ancestor."

It really was too bad about the curse. This duke took far too much responsibility for what had happened all those years ago.

His frown deepened. "She was a young woman; the third duke was a wealthy and powerful man. I know at whose door to lay the blame."

Men's minds were so narrow. "Isabelle was twenty-four years old, Your Grace. My age. Not a young woman."

He snorted. "Right. An old crone, awake on every suit, no doubt."

Could he be more annoying? "I'm sure she knew exactly how to catch the duke's interest. Women can be very wily, you know."

"I do know, much to my sorrow." He raised his eyebrows. "And I thought you were shocked when I suggested Miss Franklin might have seduced Mr. Wattles."

"You never met Miss Franklin." Yes, perhaps she wasn't being entirely rational, but looking at Isabelle's face now, she'd be willing to bet the girl hadn't been a helpless victim. "And I don't mean seduction precisely. Nothing so obvious. I've merely observed that women almost always have the cooler head when it comes to romance, even though that may not be the fairy tale men like to tell."

"Oh? This is news to me."

Of course it was news to him—he was a man.

"You should pay more attention. Watch people, though I suppose being a duke it's difficult to fade into the woodwork. But I have to imagine the game is played the same way in London as it is here."

"Indeed it is. I assure you, women pursue men most assiduously in Town." His mouth flattened. "I have far too often felt like a fox running before a pack of baying hounds."

That sounded dreadful, but she believed him. He was titled and wealthy and very, very handsome. "Yes, but I'm referring to a far more subtle game, Your Grace. A woman finds a man she thinks will make a good husband, and then she persuades *him* to pursue *her*. I've seen my sisters and many of the other village women do it countless times."

"Really?" He put his hand on one of the bedposts.

She'd like to wipe that superior look off his face. Patronizing idiot.

"Yes, really. Once a girl has selected the man she wants, she studies his habits. She'll 'accidentally' encounter him on the village green. She'll smile at him. If he smiles back, she'll arrange to bump into him after Sunday services, and they'll share a few words about the sermon. Later, she'll just happen to be walking to the store when he's on an errand in the same direction, and they'll exchange observations about the weather. Before the poor man knows it, he's completely ensnared. He's calling on her whenever he can. Finally, he has no choice but to ask for her hand in marriage."

"But then Isabelle didn't play the game very well, did she? The third duke didn't marry her." His voice was rather low. "Though he got her with child."

Her cheeks heated. The duke's words made her stomach flutter again. "That's true. I imagine she couldn't believe that anyone would tell her 'no,' so she, er, put the cart before the horse, as it were."

The sun must have gone behind a cloud, because it suddenly seemed dark and quite intimate in the room. Was the duke leaning closer?

She took a small step back.

"You describe such a calculated campaign, Miss Hutting. What about love?" His voice was little more than a whisper, dark and seductive. "What about desire?"

"D-desire?"

Oh, drat, her voice squeaked. He would think her a scared little girl.

She *was* rather unsettled. Her heart and stomach were fluttering now, and she felt light-headed. Perhaps she was going to be ill.

She grabbed the bedpost to steady herself, her fingers just below the duke's.

His hand was so much broader, so much stronger, than hers.

"Yes, desire," he said, his words weaving a spell around her. "The physical need to touch and be touched, to be so close to another person you don't know where he ends and you begin. It can be painful, that need. It can consume you."

"Ah."

She could barely breathe. It felt as if the air was being sucked out of the room.

And then he took his free hand and touched the side of her face.

Oh, God.

She should slap his hand away, but instead she wanted to grab it and press it against her cheek.

"And the longing not to be so very alone, if just for a few moments. It's a deception. A snare. We can't—none of us can—escape our solitary lives, but for a very little while we can pretend we did."

No. He was wrong. She longed to be alone. She opened

her mouth to tell him so—and saw the sadness and despair in his eyes.

She wanted to help him. To comfort him.

She stepped closer—

"Merrow!"

"Oh!" She jumped, and the duke straightened at the same time, snatching his hand back from her face. They both let go of the bedpost to turn and look at Poppy, standing on the bed. The cat glared at them and then leapt gracefully down to the floor and walked out of the room.

The bedroom. She'd been standing in Isabelle Dorring's bedchamber with the Duke of Hart doing . . .

What *had* they been doing? What had just happened?

Nothing apparently. The duke looked appalled. His expression should be funny.

She didn't feel like laughing.

"My apologies, Miss Hutting. I was . . . That is I didn't mean to . . ." The duke cleared his throat, tugged on his waistcoat, and glared up at Isabelle's painting. "I meant no disrespect. Now I believe we've accomplished everything we can here." He glanced at the bed, and she'd swear he blushed. "We should be going. I have more notices to post."

"Of course." She walked briskly toward the door. "Would you mind if I moved that portrait into the storage room when I move in, Your Grace—assuming I become the next Spinster House tenant, that is?"

"I think that is a brilliant idea, Miss Hutting."

Chapter Eight

May 5, 1617—Aunt Winifred has written again to say I should have an older lady living with me, and I have written back—again—telling her I do not need a nursemaid. Papa raised an independent daughter and gave me my head from an early age—much to Aunt Winifred's dismay. I cannot count the number of times she wrung her hands—at least in letters—and said his permissiveness would result in my coming to a bad end. Papa and I laughed over it often. Oh, how I miss Papa! But I will not have an old maid watchdog in my house. I am twenty-four years old, and this is Loves Bridge. Everyone is accustomed to my odd habits. And a companion would be very much in the way, especially now. The Duke of Hart continues to seek my company. I think an offer cannot be far off.

—from Isabelle Dorring's diary

Cat pushed an errant strand of hair out of her face as she stood in the village shop and watched Mrs. Bates, the shop owner, flutter around the duke.

"Oh, Your Grace." Mrs. Bates put a hand to her substantial bosom. "Oh, how wonderful to see you!"

He wasn't going to turn stiff and haughty with poor Mrs. Bates, was he? No. He smiled.

"Thank you, Mrs. Bates. You are very kind." He held up the Spinster House notice. "Now can you tell me where I might best post this?"

He hadn't proven himself at all high in the instep in any of his dealings with her. He'd been pleasant—friendly even—when she'd shown him the way to Randolph's office the other day, and he hadn't been at all snappish there, even when she and Jane had pulled caps a bit. And then in the Spinster House—

She bit her lip. What *had* happened in the Spinster House?

"I have a board over there, Your Grace. It's out of the way, but not *too* out of the way, if you know what I mean."

Something dark and hot and, well, *disturbing* had happened. And something more disturbing might have happened if Poppy hadn't chosen precisely that moment to get off the bed.

Yes, *bed*. She should never have been in a bedroom with a man. What had she been thinking?

But it had been completely unobjectionable until the moment he'd mentioned—she felt her cheeks flush again—desire.

She fanned her face with her hand.

When her sisters had sighed about broad shoulders and kisses, she'd thought them ridiculous. She hadn't the least wish to be pulled up against some smelly man and have his mouth mashed down on hers. Ugh! How revolting.

And yet . . .

In Isabelle's shadowy bedchamber, with the duke standing so close, she'd suddenly begun to understand. His light touch had reminded her—*all* of her—of the feel of his body against hers when he'd caught her as she'd stumbled on the path to Randolph's office. He was so big and hard, but instead of feeling overpowered, she'd felt protected.

Stupid! She did not want anything to do with the man. With *any* man. She wanted to be the Spinster House spinster. To be independent, free to write her novels without interruption.

But he'd looked so lonely in Isabelle Dorring's bedchamber.

She must have imagined that. How could the Duke of Hart feel lonely? He had an army of servants and countless friends and acquaintances, two of which had accompanied him to the castle. He didn't need her concern, and he certainly didn't need her pity.

Faugh! She'd hate to have anyone pity her.

Mrs. Bates had brought the duke over to her announcements board, where there was a faded paper about St. George's Day that Mrs. Bates hadn't yet taken down and a notice about the fair planning meeting, which Cat needed to get to soon. At least this was their last stop before Cupid's Inn.

Oh, drat. The silly Misses Wendley were giggling and peeking around the ribbon display at the duke. She had better go rescue him.

The girls saw her coming and hurried to reach the man before she did.

"Oh, look," Mrs. Bates said, beaming at the hussies. "It's the Wendley twins. I'm sure you won't be able to tell them apart, Your Grace. Even their own mother can't." Mrs. Bates chuckled. "You'll have to introduce yourselves, girls."

Then she dropped a quick curtsey. "If you'll excuse me, Your Grace, I have to get back to minding the till."

The duke inclined his head. "Thank you for your help, Mrs. Bates."

The Wendley girls barely waited for Mrs. Bates's substantial girth to pass them before stepping even closer to the duke.

"I'm Abigail," the one on the right said.

"And I'm Beatrice."

The identical blond-haired, blue-eyed, eighteen-year-old featherheads curtseyed in unison. Even though her brothers were twins, Cat had never been able to sort the girls out. To be truthful, she'd never cared enough to try.

"It's a pleasure to make your acquaintance, Miss Abigail, Miss Beatrice."

The silly chits actually sighed with delight. The corners of the duke's mouth twitched, and he glanced up, meeting Cat's eyes.

Cat grinned back. Good for him. Most men were bowled over by the girls' matching beauty.

"We're *so* happy to see you in Loves Bridge, Your Grace," Abigail said.

"We hope you'll stay now that you're here." Beatrice fluttered her eyelashes.

"Not that we don't realize London must be a wonderful place."

"We'd love to go there someday."

"Do tell us about it."

The duke blinked. Clearly he'd never before encountered anything quite like the Wendley sisters, but he recovered well. "London is rather crowded and noisy and dirty, actually."

"Oh." The girls' shoulders drooped, and they exchanged a look of dismay. However, they didn't let the duke's less-than-glowing reply discourage them for long.

"But surely there are soirees and balls," Abigail said.

"And scores of shops," Beatrice added.

"And elegant carriages."

"And riding in Hyde Park at the fashionable hour . . ."

". . . seeing and being seen."

"Well, yes, there is that," the duke said. "I suppose there's more to do in Town, but your village has its own charms."

And what would those be? London might be all the

objectionable things he'd said it was, but it had to be far more exciting than Loves Bridge. London had literary salons, theaters, museums—

Oh, what did it matter? She had as little chance of going to Town as the Wendley sisters did.

"Do you really think Loves Bridge charming?" Abigail asked.

Hadn't he just said so?

"Yes, Miss"—he hesitated slightly, clearly trying to remember which twin he was addressing—"Abigail, I do."

"Are you planning to live in the castle now?" Beatrice almost bounced with excitement.

"You must come to the village fair then," Abigail said breathlessly. "It's wonderful fun. There are games and food and dancing. Last year there was even a performing monkey."

"You can't pass up the opportunity to see a performing monkey, Your Grace," Cat couldn't resist saying. "And there will be an organ-grinder as well, I believe, though I can't promise. The committee hasn't yet decided."

He gave her a speaking look. "Oh? In that case I am severely tempted"—he returned his attention to the girls—"but I really can't say what my plans are at this time."

"Oh, we do hope you will stay, Your Grace."

"It's only a few weeks away, Your Grace."

"A few months, you mean," Cat interjected.

The girls glared at her, but she believed in accuracy, not that she thought for a moment the duke was at all interested in attending their little fair. Once the Spinster House situation was resolved, he would hurry back to London.

"I'll keep that in mind," he said, and turned to tack up the Spinster House notice.

"What's that about, Your Grace?" Beatrice peered at the sheet of paper.

"I'm required to advertise the opening at the Spinster

House, now that Miss Franklin has left." He smiled. "I don't suppose either of you is interested in becoming the next Spinster House spinster?"

He might as well have asked if they were interested in emptying the castle's chamber pots. Abigail and Beatrice shook their heads so vigorously Cat thought their hair was going to come tumbling out of its pins.

"Oh, no. Definitely not, Your Grace," Beatrice said.

"We wish to marry. All women do." Abigail glanced at Cat. "All young women, that is."

The dreadful duke managed to turn his laugh into a cough. "Yes. Just so. Now if you'll excuse us, ladies? Miss Hutting and I are off to Cupid's Inn."

"Oh, yes, of course." Beatrice looked worshipfully up at him. "It was so wonderful to meet you, Your Grace."

Cat felt like gagging. And then Abigail, the annoying baggage, smiled at her in a condescending fashion.

"How kind of you to show His Grace around the village, Miss Hutting. I'm sure you'll be so happy when he no longer needs your assistance."

"Precisely. Now, as His Grace just said, we need to be going." She turned and walked toward the door, not really caring at that moment if the duke followed her or not.

"Do come again, Your Grace," she heard Mrs. Bates call, so she knew he must be behind her.

"Are you going to make me chase you all the way to Cupid's Inn, Miss Hutting?" he said as she started across the road.

She stopped and waited for him. "No, of course not. And you could have caught up to me easily if you'd wished to."

"Yes, but I was afraid I might get my ears boxed if I did." He grinned down at her. "Which would have been a terrible injustice. All I want to do is offer you my arm so I can help an old woman totter across the green."

She had to laugh. "Those girls."

"They *are* very young."

"They are my sister Mary's age, but they act as if they have only one brain between them." She glanced at him. "And they are very beautiful. Usually that is enough."

"Enough for what?"

"To have all the males in the vicinity fluttering around them like moths around a flame."

All right, even she could hear the petulance in her voice. It wasn't that she wanted male attention herself. Not at all. It was just so exasperating to watch normally sensible men act like complete idiots over the girls.

"I, er, see."

"Oh, don't worry. I won't bite your head off." She forced a smile. "I apologize for my peevishness. I don't know what has got into me. I'm not usually bothered by the beautiful Wendley sisters."

Oh, lud, there she'd gone sounding spiteful again.

The duke stopped, causing her to stop as well.

"What is it?" She looked up into his brown eyes with their long lashes. Their soft warmth was such a contrast to the strong, masculine planes of his face.

An odd heat, a yearning almost, started low in her—

She jerked her attention back to his *ordinary* brown eyes.

"There are many beautiful women in London, Miss Hutting. The Wendley girls are lovely, but they would be only one—or I should say two—among many in Town."

"Yes, of course." How ridiculous she was. She should have realized any Loves Bridge female would pale in comparison to a London lady. "My pardon. I don't know what came over me."

He grinned. "Well, I imagine extreme irritation came over you. The girls *are* rather annoyingly inane. I was very happy to escape them."

She grinned back, her joy far out of proportion to his

comment, but she refused to examine the reason for that now. "I—"

"I say, isn't that Miss Hutting? Who's the man with her, Harold?"

"Drat it." She recognized that querulous voice all too well. Mrs. Barker was dragging her son toward them.

"Friends of yours?" the duke murmured.

"Not precisely."

Harold—Mr. Barker—had the grace to look embarrassed when he and his mother finally reached them.

"Don't just stand there, girl," Mrs. Barker said, squinting at the duke. "Introduce us."

"I will be delighted to do so, if you will give me the opportunity." She didn't even try to keep the annoyance out of her voice. With luck, Mrs. Barker would take a complete disgust of her—not that the woman didn't already thoroughly dislike her—and forbid her son to have anything more to do with her. "Your Grace, may I present Mrs. Barker and her son, Mr. Barker. Mrs. Barker, Mr. Barker, His Grace, the Duke of Hart."

The duke and Mr. Barker bowed; Mrs. Barker stared.

"I should have guessed," she said. "You look very like your father."

"Indeed, madam?"

The duke examined Mrs. Barker as if she were some repulsive insect he'd just discovered under a rock. Cat wished she could copy the expression to use herself.

"Oh now, don't stiffen up." The woman sighed, and what looked like a nostalgic smile flitted over her lips. "He was quite something, your father. We were all enamored of him."

Mr. Barker, unlike his mother, was not oblivious to the duke's chilly demeanor. "Delighted to make your acquaintance, Your Grace." He bowed again and tugged on his mother's arm. "Come along, Mama. I'm sure Miss Hutting and the duke need to be on their way, and you will wish to do your shopping."

His mother tugged back, refusing to move. "Part of the attraction was the curse, of course. It made your father seem so mysterious. Dangerous." She giggled—at least that was what Cat thought the odd noise was. "We all wanted him, even if for just a slip on the shoulder."

"Mama!" Mr. Barker's face was now bright red.

Cat was quite certain her eyes were starting from their sockets. To think old, dumpy, cantankerous Mrs. Barker had lusted after anyone, let alone a Duke of Hart. . . .

It was more than her poor brain could comprehend.

The current duke stiffened even more, if that were possible.

"Oh, don't be such a namby-pamby, Harold," Mrs. Barker said. "I was young once. How do you think you made your appearance on this earth?"

If Cat hadn't been afraid the duke would explode at any moment, she might have found Mr. Barker's dumbfounded expression funny.

"Mama, surely you didn't play Papa false!"

Good God—Mrs. Barker blushed!

"So I'm . . ." Mr. Barker swallowed again so hard, his Adam's apple bobbed violently. "I could be—"

"Of course you couldn't, you nod cock. The duke died almost three years before your birth." She shook her head, exasperation writ large on her face. "You are clearly Mr. Barker's son."

The current Mr. Barker at first looked relieved—and then, as he registered his mother's tone, vaguely upset. He must know there was an insult there somewhere, but he couldn't quite put his finger on it.

"Madam," the duke said, "I really must—"

"You have the look of your mother, too, though," Mrs. Barker said.

The duke froze.

A woodpecker drummed in a tree somewhere; a hammer clanged on metal in the blacksmith shop; farther down the lane, a horse snorted.

"You knew my mother?" The words were stilted, as if the duke hadn't wished to say them.

"Oh, yes. Miss Clara O'Reilly. I didn't know her well, you understand. She was Mrs. Watson"—she glanced at Cat—"the village dressmaker before Mrs. Greeley—Mrs. Watson's poor Irish niece. The girl hadn't been in Loves Bridge more than a day or two before the duke saw her." Mrs. Barker snorted.

This cannot be good. I should try to get the duke away.

Cat glanced up at him. He was staring at Mrs. Barker, his face impassive.

If he doesn't want to hear the woman, he'll stop her. He's a duke. He won't suffer fools.

"Clara was beautiful, so of course your father wanted her, but she was also terribly religious. He couldn't have her unless he married her." The woman sniffed. "He tried for weeks to seduce her—everyone was making bets on when her walls would finally come tumbling down—but she held firm." She shrugged. "The duke was desperate, so he did indeed meet her at the altar."

"I see." The present duke might well have been carved from stone.

"I will say Clara loved him—that was clear. And she didn't believe in the curse, not having grown up in the village, so she was quite shocked and rather brokenhearted when he died, though you must know that, Your Grace." She smiled. "How is your dear mother?"

A muscle jumped in the duke's cheek. His nostrils flared. "I have no idea. If you'll excuse me, madam?" He turned on his heel and strode off across the green.

"Well." Mrs. Barker rose to her full height. "That was rather rude."

Cat opened her mouth to tell the old harridan exactly what she thought of her behavior, but for once Mr. Barker spoke first.

"You were the one who was rude, Mama. I thought the duke showed admirable restraint."

"Harold!"

He ignored her to bow briefly to Cat. "Please extend my apologies to His Grace, Miss Hutting." Then he frowned down at his mother. "I think we'd best do your shopping another day."

"But I wish to do it today."

"I, however, do not wish to spend any more time in your company. We shall return home, if you please."

"Harold! How can you speak to me that way?" Mrs. Barker sputtered and argued as her son led her away.

Cat had to almost run to catch up to the duke. She would not have caught him at all if he hadn't stopped at the far edge of the green.

She put a tentative hand on his arm. "Do you really not know how your mother goes on?" She knew she shouldn't ask. She hadn't intended to—the words just tumbled out.

She might wish for some privacy and distance from her parents and siblings, but she couldn't imagine not having any contact with them at all.

At first she thought he wasn't going to answer. He was staring across the road at the inn—he'd barely glanced at her when she'd come up—and the arm under her fingers was as hard as granite. She bit her lip and waited.

"I do not," he finally said. "I told you my mother gave me up when I was an infant."

Dear heavens, how terribly sad. She wanted to wrap her arms around him and comfort him. Instead she grasped her hands tightly together.

"I see." She knew he didn't want her sympathy, but she couldn't keep from giving it to him anyway. "I'm sorry."

He looked at her then and smiled, though his eyes were bleak. "Don't be. It doesn't matter."

He was wrong. It did matter. She might not wish to be a mother herself, but she knew how important a mother's love was to a child. Mama had been a constant presence in her life—too constant lately with her talk of marriage, but her heart was in the right place. She truly thought a woman couldn't be happy without a husband and children.

The duke looked back at the inn. "I must post this last notice. My friends must be wondering what has become of me." He smiled with some good humor finally. "More likely they'll have drained the tap dry, and I shall have to haul them back to the castle in a wheelbarrow. Shall we go?"

He offered her his arm, and they crossed the road.

That Barker woman is intolerable.

Marcus tried to rein in his temper as he opened the inn door for Miss Hutting. "Is there a specific place I should hang this paper?"

And her son is the biggest lobcock it has ever been my misfortune to encounter. No wonder Miss Hutting has sworn off marriage, if that fellow is the best the village has to offer her.

"Mrs. Tweedon—the innkeeper's wife—will know the best spot."

And to say with a straight face that my mother had loved my father—

No, he could not think about that now.

"I imagine I should ask her permission before daring to hang something in her husband's hostelry, shouldn't I?"

Miss Hutting laughed. "Yes, indeed."

The inn was as old as the castle, but it looked far more

inviting. The furnishings, while worn, had clearly been purchased within his lifetime.

Blast it, he'd like to haul every stick of furniture and every depressing painting out of the castle and have a huge bonfire. He'd invite all the villagers to come dance round it, and he would lead the steps.

"And here she is," Miss Hutting said. "Good morning, Mrs. Tweedon. I've brought the Duke of Hart with me, as you can see."

A stout woman with graying brown hair had emerged from another room, balancing a teacup and a plate of assorted cakes and biscuits in her hands. In age and shape, she was not unlike Mrs. Barker, but Mrs. Tweedon's face had deep smile lines by her mouth and eyes.

She put down her burden and curtseyed. "Welcome to Cupid's Inn, Your Grace. Your friends are in the taproom." Her smile broadened. "You must know that news of your presence has spread like wildfire through the village." She studied him intently.

Oh, God. Did she sleep with my father as well?

Now he was going to wonder that every time he met a woman of a certain age.

He bowed. "I hope I am not too much of a disappointment, Mrs. Tweedon."

"Not at all." Her eyes twinkled. "I'm delighted to say you have your father's formidable good looks and your mother's sweetness of expression."

Bloody hell.

It hadn't occurred to him that at every turn he'd encounter villagers who'd known his parents.

"Ah, I see I shouldn't have said that. I am so sorry, Your Grace."

Mrs. Tweedon looked as if she'd like to give him a hug. He braced himself, but fortunately she thought better of the notion. Instead, she shook her head and frowned.

"That terrible curse. I don't wish to speak ill of the dead, but it isn't as if Isabelle Dorring didn't bear some responsibility for the situation she found herself in."

"Exactly what I told His Grace, Mrs. Tweedon. And even if the entire blame could be laid on that duke's doorstep, *this* duke is not at fault." Miss Hutting did go so far as to try to put her hand on his shoulder.

He stepped slightly to the side to avoid her touch. He didn't wish to snub the girl, but he couldn't allow such familiarity to continue. There was no future in it.

Unfortunately.

"Yes, well, that is neither here nor there, is it?" He held up the last notice. "Mrs. Tweedon, Isabelle Dorring's instructions say I must post this announcement concerning the Spinster House opening at the inn. Where do you suggest I put it?"

"Let's see, when Miss Franklin was selected, we posted it in the red room. I suppose that will do again." Mrs. Tweedon chuckled. "There are several spinsters there now."

"Splendid." He would finally get this last notice up and start the clock running. In three days, the new Spinster House spinster would be chosen, and he'd be free to leave Loves Bridge for another twenty years.

No, forever. He'd be dead long before there was another Spinster House vacancy.

"Come along, Your Grace," Miss Hutting said. "This way."

He followed Miss Hutting through several rooms, closer and closer to a hubbub of female voices. When they finally reached the aptly named red room, however, silence descended like a door had been slammed shut. Six pairs of female eyes—and one infant's—turned to regard him.

Miss Hutting made the introductions. "You know Jane—I mean, Miss Wilkinson," she said. "May I make known to you the Misses Boltwood"—two white-haired ladies smiled, ogled his person, and then leaned toward each other to giggle behind their hands like schoolgirls—"Mrs. Latham and Mrs. Simmons"—two young matrons, Mrs. Latham being the one with the baby on her lap—"and Miss Davenport." The last woman looked to be close in age to Miss Wilkinson and Miss Hutting.

His eyes drifted back to the child, who gave him a wide, toothless grin. His heart clenched.

The sooner he got out of Loves Bridge, the better.

"Ladies," Miss Hutting said, "this is the Duke of Hart. He is here to post the notice advertising the Spinster House opening."

Marcus bowed to the assembled females. "My pleasure."

"Oh, no, it is *our* pleasure, Your Grace." One of the Misses Boltwood waggled her eyebrows at him.

"Behave yourself, Cordelia," her sister said, cuffing her playfully on the shoulder. "What will His Grace think of you?"

His Grace smiled and hoped he would not be compelled to say what he was thinking.

"There's the notice board," Miss Hutting said, gesturing. Did she sound annoyed?

"Thank you, Miss Hutting." She looked annoyed. "I'll just tack up this paper, then, and leave you ladies to your meeting."

He turned to the board. The sooner he posted this, the sooner he could find Nate and Alex and have a well-earned glass of ale.

"I'm not surprised Miss Franklin and Mr. Wattles—that is, the new Duke of Benton—made a match of it," he heard one of the Misses Boltwood say. "My word, how the temperature rose whenever they were in a room together. I almost had to pull out my fan to keep from roasting."

"And the way they looked at each other when they thought they weren't being observed." That was the other Miss Boltwood. "It was very, er, *stimulating*."

The two ladies giggled again.

"I didn't notice anything," Miss Hutting said.

"*You* wouldn't."

The sooner he got out of here, the better.

"At least they didn't take to rolling in the bushes."

Good God, they can't know about Miss Rathbone, can they?

He made the mistake of looking at the sisters. They were staring at him, their eyebrows now waggling simultaneously.

Blast. They do know.

He *had* to leave. Immediately. "Thank you, Miss Hutting, for your help. Now if you'll excuse me, I shall—"

"A moment, Your Grace," Miss Davenport said. "I can't read the paper from here. Would you mind telling us the gist of it?"

"Yes." Mrs. Latham laughed. "Perhaps Miss Cordelia or Miss Gertrude would like to apply."

"Oh, no," Miss Cordelia said. She looked at Marcus with what he feared was intended to be a coy expression. "We're still looking for the perfect mates." Her eyes examined him from his head to his, er, hips.

Dear God, don't let me blush.

He felt his face turn red.

Of course the Almighty would not suddenly concern Himself with the Cursed Duke.

Gertrude elbowed her sister. "Now you've embarrassed the poor boy, Cordelia."

Miss Davenport frowned at the sisters. "Neither of you may be interested in the Spinster House, but I am." She looked at Marcus. "Extremely interested."

Miss Hutting sucked in her breath. "Anne! Your father's a baron. You have no need to live in the Spinster House."

"Oh, yes, I do," Miss Davenport said, her eyes narrowing. She looked fully as determined to win the position as Miss Hutting and Miss Wilkinson.

Damnation.

Chapter Nine

May 10, 1617—I encountered the duchess on the village green today. I wished her a good morning very pleasantly, and she walked right past me, refusing even to look at me, the witch. Just wait until I marry her son. Then she'll be sorry.

—from Isabelle Dorring's diary

The duke left as soon as he'd answered Anne's questions. Of course it also came out that Cat and Jane were interested in the position as well.

"I don't understand why you girls don't want to marry," Miss Gertrude said as she watched the duke depart. "Men can be quite, er, *entertaining*."

Cat would swear the duke suddenly picked up his pace, darting through the door and out of sight.

"*You* aren't married." Anne sounded uncharacteristically mulish.

Why did Anne want to live in the Spinster House? She'd never said anything about wishing to be a spinster before.

Well, yes, she'd never said anything about wanting to

marry, either. In fact, she'd been rather reluctant to attend many of the *ton* parties she'd been invited to. But she was a baron's daughter, for goodness' sakes. Of course she would marry and marry well. *She* wouldn't be stuck in Loves Bridge for the rest of her life, producing baby after squalling baby, hearing the same gossip, seeing the same people, doing the same thing day after day after day until she died and got buried next to all her ancestors.

"I may not have a man in my life at the moment," Gertrude said, "but—"

"But I think we had better get on with planning the fair," Viola Latham said quickly. "Malcolm won't be quiet forever." To underline her point, Malcolm began to fuss, likely the result of a surreptitious poke administered by his mother. "He's teething, you know."

Malcolm had been teething for the last two months—as long as they'd been having meetings. He'd yet to produce a single tooth, but he could be counted on to provide a well-timed squawk when the discussion meandered too far afield.

Gertrude sniffed and gave Cat a pointed look. "We'd be much further along if everyone had arrived on time."

Everyone turned to look at her, varying degrees of speculation in their gazes.

"I was just helping His Grace put up the Spinster House notices. He didn't know where best to post them."

"How very kind of you," Viola said, exchanging an annoyingly speaking look with Helena Simmons.

"Yes. You've certainly taken the duke under your wing," Helena said. Helena's husband and Cat's sister Tory's husband were brothers, and Helena and Tory were as thick as inkle-weavers. "I understand you also helped the poor fellow find Mr. Wilkinson's office the other day."

"Yes, she did." Jane's eyes narrowed in suspicion. "I was

there, of course. I saw them, and I'd say they were on very good terms."

"You'll also recall I had almost convinced the duke to give me the keys to the Spinster House." Good Lord, what was the matter with these women? They knew she had no interest in marriage.

Gertrude snickered. "I didn't know you were so clever, lulling the fellow into thinking you're no threat to his comfortable bachelor existence."

"I'm not a threat."

Cordelia ignored her. "When are you going to let him know he'd better make room for you at the castle"—she winked—"and in his bed?"

"Just don't venture into any bushes with him," Gertrude said. "Make him wait for his fun until he's paid for it with a wedding ring."

Good God.

"This duke is not about to follow in his ancestor's footsteps."

The Boltwoods exchanged a glance. "Tell that to Miss Rathbone."

Who in God's name is Miss Rathbone?

She didn't want to know.

"And I would never allow the man—any man—such liberties."

If Poppy hadn't distracted us in Isabelle Dorring's bedchamber . . .

Nothing would have happened.

"I assure you I'm no threat to the duke's unmarried state." She shouldn't have to justify her actions, but perhaps that would stop this ridiculous speculation. "My father told me to help the man find Mr. Wilkinson's office when he stopped by the vicarage for directions. And I just happened to encounter him this morning. It would have been rude not to offer my assistance."

Helena chuckled. "'The lady doth protest too much, methinks.'"

Cat looked at Malcolm. *Squawk, why don't you?*

Malcolm smiled at her around the fingers he was contentedly sucking. There would be no help from that quarter.

"*Could* we get on with planning the fair?"

Viola raised a brow at Cat's rather desperate tone, but did take pity on her. "Of course. Just before you arrived, Miss Cordelia suggested we include a treasure hunt this year."

Cordelia suggested they include a treasure hunt every year, and every year Miss Gertrude was the only other committee member to support the notion. Everyone knew the sisters only wanted an invitation to snoop through people's houses.

"Yes." Cordelia grinned at Cat. "And since you are so, ahem, *friendly* with the duke, you can persuade him to include the castle in the hunt!"

"I. Am. Not. Friendly. With. The. Bloody. *Duke!*"

The ladies inhaled sharply.

She must *not* lose her temper. "Pardon me." She turned toward Cordelia. "You know Mr. Emmett will give you a tour anytime you like and let you poke your nose into every blast—I mean every *last* cabinet and corner."

Gertrude elbowed her sister. "Shows great passion, eh? The duke is a lucky man."

"The duke is not a lucky man!"

"No need to get snappish, Miss Hutting," Cordelia said.

Deep breath. "Even if I was interested in marriage, *which I am not*"—another deep breath—"the duke would not wed me. Remember the curse."

Helena laughed. "Nobody believes in the curse anymore."

"The duke does."

Viola's eyebrows went up. "Oh? So you're familiar with the duke's thoughts on the matter, are you, Cat?" She looked at Helena. "Perhaps there *is* something between them."

"There is *nothing* between us." How could she convince them? She looked around the room—oh, right. "Jane knows the duke believes in the curse, too. It was quite clear when we were in her brother's office discussing how the Spinster House opening needed to be announced. Isn't that right, Jane?"

Jane was too honest to lie. "He did seem very anxious to follow the rules precisely."

"See?" Cat let out a long breath. "Now let's drop this foolish subject and—"

"The curse didn't keep his father from marrying Clara O'Reilly," Gertrude said.

"No, indeed it didn't." Cordelia sighed. "That courtship—if one could call it a courtship—was almost painful to watch."

Gertrude nodded. "The duke—this duke's father—was so very handsome. He could have had anyone he wanted—except Clara. She wouldn't let him under her skirts without a ring on her finger."

"He tried," Cordelia said. "He gave her lavish gifts."

"Which she refused."

"And he invited her to glittering parties at the castle."

"Which she would not attend."

"Finally he was so mad for her that he showed up for Sunday service." Cordelia laughed. "We all thought the poor vicar was going to faint."

"And do you remember, Cordelia? As soon as the vicar said the final blessing, the men—and some of the women—rushed out to change their bets to favor marriage over a slip on the shoulder."

"So you see," Cordelia said, leaning over to poke Cat's arm. "Play your cards right, my dear, and you could be a duchess."

Cat jerked back out of Cordelia's reach. "You can't think . . . I would never . . ." How horrible to lure a man into marriage in any situation, but especially if he thought he'd die as a result. "I don't want to be a duchess. I don't want to be a wife."

"But would you mind being a widow?" Gertrude asked.

Malcolm started wailing. Thank God.

"We'll have to continue the meeting next week. Perhaps we can be more productive then." Viola had to shout to make herself heard over Malcolm. "And this time, everyone, please try to be prompt." She looked directly at Cat.

Cat nodded. She didn't have time to argue the matter. She had to get to Anne.

"You don't really mean to apply for the Spinster House position, do you?" Jane was asking Anne when Cat reached them.

"I certainly do." Anne started for the door.

"But why?" That was what puzzled—and, all right, infuriated—Cat. "You don't need the Spinster House."

Anne glared at her. "Yes, I do."

"But your father's a baron," Jane said as they went outside.

"A baron—yes. And a beef-witted, beetle-headed, coxcomb." Anne's voice was suddenly high and thin. She sniffed and blinked rapidly.

Oh, dear. Anne was going to start crying, and she never cried. Something must be seriously amiss.

"Did you see the legs on that man?"

Gertrude Boltwood's voice preceded her as she pushed open the inn door. It would be fatal if she and her sister saw Anne on the verge of tears.

"Come on." Cat grabbed Anne's arm, and she and Jane towed her down the street.

"Oh, lud," Jane said, glancing back. "The Boltwoods are coming this way."

"Let's go to the willow," Cat said. Anne was still fighting tears. She needed to unburden herself, and the willow was where they had always gone to share secrets.

They turned the corner and hurried down the narrow

lane, over the stile at the stone fence, along the edge of Farmer Linden's field—observed by a few placid cows and a sprinkling of sheep—and across the wooden bridge to the willow. Cat pulled Anne down to sit next to her on a bench someone had placed under the willow's drooping branches ages ago, and Jane sat on Anne's other side. The stream burbled comfortingly near their feet.

"All right, Anne," Cat said. "Tell us everything."

Anne fished her handkerchief out of her pocket and blew her nose. "You already know Papa dragged me off to Viscount Banningly's house party."

"Yes," Cat and Jane said in unison.

Anne had complained bitterly about it for weeks beforehand. On her twenty-sixth birthday several months ago, the baron had suddenly decided Anne was in danger of remaining permanently on the shelf. He'd started pushing her to attend *ton* house parties, and when he discovered she'd been spending more time reading in the library than trying to charm eligible men, he started attending with her.

Anne sniffed and then gave up and blew her nose again. "Lud, how I hate those things. The men are dead bores. All they talk about are horses and hunting, and if they have a title or money—and most have at least one of those—they are even more insufferable, expecting you to bat your eyes and sigh and admire them. Faugh!" She pushed her hair out of her face and scowled. "And they look you over as if they're at Tattersall's and you're a horse they're considering buying."

"That sounds dreadful," Cat said. But Anne had been to many parties over the years and had never come home in such a state. "Did one of them ask your father for your hand, then?"

"No." Anne's mouth tightened. "It's far, far worse than that."

"Good God!" Jane paled. "Never say someone . . . Surely

your father being there would have kept anyone from . . ." Jane put a comforting hand on Anne's arm. "Did some dastard try to take your virtue?"

"Good God, no!" Anne shook off Jane's hold. "Of course not. I'd like to see any man try. The fellow wouldn't be able to sit a horse for many days afterward."

Jane scowled at Anne. "Then what is the problem?"

"Papa!" Anne started crying again. "He's a randy old goat who, at fifty, fancies himself a lusty lad of twenty."

"Oh." Cat stared at Jane. Jane's mouth was hanging open as wide as Cat's must be. "But I thought he'd been seeing the Widow Conklin for that sort of thing."

The widow was an accommodating woman of indeterminate age who lived on the edge of Loves Bridge. She'd moved into her little cottage before Cat was born and had become very popular with the local men. It was doubtful that there had ever been a Mr. Conklin, but as the widow was pleasant and polite and never put herself forward— *and* refused to entertain married men without their wives' permission—the village women accepted her without much complaint.

"He had been," Anne said, "but now he's decided he's in l-love. He wants to remarry."

"I see." Jane looked at Cat for help.

What was she to say? Neither she nor Jane had experience with this. Cat's parents were still married, of course, and Jane's parents had perished in a carriage accident when Jane was young.

"Perhaps your father wants a companion for his old age, Anne," Cat said. "He must be lonely."

Anne's mother had died at the end of Anne's first Season, almost ten years ago, so one might wonder why the baron suddenly felt the need for a wife.

There was no comprehending the male mind.

Anne glared at her. "Mrs. Eaton is Lord Banningly's

widowed, *much* younger sister. She's only twenty-five—a year younger than I am."

"Oh." Cat couldn't think of a single thing to say.

Well, a single polite or helpful thing.

She looked at Jane. Jane shook her head and shrugged. Apparently she had nothing to add either.

"Papa wishes to get an heir, and Mrs. Eaton has two young sons. That is one of her main selling points."

"There are others?" Jane asked.

Anne flushed. "I suppose she's rather beautiful."

"I just can't imagine your father telling you all this, Anne." The baron could be gruff and sometimes tactless, but Cat wouldn't have thought him callous.

"He didn't need to tell me. It was painfully obvious—he was casting sheep's-eyes at the woman the entire party."

"Ah, but was the woman casting sheep's-eyes back at him? If she's not interested—and pardon me for saying so, but the baron *is* old enough to be her fa—" Jane caught herself and coughed. "That is, the baron is quite a bit older than she."

Anne balled her handkerchief tightly in her hand, her jaw hardening. "I suspect she is looking for a home for herself and her sons. She seemed perfectly willing to entertain Papa's attentions. In fact—" Anne pressed her lips tightly together.

Cat was afraid to ask, but Jane wasn't.

"In fact what?"

"I stepped into the library one rainy afternoon, trying to avoid an especially annoying viscount, and found Mrs. Eaton on Papa's lap, her bodice drooping and her skirts in disarray."

Eew!

Blast, Cat hadn't said that aloud, had she? No, she didn't think so. And clearly it was exactly what Jane and Anne were thinking anyway.

"So you see," Anne said, "I *have* to win the Spinster House."

Marcus sat with Mr. Emmett in the castle study. It was the morning after he'd posted the notices. In just a few days, he could leave Loves Bridge forever.

Except there was a lot of work to be done first. His friends were right. Even the best steward wasn't the same as the landowner.

"Your Grace, if you will only look at this report, you will see that the drainage in the south field needs improvement."

The paper fluttered as if it were a captured bird in poor Emmett's shaking hand. He waited for Emmett to lay it on his desk. He'd tried earlier to take something directly from the elderly steward, but that had seemed only to make the man's infirmity more pronounced.

"I can ride out with you to inspect the area, if you like, Your Grace."

"Thank you, Mr. Emmett."

He was not at all certain Emmett should be on the back of a horse. Miss Hutting had been correct: mentally, the man was as sharp as one could wish. His knowledge of the castle and its contents was encyclopedic. But physically . . .

Physically he was probably in excellent shape for a man who was eighty years old. Hell, he'd be happy to be as fit as Emmett if he could hope to live to that age. But no matter how robust, an eighty-year-old man with a touch of the palsy should likely not be spending hours in the saddle, galloping around a vast estate.

"This seems reasonable, but you are right—I probably should see the area myself." Since he was stuck here until the Spinster House issue was resolved, he might as well use his time productively.

"That would be splendid, Your Grace."

Good God, Emmett was almost bouncing in his chair. Was he really that eager to go look at some ditches?

"That is, it is splendid that you are taking a personal interest in the land, Your Grace. I don't mean to be critical—I completely understand why you've not wanted to visit the castle. But your tenants do sincerely wish to see you, if for no other reason than to see who it is their rents support."

Yes, he would grant he did owe them something for that.

He regarded Emmett. Hmm. "When did you come to work at the castle, Mr. Emmett?"

"When I was twenty, Your Grace."

So the man must have known his father and mother. Emmett could tell him if there was any truth to that harpy Mrs. Barker's tale.

Did he *want* to know about his parents?

It felt cowardly not to inquire.

"How old was my father when you arrived, Mr. Emmett?"

"Seven, Your Grace, and his sister—your aunt, Lady Margaret—was twelve. Not that they spent much time here. The duchess preferred the London house."

"Of course."

Emmett sighed. "It is the way of it."

Marcus straightened the report Emmett had given him so it was at right angles to the edge of his desk. "And once my father reached his majority, did he take more of an interest in the estate?"

He glanced back up to see Emmett frown, a blush coloring his wrinkled cheeks. Blast.

"He came somewhat frequently, Your Grace, but not to attend to estate business, I'm afraid."

Ah. He could guess what sort of business his father had been attending to. "I encountered Mrs. Barker this morning, Mr. Emmett."

The man's frown descended to a scowl. "That woman is most unpleasant."

"Yes, she is."

He should let the subject drop. Nothing good could come from poking into this long abandoned dunghill, and yet he found he didn't like the notion that the villagers knew more about his family than he did.

"She gave me the impression that my father visited Loves Bridge when he wanted some female, er, companionship."

He'd hoped he'd somehow misunderstood the woman, but Emmett was nodding.

"Aye. I'm sorry to say it, Your Grace, but your father was a rake."

Zeus! His father had been more than a rake. It was one thing to frequent the beds of jaded London ladies who knew how the game was played. But consorting with village girls, especially when you were the lord of the manor? That was unconscionable.

Apparently he came from a long line of blackguards.

His aunt and uncle must have known what the man had been like. Had they told Nate? Was Marcus the only one in the dark?

The scoundrel was his *father*. Someone should have told him the man's history. It might have explained his mother's absence. . . .

No. Nothing could explain that.

Oh, God, what did it matter? His father could have been a saint. The curse would still have killed him.

"I had such great hopes that your father had fallen in love with Clara," Emmett was saying. "And Clara was so obviously in love with him."

Bloody hell, there it was again. Why did Emmett think his mother had loved his father?

And why was he calling her by her Christian name?

"How well did you know my mother, Mr. Emmett? I believe the Barker woman said she was new to the village."

"She was. She was Mrs. Watson's brother's daughter. Mrs. Watson used to be the village dressmaker here, and her brother had sent Clara to her to learn the trade, though I suspect the real reason was his new wife didn't care to have the girl in her house. She was very beautiful."

"So Mrs. Barker said." He'd never seen his mother. A painting hadn't been done of her, or, if it had, it had been stuck away in an attic and forgotten. "I can't imagine my father would have married an ugly woman."

"Yes, well, being beautiful and without funds isn't easy for a woman." Emmett frowned. "Watson was a particular friend of mine and shared the details of Clara's visit over a pint. When the duke began to pursue her, Watson asked me to determine your father's intentions, not that it was my place to ask such a thing. I tried once and was firmly rebuffed, and rightly so, I suppose. I *am* only the steward."

He'd always assumed his mother had trapped his father, but both the Barker woman and Emmett indicated otherwise.

"The courtship was far too brief, in my view. And then they were married in the village church and went off to London. I believe—" He pressed his lips together. "Well, that is neither here nor there."

"What is neither here nor there, Mr. Emmett?"

Emmett's brow furrowed, and he leaned toward Marcus. "Your Grace, I know it is none of my concern, but, well, I'm sorry to tell you I don't believe the duke treated Clara well."

"You think he beat her?" Good God, was there no end to his father's perfidy?

Emmett looked horrified. "Oh, no, Your Grace. Nothing like that. I think he merely went back to his old ways, frequenting brothels and the like. I suppose it was to be expected—he was a duke, after all—but Clara didn't expect it. For her, marriage meant fidelity." He shook his head. "She was only a country mouse, and an Irish one at that."

"The man knew what she was when he married her."

"Yes, but knowing and *knowing* are somewhat different, if you take my meaning. And, frankly, your father was too infatuated with Clara to think clearly . . . until he got what he wanted, that is."

Yes. His blasted father had been thinking with his cock instead of his head.

"And there is this—I've often wondered if the curse didn't cause your father to go a little mad both in pursuing Clara so single-mindedly and afterward, once he knew Clara was increasing."

Marcus could understand the dread—perhaps even the panic—his father must have felt. It could not be pleasant to have death breathing down your neck. He only hoped he'd find the courage to live with honor and dignity when his turn came.

Emmett shifted in his chair. "I can't lay all the blame at your father's door, however. I expect Clara wed him thinking she could change him, and, of course, she soon discovered she couldn't." He sighed, shaking his head.

"In any event, when she came back to Loves Bridge after he died, she wanted nothing to do with the dukedom. She even insisted on staying with the Watsons, but we were able to persuade her that would cause too much talk. The next duke had to be born in the castle."

So his mother had abandoned him because she held his father's sins against him. Hell, of course she had. That's what the curse was all about, wasn't it? Punishing the heirs for the sin of the third duke.

Emmett was fidgeting as if there was something else he wished to say.

Might as well say it for him.

"And then my mother took me to my aunt and uncle's and left me there so she could be free of the curse at last."

On a dispassionate level, he could understand that. He'd get free if he could.

Emmett's eyes widened in what appeared to be shock. "No, that's not what happened at all, Your Grace. Your aunt and uncle came here. They persuaded Clara that it would be best if she gave you to them to raise."

"What?!"

That wasn't possible. Aunt Margaret and Uncle Philip would never have done that. It was his mother who'd decided she didn't want him.

"Please try to understand, Your Grace." Emmett's rheumy eyes held his without wavering. "Clara had been dragged to London, away from the few people she knew, and thrust into a society that taunted her, both because of the curse and because of her Irish accent. Her husband ignored her, flitting from one woman's bed to another, and when he died unexpectedly—"

"Unexpectedly?!"

"To Clara, Your Grace. She'd not really believed in the curse until then." Emmett sighed, his shoulders drooping. "She came back to Loves Bridge brokenhearted, heavy and awkward with child. And then, just days after your birth, your aunt and uncle arrived. They were part of the world you were born to inhabit, a world that was completely foreign to Clara. Your uncle was even your guardian. So when your aunt said it would be best if they, in effect, adopted you, Clara agreed."

Good God, this turned everything on its head. "So are you saying my mother gave me up for *my* benefit?"

Emmett sat back, clearly puzzled. "Of course. What other reason could she have had? She cried for days after your aunt and uncle took you away."

Emmett *must* be wrong. "That doesn't explain why she hasn't contacted me since."

"I suspect she thought you wouldn't welcome it, Your

Grace. I believe your aunt and uncle persuaded her it would be best if she forgot she'd ever given birth to you, that having an Irish mother would be worse than having no mother at all." He shook his head. "I must admit, I didn't agree, but then I know very little about the *ton*. And, if you'll forgive me, what little I do know I cannot like."

Emmett was wrong. He must be, but . . .

An odd bubble of what felt like excitement formed in his chest. *Could* he be right?

No. The real reason his mother hadn't contacted him was that she was too busy enjoying herself. If she'd been a country mouse when his father had married her, she was one no longer.

"What about the Italian count?"

"The Italian count?" Emmett's brow wrinkled. "What Italian count?"

"The one my mother married. And don't tell me there isn't someone supporting her. As long as I've been in charge of her funds, she hasn't drawn a single penny."

Emmett was still giving him a puzzled look. "Yes, it's true she remarried, but her husband is neither Italian nor a count. She returned to Ireland once she'd recovered from your birth and, after several years, met and wed an Irish physician. She lives in Dublin now and has three sons."

I have half-brothers.

He looked away from Emmett to collect his thoughts and found himself regarding the third duke's portrait. He itched to snatch the painting off the wall and ram his fist through the bloody hellhound's face.

"So you are in contact with her?" He was able to keep his voice level.

"Yes, Your Grace. Due to my friendship with her aunt and uncle and the rather, er, emotional time surrounding your birth, I've come to look upon her as the daughter I never had."

"I see." He picked up a round, brass paperweight. It was good to have something solid to hold. His thoughts were spinning.

I have half-brothers.

"How old are her sons?"

"Oh, they are grown now. I believe the youngest is twenty."

"And the oldest?"

"Twenty-four. She waited a number of years to remarry."

I have relatives I never knew about. Irish, not Italian. Those both begin with I. Could I have got the story confused?

Impossible.

"Very well, Mr. Emmett. Thank you. That will be all."

I need to talk to Nate, find out if he knows the truth of Emmett's tale.

Emmett slowly pushed himself to stand. "And the drainage problem, Your Grace?"

Oh, right. He'd forgotten about that. "I'll take a look at it tomorrow, but . . ." How to say this gently?

"Yes, Your Grace?"

"I value your knowledge, Mr. Emmett, but perhaps it would be better . . . that is, perhaps it would help me gauge the knowledge of your assistant if I took Mr. Dunly with me."

Emmett laughed. "And you're afraid to ride out with an eighty-year-old man."

"I don't mean to—"

Emmett held up his hand—his visibly shaking hand. "No, you are quite right, Your Grace. I can still ride, but I know I could never keep up with you. Take Theo. He understands the problem perfectly. When should I tell him to be ready?"

"Shall we say at eight in the morning?"

"Very good." Emmett bowed and turned to leave, but

stopped with his hand on the door latch. "Oh, I almost forgot, Your Grace." He reached into his pocket and pulled out a folded sheet of paper. "This came for you from the vicarage just before our meeting. Henry, the vicar's oldest son, brought it by. Said it was an invitation to dinner tomorrow for you and Lords Haywood and Evans."

Marcus took the paper. "Thank you. I'll ask my friends and send a reply."

Emmett chuckled. "You can send it with Theo. He's wearing out his poor horse going between the castle and the vicarage. Young love is something, eh?"

"Er, yes, I suppose it is." *Not that I've experienced the emotion*, he thought as Emmett closed the door behind him.

The door had barely latched before it swung open again, and Nate and Alex walked in.

"We saw Emmett leave," Nate said, "and wondered if you'd like to go riding with us."

"It would do you good to get out of this fusty old room"—Alex inclined his head toward the third duke's portrait—"and away from that fellow's unpleasant stare."

Marcus glanced up at the painting. "I should pull him off the wall and consign him to the farthest, dustiest corner of the attic."

Nate nodded. "An excellent idea."

"Nate, Emmett just told me an incredible story. He said my mother married an Irish physician and lives in Ireland."

Nate's brows shot up. "This is the first I've heard of it. My parents—and the *ton*—believes she wed an Italian count."

"Yes." Marcus rubbed the back of his neck. "But Emmett was quite convincing. He even told me I had Irish half-brothers."

Alex gave a long, low whistle. "The fellow *is* quite elderly. Perhaps his mind is going. Remember Childwich?"

"Lord, yes. The count who could speak 'canine,'" Marcus said. "I was there when he told the Countess of Fontenly that her pug's greatest wish was to be an opera singer. But Emmett isn't as bad as that. He was completely lucid about the estate's drainage issues."

"So was Childwich about anything but conversing with dogs."

Nate was frowning. "I'd say the situation bears watching, Marcus. At least you've got Mr. Dunly ready to step in if Emmett falters too much."

"Yes." Emmett *must* be confused—and yet his story had been so detailed.

"Don't worry about it." Alex clapped him on the shoulder. "Come for a ride with us instead. Breathe some fresh air; feel the sun on your face. Remember: *All work and no play makes Jack*"—he grinned—"or, in this case, Marcus, *a dull boy*."

"Perhaps you're right." Marcus leaned back in his chair and stretched. He felt an odd mixture of disappointment and relief. Disappointment that he didn't have a family of half-brothers in Ireland, but relief that he hadn't grown up believing a lie. And Nate was right—he did have Dunly in place if Emmett needed to be relieved of his duties.

He stood—and saw the invitation lying on his desk.

"If you want to get out of the castle," he said, "we've been invited to dine at the vicarage tomorrow."

Alex's brows went up. "Doesn't the vicar have ten children?"

What did that have to say to the matter? "Yes, though two of them are married."

"They will probably come and bring their progeny." Alex pretended to shudder. "You and Nate go ahead; I think I will skip that chaos."

"Alex is right, Marcus. It does sound very uncomfortable. I believe I'll pass as well. Why don't you send your regrets?"

Because Miss Hutting will be there.

No. That was not his reason. Definitely not.

"Surely the children will eat in the nursery. The vicar is an important man in the village. Weren't you two just telling me I should become more involved here?"

"But not at the expense of your stomach, Marcus," Alex said. "Go to services if you must—not that I plan to accompany you there, either—but don't court indigestion."

Marcus looked down at the invitation again. It seemed wrong to decline. "I think my stomach will survive."

It was his heart—and another organ—that concerned him more.

Chapter Ten

*May 20, 1617—The witch has left for London, so
Hart can finally spend more time here. He slips in
the back door—we don't want to get the gossips'
tongues wagging. The duchess has ears everywhere.*

—from Isabelle Dorring's diary

Apparently the vicar did not believe in relegating his
children to the nursery for the evening meal nor in following any sort of etiquette in seating arrangements. Marcus
took his place on the vicar's right, and then everyone else
sorted themselves out however they pleased. Miss Hutting
was directly across from him with one of her four-year-old
brothers on her left. The other twin was on his right.

He'd never been around children. None of his acquaintances had them, not that they would have trotted them out
for company in any event. And, well, one would think the
vicar might consider how uncomfortable and, ah, *painful* a
family meal would be for him, given that his chances of
having a family himself were close to zero.

He felt a tug on his sleeve and looked down at . . . which one was this?

"Mikey, don't pull on the duke's coat," Miss Hutting said.

Well, that answered his question.

Mikey ignored his sister. His large brown eyes looked up into Marcus's. "What's your horse's name, dook?"

"George."

A boy's face is so much softer than a man's.

In a few years this child's rounded cheeks would vanish under sharp cheekbones, and his smooth, fine skin would weather. His nose would lengthen, his chin would sprout whiskers, and his sweet innocence would be lost to disappointment and disillusion.

"George?" The other twin wrinkled his nose. "That's no name for a horse."

"It's a fine name," Mr. Hutting said. "It's the king's name, Tom, as well as the Regent's. Here, Your Grace, have some peas. And would you mind spooning some out for Mikey? If he does it himself, we'll have peas all over the floor."

"Thank you, sir." Marcus took some peas for himself and then turned to serve the boy.

"Not many, dook," Mikey said. "I don't like peas."

"I think you should call him . . ." Tom was still on the topic of his horse's name. The boy wrinkled his brow. "Rex or Thunder or Peg . . ." He looked at his father. "You know, Papa. The flying horse."

"Pegasus." The vicar smiled at Marcus. "Thomas and Michael love Greek and Roman mythology, Your Grace." He offered him another bowl. "Have some buttered prawns. Our cook's buttered prawns are very good."

"I like it when Cook leaves the heads on," Mikey confided as Marcus put some prawns on his plate. "But Sybbie and Pru think it's repul-pul . . ." His small face screwed up.

"Repulsive?"

"Yes." The boy grinned at him. "That's the word."

"Tom and Mike like the stories because they don't have to spend hours translating them," Henry said. He was sitting on the other side of Michael.

The vicar's brows rose. "And you wouldn't have to spend hours, either, if you applied yourself more, Henry."

"I don't need to know Latin or Greek to be a cavalry officer."

"You're not going to be a cavalry officer," Mrs. Hutting said. She was at the far end of the table with Dunly on her right and Mary on her left. Prudence and Sybil, Miss Hutting's younger sisters, sat between Tom and Dunly and were staring at Marcus as if *he* were a god of ancient mythology.

He smiled at them; they blushed and looked down at their plates.

Marcus felt another tug on his sleeve.

"Does George bite, dook?"

"No, indeed. George has excellent manners."

Mikey grinned. "That's good. Mr. Barker's horse bites."

"And does your cook make good biscuits?" Tom asked.

How had biscuits entered the conversation?

"Thomas, I'm sure His Grace has no interest in his cook's biscuits," Miss Hutting said.

Marcus would swear she sounded nervous. Why?

"Actually, I'm rather fond of sweets." He smiled at Thomas. "So I can tell you with certainty that Mrs. Chester is an excellent baker. Isn't that so, Mr. Dunly?"

Dunly tore his eyes from Mary's. "Yes, indeed." He grinned at Tom. "She makes splendid seedcakes, too, Tom, and plum cake and all sorts of treats. And she's always urging you to have another."

"By Jove," Walter, on the other side of Henry, said. "That's capital!"

"Yes." Tom nodded enthusiastically and then looked at Marcus. "So would you marry Cat, dook?"

Miss Hutting made a strangled sound while the rest of the table, except for the twins, gasped—or giggled.

Michael tugged on Marcus's sleeve again. "Yes, dook. I like you much better than Mr. Barker. His horse bites, and his cook makes nasty, dry biscuits."

"And his mother looks like a witch," Tom said. "She even has a wart on her nose."

He could certainly agree with that assessment. The woman looked and acted like an evil old crone.

"Michael, Thomas, you must not say such things to His Grace," Mrs. Hutting said.

"But, Mama, you want Cat to have a husband, and dook doesn't have a wife"—the boy looked back at Marcus—"do you?"

He should be furious, but how could he be angry at this little boy who looked so angelic and sincere? "No, I don't have a wife."

Michael beamed at him. "Then *would* you marry Cat, please, dook? I know she's old, but she's nice."

"Michael!" Miss Hutting's face was bright red, her expression an interesting mix of mortified, horrified, and furious. "You cannot ask His Grace to marry me."

"Then you ask him, Cat," Thomas said. "You must like him better than Mr. Barker." The boy looked back at Marcus. "She hates Mr. Barker, dook."

"I see." Poor Miss Hutting. One might think the other members of her family would come to her rescue, but they appeared to be struggling not to laugh—as, he must admit, was he. There'd never been this sense of fun in Nate's family. Well, he and Nate had never eaten with Nate's parents when they were children. "And what makes you think your sister would find me any less objectionable, Thomas?"

It wasn't Thomas who answered him.

Prudence—the sister who he'd been told was ten years

old—snorted. "It's hardly a secret, Your Grace. Cat's been casting sheep's-eyes at you ever since you arrived."

Had she? And, perhaps more to the point, why did the thought generate a jolt of anticipation instead of annoyance?

He glanced at Miss Hutting. If looks could kill, Prudence would be stretched out on the floor.

"Prudence!" Mrs. Hutting scowled at the girl. "What a thing to say."

"Well, she has," Prudence said rather sulkily.

The vicar finally jumped into the fray to change the topic. "I say, Your Grace, have you found things in order at the castle?" He looked down the table at Dunly. "I certainly hope so. Theo works very hard."

"Yes, he does," Mary said, while Theo blushed.

"It's Mr. Emmett, Your Grace. He tells me how to go on."

"Indeed," Marcus said, "but I can see how he relies on you—and he is wise to do so. You were very knowledgeable when we examined that drainage issue this morning."

Dunly's blush deepened, and Mary grinned with obvious pride.

It felt good to be able to praise Dunly. He'd enjoyed their ride and talking about estate issues. Certainly it had been a far more satisfying way to spend his time than wasting it in idle activities in Town.

Maybe he *had* let the curse overshadow his life. No one lived forever. He just had a more defined exit point.

"Dare we hope you might stay for a while then, Your Grace?" Mr. Hutting asked. "Everyone in Loves Bridge would be delighted if you chose to extend your visit."

"I haven't made a firm decision on that matter, sir." He carefully did not look at Miss Hutting. He should leave the village the moment the Spinster House issue was resolved. It was by far the safest choice. He *was* only thirty.

But he was very tempted to stay.

"And what about the Spinster House, if I may ask, Your

Grace?" Mrs. Hutting gave her husband a dark look. "You might imagine my surprise when I learned that Miss Franklin had married Mr. Wattles—or I should say the Duke of Benton—in the dead of night."

Mr. Hutting took a sudden interest in his meal.

"I've seen the notices posted throughout the village," she continued. "Have you had anyone express an interest?"

"Yes, indeed. Three women actually."

"Three!" Mrs. Hutting's eyes widened. "Who are they?"

He opened his mouth to answer—and felt a sharp pain in his shin. Someone had kicked him.

He glanced across the table. Miss Hutting's eyes pleaded with him, as she gave her head the slightest shake.

Apparently she had not informed her parents that she wished to be the next Spinster House spinster.

"I'd best not say, Mrs. Hutting. The unsuccessful candidates might not wish their identities to become common knowledge." Though he'd wager keeping such a secret in a small village like Loves Bridge would be next to impossible.

"Oh, yes. You are quite right, of course." Mrs. Hutting's eyes slid over to regard her eldest daughter, who was now studying her meal as assiduously as her father had his. "I can't imagine why any girl would want to be a spinster."

"If there are three candidates," Mr. Hutting asked quickly, likely noting the direction of his wife's gaze, "how is a winner determined, Your Grace?"

"The ladies draw lots, sir."

"Lots?" Mrs. Hutting laughed. "Are you certain they don't pull caps, Your Grace?"

From the corner of his eye, he saw Miss Hutting bristle.

"Just lots, madam. It is all set out in Isabelle Dorring's papers."

Mrs. Hutting frowned. "Oh, dear. Isabelle Dorring. Perhaps you know she is a distant relation of mine?"

"Yes, Miss Hutting told me."

Mrs. Hutting leaned forward. "If I may, Your Grace, I'd like to apologize on behalf of Isabelle. I've always thought the situation"—she paused as if looking for the appropriate word—"unfortunate. Well, rather more than unfortunate from your point of view, of course."

He inclined his head. "No apologies are necessary, madam. My ancestor was very much to blame."

"Gammon!" Miss Hutting frowned at him. "It took two people to accomplish that particular sin."

Which was not an appropriate subject for the dinner table, especially one with a number of young, interested ears. "Yes, but their positions were not equal, Miss Hutting." He didn't need to point out their obvious difference in rank. "Women are the weaker sex."

Henry let out a long, low whistle. "You might want to consider diving under the table right about now, Your Grace."

Indeed, Miss Hutting looked as though she was going to wing her plate at him.

"Even if your ancestor had been the devil incarnate," Mrs. Hutting said, shooting Henry a quelling look, "the consequences of his actions should not govern you two hundred years later."

"Perhaps they should not, madam, but they do. Every duke since the one Miss Dorring"—he glanced down at Thomas and Michael—"er, met has died before his heir was born."

"That sounds like something from one of Mrs. Radcliffe's novels," Prudence said.

"Prudence!" Mrs. Hutting frowned at her daughter. "Where did you get any of Mrs. Radcliffe's books?"

"From Mary."

"Mary . . ."

"I got them from Ruth, Mama. She left them behind

when she wed." Mary glared at Prudence. "And I didn't give them to Pru. She must have stolen them from under my bed."

"I was just looking for something to read."

"Under Mary's bed?" Mrs. Hutting's frown returned to Prudence.

"It's Cat's bed, too."

It was Miss Hutting's turn to frown. "What were you looking for that's mine, Pru?"

Prudence ignored her. "You should be glad all I borrowed were those old books, Mary. I could have taken your diary."

Mary gasped and lunged across the table. "You better not have read it."

Prudence leaned back out of reach. "Why? Would I have found something interesting?"

Dunly tugged at his cravat and shifted in his seat.

Ah. Well, marriage absolved all sins.

"Stop it, girls," Mrs. Hutting said. "I'm sure His Grace is not used to such unseemly behavior at his meals."

That was certainly true. None of the dining room events this evening bore the slightest resemblance to his normally staid and, frankly, boring repasts.

Mary resumed her seat, her expression promising her sister retaliation later.

Mrs. Hutting smiled at him. "Your Grace, as you know, Theo and Mary are going to be wed in less than two weeks' time. I do hope, if you are still in residence, you will join us for the celebration."

He usually avoided weddings like the plague, but Mrs. Hutting was looking at him so hopefully, he didn't have the heart to decline outright.

"Thank you, madam. If I'm still here, I would be happy to attend."

"And your friends, Lords Haywood and Evans, are welcome, too, of course."

"I will tell them." There was virtually no chance Alex

and Nate would come, but he'd leave it to them to send their regrets.

"And, er . . ." Mrs. Hutting looked down to arrange the angles of the knife and fork on her plate.

Oh, hell. What's coming now?

"I've been meaning to ask you, Your Grace, since London is not so far away, whether you know of anyone who might be willing to come down to play the pianoforte for the festivities." Mrs. Hutting smiled at him. "Mr. Wattles's—that is, the duke's—departure has disrupted our plans, I'm afraid."

Mr. Hutting nodded. "Indeed. We would never wish to stand in the way of true love, of course—"

There was no "of course" about it. Marcus caught the grim look Mrs. Hutting sent the vicar. He'd wager the good woman would have thrown herself between Miss Franklin and the Duke of Benton gladly if it would have kept the duke in Loves Bridge for Mary's wedding.

"—but we could wish the timing had been better." The vicar smiled. "For us. I assume the timing was just right for the duke and his new duchess."

"It's all right, Papa," Mary said. "We don't need anyone to play the pianoforte."

Dunly wisely kept out of the discussion.

The vicar frowned. "I suppose we can forgo music at the ceremony, though I was hoping to find someone to play the organ, but what about the dancing afterward, Mary?"

"Mr. Linden is quite a good fiddler and—"

"We cannot dance to Mr. Linden's fiddling." Mrs. Hutting looked as if she'd bitten into a lemon.

"We do at every other party, Mama."

"Well, we won't at your wedding." She sighed. "At least I hope we won't."

He shouldn't say anything, but the words were out before he could stop them. "Lord Haywood is an accomplished musician, madam. I don't know if he'll still be in Loves Bridge by the time of the wedding—he and Lord Evans had planned to go walking in the Lake District." *Which hopefully they will still do—with me.* "But I can inquire."

"Oh, would you, Your Grace?" Mrs. Hutting looked at him as if he'd just offered her the crown jewels. "That would be wonderful, if Lord Haywood is available and willing, of course."

"Yes, well, I can't promise anything."

"I completely understand, Your Grace."

But she was beaming at him. He felt committed to dragging Nate to the wedding or finding some other musician.

"Now if you'll excuse me, Your Grace, I need to get the younger children to bed. Come along Thomas, Michael, Sybil, Prudence. Say good night to His Grace."

The girls curtseyed; Thomas managed a bow.

Michael grabbed Marcus's large hand with his small one and looked anxiously into his eyes. "I like you, dook," he whispered. "Please marry Cat."

"Come along, Michael," Mrs. Hutting called as she shepherded the others out of the room. "Stop teasing His Grace."

"He's not teasing me, Mrs. Hutting." But what answer could he give the boy? Marcus gently squeezed Mikey's fingers. "We'll see. Now, go along. Sleep well."

Mikey started to leave and then, all at once, turned back and flung his arms around Marcus's neck, hugging him tightly before running off to join his mother. It happened so quickly and was so unexpected, Marcus didn't have time to react.

"I'm sorry, Your Grace," the vicar said, worry clouding his eyes. "I hope Mikey didn't give offense."

Marcus struggled to control his emotions, but he was afraid his face reflected the shock he felt. At least, he hoped that was all it revealed.

"Of course Michael didn't give offence, Mr. Hutting." He thought that came out rather well.

Oh, God. The feel of those small arms around my neck, the soft cheek brushing against my . . .

He wished he'd hugged the boy back.

Nate's parents had not been overtly affectionate. They'd loved each other—Marcus had never doubted that—but their love had been a restrained, formal love as befitted the Marquess and Marchioness of Haywood. He and Nate had spent most of their time with servants—nurses and governesses and tutors.

This family was very different.

Of course it was. Mr. Hutting might have been born to an earl, but he was now a vicar. He didn't have the funds for an army of servants to care for his sizeable brood.

"Boys," the vicar told Henry and Walter, "you may be excused. Make your bows, and don't forget you each owe me translations in the morning." He raised an eyebrow. "I hope the work is well under way, if not completed."

"Yes, Papa."

"I was just going to finish it, Papa."

The vicar watched them go and then turned back to Marcus. "They are good boys, Your Grace. Perhaps not scholars—though I actually have some hope for Walter—but good-hearted." Pride shone clearly in his eyes.

An emotion I'll never have the opportunity to feel.

"They're hellions," Miss Hutting said. "Always kicking up some sort of lark."

The vicar laughed. "They're boys, Cat. That's what boys do."

Miss Hutting frowned. "And, Papa, they've been teasing me unmercifully about—" She looked over at Marcus and flushed.

Interesting.

She jerked her eyes back to her father. "That is, they've

been teaching Thomas and Michael the most inappropriate language."

"As my brothers taught me." The vicar laughed again. "I hate to say it, Cat, but that's probably the least objectionable thing that Walter and Henry will pass on to the twins." He looked at Marcus. "I'm the fourth of four boys, Your Grace. I'm afraid I speak from experience."

"Your daughter told me you're Penland's brother, sir. I can't say I'm well acquainted with the earl, but I do know his son. I wouldn't have thought either of them hellions. On the contrary, I believe they have a reputation for being very strict and proper."

"Yes, now. That's the work of the countess. She—" The vicar pressed his lips together and shook his head. "And here I am, a man of the cloth on the verge of speaking ill of my sister-in-law. That will never do." He put his hands on the arms of his chair. "Let's adjourn to the drawing room, shall we, and have some brandy"—he smiled—"and tea for the ladies?"

Marcus stood with the rest of those left in the dining room—the vicar, Miss Hutting, Mary, and Dunly.

"I'm afraid I have to decline your offer, sir. I need to return to the castle." He'd had about all he could bear of such a comfortable family life. "I've left my friends to their own devices long enough."

Dunly's face fell. "Of course, Your Grace. I'll—"

"Oh, no, I don't wish to curtail your visit with your betrothed, Mr. Dunly. I can find my own way back to the castle."

"If . . . if you're certain, Your Grace."

He'd better be certain. Dunly was trying manfully to mask his relief, but Mary wasn't. Her smile almost blinded him.

Such simple, straightforward love.

"Of course I am. Good night." He bowed.

"I'll see you to the door, Your Grace," Miss Hutting said.

Some emotion, rather darker and more complicated than Dunly's, stirred in his gut, turning to an intense ache in the most predictable part of his anatomy as he followed Miss Hutting and watched her hips sway.

My heart aches, too. Is this what love feels like?

Of course not. This emotion wasn't the chaste and virtuous one lauded by poets. It was intensely, *painfully* carnal.

He must have an especially bad case of lust.

Miss Hutting led him to the door—and then outside and down the walk.

Hmm. What is she about?

"Do you plan to escort me all the way to the castle, then?"

She looked over her shoulder at him. "Of course not. I just wish to speak to you in private." She headed for a clump of tall bushes that appeared not to have benefitted from a gardener's attention recently, if ever.

"We can converse here without being overheard or observed," she said, and stepped through a narrow gap in the foliage.

His eyebrows almost shot off his forehead.

My, my.

If this were bold Miss Rathbone, he'd be certain his freedom—and thus his life—was in danger. But this was Miss Hutting, one of the most determined candidates for the position of Spinster House spinster.

"Are you coming?" Her voice hissed from the greenery. "Or are you going to stand there like a complete lobcock all evening?"

Such seductive words.

He should stay where he was, but his raging lust moved from his . . . heart to his head, sending rational thought packing.

"I'm coming." He stepped into the small, shadowy space. "I'm here."

There was hardly enough room for both of them—or maybe it was merely his intense awareness of Miss Hutting that made the place feel close and intimate and tempting.

He could *not* be tempted.

Temptation was thick in the air, in the light scent of her hair, in the curve of her cheek . . . of her breast.

"What did you wish to discuss?" That had come out rather harsher than he'd intended.

"*Shh!* If you don't keep your voice down, we'll be discovered."

"Yes." And then they'd be marched lock-step to the altar. It was a *very* bad sign that the thought didn't cause him to run for the castle.

"So why did you drag me into these bushes?"

"I didn't drag you," she whispered. "You came of your own accord."

No, it was the lust that agreed to this, not me.

"I needed to talk to you privately, and I couldn't do that inside. I want to be sure you understand why I *must* win the Spinster House position tomorrow."

Was Prudence correct? Had Miss Hutting been casting sheep's-eyes at me?

"But my understanding isn't necessary, Miss Hutting. Isabelle determined how the matter would be settled two hundred years ago. It is all to be left to chance." She had no more control over her fate in this instance than he had ever had over his. "To luck, good or bad."

He moved a little closer. She put a hand on his chest.

"Be careful. You're about to step on my toes." She frowned. "I never realized how large you are. You take up a lot of space."

"Mmm." He covered her hand with one of his. He expected her to jerk away, but she didn't. "Why do you want the Spinster House so badly, Catherine?"

He hadn't meant to use her Christian name, but it felt very good on his tongue.

Other things would feel good on his tongue, too. Her lips, her breasts, her—

She'd stiffened. Was she going to slap him? She would be wise to do so.

"Everyone calls me Cat, Your Grace." Her voice sounded husky.

She hadn't bothered to put on her bonnet when they'd left the vicarage. He wanted to touch her hair, to undo its pins and watch it tumble down over her shoulders. He wanted to bury his hands and face in the silky mass.

"But I will call you Catherine." He brushed his thumb over her cheek. It was almost as soft as her little brother's. "And you must call me Marcus."

"M-Marcus? I could never do that."

Did she realize her other hand had also come up to rest on his chest? He covered it, too. "You just did."

"No, I . . ." She shook her head as if to clear it. She must feel the same drugging heat clouding her thoughts that he did. "Why are you—"

"Shh." He put his fingers over her lips. They were softer than her cheek. "You don't want to be discovered, remember?"

What would happen if I put my mouth where my fingers are?

Need throbbed in him—in his cock, but also in his heart and in his mind. He shouldn't do this. He knew he shouldn't, but he *wanted* it. Just a taste. That was all.

If only he were an ordinary man like Theo Dunly. A man who could court a pretty girl, who could steal a kiss, who could think about marriage and dream of a future with a wife and children and perhaps someday even grandchildren.

"Didn't you see how it is with my family? How crowded and noisy? How it's impossible to have any privacy? I never have a moment to myself." Catherine leaned into him, completely caught up in her need to persuade him.

She *was* persuading him, but not to the action she wished.

"I have too many moments to myself," he said.

"Oh. Yes. Well, I suppose so, but your situation is vastly different, Your Grace."

"Marcus. Please, Catherine. Marcus."

Her tongue peeked out to moisten her lips, and he was lost.

"M-Marcus," she said.

And then he kissed her.

Chapter Eleven

May 25, 1617—Marcus kissed me! He was taking his leave, and just before he opened the door, almost as if against his will, he bent and brushed his lips over mine. My first kiss! I believe I'm well and truly in love.

—from Isabelle Dorring's diary

Cat turned over in bed and stared up at the shadowy ceiling. The candles had been blown out and the fire banked. The house was quiet. She should be asleep. She had to have her wits about her tomorrow when they drew lots for the Spinster House.

Oh, God. She closed her eyes. The Duke of Hart had *kissed* her. It had been nothing like she'd imagined kissing to be. There'd been no mashing mouths or bumping noses. It had been just the briefest brush of his lips against hers, but she'd felt it all the way to her soul.

She felt it now, but in a rather more carnal location.

Her eyes flew open. Heat flooded her face—no, her entire body. Very odd bits of her ached.

She'd never thought he'd kiss her. She hadn't thought of kissing at all when she'd brought him into the bushes. She'd been thinking only of the Spinster House.

He was so tall and broad. He'd smelled of wine and wool and something dark and musky and exciting. Tempting. And when he'd whispered her name—*Catherine*—his voice had been so warm and—she grew even hotter—seductive.

She was glad now that no one else ever called her by her full name.

"Will you stop tossing and turning?"

Oh, drat. Mary was awake.

Her sister leaned up on her elbow. "What is the matter with you, Cat?"

"Nothing. I'm sorry. I'll try to lie still."

"Why don't you try to *sleep*?" Mary pushed her hair back off her face and then sat up all the way, wrapping her arms around her knees as if she planned to have a long chat. "It's the duke, isn't it?"

Perhaps if she ignored her, Mary would lie down again. Cat closed her eyes.

"It must be the duke. You've never had any trouble sleeping before. It's quite disgusting how easily you drop off—and then you snore to wake the dead."

Her eyes flew open again. "I do not!"

Did she snore? What if the duke—

Good God, she was losing her mind. The duke was never going to be in a position to hear whether she snored or not.

"Yes, you do. I always try to fall asleep first or else I have to wait until you stop. After a while you sort of snort and snuffle and quiet down."

Cat glared at Mary. "You're mistaken."

"How would you know? You're asleep. You can't hear yourself."

Cat contemplated the ceiling again. With any luck, she'd

be sleeping at the Spinster House soon and would never have to share a bed again.

Except with Marcus. . . .

No! Good God, no! "I'm not snoring now. This is your golden opportunity. Go back to sleep."

Of course, that's not what Mary did.

"Pru was right, you know. You *were* casting sheep's-eyes at the duke all during dinner."

Ignore Mary. Ignore Mary.

"Did he kiss you?"

"What?!" Cat sat up. Mary couldn't have seen them. She'd been inside with Theo . . . hadn't she? "Why do you think that?"

"Because the duke looked like a man who'd just been kissing someone."

"Uhh." Her hands started up to cover her face, but she forced them back to the bed. She must brazen it out. Remain calm. Not admit anything. Mary might suspect, but she couldn't know for certain.

Cat took a deep, steadying breath.

"How do you know how the duke looked? Weren't you in the drawing room with Papa and Theo?"

"Oh, no. Theo and I told Papa we were going for a stroll. Which we were—to that clump of bushes. You know it's a favorite trysting spot, don't you? Tory and Ruth used to spend lots of time there with their husbands—before they were their husbands, of course."

"They did?" All she'd known was that it was a splendid place to hide in hide-and-go-seek.

"So you *didn't* know."

Was that pity she heard in Mary's voice? It had better not be. Simply because she chose not to frolic with men in the foliage. . . .

Except that was exactly what she'd just done.

"He didn't force you in there, did he?" Mary frowned.

"Theo told me there'd been some scandal involving the duke, an unmarried lady, and some bushes in London, but after meeting His Grace, he decided it must have been malicious gossip."

Didn't Gertrude Boltwood tell me not to go into the shrubbery with the man?

Ridiculous. Nothing especially shocking had happened.

"Of course the duke didn't force me. The bushes were my idea."

That didn't come out quite right. Mary's eyes widened as if they were going to pop out of her head.

"But only so I could have some privacy to push my candidacy for the Spinster House with him."

Mary actually gasped. "You want to live in the Spinster House?"

Oh, God, that let the cat out of the bag. "Yes, but don't tell Mama and Papa."

"Of course I won't tell, but if you still want to be a spinster, why were you kissing the duke?"

"I wasn't." He'd kissed her. She'd been too stunned to return the favor.

Mary frowned. "The duke certainly looked kissed. Theo and I weren't more than ten feet away from him when he came out of the bushes. You can imagine our surprise." She giggled. "And relief. It would have been beyond awkward, especially for Theo, to stumble on you and the duke in a passionate embrace."

"There was no passionate embrace!" That, at least, was true. There'd been no embrace at all. The duke had merely touched his lips to hers.

And changed everything. She'd felt the shift as clearly as if the ground had moved under her feet.

"We were only discussing the Spinster House."

That earned her a snort. "The duke did not look like a man who'd been discussing a house or spinsters. He looked"—

Mary sighed dramatically—"bewitched. So much so that he didn't notice us standing there. Nor did you, but by the time you came out, we'd hidden behind the oak tree."

Cat didn't like that at all. "So you admit you were spying on me?"

"No." Mary suddenly sounded very serious. "When I saw the duke come out of the bushes, well, I wanted to see who he'd been cavorting with. I was glad it was you." Mary touched Cat's arm. "There *is* the London rumor, and it's clear you care for him. I don't want you to get hurt."

Oh. Mary's concern almost undid her. She bit her lip and blinked back tears. She wasn't normally so emotional.

It was all the duke's fault. If only he were the evil villain his ancestor had been. Then her life would still be following a rational plan, and she wouldn't be so confused and upset.

"There's nothing between me and the duke, Mary."

"I think there is." Mary bounced with excitement, shifting the mattress and making Cat feel slightly ill. "I think he's going to offer for you. Theo thinks so, too."

Theo was so besotted, he'd agree with anything Mary said.

"A duke is not going to marry a vicar's daughter."

"But Papa is an earl's son. Your birth is perfectly respectable, Cat."

If only she *could* marry him. . . .

No! What was she thinking?

"I'm a confirmed spinster."

"You didn't look like a confirmed spinster at dinner—and especially not when you came out of those bushes."

There was no point in arguing that. Mary would never concede, and Cat was very much afraid she *had* looked a bit dazed.

Of course she had. She'd never been kissed before.

"The duke won't offer for me. He's too young."

"Thirty isn't young."

"It is if you think you'll die shortly after you marry."

She must not forget that. Even if she fell madly in love with the man, he looked upon marriage as a death sentence. He had many more years before he had to do his duty and get an heir.

It was so unfair! Not for her, but for him. He should have the opportunity to be a father. He'd been so kind and patient with the twins at dinner. Lud, she hadn't known where to look when Mikey had asked Marcus to marry her. She'd been mortified, but terrified as well that the duke would cut up rusty—with good reason—and say something cruel to Mikey. But he hadn't. And later, when Mikey had hugged him . . .

Oh, God. That had made her heart ache. Marcus had looked surprised, but she'd swear she'd also seen yearning in his eyes.

He'd make a wonderful father.

"I hate Isabelle Dorring."

Mary nodded. "She has certainly caused far more trouble than any one person should be allowed to. But I have to say it seems so silly that a man as intelligent as the duke should believe in curses." Mary dropped her voice. "I tell you in strictest confidence that Theo wasn't best pleased when he heard the duke was coming to Loves Bridge. I'm afraid he judged him a bit harshly for being an absent landowner." Mary shrugged. "Well, I agree that wasn't good for the estate."

Cat bit her lip. Mary knew nothing about the estate; she was just parroting Theo.

"But in the little time the duke's been here, he's impressed Theo with his shrewd questions and well-considered opinions. So we are even more surprised he's so superstitious."

Cat was, too, but perhaps she'd feel the same way were she in his position. "It's hard to ignore history. Every duke since Isabelle's time has died when his wife was increasing with his heir."

"Coincidence."

"That's a lot of coincidences."

"What else could it be?" Mary asked. "*You* don't believe in the curse, do you?"

"N-no." Cat wasn't sure what she believed any longer.

"Of course you don't." Mary grinned, and then finally lay back down and pulled the coverlet up. "So persuade the duke. He'd be much happier if he overcame his fears and married you."

Could she persuade him?

No. It would be wrong even to try. In his mind, she would be asking him to sacrifice his life for her. That was too much to ask of anyone, especially someone you loved—

Oh, lud. She *did* love him, didn't she?

No. She couldn't. She'd only known him a few days.

What am I thinking? I don't want to marry anyone.

She closed her eyes. She *had* to go to sleep. Tomorrow she would draw lots and, with luck, win the Spinster House. Then Marcus—the *duke*—would leave and everything would get back to normal.

Normal suddenly felt like a hollow, joyless trudge to the grave.

Cat sat at one of the schoolroom desks, a still-blank sheet of paper in front of her, and watched Thomas and Michael play with their soldiers. Sybil had gone down to the garden to paint, and Prudence was curled up who-knew-where reading.

She should be writing. She picked up her quill . . . and put it down again. She didn't feel at all needle-witted this morning. She hadn't slept well and in just—

She checked her watch once more. Time was passing so slowly this morning. Would it never be eleven o'clock?

In just thirty more minutes she'd go over to the Spinster House. Well, twenty-five. No, twenty. In just twenty minutes, she'd go. She'd be a little early, but with luck, the house would be open. If not, she'd stroll around the gardens, out of sight of the vicarage. She'd tell Mama and Papa her plans once she knew for certain that she'd won the lottery.

After today she should have hours and hours of lovely, uninterrupted time to work on her book.

Unless Jane or Anne won.

They *couldn't* win.

"Oh, there you are, Cat."

"Eek!" Drat, she shouldn't be so jumpy. Mama would suspect something. She stood at the schoolroom door now, looking at Cat rather closely.

Cat forced herself to smile. "You startled me."

"Obviously."

Mama came in and sat in the hard, uncomfortable chair next to Cat. This could not be good. Had Mary told her about the Spinster House?

No, Mary wouldn't snitch on her, though it wouldn't be surprising if Mama had guessed on her own. There weren't that many unattached women in Loves Bridge.

Cat kept smiling. "You don't have another basket for Mrs. Barker, do you, Mama?"

"No." Mama picked at an imaginary bit of lint on her skirt. "I've given up on that plan. I can see Mr. Barker won't suit."

"Cat's going to marry dook, Mama." Mikey didn't even bother to look up from his soldiers.

"No, I'm not." *Lud, am I blushing? Hopefully Mama is still looking at her skirt—*

Of course she wasn't.

Cat forced herself to return her mother's gaze. It wasn't

easy. Mama's expression was a terrifying mix of hopeful, worried, and determined.

"Papa thinks His Grace is interested in you, Cat."

Mama had never invoked Papa's name before when discussing potential mates. Did Papa really think—

It made no difference what Papa thought. Papa didn't believe in the curse, but the duke did.

"His Grace is merely polite."

Mama kept looking at her.

Don't flinch. Don't look away. You've stood up to Mama before.

"And I think you're interested in the duke, Cat."

She didn't have *that* much control. She glanced over at the boys playing with their soldiers.

Unfortunately the boys weren't as involved in their game as she'd thought.

"Dook likes you, Cat," Mikey said.

Tom nodded. "And we like him. He's much better than Mr. Barker."

She felt trapped.

Ridiculous! She couldn't be trapped by two four-year-olds and her mother.

"I am not marrying the duke or Mr. Barker. I'm not marrying anyone."

She felt Mama touch her hand.

"What of the duke's friends, Cat? Can you like one of them?"

Horror exploded in her gut. Marry one of Marcus's friends? Good God! "No."

"But you need a husband, dear," Mama said softly.

"No, I don't."

Mama pressed her lips together and forced herself to change tactics.

"Very well, but have you looked ahead to what life holds

for an unmarried woman? Have you given any thought to where you'll live, for example?"

If Mama wasn't going to mention the obvious answer, she wasn't either.

What if Anne or Jane wins the Spinster House? What will I do then?

Her stomach lurched, and she swallowed the bitter taste of panic. The Spinster House tenancy was for life.

Or until marriage.

Hmm.

She wasn't ready to commit murder, but she was willing to try her hand at matchmaking, if necessary. Mama had mentioned Marcus's friends. They were attending Mary's wedding—Marcus had sent word that Lord Haywood had consented to play the pianoforte. True, she hadn't actually met either of them, but from a distance they appeared pleasant enough. Perhaps one of them would be a suitable husband for Anne or Jane.

Though hopefully *she* would win the house.

Annoyance crept into Mama's voice, even as worry creased her brow. "You'll always have a place with us, of course, but we won't live forever. I can't imagine you'd be comfortable with Tory or Ruth or Mary. Or with Henry or Walter or Pru or Sybbie. They'll all grow up and wed, you know."

Cat nodded. If she couldn't mention the Spinster House, she had nothing to say.

"A husband does more than provide a roof over your head, Cat. He's a companion." Mama leaned closer, blushing a little. "A lover."

"Er, yes. I know." Mama wasn't going to pursue *that* discussion, was she?

She was.

"I realize you haven't known a man's touch yet—"

The memory of Marcus's mouth on hers suddenly made her lips—and other parts—tingle. She felt herself flush.

Mama's eyebrows shot up. "Have you kissed Mr. Barker, then?"

"Of course not! You know I can't abide the man."

"That is what I thought, but it wouldn't be unusual if you'd been curious—"

"I would not be curious with Mr. Barker."

Mama's eyes narrowed. "Then with whom?" A brow arched up. "The duke?"

"Mama!" It hadn't been curiosity in the bushes. She'd only meant to have a moment of privacy with the duke to argue her case for the Spinster House. She'd never dreamed that anything of an amorous nature would occur.

Mama still looked suspicious, but, blessedly, chose not to argue the matter. "Then if you haven't kissed anyone, dear, you have no idea what you are missing." She cleared her throat and glanced over at the boys—they were still playing, but the battle was suspiciously quiet. She leaned close again and dropped her voice to a whisper.

"Normally I'd wait until the night before your wedding to tell you how it is between men and women but—"

No!

Cat bounded to her feet. "I'm so sorry, Mama, but I have to be going." She glanced at her watch. Yes, indeed. She should have left several minutes ago. She was almost late.

Mama caught her hand and stood, too, being careful to face away from Thomas and Michael. "Married love is nothing to be afraid of, Cat. A man's love is wonderful." She chuckled. "I wouldn't have ten children if it weren't."

Cat's stomach twisted. She knew Mama and Papa must have done whatever it was that produced children, but she didn't want to think about it.

She'd seen dogs and other animals copulate. It looked embarrassing—disgusting really—and most uncomfortable for the female. It was not something she ever wished to do.

But after kissing Marcus—

She would *not* think about kissing the duke, especially with Mama watching her. Mama's eyes were far too sharp.

"I'm sure you are right, Mama. And now I'm afraid you really must excuse me. I, er . . . I have to meet Jane and Anne." That was true. "And I'm almost late." She tugged on her hand, but Mama squeezed it instead of letting go.

"I don't want you to go through life alone, Cat. I know I've thrown Mr. Barker at your head—well, and other men before him—but I only want your happiness. Life without a husband and children would be unbearably lonely."

An ache bloomed in Cat's chest, and she squeezed her mother's hand back. "How can I be lonely with nine brothers and sisters and countless nieces and nephews, Mama?"

"Your brothers' and sisters' lives will be centered on their own families. What will you have?"

What *would* she have?

What she'd always wanted. "My writing."

Mama's brows snapped down. "Pish! Your writing won't keep you warm in bed at night."

No, it wouldn't. *Was* Mama right?

Drat it, this was all the duke's fault. What had he been thinking to kiss her?

"I wish to be an author, Mama. I always have."

Mama's patience was at an end. She dropped Cat's hand to throw her own into the air in disgust. "Author! You'll be the old spinster aunt, that's what you'll be, sitting in the corner while life passes you by."

"Cat can come live wif me, Mama, if dook doesn't marry her," Mikey said, coming over to wrap his arms around Cat's legs.

"Or you can live with me, Cat," Tom said, tugging on one of her hands, "and write your books."

Mama smiled. "That's very sweet of you, boys."

"Yes." Cat swallowed the lump that had suddenly appeared

in her throat and hugged her little brothers. "Thank you, both." If she didn't leave now, she'd start crying—*and* she might miss the lottery. "And now I *really* must go."

She rushed down the stairs and out of the vicarage. They wouldn't start without her, would they? She walked faster. Thank heavens the Spinster House was so close. She dashed across the street—and almost tripped over Poppy.

"Merrow!"

"Oh! I'm sorry, Poppy. I didn't see you." She bent to give the cat a quick pat.

Poppy glared at her for a moment and then apparently forgave her, rubbing herself against her ankles before running off toward the back gardens. At least if she was lucky enough to win the Spinster House tenancy, she wouldn't have a disgruntled housemate.

She hurried up the walk. Incipient panic made her rap on the door rather more forcefully than necessary, but if they'd held the drawing without her . . .

Randolph opened the door. "No need to knock the house down, Cat." He looked behind her as she came in. "You haven't seen His Grace, have you?"

"No. Isn't he here yet?"

A stupid question. Randolph wouldn't have asked if the duke had already arrived. Cat stepped farther into the sitting room—and into the narrowed gazes of Jane and Anne.

"We thought he was with you," Jane said. "You and he seem to be such good friends."

"What do you mean by that?" The sitting room felt much larger than it had when she'd been here with the duke. She sat gingerly on the edge of the red settee, as far as possible from Anne at the other end. Jane had taken the armchair.

"I saw you dart into the bushes with him yesterday," Anne said.

Cat's stomach dropped. She wouldn't admit anything.

"How could you have? The vicarage is nowhere near Davenport Hall."

"I wasn't at home. I was here, looking around, planning what I would do with the garden once I move in."

Jane snorted. "A waste of your time, since I'll be the one living here." She smiled. "I'll invite you both to visit, however."

The panic she'd felt at the door thudded in Cat's chest again. "We all have an equal chance."

"Unless the duke manipulates things to give *you* the advantage. He probably wants you to win so he can sneak in and out to visit."

"Jane!"

That had been Randolph's voice. Cat had been too shocked by Jane's venom to do more than gasp. Jane had never been like this before.

Jane flushed. "I'm sorry. I didn't mean that. It was a horrible thing to say. I just want to live here so badly."

"That is no excuse to forget your manners and even common decency," Randolph said.

Did the man truly wish for Jane to strangle him?

"You are not my father, Randolph. I don't need you to tell me how to behave."

"You apparently need someone. I've never seen you act like such a shrew."

Jane glared at Randolph, her jaw clenched so hard it looked like it might shatter.

"Jane has a point," Anne suddenly said into the tense silence. "It will look very odd if you win, Cat."

Good God, what was this? "Why? I have as much right to live here as you or Jane." More right, since Isabelle was her ancestor, but that didn't seem like a good thing to say at the moment.

"The duke compromised you when he took you into the

bushes," Anne said. "You are more a fallen woman than a spinster."

"I am not." How could Anne say such a thing? "And the duke didn't take me into the bushes. I took him."

Anne, Jane, and Randolph gasped in unison.

Drat! She'd not intended to admit that. "Only to have some privacy to discuss the Spinster House."

Jane sniffed. "That must have been an interesting 'discussion'."

Dear God, don't let her blush.

Anne tittered and then her brows rose. "Indeed. And nothing else happened?"

"Of course not."

God didn't like liars. Cat felt heat sweep up her neck to cover her face.

Jane and Anne exchanged an unpleasant, knowing look, and then turned their eyes toward her. She felt like a bug pinned to a board.

"Everyone knows your sisters have used those bushes as a trysting place for years," Anne said. "No one will be surprised to learn that you used them, too."

Cat suddenly had trouble drawing an adequate breath. Spots danced briefly before her eyes. What would Papa say? And Mama? She'd be disgraced—

No. She must not panic. Nothing had happened.

Well, nothing much.

"Our conversation was perfectly innocent." It was what had happened after the conversation that had strayed toward the scandalous. "And, in any event, no one but you saw us, Anne. Surely you will not spread unpleasant rumors about me."

"I wasn't the only one to see you. Lord Haywood observed the scene as well." For some reason Anne's color was suddenly very high. She dropped her gaze to her hands.

"But he's the duke's cousin. He won't say anything."

Anne smoothed her skirt. "And someone else might have

seen you. The Boltwood sisters were out walking." She shrugged, still not meeting Cat's eyes. "It's a small village. You know how quickly gossip travels."

Desperation—and then anger—twisted in Cat's chest. She gripped her hands tightly together, forcing herself to take a slow, deep breath. She would not lose her temper. She would—

"Good morning, Wilkinson, ladies."

The voice wrapped around her heart and sent her pulse racing. She turned to see the duke standing just inside the doorway.

The room suddenly got smaller, as small as when she'd been here with him before, and she felt warm and breathless as she got to her feet.

"Sorry I'm late. I ran into a small problem." The duke looked at Randolph. "Shall we get this over with?"

"Yes, Your Grace. I have the lots in the kitchen. If you will—"

"Just a moment, Randolph," Jane said. "How are you going to ensure His Grace doesn't favor Cat?"

The duke's expression froze. "Are you calling my honor into question, Miss Wilkinson?"

Cat shivered. The temperature had dropped several degrees.

"Jane!" Randolph could not have sounded more appalled. "What are you thinking?"

Jane, hands on hips, faced her brother. "I'm thinking I want to be completely certain I've got a fair chance to win the Spinster House." She turned to regard the duke. "I'm sure you're the epitome of honor, Your Grace, but this might be my only opportunity to escape my brother's home."

"Good *God*, Jane, you make me sound like a bloo—like a blasted jailer."

"I often feel like I'm incarcerated, Randolph."

Randolph's face grew very red, and a vein in his forehead began to pulse.

"I have to agree with Jane," Anne said. "I, too, want to be certain everything is aboveboard."

His Grace's eyebrows were up by his hairline. He managed to look insulted and disdainful simultaneously. "And why, may I ask, do you ladies think I would favor Miss Hutting?"

"Anne saw us go into the bushes, Your Grace." There was no point in trying to hide that. In fact, Cat was very much afraid that if she did indeed win the lottery, Anne would spread the story throughout the village. Anne had never been vindictive before, but this situation seemed to be bringing out the worst in all of them. "And though I explained I merely wished to have a private word with you, she seems to think something else happened."

Oh, dear Lord, had she seen a smile flit over the duke's lips?

"I'm sure the ladies didn't mean to call your honor into question, Your Grace." Randolph glared at Jane in particular, but she glared right back at him. "Emotions have been running a bit high, as you might imagine, since each of the ladies is very eager to reside here."

"I see. And I suppose I must be the one holding the lots?"

"I believe so, Your Grace." Randolph's mouth twisted. "I'm not certain that Miss Dorring's instructions specify, but since I'm the only other person available to do it, and my sister will likely accuse me of arranging things against her if she loses, I think it will have to be you."

"*Would* you accuse your brother, Miss Wilkinson?"

Jane didn't even flinch. "Yes, Your Grace, I would."

The duke nodded. "Then I suppose I must take comfort in the fact that mine are not the only motives you question. Very well. Tell us how you had planned to go on, Wilkinson, and we can then adjust the procedure to meet the ladies' requirements."

"Thank you, Your Grace." Randolph scowled at Jane. "I believe I've already devised things to guard against any favoritism. I put clay in the bottom of an old ceramic vase and carefully arranged the three sticks in it so they appear to be of equal length. Unless you can see through solid objects, you will not know yourself which is the shortest straw and thus have no way of favoring one candidate over another."

The duke nodded. "That seems sufficient, but in an abundance of caution, I will blindfold myself as well. Will that do, ladies?"

Jane frowned. "I suppose so. Do you agree, Anne?"

Anne looked as if she'd like to find fault, but finally said, rather reluctantly, "Yes, I guess so."

Of course no one asked Cat, not that she would disagree. What else could the duke do? The entire situation was ridiculous.

The duke pulled a large, white handkerchief out of his pocket. "If you will be so good as to tie this around my eyes, Wilkinson? And then please let the ladies inspect your handiwork to be certain they feel confident everything is in order."

"I'm sorry, Your Grace," Randolph said as he took the handkerchief. "I never guessed this would turn into such a farce."

The duke had beautiful eyes, but once they were covered, Cat found herself focusing on his lips. Lud! Her body remembered in exquisite detail exactly how they had felt on hers.

She looked away as Jane and Anne stepped closer to assure themselves that the duke couldn't see.

"Don't you wish to examine the blindfold, too, Cat?" Randolph asked.

"No. I trust you to be able to tie a knot."

"Thank you." Randolph looked at Jane and Anne. "Does everything meet with your approval, ladies?"

Anne nodded.

"Yes," Jane said. "Let's get on with it."

Randolph fetched the vase and put it carefully in the duke's grasp. Cat's stomach twisted, and her legs started to shake. In just a moment, she'd know if she'd won the Spinster House or if she was condemned to continue living in the vicarage's chaos.

"May I suggest I count to three and then each lady put her hand on her chosen lot? However, before anyone pulls one out, I will give the vase to you, Wilkinson." The duke's beautiful lips turned up into a grim smile. "I should like to have removed my blindfold before the result is known in case I need to defend myself."

"I hope we have more control than to attack you, Your Grace," Jane said.

"I hope so, too, but I find myself strangely reluctant to wager my safety on it." The duke extended his arms, holding the vase well away from his body. "Here we go, then. One. Two."

Cat's heart raced. She tensed, ready to dart her hand out the moment the duke said "three." She had her eye on the lot she was going to choose.

"Three."

She reached out—and had her fingers knocked away by Anne's.

"Anne!"

"I got to it first."

Cat had no choice. She had to take the last lot.

"Wilkinson," the duke said, "if you will hold the vase?"

Randolph took it, and the duke stepped back, ripping off his blindfold.

"Very well," His Grace said. "Let us see who will be the next Spinster House spinster."

Cat pulled her stick out of the vase and then looked at the others. Oh! There was no question—hers was far shorter than Jane's or Anne's.

"I won!" She grinned at the duke.

His Grace did not return her smile. "Congratulations, Miss Hutting. And may I advise you to watch your back if you wish to maintain your position?"

"What? Why?" She looked at Jane and Anne. "Oh."

Her friends were scowling at her as if she were their mortal enemy.

Chapter Twelve

May 30, 1617—The gabble grinders are whispering about me. Mrs. Bidley even gave me the cut direct at church Sunday. But I don't care. All I want is for my dear Marcus to return from London. His dreadful mother insisted he dance attendance on her last week, but he promised to come back as soon as he is able. I'm counting the days.

—from Isabelle Dorring's diary

"You're moving into the Spinster House?"

"Yes, Papa."

Cat had waited until dinner when the entire family was gathered to make her announcement. It had not gone well.

No, that was a colossal understatement. It had gone terribly. It had been like tossing a bomb into the middle of the dinner table. All conversation stopped, and everyone stared at her, mouths agape. Even Mama, for the first time in Cat's memory, was speechless.

And then Mama . . . well, drooped was the best way Cat

could describe it. Her shoulders, her mouth, her eyes— everything slid downward as if pulled by unbearable disappointment.

Mikey started to cry, and even Tom sniffled.

"But why, Cat?" Papa sounded completely bewildered. "Aren't you happy here?"

"Of course I'm happy, Papa." On one level, that was true. She did love her family. "But I'm twenty-four years old. It's time I moved out." She forced a smile. "I don't even have my own bed here."

"You will soon," Mary said, "when I wed Theo."

"Yes, and then Mama will move Pru in." Cat tried to laugh and almost managed it. This was much, much harder than she'd thought it would be.

"No, Cat." Mama finally found her voice. "I would have let you have the bed—and the room—to yourself if you'd told me that was what you wanted. We have enough space now. Pru and Sybbie can keep sharing."

"Yes, Cat. I don't mind," Pru said, her voice quavering. "Please don't leave."

Good God! She'd thought Pru would be the one opening the door and giving her a sisterly shove to hasten her departure.

Sybbie was sobbing into her napkin now, and Walter and Henry just stared at their plates. They must be extremely upset—they'd stopped eating.

This was silly. "It's not as if I'm moving to London. I'll be just across the street."

It was the right decision. She'd wanted this for years. So why did she suddenly feel as if she was making a terrible mistake?

She just hadn't expected this reaction, that was all. It was unfortunate, but change was always hard. Once everyone got used to her living in the Spinster House, things would settle down.

And, really, when Tory and Ruth had moved out, there hadn't been this great fuss. And Mary was leaving in just over a week—no one was crying about that.

No, the problem wasn't Cat moving out. It was her leaving without marrying.

"How could I not take advantage of this opportunity? I never guessed Miss Franklin would wed and open up the Spinster House position."

"But I thought you lov"—Mary caught herself—"liked the duke, Cat."

"Of course I like him." She gave Mary a look that threatened slow dismemberment if she said one word about their nighttime conversation. "What does that have to say to the matter?"

Mikey had come over to wrap his arms around her waist and soak her dress with his tears. Now he wiped his streaming nose on her. "You're supposed to marry dook, Cat."

She hugged him tightly. "No, I'm not, Mikey."

"Yes, you are." Tom had stayed in his seat, but his eyes were red and his lower lip stuck out as it always did when he was fighting tears.

"Oh, Tom." She smiled at him, and then looked around the table and forced a laugh. "This is ridiculous. The duke hasn't even offered for me."

"But he will."

"Papa!"

"I saw how he looked at you during dinner last night, Cat. And how you looked at him. You can't say you're totally indifferent to the man, because I won't believe it."

"She's not indifferent to him, Papa." The words burst out of Mary. "She—"

"I *said* I liked him." Cat glared at her sister, and Mary flushed and held her tongue.

Mama shook her head, clearly baffled. "I can understand your reservations about Mr. Barker, but the duke is nothing like him."

"I know that." Of course she knew it. In other circumstances—

But the circumstances were as they were. The duke was bedeviled by the curse, and she wished to write books. A husband—even a husband such as the duke—would be a tremendous distraction. Living in the Spinster House was the perfect way to ensure she actually wrote rather than merely wished to do so.

"I've told you, Mama, and you, too, Papa, that I have no plans to wed. I want to write. I need time and a quiet, solitary place to do that."

"I don't know why," Papa said. "I would think all you'd need was some paper and a pen."

Of course Papa didn't understand. No one had ever understood, except perhaps Miss Franklin. Writing a novel was far more than just scribbling words on a sheet of paper.

"It's not that simple. If I married, running a household, especially one with children, would take all my time." She looked back at Mama. "Isn't that true?"

Mama raised an eyebrow. "I suspect as the Duchess of Hart, you'd have an army of servants ready to do whatever you needed at the crook of your little finger."

"Oh!" Prudence's eyes widened. "That's right. If you marry the duke, you'll be a duchess." She almost bounced in her chair. "My friends will be *so* jealous."

"And I wager the duke has a bang-up stable," Walter said. "Or he will once he decides to live at the castle."

"And he has a cook that bakes good biscuits," Tom said.

"And a horse that doesn't bite," Mikey added.

"And he can buy me my cavalry commission—"

"No, he cannot, Henry." Mama scowled. "You are not going into the cavalry."

"But, Mama—"

"Stop!" Cat took a deep breath. "I am not getting married."

"But Mama is right," Prudence said. "If you married the duke, you'd have servants to take care of everything. And the castle is so large, you could probably go days without seeing him if you wanted to."

But that was *not* what she wanted. She wanted to share her life with Marcus. She wanted to wake up with him every morning and go to bed with him every night.

And now she was blushing. She could not think about beds and Marcus.

"I am *not* marrying the Duke of Hart. How many times do I have to say it?" She struggled for control. "Contrary to what you say, Papa, he will not propose. Are you forgetting the curse?"

Walter shrugged. "Even better. If you marry him, you'll be a wealthy widow in just a little while. Then you'll have the castle and money and plenty of time by yourself to write. I should think that would be exactly what you'd want."

Cat surged to her feet. "It is *not* what I want! What an awful, hateful thing to say." She threw down her napkin and ran from the room.

Mama found her later sitting on the bed she shared with Mary.

"Walter should not have said that." Mama sat down next to her.

"No, he should not have."

"Papa has him translating Latin and Greek phrases as a punishment, but he'll be up to apologize himself shortly. He's truly contrite."

"He should be." Cat refused to meet Mama's gaze, not that Mama needed to see her eyes to know what she was feeling. Cat had shown the entire family that.

Mama laid her hand on Cat's. "I'm sorry, Cat. I wish I could do something to fix this."

Cat's throat clogged with tears. She swallowed determinedly.

Mama's fingers tightened on hers. "If Isabelle wasn't dead already, I'd drown her myself. The pain she's brought you and the duke is unconscionable."

Cat managed to force some words past the lump in her throat. "There is nothing between me and the duke."

Mama let that lie pass unremarked upon.

"Walter said he'd help you move in the morning."

"I don't need help."

"Perhaps not, but it would be kind of you to let him make amends this way. I believe he really didn't understand your feelings."

Likely not. *She* didn't understand them. "All right."

Half an hour later, someone knocked on her door.

"Come in."

Walter edged into the room.

"I'm sorry for saying what I did, Cat. I didn't know—I mean, you said—" His voice broke—he was at that age when it broke often—and he shrugged, staring down at his feet. "I really am sorry."

"I know, Walter. It's all right."

"And you'll let me help you in the morning?" He glanced up and then back down. "Mama said you would."

"Yes, of course."

By morning, Walter had regained his swagger. He chattered away about something—Cat was listening with only half an ear—while he carried her valise to the Spinster House. They passed Mrs. Bates on her way to her shop.

Cat smiled and nodded. "Good morning, Mrs. Bates."

Mrs. Bates didn't answer or even meet Cat's eyes. Instead

she pulled back her skirts and crossed to the other side of the road.

Walter stopped and stared after the woman. "Why'd she do that?"

"I don't know." It was very odd. Mrs. Bates was usually quite friendly.

"It was like you had the plague or something."

"Perhaps she is the one who is ill." Cat didn't have time to stand on the walk and puzzle over Mrs. Bates's peculiar behavior. The key to the Spinster House was heavy in her pocket. "Come along, Walter. I want to get settled as soon as I can, and Papa said you weren't to dally. You have more translations to do."

Walter scowled. "Papa has no mercy. You'd think he'd give me the day off since my oldest sister is moving out."

Cat snorted. "Doing it rather too brown, Walter. You aren't going to miss me. And if you do, I'll be just across the road, for goodness' sakes."

"It won't be the same."

"Yes, it will." They'd reached the Spinster House door. Cat fitted the key into the lock and turned it. The door swung open noiselessly to reveal Poppy sitting in the entryway cleaning her paws, as if she'd been awaiting their arrival.

The cat took one look at Walter, arched her back and hissed, and then darted past their legs and down the walk.

"And I don't like you either!" Walter called after her. Most animals loved Walter, so he was especially offended by Poppy's rejection.

"She's only a cat, Walter."

"And a stupid one, at that. I'd evict her if I were you."

"I doubt I can. This is her house more than mine—or at least I'm sure that's what she thinks. Now give me my bag, and you can be on your way."

"I'll take it up to your bedchamber for you. You don't want

to hurt yourself lugging it up the stairs." Walter wandered farther into the sitting room.

Clearly he was not anxious to return to the vicarage and his translations.

"I am not so delicate, Walter, and the bag's not that heavy—I packed it, remember?" She could let him carry it up, but she was strangely reluctant to have him see the rest of the house. This was her place, her new life. She wasn't ready to share it.

"All right." Walter set the bag down, but made no move to leave.

"Have you forgotten where the door is?"

"No." He still didn't move, except to shift from foot to foot. He glanced around the room, his eyes stopping at the dreadful picture of the dog with a dead bird in its mouth. "Look at that painting."

"Yes, I've seen it before. Now I'm sure Papa is waiting for you."

He frowned at her. "Want to get rid of me, do you?"

She did. She was eager to revel in her solitude. But she thought she heard a hint of bravado in his voice. "You aren't really going to miss me, are you, Walter?"

"Of course not." His words said one thing, but the hesitation in his voice said something else.

Heavens! He *was* going to miss her. "You know you can visit whenever you want."

Oh, drat. She hadn't wanted to say that. She was here for the solitude. She wouldn't get much writing done if her siblings kept popping in.

But it had been the right thing to say. Walter's sudden grin was blinding. However, being a thirteen-year-old boy, he was not about to admit to any feelings.

"Why would I want to do that? You're just across the

street, remember." He paused and shifted on his feet again. "You'll be coming home for dinner, won't you?"

"Yes, from time to time." She started for the door to encourage him to do likewise. "Now go along. You don't want to keep Papa waiting."

Walter sighed. "Blasted translations. Why couldn't those ancient chaps have written in the King's English?"

"Perhaps because they were Greeks and Romans."

Walter made a face at her, and then waved and headed back toward the vicarage.

She closed the door firmly behind him and rested her forehead briefly against it.

Finally! For the first time in her twenty-four years she couldn't hear someone talking or crying or arguing or just thudding around. There was no one asking her to play games or run errands. She was completely, blissfully alone.

It *was* rather quiet—

Of course it was. That's what she wanted. Quiet. Room to think.

She picked up her valise and climbed the stairs, her footsteps echoing through the house. She could invite Anne and Jane over for a cup of tea—

No, they wouldn't come, not while they were still smarting from their failure to win the Spinster House. But in a few weeks they might accept an invitation. She'd hate to lose their friendship. Meanwhile she'd spend the time when she wasn't writing, arranging things the way she wanted them.

She put her bag down in her bedroom. The very first thing she was going to do was open a few windows and let in some fresh air and sunlight. She looked at the painting of Isabelle Dorring.

"And the second thing I am going to do is put you in storage."

Marcus stood in the morning light and looked out the study window.

No. He stood at the window, but he wasn't looking at anything. He was lost in the quagmire of his thoughts.

He was free. He'd finished dancing to this part of Isabelle Dorring's tune and could leave Loves Bridge forever. Miss Hutting was only twenty-four. She might well live to be sixty or seventy.

But he wasn't free. The Spinster House tenancy had been decided two days ago—Miss Hutting, not one to waste time, had probably moved in yesterday—but he was still here. Nate and Alex had left for London. He should have gone with them, but he'd told them he had estate business to keep him busy until they returned for Miss Mary Hutting's wedding—Nate had agreed to play the pianoforte—and then they could all three go off to walk the Lake District.

Perhaps.

He did have estate business, but that wasn't the real reason he was staying—or at least not the main reason.

He was staying because he couldn't bring himself to leave Catherine.

He squeezed his eyes shut. Blast it, Nate had been spying on him again. He'd seen him go into the bushes with Catherine after dinner at the vicarage. Later that night, back at the castle, and again the morning after, Nate had gone on and on, lecturing him about the curse and the need to be careful. He'd made Marcus late to the Spinster House lottery.

He sighed. Nate only wanted to protect him. He understood that. But he had to live his own life. Make his own choices.

Even if those choices led to disaster.

So he'd lied to Nate. God. He'd never lied to Nate before. But he hadn't seen any other option. Telling Nate the truth—the complete truth—would only have set them at loggerheads and kept Nate here, breathing down his neck and sticking his nose into his business.

So he'd told Nate he and Catherine had gone into the bushes to discuss the Spinster House.

True.

And that nothing had happened.

Not true.

That she was a dedicated spinster, with no thought or wish to marry.

True, but he hoped to be able to persuade her to change her mind.

Nate had been delighted when Catherine had won the lottery. It had likely been the only reason he'd allowed himself to go back to London. He'd considered the danger over.

But it wasn't over.

Marcus leaned his forehead against the glass. He couldn't bear the loneliness much longer. It had become a howling wind rushing through him—and all because of Catherine, the new Spinster House spinster, a woman who had absolutely no interest in marriage.

But she had kissed him there in the bushes. She'd leaned into him, and her lips had softened under his. It had been unbearably sweet.

God, he wanted her here now. He wanted to crush her against him, to plunge his tongue into her mouth and—

He turned away from the window and sat down at his desk. He should try to think of something else. Perhaps he could get some work done. He picked up one of the papers on his desk and read the first paragraph.

And then he read it again.

It wasn't working. All he could think about was Catherine—

her face, her voice, her body, the touch of her hands, the scent of her skin. He was a besotted idiot.

He had to do *something* productive. Perhaps he could answer some of his simpler correspondence. He'd just—blast, his pen needed trimming.

He started pulling open drawers. They were all empty. Emmett had said the desk had been cleaned out years ago—it hadn't been used since the notorious third duke's time—but a small penknife might have been overlooked. He stuck his hand deep into each drawer, earning only a covering of dust on his coat sleeve for his trouble.

Until the last drawer. There was something long and thin wedged into one of the back corners. He peered inside, but he couldn't quite make out what it was. It *might* be a penknife.

He reached back in and pulled and twisted. Whatever it was, it was stuck fast. Perhaps if he pressed down . . . Yes! The thing finally moved—

And the back of the drawer swung forward. Zeus! A secret compartment—with something inside: an old, worn, black book, about the length and width of his hand and roughly about half an inch thick—

"Y-Your Grace?"

His head snapped up as he slipped the little book into his pocket. He didn't want to share his discovery, at least not until he knew what it was.

A nervous Theodore Dunly stood in the doorway.

"Come in."

"Thank you, Y-Your Grace."

Dunly walked hesitantly into the room. He looked as if he might bolt if Marcus said the wrong thing. Odd. Dunly had never before struck him as high-strung.

"How may I help you, Mr. Dunly?"

This appeared to be too difficult a question for the man to answer. He stared at Marcus, his jaw flexing.

"Have a seat." Marcus gestured to the two wing chairs facing his desk.

"Thank you." Dunly perched on the edge of one of them. "Your Grace."

Silence.

This was ridiculous.

"Mr. Dunly, please. You clearly have something to say. Just say it and put us both out of our misery."

Dunly nodded. "Yes, Your Grace." His Adam's apple bobbed, and then his jaw hardened. "Mary—Miss Mary Hutting—urged me to speak with you, Your Grace." He took a deep breath. "About her sister." Another breath. "Miss Catherine."

Oh, hell. "Yes?"

"She . . . that is, they . . . I mean Mary, er—"

"Just say it, for God's sake!" Marcus took his own deep breath. "My apologies, Dunly. I shouldn't have shouted. However if you don't come to the point immediately, I cannot answer for my actions."

"Yes, Your Grace." Dunly fixed his eyes on a spot just above Marcus's right shoulder and spoke in a rush. "Mary wanted me to be certain you were aware of the rumors."

This did not sound good. "What rumors?"

"The rumors about you and Cat."

He'd swear his heart stopped beating in his chest.

"Dunly, I have not been back to the village since Miss Hutting won the Spinster House, and even if I had been, no one would gossip to me. Tell me what the *hell* you are talking about."

Dunly's eyes met Marcus's and then darted back to the spot over his shoulder. "Someone—someone besides Mary and me, that is—saw you and Cat go into the bushes the other day, Y-Your Grace. Now everyone is saying you and she are . . . that Cat is . . ." Dunly blushed furiously. "Everyone is saying Cat is no better than she should be, especially since she is living without a chaperone in the Spinster House. All the women are giving her the cut direct."

"Bloody hell!" Marcus surged to his feet. How dare they treat Catherine that way? He'd beat the miscreants into the ground—except he couldn't very well attack a gaggle of gossiping females, no matter how much they deserved it. He knew damn well Nate hadn't breathed a word. "The vicar and Mrs. Hutting don't believe this calumny, do they?"

"No." Dunly stood, too, and smiled briefly. "They know Cat too well. Mary said Mr. Hutting is planning to preach about the evils of gossip in his next sermon, and Mrs. Hutting—" He shrugged. "I'm afraid Mary thinks her mother would be happy if Cat *was* misbehaving with you, Your Grace. Mrs. Hutting cannot understand Cat's determination not to wed. Well, Mary can't either. Mary's certain Cat loves—" Dunly caught himself and snapped his jaws together.

"Yes, Dunly? Miss Hutting loves . . . ?"

Him?

Something hot and fierce coiled in his chest.

"Er . . ." Dunly's face flushed painfully red. "Ah . . ." His eyes suddenly brightened like a fox's might when he spies a way to avoid the hounds. "Independence. Mary is certain Cat loves her independence."

Damnation. That was true, but he would swear Dunly had been going to say something very different.

"I hope I didn't give offense, Your Grace. I know it's a bit of meddling, but Mary insisted I speak to you. She felt you should know if you didn't already." He cleared his throat. "She felt you would *want* to know."

"Quite right. Thank you for telling me." He would

have to offer for Catherine now or she'd be ostracized by everyone she knew.

Dunly's shoulders relaxed, and he sighed with relief. "I'll admit I didn't want to say anything, Your Grace. Not really my place, don't you know? But Mary insisted."

"Yes, indeed. She was quite right to do so."

If he wed Catherine, he could start counting the days to his death. He was only thirty. It was too soon.

He waited for the crushing dread that always came whenever he thought of marriage.

It didn't come. Instead he felt anticipation. He wanted Catherine, and now he'd be able to have her, even if only for a few months.

"I'm going to ride into the village, Dunly, in case anyone asks for me."

"Yes, Your Grace."

He went to the stables and had George saddled. Was he mad? He'd just refused to be trapped into marriage by Miss Rathbone and her father, and yet here he was on his way to step into parson's mousetrap voluntarily.

Perhaps he didn't have to. The gossip might subside, especially if he left Loves Bridge.

He didn't want to leave the village. He didn't want to leave Catherine.

He felt an odd sense of relief. He was finally going to turn and face the thing he'd been running from his entire life. There was freedom in doing that.

He rode to the vicarage first. Mrs. Hutting, the twins at her side, opened the door.

"Dook!"

The boys rushed at him to wrap their arms around his legs. He put his hands on their heads. God, how he wished he could touch his own son someday.

One of them—Michael; he was coming to be able to tell

them apart—looked up at him. "People are being mean to Cat, dook."

"I know. Mr. Dunly just told me."

"Are you going to make them stop?" Tom asked.

"Yes."

Mrs. Hutting snorted. "That will be a trick. Boys, let His Grace go. The poor man can't move."

The twins stepped back, and Marcus felt strangely bereft.

Nonsense. He straightened and looked at Catherine's mother. "I've come to have a word with the vicar, Mrs. Hutting."

She nodded. "He's in his study." She looked down at the twins. "We'll go out later, boys. Right now Papa and I need to discuss a few things with His Grace."

He was certain he'd mentioned only the vicar. Perhaps Mrs. Hutting had not discerned his intent.

Or perhaps she had. The boys definitely understood.

"Huzzah!" Thomas jumped up and down. "Dook is going to marry Cat!"

Michael's brows wrinkled. "Cat likes you, dook, but she might not say so the first time. She can be as stubborn as a mule."

"Michael," Mrs. Hutting said, "where did you hear that?"

"From you, Mama."

"Oh." Mrs. Hutting laughed. "I suppose I might have said such a thing on occasion. Now run along so that His Grace and Papa and I can arrange things."

It wasn't his place to tell the woman that mothers were not included in such discussions. That was the vicar's job, though somehow he doubted the man would discourage his wife from joining them.

Nothing about this family followed his expectations.

"Yes, Mama," Tom said. He looked at his brother. "Let's go tell Mary."

"Yes, let's."

"Nothing's decided yet, boys," Mrs. Hutting called after them as they dashed up the stairs. She smiled and shook her head. "Those two will be the death of me. Now, if you will come this way, Your Grace, we can be comfortable."

She led him to the study. "I admit I am very happy to see you, though I must warn you, Michael is right about Cat. The entire village could turn its back on her, and she wouldn't care." Mrs. Hutting frowned. "Or in any event, she would pretend she didn't care. She can be maddeningly obstinate. Can you believe she has this silly idea that she wishes to be a novelist?"

Since Mrs. Hutting opened the study door at this point, Marcus wasn't required to comment on Catherine's literary aspirations.

"William, His Grace is here to see you."

"Ah." Mr. Hutting put aside his books and papers to stand and smile at Marcus. "Come in, Your Grace. Have a seat." He looked at his wife. "Perhaps you could bring us some refreshments, my dear?"

"Oh, no," she said, taking the chair next to Marcus. "You are not getting rid of me that easily, sir. If you are thirsty, you can have some of the brandy I know you've got tucked away behind Aristotle and Plato. I'm sure His Grace would rather have that than tea anyway."

He knew where Catherine got her strong will.

"Very likely," the vicar said. "Would you care for a glass, Your Grace?"

"Thank you, sir, but I must decline. I plan to go from here to the Spinster House, and I wish to have all my wits about me when I speak to your daughter."

"Very wise." Mrs. Hutting nodded with approval.

The vicar, however, was frowning. "Am I correct in

assuming you are here to ask for Cat's hand in marriage, Your Grace?"

"Yes, sir, I am." Thank God his voice hadn't wavered. "I came as soon as Mr. Dunly told me about the gossip." He cleared his throat. "How is Miss Hutting taking it?"

The vicar laughed. "Not well, of course. She's furious. Got into a shouting match with Mrs. Barker on the village green yesterday. Henry had to pull Cat away, while Mr. Barker took his mother home."

"Ah." That was not the answer he'd expected, though if he'd considered more carefully, he should have expected it. Catherine was not a typical female.

Mrs. Hutting leaned toward him. "Cat says Anne Davenport saw something perfectly innocent and decided, once she lost the Spinster House lottery, to spin a tale, hoping to force you into marrying Cat and thus opening the Spinster House position again."

"But Cat laughed at how silly Anne was to think she would marry anyone because of a little gossip," the vicar added. "Or even a lot of gossip." He smiled with what looked like pride. "Cat is very principled."

"And strong willed," Mrs. Hutting said.

Marcus nodded. "Yes, I noticed that."

The vicar looked down at his hands clasped on his desk. "I confess I am curious, however. The rumor is just that you went into the bushes with Cat, and everyone has then embroidered on that to a ridiculous degree. Cat says she took you there to have a private conversation, but I don't think she's telling the complete truth." He looked up. "What did happen?"

Marcus shifted in his chair. "I kissed her."

"And then she slapped you?" the vicar asked.

"No."

Mrs. Hutting put her hand on his arm. "Did she kiss you back?" She sounded as if she hoped the answer was yes.

He was not one to tell tales.

"The encounter was quite chaste."

Mrs. Hutting's face fell.

He cleared his throat. "But I realize I shouldn't have gone with your daughter. Her intentions were innocent, while mine were . . ." He hadn't intended to do anything improper, precisely, but he'd certainly known better than to go into the vegetation with a female. "Not entirely so."

Mrs. Hutting actually bounced a bit and clapped.

"I am willing to offer for your daughter's hand in marriage."

"Oh, dear." Mrs. Hutting frowned. "You don't sound very happy about that."

"Of course he doesn't," the vicar said. "Remember Cat told us he believes in Isabelle Dorring's curse."

"Oh, that's right. That horrible curse."

They both looked at him with eyes full of concern.

He forced a smile. "Everyone has some unfortunate, er, burden to bear, I suppose."

"But not everyone thinks his wedding will be followed so closely by his funeral." The vicar sighed. "You have my permission to court Cat, Your Grace, but there is no need to do so. If everyone who ever stole a kiss in the shrubbery was forced to marry, there would be no single people left." He shrugged. "The gossip is silly. It will pass."

Mrs. Hutting touched his arm again. "You should only ask Cat to marry you if you really love her, Your Grace. That's what she needs. Not a husband, but a man to love her."

As he needed a woman to love him.

But things were never that simple, were they?

"Thank you." He stood. "I'm off to see your daughter now. I hope you may wish us happy shortly."

"I hope so, too." The vicar smiled. "And I hope someday to see you dandle your sons and daughters on your knee."

There was no chance in hell of that. "Thank you, sir." He turned to leave.

"Oh, and one more thing."

"Yes, sir?"

The vicar grinned. "Cat has a powerful right arm. You might wish to be prepared to duck after you pop the question."

Chapter Thirteen

*June 10, 1617—Marcus is back! I'm so happy.
Except something is troubling him. I wish he would
tell me what it is.*

—from Isabelle Dorring's diary

Cat sat at the desk in the Spinster House library, a stack of papers at her elbow. True, most of the sheets had many of their words crossed out, but the story was beginning to take shape. Her poor, meek, *boring* heroine had finally seized control of her life. Instead of simpering in a corner, hoping the handsome Duke of Worthing would notice her, she was planning how to save him from an evil witch and the witch's familiar, a sly cat.

Poppy, stretched out in the sun on the window seat, yawned.

Cat grinned. All right, perhaps the story was inspired somewhat by current events. The point was, she'd got beyond the dreaded first sentence. It might all be complete balderdash, but at least she was finally writing *something*. Surely the lady who'd authored *Sense and Sensibility* and

Pride and Prejudice hadn't been able to get her stories perfect the first time either.

She dipped her pen into the inkwell and prepared to skewer a character who bore a marked resemblance to Mrs. Barker. First she would—

Drat! Someone was knocking at her door.

Perhaps the person would go away. She leaned over her paper again.

No. More knocking. She frowned, brushing her pursed lips with her quill. It could be Mama or Papa or one of the boys—she'd persuaded them to knock rather than just walk in.

Well, yes, locking the door had helped with that.

The knocking was getting louder. Clearly whoever it was wasn't going to stop until she opened the door. She sighed and got up. "Why can't people just leave me alone, Poppy?"

Poppy stared at her.

Yes, all right. Thanks to Anne's maliciousness, people *were* leaving her alone. Apparently her reputation was now as black as possible, though it was hard to see how a single kiss in the shrubbery could be such a mortal sin.

She flushed. Likely she was now accused of far more than a kiss. She didn't precisely fault Anne, though her betrayal did hurt. But then she might have done something similar if she'd lost the lottery. Despair spawned desperation.

She'd just have to weather the storm. Everything would calm down once the duke left Loves Bridge.

She hurried across the sitting room. The blasted knocking was getting even louder and more insistent. "I'm coming, I'm coming." She flung open the door. "What do you—"

Good God. It was the duke. Her heart attempted a very uncomfortable pirouette in her chest as she looked into his handsome face.

"What are you doing here?"

Not the politest of greetings, but apparently surprise and a far more carnal emotion didn't result in the best of manners.

"I am here to speak with you, of course. May I come in, Miss Hutting?"

"No!" That was all she needed. Reasonable people might question how much she could have sinned in the bushes with the man, but alone in a house . . . Not that *she* had any idea of what sins were possible, but the duke certainly must. He likely had a long list of shocking activities he could pursue.

A disconcerting heat flooded her, and she moved to slam the door in his face.

He blocked her easily by simply putting out his hand. "Thank you," he said, and stepped past her.

Was that the scandalized breath of the Loves Bridge gossips she heard drawn in sharply?

No, it was her own breath. She glanced outside. Oh, dear. Mrs. Greeley, likely arriving at the vicarage to put the finishing touches on Mary's wedding gown, was staring at her from across the street.

"You need to leave *now*. You've been seen."

"I have?" The duke leaned over her. "So I have." He waved at Mrs. Greeley.

Mrs. Greeley, clearly dazed, waved weakly back.

"Ohh." Mortification flooded Cat, and she backed away as the duke closed the door—with him still on the inside.

Lud! He was doing the same trick he'd done when he'd been here before—filling up all the available space. She felt a bit light-headed.

I have to marshal my wits before they are completely scattered.

"Perhaps you aren't aware of it, Your Grace, but someone—I suspect Anne—has been spreading the tale of our brief discussion in the shrubbery, except everyone has embroidered the story past recognition. And while the village is giving me its collective back now, if you will only leave, I'm sure—"

He put his hands on her shoulders. "I know about the gossip, Catherine. I'm so sorry. I just found out, or I would have been here sooner."

"Ah." Just as she had feared, her poor brain was suddenly scrambling around like a mouse trapped in the bottom of a deep, slippery pot. It couldn't hold on to any one thought. Her body, however, knew exactly what it wanted—to press up against Marcus. She breathed in his scent, felt the comforting weight of his hands, and ached to taste his lips again, to—

"I've spoken to your father, and he's given me permission to pay my addresses."

"What?" Marcus wasn't making any sense. Why wouldn't he stop talking and kiss her?

He laughed and shook her gently. "I will go up to London tomorrow for a special license, and we can be married—"

"Married?!" She jerked back, and he let her go. "Have you lost your mind?"

More to the point, had she lost hers? She'd dreamed for years of this freedom she'd just won—to live alone on her own terms and be able to write without constant interruption— and at the duke's words, her first impulse was to throw it all away as Miss Franklin had done.

His brows snapped down so they met over his nose. "No, of course I haven't lost my mind."

"Then why are you talking about marriage?" She couldn't stand still, so she paced back and forth, being careful to stay well beyond arm's reach—*her* arm's reach— of the duke. The temptation to go along with his plan was shockingly strong. Her body hummed so loudly with need, it was drowning out every other thought.

Remember—the duke thinks marriage is a death sentence.

He's wrong. The curse is a silly superstition.
But if he's right . . .

She did not want to cause Marcus's death.

The duke was still scowling. "I've compromised you. I've ruined your reputation. Of course I'm talking about marriage."

"Nonsense. You didn't ruin my reputation; Anne did." That didn't come out right. "I mean my reputation is not ruined. People may talk for a while, but they'll realize soon enough that they are making a great deal about nothing. I even think Anne—and Jane, too—once they get over their disappointment at losing the Spinster House, will come about and mend our friendship." She hoped so, at least.

"And even if my reputation remains in tatters, I was the one who dragged you into the bushes, so it could be argued I'm responsible for my own ruination." She forced a smile. "See? You can absolve yourself of all culpability."

He was still frowning at her. What was the matter with him? He should be grinning and cutting a caper.

"But what about that woman with the ugly bonnet? She saw me come in here just now. I even waved at her."

What woman? Oh! "You must never say that to her!"

He blinked. "Say what to whom?"

"To Mrs. Greeley—the woman who saw you come in. You must never tell her you think her bonnet is ugly. She's our village dressmaker and cares about such things." The poor woman would be devastated if she discovered the London duke found her headgear lacking. Not that it should be any surprise to her. Mama, at least, had been trying tactfully to tell her for years that her fashion sense left something to be desired.

"Then she shouldn't put such a hideous hat on her head. I hope her taste in dresses is better."

"Well, not much, but she does take instruction well. She got quite carried away with Mary's wedding dress, but agreed to remove all the furbelows when Mama insisted." Cat laughed. "You should have seen Mama's expression when Mary's head finally emerged from the froth of flounces and pleats and ribbons and knots. Papa said it looked like a haberdashery had vomited all over her."

The duke stared, and then shook his head as if *he* was trying to free himself from festooned fabric. "That is neither here nor there, Miss Hutting. My point is the woman has a tongue in her head and will likely use it. Everyone will know about this visit."

"Precisely. Which is an excellent argument for bringing it to a quick end." She strode toward the door.

The duke stood where he was. "But what about your reputation?" The poor man sounded extremely frustrated. He must be used to everyone falling in line with his plans.

"I told you, any injury to my reputation is of my own doing." She shrugged. "And reputations are of most concern to young ladies hoping to catch a husband. I don't want a husband"—*other than you*—"so I don't need a reputation."

She could almost hear his teeth grinding.

"Now if you will be so kind as to—"

She started to open the door, but the duke moved at the same time, so quickly he took her completely by surprise. One second her hand was on the latch, and the next her back was against the door, shutting it firmly.

She gawped up at him as she tried to comprehend her sudden change in position. It didn't help that his body was pressed against hers from her shoulders to her knees.

"You didn't give me time to slap you." She should be furious. She couldn't move.

She didn't want to move, unless it was to press more tightly against him. She tried instead to press against the door, and the evil man just moved in closer.

The tiny part of her brain that still functioned knew he would let her go if she asked him.

If only I could muster the will to do so.

"Of course not." He smiled. "I'm not stupid."

And then his mouth came down on hers.

This kiss was much different from the one they'd shared in the bushes. His lips didn't just brush lightly over hers. They clung. They stroked and nibbled and explored.

His hands were off exploring, too, tracing their way from her hips to her waist, up her sides to just under her breasts. Hot, drenching pleasure coursed through her, pooling low in her belly, throbbing between her legs, causing her nipples to tighten and ache. She was suddenly very, very hot.

Thank God Marcus and the door were supporting her, or she'd melt into a puddle on the floor.

She wanted to touch him. She moved her hands up under his coat, but his blasted waistcoat was in her way. She wanted it off. She wanted everything off—his clothes and her clothes. She wanted to feel his naked flesh against hers.

His lips and tongue traced the line of her jaw and then nuzzled a sensitive spot just under her ear.

She moaned and rubbed the part of her that ached the most against his legs and the bulge that had appeared between them. If she were only a few inches taller, that bulge would fit perfectly against her. She stretched and wrapped her arms around his neck.

His mouth moved back to hers, and this time his tongue traced the seam of her lips. Did he want her to open her mouth?

She did.

Ohh. His tongue slipped in, making the throbbing grow until her body felt hollow, aching for something only he could give her.

Her fingers slid deep into his hair, his thick, silky hair that had the slightest bit of curl, and she moaned again, her heart pounding in her ears.

Which is probably why she didn't immediately hear someone pounding on the door behind her.

Marcus heard, though. He lifted his head. "Are you expecting company?" he whispered.

"Huh?"

He looked at the door just as whoever it was knocked again.

"Oh!" She tried to shove him away.

"Wait," he murmured by her ear. "Whoever it is will leave eventually."

"And how will that look?" she hissed back at him. "You know Mrs. Greeley saw you come in. People will imagine the worst."

He grinned, looking at once seductive and boyish and oddly happy. "Then let's do the worst."

Oh, no. Tempting as that was, it would be a serious mistake. The sort of activity she suspected he meant could lead to a child, which would make it harder to decline his offer of marriage.

He saw her answer in her eyes and let her go. She jerked open the door. Her sister Mary was just leaving, Michael and Thomas by her side. They turned back, and Mikey and Tom broke into wide grins.

"It's true. Dook is here!" Mikey said, rushing past Cat to give Marcus a hug.

"We almost gave up," Tom said, following Mikey.

"Where's Poppy?" Mikey asked. "We thought we heard her meowing just inside the door."

Cat felt her face flush—and Mary's eyes study her. "I think she's in the room with the harpsichord, Mikey. Or maybe she's gone off somewhere. You know Poppy's a bit afraid of you and Tom."

"Silly cat." Mikey grabbed Marcus's hand. "Let's go look for her, dook."

Marcus let the two little boys tow him away.

"I wonder what happened to the duke's hair," Mary said, watching the small group vanish into the other room. "It's rather untidy."

"Umm." It was probably safer not to venture an opinion.

"Your hair is rather untidy as well."

Cat's hands flew up to assess the damage. Oh, dear. How had so many strands come loose? She'd need a mirror to put everything to rights.

"We were, er, in the midst of a discussion."

Mary snorted. "*Discussion*. That's an interesting term for it."

Mary could be very annoying.

"The duke heard about the rumors. He asked Papa for my hand in marriage."

"Oh, Cat, that's wonderful!" Mary threw her arms around her and hugged her tightly. "I'm so happy for you. See? He didn't let that silly curse prevent him from proposing."

When Cat didn't hug her back, Mary pulled away, frowning. "What's the matter?" Her frown deepened. "You aren't going to hold to your mad decision never to marry, are you?"

That's what she should say, but she didn't have the heart at the moment to put on a brave face.

"I can't marry the duke."

"Why not?"

"Because he still believes in the curse, Mary. I can't ask him to give up his life just because people are talking about me."

"But he won't die. You know that"—Mary's eyes widened—"don't you?"

Icy fear chilled any lingering passion. "I don't know what I believe."

Marcus walked up from the stables to the castle. The day had not gone at all how he'd expected. When he'd left for the village, he'd been certain the vicar and his wife would fall on his neck in gratitude that he was willing to do the right thing by their daughter. He'd thought Catherine would be relieved to be saved from scandal. He'd thought he'd be betrothed now and contemplating his own mortality.

He'd forgotten he was dealing with a family of lunatics.

He slapped his hand against his thigh. What the hell could he do? He couldn't force Catherine to the altar.

And why would he wish to? He should be delighted with the outcome. He'd done what honor demanded. Now he was absolved of all blame, not that the situation was his fault to begin with.

He clenched his teeth. But people *would* blame him. They'd assume he hadn't offered, because what woman in her right mind would turn down the chance to be a duchess, even the duchess of the Cursed Duke? And he *had* been the one to initiate that kiss in the bushes. And the kiss in the Spinster House . . .

He started walking faster.

What the blazes was the matter with him? He'd never cared about public opinion before. He certainly hadn't lost a moment's sleep over Miss Rathbone's ruined reputation.

But Miss Rathbone hadn't had a reputation except as an unpleasant, unscrupulous, scheming harpy. She'd earned every bloody aspersion cast her way. Catherine, on the other hand . . .

Oh, God. His mindless cock stiffened, making it painfully clear why he was in such an agitated state. It had nothing to do with Catherine's reputation. He'd been so blasted happy to see her when she'd finally opened the door that his heart—and his cock—had literally leapt for joy. He shouldn't have waved at Mrs. Greeley, but he'd *wanted* to be seen with Catherine. He'd wanted everyone to know that she was his.

Except she wasn't.

But she *had* responded to his kiss.

At least, he thought she had. He slowed his steps, going back over the scene in his mind. Perhaps he'd been a little too overwhelmed by it himself to know for certain.

But no, she hadn't pushed him away. On the contrary, he'd felt her hands moving under his coat and then through his hair. She'd moaned and rubbed against him—

Zeus, he was going to embarrass himself here in the middle of the lawn. He needed to think about something else, something like drainage issues and . . .

And Catherine's body had fit perfectly against his. Her mouth had welcomed him, and all he'd wanted was to get lost in its warm, wet depths.

And then he'd wanted to strip her naked and have her under him, his cock plunging deep while she screamed his name—

No. Think of dry rot. Crumbling mortar. Leaking roofs.

This insane attraction was all the curse's fault. Now that he was thirty, the need to see to the succession was growing, pushing him toward the cliff that was marriage. Finch and Kimball had warned him. Nate had tried his best to save him.

It was time to save himself.

He needed to put as much space as possible between himself and Miss Hutting as quickly as possible. He'd leave for London at once. Emmett and Dunly had been taking care of the castle quite competently all these years; they could continue to do so. They didn't need him. Hopefully by the time he returned for Mary's wedding—unfortunately, he couldn't skip that, not with Nate committed to play the pianoforte—he'd be cured. Several visits to his favorite brothels should do the trick.

He tried to ignore the nausea suddenly roiling his stomach at the thought of taking anyone but Catherine to bed.

Thank God Mary and the twins had shown up when they

had. He would miss Thomas and Michael—he would miss all the Huttings—but it could not be helped. Sometimes retreat—hell, out-and-out flight—was the only option.

Emmett met him at the front door.

"Your Grace, I'm happy to see you've returned." Emmett did not look happy; he looked nervous. "You have a visitor." He cleared his throat. "In the study."

Who the hell could be visiting him here? "Did the person give you his name?"

"Yes."

Marcus waited. Emmett stared back at him, a panicked smile pinned to his face.

"So who is it?"

"Er . . ." Emmett swallowed. "Um, Mrs. Cullen." His tongue was finally loosened. "She arrived an hour ago. I put her in the study and gave her some tea and cakes. She's very anxious to see you, Your Grace. I would suggest you go right in." He smiled weakly. "Straightaway, if that would be convenient." He swallowed again. "Your Grace."

"I don't know a Mrs. Cullen. Emmett, what are you hiding from me?"

Emmett's face lost what little color it had, but then his chin hardened with resolve. "Your Grace, I think it best if you let Mrs. Cullen explain things."

Oh hell, hadn't this day been bad enough? He didn't want to deal with another difficult woman; he wanted to flee to London, but he didn't have the heart to vent his spleen on old Emmett. For some reason it was important to the man that he hear this Mrs. Cullen out.

"Oh, very well, but I hope this won't take long."

"Indeed, Your Grace." Emmett wouldn't meet his gaze. "I'm certain Mrs. Cullen won't waste your time."

The man was clearly hiding something, but what? The woman purported to be married, so she couldn't be planning to claim he'd compromised her—not that he would fall in with such a scheme in any event. And surely Emmett wouldn't be part of something so underhanded.

He would go along and find out what she wanted. If it turned out she had nefarious intentions, he'd send her on her way with a flea in her ear.

When he reached the study, he paused just outside the room to observe the woman. She was tall and slender, her black hair threaded with gray. She did not look to be a member of the *ton*. Her blue, unremarkable frock wasn't precisely dowdy, but it certainly wasn't of the first stare. He doubted it had been made in London.

At the moment, she was frowning up at the third duke's portrait. Hmm. Something about her profile was oddly familiar. He was certain he'd never seen her before, but perhaps he'd once met a member of her family.

"Good afternoon, Mrs. Cullen," he said, coming into the room. "I'm sorry to have kept you waiting."

At his voice, the woman sucked in her breath and whirled to face him, her right hand going to her breast as if to keep her heart from leaping free. "M-Marcus," she breathed.

He frowned. "I'm sorry. Have we met before?" He would swear they had not, and yet the woman was bold enough to use his Christian name. And she was looking at him in a very . . . unusual way, as if she wished to memorize his every feature.

She smiled, the corners of her blue eyes crinkling. "Yes, we have, Your Grace, but only briefly and many years ago. You would not be remembering it."

She had an Irish lilt to her voice.

"Ah. I see." Though of course he didn't. "Did you come with a specific purpose in mind, then, Mrs. Cullen?" *Other than to stare at me.*

She laughed at that. "Oh, yes. I'm sorry. You must think me very odd. May we sit down, Your Grace? And then I'll be telling you my story."

"Of course. Shall I ring for more tea?"

"No, thank you. I've had quite enough."

Unfortunately *he* would like a large glass of brandy. Something told him he'd need the alcoholic support. But it would be rude to drink when the woman wasn't, and she didn't strike him as the sort of female who would be partial to spirits.

She sat gracefully on the uncomfortable settee while he took the uncomfortable chair. If he were going to stay here—which he wasn't—he'd make getting rid of this furniture a top priority.

The woman was studying him again in that oddly intent way. Was she never going to get to the point of her visit? He'd best prompt her.

"You were about to tell me why you are here, Mrs. Cullen."

She nodded—and then sighed. "Yes. I'm afraid there's no easy way to be saying this, Your Grace." She hesitated again.

"Then just say it, madam." He couldn't keep the thread of annoyance from his voice. He'd had enough emotional drama for one day.

She nodded. "You are quite right." She took a deep breath, smiled, and said, "I'm your mother."

"What?!" He felt his jaw drop, and then he surged to his feet and started to pace.

The woman was lying. She was here to pick his pocket; that was it. Somehow she'd got wind he was in residence. Perhaps she was in league with Emmett. The man had made a point of telling him that wild tale about an Irish mother. He'd even admitted to knowing her.

He looked back at her to tell her exactly what he thought of such machinations—

And suddenly realized why she looked familiar. He'd seen a male version of her face in his own looking glass.

"I'm sorry," she said. "I'm sure it's a shock."

"Yes." He sat again. He *really* would like a glass of brandy. "It is. How do you come to be here, madam?" He wouldn't call her Mother. He couldn't, not yet. Perhaps not ever. Nate's mother—his aunt—had earned that title.

But why had Aunt Margaret told him his own mother had married an Italian count and gone to Italy?

"I believe Emmett told me you live in Dublin?"

Mrs. Cullen nodded. "I do. My husband is a physician there. He's been corresponding with a doctor outside London for years and finally decided to visit. Since we were so close to Loves Bridge, I asked if we might stop and see Mr. Emmett as well. It was amazing luck"—she smiled—"or fate to find you here."

Neither luck nor fate had ever favored him. "And your husband? Where is he at the moment?"

"Shortly after we arrived, Mr. Emmett got word that a tenant's child had taken ill, so my husband went off to see what was amiss. He always travels with his bag of medical supplies. You'd be surprised how often he is called upon to help someone."

Mrs. Cullen was clearly proud of her husband. Marcus would even guess that she loved the man.

It was nothing to him, of course. He only felt this twinge of . . . discontent because he'd had a stressful morning.

She leaned toward him, determination suddenly in her eyes. "My husband will be back shortly, I'm thinking, Your Grace, so I should say this now." She picked at an invisible speck of lint on her dress. "Please understand I don't wish to criticize your aunt—"

"I would hope not, madam. I will not brook any censure of the woman who raised me."

Mrs. Cullen flinched at his words. He was sorry for it—sorrier than he would have guessed, actually—but it seemed best to be frank.

"Yes, she did raise you. And I do believe it was for the best—at least, that is what I have always told myself. But I never realized—" She paused, frowning. "That is, I never imagined . . ."

She leaned toward him again. "Your Grace, Mr. Emmett told me it was his impression that you thought I didn't want you, that I'd been happy to give you up. That is not true." She sighed. "Or not completely true. It is far more complicated than that."

It had happened a long time ago. It was likely best they leave it in the past. "Now, Mrs. Cullen, there is no need to—"

She spoke over him. "I loved you, Marcus. Giving you to your aunt and uncle was the hardest thing I have ever done. It was like tearing my own heart out. I did it because I was persuaded it was what was best for you."

"And is that also why you've never contacted me in thirty years?" Blast it, he should hold his tongue. None of this mattered. It was ancient history.

So why did he have this crushing ache in his chest? He wasn't a child any longer. He was a grown man. He didn't need a mother.

"Yes, that was part of the reason. I said it was complicated." She pushed an errant strand of hair off her face. "I don't know if you can possibly understand."

"Then don't feel the need to explain, madam. I've survived quite well without you."

Perhaps that was not completely true.

She swallowed and looked down at her hands. "Still, I hope you will allow me to try. I think it would be helpful for you to know my side of the tale."

"Very well." He made a show of consulting his watch. It was very rude of him, but his emotions were an unsettling, churning stew in his gut. He both wanted and didn't want to hear what she had to say.

"Thank you." She clasped her hands together. "When I look back on those days, I try to remember that I was very young and rather naïve. And, well, stupid. I thought I could shape the world to my liking—silly since I was only in Loves Bridge because my father's new wife didn't want me underfoot. Even now my husband tells me I always think things will go the way I wish."

He looked at his watch again. He didn't mean to be rude this time. He just wanted this over and a large glass of brandy in his hand. He'd given up any hope of setting off for London today.

"I should get to the point, shouldn't I?"

"Yes." He couldn't manage more than the one word.

She frowned, but continued. "I was only seventeen when you were born."

That young? That's hardly more than a girl.

And the duke had been well over thirty.

"I loved your father, but I'll admit our marriage was a mistake. I thought if I loved him enough, he would come to love me and we would live happily ever after." She sighed.

"Of course I was wrong. As soon as we said our vows, we left for London. It was a nightmare. Many of the young women in Town had hoped to win your father—or, more to the point, his title and wealth—for themselves. They were not, ah, welcoming."

No. They had probably been quite vicious.

"My Irish accent and country ways just made things that much worse. So I'm sorry to say that instead of coming to love me, your father became more and more embarrassed by me." She smiled slightly. "Well, I'm certain I *was* embarrassing. And then I conceived you almost at once. The poor man must have heard the banshees wailing in his ears." She looked up at Marcus. "I thought the curse was just a story, you see, but it was a true story for your father."

"It's a true story for every Duke of Hart, madam."

"Yes, I understand that now." She shook her head. "So after he died, I came back to Loves Bridge, pregnant and heartbroken and feeling that I'd ruined my life. There were indeed days when I wished I could turn back the clock and be Miss Clara O'Reilly again."

And if she could have done that—if she could have undone her marriage—he'd not be here.

He might at one time have thought that was something to be wished for, but, after kissing one very prickly spinster, the notion was now not at all appealing.

"You'd hardly ruined your life, madam. You were the Duchess of Hart with all the wealth and privilege you could want."

She scowled at him. "And I didn't want any of it. London taught me I didn't belong among the *ton*."

She took a deep breath, clearly getting a tighter rein on her emotions, and then continued. "So when your aunt and uncle visited shortly after your birth, it didn't take much to convince me that having a baseborn Irish mother could only be a detriment to your consequence. When they said they'd raise you with their son, who was almost exactly your age, it seemed like the perfect solution—the best thing for you, and perhaps the best thing for me as it would allow me to escape this." She gestured to the shabby room, but he knew she meant all of it, all the burdens and expectations that came with being the Duchess of Hart.

And I would have been trapped here, too.

Yes, he would have had his mother, but it was unlikely she'd have been happy. And he wouldn't have had Aunt Margaret and Uncle Philip and Nate. They would have visited—Uncle Philip was his guardian—but it would not have been the same.

He would have had a very lonely childhood.

"And, remember, your aunt had seen the terrible effects

of the curse better than anyone. She was five years old when her father died and your father was born. She lived with your grandmother until she married your uncle." Mrs. Cullen frowned. "Well, no, she lived with a succession of nannies and governesses. The duchess was too busy attending parties and other social events to be bothered with her children. When I considered how she'd grown up, I found I really couldn't fault her for assuming I would be the same sort of mother."

"The women who marry the Cursed Duke have always been more interested in being widows than wives."

Her frown turned into a scowl. "Not me. And perhaps not the others. One never knows what occurs in someone else's marriage or how another person copes with grief."

He was willing to grant that Mrs. Cullen hadn't married for greed, but he was not so quick to give the other duchesses that benefit of the doubt.

She sighed as if conceding she'd not convince him. "So as to the Italian count—your aunt came up with that story to explain to the *ton* where I'd gone. She said everyone would believe it, and I could vanish back into anonymity, which is exactly what I did. As soon as I could travel after your aunt and uncle took you, I left Loves Bridge and went home to Ireland. Not to my old home, of course. My father's wife still didn't want me there. I rented a house in Dublin.

"I wrote to your aunt regularly, and she wrote back, telling me how you got on." Her smile was rather sad. "You seemed to be flourishing without me. And then I met and married my husband and got very busy helping him with his medical practice and raising our sons and I . . ." She sniffed and pulled out her handkerchief, dabbing at her eyes. "I let you go. I believed you'd found a better home than I could ever give you. Your uncle was your guardian, after all. You needed to be brought up as the Duke of Hart."

That was true.

She leaned toward him then, opening a locket she wore and showing him the picture inside. "And I never forgot you, Marcus. See? This is a miniature your aunt sent me, painted when you were ten years old."

He looked at his young face. He remembered when that was done, just a month or two before he'd come to Loves Bridge and sat through his uncle's interview with Miss Franklin.

Mrs. Cullen grinned. "And I'll confess I do have a few friends in London besides your aunt. I hear things—like your recent experience with a Miss Rathbone."

Did she think to criticize him? "I was not about to marry that scheming hussy."

"Of course not. The girl didn't love you. And, more importantly, you didn't love her."

"Er, yes." He shifted in his seat. He hadn't expected Mrs. Cullen to support him in his handling of Miss Rathbone.

"Well, I have taken enough of your time, I'm sure, Your Grace." She stood and shook out her skirts. "But I hope you believe me. I have told you the truth."

He stood when she did. "Yes, Mrs. Cullen, I do believe you." Even though her story made his head spin.

He glanced up to see the third duke's portrait. But there was one question his mother had yet to answer. "Perhaps you could tell me one more truth. If you cared for me as you say you did, why did you saddle me with that popinjay's name? Wasn't bearing his title punishment enough?"

She looked up at the painting, too. "Your father wished you to be named Marcus," she said. "I don't know why." She looked back at him. "But I do know why I agreed to it." She smiled and touched his arm. "I hoped you would be the one to break Isabelle Dorring's curse."

Chapter Fourteen

June 15, 1617—Rosaline just got betrothed to the blacksmith. I overheard it at the market—she and Maria don't talk to me any longer. They say I'm no better than I should be. Nasty cows! I can't wait to see their faces when I become the Duchess of Hart. I know Marcus is on the verge of proposing.

—from Isabelle Dorring's diary

Marcus had never been so happy to close his bedchamber door in his life. He had a pounding headache.

Mrs. Cullen was still here. He'd invited her and her husband to stay at the castle, and she'd accepted, though only for tonight. Tomorrow they would set out to return to Ireland.

He poured himself a healthy dose of brandy and collapsed onto what might be the only comfortable chair in the entire castle, closing his eyes and resting his head on the chair's upholstered back.

God! His mind was still reeling from the day's events. His interview with Catherine had been bad enough, but then to meet his mother . . .

He felt like a newly blind man stumbling through an ever-changing maze. Everything he thought he'd known was now in question.

He stared into the fire, taking a sip of brandy, hoping the alcohol's warmth would melt the cold knot in his stomach.

He should go back to London. His life there was much less confusing. In Town, he knew who he was and what was expected of him. He hated it, but at least he didn't feel so powerless.

God! He pressed the fingers of his free hand into his forehead, his thoughts tumbling over each other.

His mother and his aunt had lied to him. They'd made up the Italian count.

But the lie had served its purpose. It had freed his mother from the nasty London gabble grinders. And in an odd way, it now freed him. The shallow woman he'd been embarrassed to acknowledge wasn't his mother at all—she was just a story, brought to life by the *ton*'s groundless speculation.

Still, his mother had admitted she'd given him up, and with some relief.

But what else could she have done? If she'd been forced to live as the Duchess of Hart would she have ended up as cold and heartless as her predecessors? And if she hadn't given him up, he wouldn't have grown up with Nate and Aunt Margaret and Uncle Philip.

She'd never written him, yet she wore a locket with his miniature.

He was a grown man. He didn't need a mother.

So why did he feel as if some empty place inside him had been filled?

He took a large sip of brandy and sunk lower in the chair.

He liked her. He hadn't expected to, but he did. He'd enjoyed dinner very much. She and her husband had been entertaining companions, talking knowledgeably about all sorts of subjects, none of which had anything to do with the *ton*.

He swallowed the last of his brandy. There was no point in stewing over things anymore tonight. He'd go to bed. A good night's sleep, if he could manage it, should put things in perspective.

He started to remove his coat and felt something in one of his pockets. Oh, right. With everything that had happened today, he'd completely forgotten about the little book he'd found in the desk's secret compartment.

He pulled it out to examine. It was old, its pages yellowed and brittle. He carried it over to the light.

It was a diary. The handwriting looked like a man's. And the date—

1617.

Zeus! It must have belonged to the third duke.

He put it on the table and pulled his hands away as if burned. He didn't want to know what twaddle that blackguard had committed to paper.

Or did he?

The man had haunted his life, casting a pall over even the simplest pleasures. Perhaps he *should* know the fellow's thoughts. He might better understand what had happened two hundred years ago.

He opened the book again and read the first entry. Yes, the diary had indeed belonged to the third duke. The man's handwriting was large and bold and confident. He was obsessed with the typical things a London buck cared about: horses and hunting and women and various court intrigues. Not much had changed in two hundred years. There was a long diatribe about his tailor and almost two pages describing an opera singer the man was lusting after.

But had the fellow written about Isabelle?

Marcus turned a few more pages. Ah, yes. Here it was.

*April 16, 1617—I should come down to the castle
more frequently. The girls in Loves Bridge admire
me greatly. One comely baggage is pursuing me—
she manages to turn up wherever I go. Her name is
Isabelle Dorring, and her dead father was a rich
merchant. And she lives alone—no chaperone—in a
house across from the vicarage. I think I shall
further our acquaintance. I could do with a little bit
of fun.*

His ancestor was exactly what he'd thought him—a
complete blackguard. What sort of man takes advantage of
a country miss?

Your sort.

At least that is what the villagers must think.

Damnation. He'd tried to do the right thing by Catherine.
He'd offered for her. He couldn't help it if she refused to
have him.

*But when I kissed her, she kissed me back. Perhaps
I can—*

Perhaps he should leave well enough alone. She'd said
she wanted to live by herself. He should respect her decision.

But that didn't mean he couldn't keep his ears open. He'd
ask Dunly to let him know how she went on. If she was
wrong about the gossip dying down, he would ask her again
to marry. Then she might be willing to accept him.

He scowled down at the diary. *I should put it away.*

No, I should burn it.

If he was going to burn it, he might as well read a little
more.

Hmm. By April 20, the duke's tone had changed. Now he
was writing of Isabelle's beauty—her lovely eyes, her en-
trancing dimples, her wondrous form. He was beginning to
sound rather besotted.

Oh, God, the fellow had even tried his hand at poetry. Marcus turned that page quickly.

This was interesting. The duke wrote that his mother did not like Isabelle. She thought the girl quite common—a merchant's daughter, don't you know. Fine for a quick tumble, but not at all acceptable as a duchess. She forbade him seeing her again and dragged him up to Town, thrusting him into the company of the female *she* had selected for him: Lady Amanda Mannerly, the Duke of Blendale's daughter, who, if memory served, had indeed become the third duke's wife.

Clearly the mother had the stronger will of the two, though the milksop son spent a number of diary pages protesting. He sneaked behind his mother's back, visiting Isabelle—and Isabelle's bed—when the duchess was in London. The final entry was written with slashing strokes, full of cross outs and splotches that might be—though Marcus hoped were not—evidence of tears.

> *July 10, 1617—I love Isabelle. I am going to marry her. I don't care what Mama says. She can't force me to wed Lady Amanda. If she drags me up the church aisle, I shall refuse to say my vows. I have given myself—soul, body, and mind—to my Isabelle. I will never love another.*

Eh. If only the Minerva Press had been in existence back then. The fellow could have had quite a career penning overwrought novels.

The fact was, for all his protestations to the contrary, the third duke *had* married Lady Amanda even though Isabelle was carrying his child. There was no excuse for that, but it was somewhat comforting to learn his ancestor hadn't been a cold-blooded devil. He'd apparently cared for Miss Dorring. Too bad he hadn't had more backbone. Two hundred years of misery could have been averted if he'd only had the will to tell his mother *no*.

Marcus put the diary on his dresser and finished getting ready for bed. *He* had a backbone. He wouldn't force himself on Catherine, but he would make very certain she was happy with her decision to remain unwed. He wouldn't leave Loves Bridge until he'd spoken to her about it once more.

Someone knocked at the front door.

Cat's heart jumped, and she looked up from her writing. "Who could that be?"

Poppy yawned and scratched her ear. She was in her favorite spot on the window seat again, watching the birds in the garden.

Could it be Marcus? Cat's heart started again in slow, painful thuds. She'd tossed and turned all night, remembering his kisses.

She couldn't see him again, not yet.

"No, I don't think it's the duke. The knocking is different from yesterday's." It was insistent, but not as forceful. "It's probably Mary. I'll ignore her, and she'll go away."

Poppy gave her a disdainful look before jumping down and running into the other room.

"You're not going to sit in the front window, are you?" Cat called after her. "That will make whoever it is think I'm at home."

Poppy did not reply.

"Drat!" She put down her pen. She supposed she should go see who it was.

Poppy was indeed in the window when Cat crossed the sitting room, and their mysterious visitor was still knocking. She put her hand on the latch. Did she want it to be Marcus or not?

She wasn't certain.

Well, she couldn't stand here like a statue all day. She took a deep breath and opened the door.

"Oh." It wasn't Marcus. It was a tall, thin woman with kind eyes.

The woman smiled. "Good morning. I'm looking for Miss Catherine Hutting." Her voice had an Irish lilt.

"I'm Miss Hutting."

"Splendid. Might I come in?"

Oh, dear, she suddenly realized who this must be. "Er, of course."

"Thank you." Her guest stepped inside and removed her bonnet, revealing black hair threaded with gray.

"You're the Duchess of Hart, aren't you, Your Grace?" Theo had told Mary last night that the duke's mother was visiting, and Mary had hurried over to tell her. Though why Mary would think she was at all interested—

All right, she knew why Mary thought she'd be interested. Mary was a romantic at heart. She still hoped Cat would marry the duke.

"I was the duchess a long time ago, Miss Hutting. I've since remarried and am now known as Mrs. Cullen."

"I see." Theo had told Mary that, too. Cat glanced back out the door. "Is your husband with you?"

"He's over at the vicarage, talking with your father. He thought—quite rightly—that I'd like a private word with you."

"Ah." Cat reluctantly closed the door. Why would Marcus's mother wish to speak privately with her? Hopefully the woman would be quick about stating her business.

Mrs. Cullen had finished looking around the room and was smiling at her again. Sadly she did not appear to be at all anxious to come to the point.

She could ask her the reason for her visit.

No, that felt rude. Cat forced herself to smile. "Would you like a cup of tea?"

"That would be lovely."

Poppy came over meowing, and Mrs. Cullen smiled. Something about her expression reminded Cat of the duke.

"What a beautiful animal," Mrs. Cullen said, stooping to scratch Poppy behind the ears. "Is she yours?"

"Oh, no. Poppy lives here, but she doesn't belong to me. She doesn't belong to anyone."

Mrs. Cullen laughed. "Isn't that the way of all cats?"

"I suppose so. Poppy's the only cat I've had much contact with."

Poppy sounded like a swarm of bees, she was purring so loudly. Mrs. Cullen must know the precise spot to rub.

"If you'd like to have a seat, I'll just go put some water on." The house came with a generous stipend, but Cat hadn't felt the need—or the desire—to hire a servant. Miss Franklin had done for herself well enough. Cat could, too.

"Wouldn't it be easier to take our tea in the kitchen?" Mrs. Cullen gave Poppy one last stroke and straightened. "You mustn't think I live like an English duchess, Miss Hutting. I'm not used to being waited on. My husband is a physician, and we had three boys together, so I've lived most of my life in happy chaos. A quiet cup of tea in a cheery kitchen sounds splendid."

"Oh. Yes. All right. If you'll come this way, then."

Cat led Mrs. Cullen into the kitchen, which wasn't particularly cheery, though the sun streaming in the window made it tolerable. Poppy went straight to a warm patch on the stone floor and stretched out. Thankfully it was early enough in the day that the sun had not yet reached the middle of the room. That would have been all Cat needed. She'd tripped over Poppy several times since she'd moved in. She did not care to do her frantic balance-saving dance to the tune of an annoyed Poppy's caterwauling in front of Marcus's mother.

"I've never seen the inside of the Spinster House. It's rather"—Mrs. Cullen sat at the old wooden table—"cozy."

Old and *dilapidated* were better adjectives. Cat put the water on to boil and then sliced the seedcake her mother had sent over the day before. Once she had everything ready, she put it on the table, sat down, and mustered her courage.

"Mrs. Cullen, I don't mean to be unmannerly, but—"

The woman smiled as she took a slice of cake. "But you are wondering why I've come to see you."

"Well, yes."

"Of course you are." Mrs. Cullen broke off a bit of her seedcake. "You see, I'm a meddler, Miss Hutting. I didn't begin life that way, but raising my three younger sons has taught me that sometimes it's important to give people a push in the right direction." Something that looked like sadness shadowed her eyes briefly. "And I suppose I feel that since I wasn't there to raise Marcus, I owe it to him to help him find happiness."

"Oh?" Cat shifted in her seat. This conversation—or, more likely, monologue—looked to be going in a very uncomfortable direction. She should show the woman the door. Her writing time was slipping away.

"Indeed." Mrs. Cullen leaned toward Cat. "I love Marcus, Miss Hutting. Yesterday might have been the first time I'd seen him since shortly after his birth, but I assure you not a day has gone by these last thirty years that I haven't thought about him."

She'd abandoned her poor baby, and now she said she loved him? "But you gave him up."

Oh, lud, she shouldn't have said that. She should have kept her tongue between her teeth and let the woman talk. The sooner she said her piece, the sooner she'd leave.

Mrs. Cullen's brows slanted down. "I did, but I was persuaded it was for his benefit." She sighed. "And, really, what could I have offered him beyond my love? The world

Marcus was destined to live in was totally foreign to me, and I would never have been allowed to take him with me to Ireland." She laughed. "Can you imagine the great Duke of Hart growing up in a little Dublin town house?"

"No." Put that way, yes, she could see why the woman had done what she had, though remaining absent for so long—

That was none of her concern. "Mrs. Cullen, I still don't understand. What does any of this have to do with me?"

"I think my son might love you—or at least come to do so."

"What?!"

Poppy did not care for Cat's sharp tone. She lifted her head off the sunny spot on the floor and growled.

Mrs. Cullen, however, laughed. "I told you I was a meddler. I asked Mr. Emmett how Marcus went on and, after that conversation, I spoke to Mr. Dunly. They mentioned you—and some interesting rumors that are going through the village."

Oh, drat.

"And then I chatted with your parents before I came over here. Your father told me he gave my son permission to court you."

No wonder Mrs. Cullen had sought her out. "Yes, but you needn't worry I'll marry him. I won't."

Mrs. Cullen's brows rose. "But he's compromised you."

"No, he hasn't. That story was started by one of the women who lost the Spinster House lottery. It'll die down soon."

Marcus's mother studied her. "So the rumors are completely groundless?"

"Er, y-yes." She did wish she was better at lying. "It was just . . . that is . . . well, you see . . ."

Cat took a large bite of seedcake to keep her unruly

tongue from leading her deeper into the hole she was digging.

Mrs. Cullen smiled. "My son would not have talked to your parents if he didn't feel something for you, Miss Hutting."

Cat choked on a crumb that went down the wrong way. "Oh, no. You are mistaken."

If only it were true.

It wasn't true, of course. The woman knew nothing of the matter. She might be Marcus's mother, but she'd only just met him. "He talked to my parents because of the gossip. You can be sure I quickly disabused him of the notion that he was under any obligation to me."

Mrs. Cullen shook her head. "Oh, no, Miss Hutting. You must know the Duke of Hart would not be offering marriage simply because people think he's compromised you. Many women have tried to trap him over the years, and he has always refused to be trapped."

"I thought you said you hadn't seen the duke since his birth, Mrs. Cullen."

She smiled. "Ah, but I'm his mother. I have eyes everywhere. I did make a few friends when I was the duchess, and they, as well as his aunt, write to tell me what he's doing, especially now that he's turned thirty." Her expression darkened. "The urge to marry grows stronger once the Duke of Hart reaches that age."

Drat. So that dreadful curse was behind this, too. "All the more reason not to accept his offer—not that I'm at all interested in marriage with him or anyone."

"Really? You've no desire for a man's touch?"

"No! Of course not." If only her face wasn't burning.

And if only Mrs. Cullen's gaze wasn't so probing. "It's true some women don't feel desire, but I'm thinking you're not one of them."

Cat rearranged the cake crumbs on her plate. "I've no time for marriage. I wish to write novels."

Mrs. Cullen frowned. "Can't you do that as a married woman?"

People who had never tried to write a book had no idea what was involved. "No. A husband and children take up far too much time and energy, Mrs. Cullen, as I'm sure you must know."

The woman's frown deepened. "I cannot agree with you. I may never have tried to write a book, but even when our sons were very young, I helped my husband with his work." A note of pride crept into her voice. "Besides seeing patients who can pay, Dr. Cullen treats many of Dublin's poor."

She took a sip of tea and regarded Cat over her teacup. "You have to live life so you have something to write about, don't you? How can your characters feel joy or sorrow or love or hate if you've not felt those emotions yourself?"

She *had* felt those things, rather more often since she'd met the duke. "Are you saying single women can't be writers, Mrs. Cullen?"

"No. But the question is, Miss Hutting, where are *you* going to feel more intensely—alone in this house or to-gether with my son?"

Together with Marcus.

She couldn't say that. "Here, of course."

Mrs. Cullen's right brow flew up. "That is not what your parents and your sister Mary think." She smiled. "In fact, your entire family—including your charming youngest brothers—think you belong with my son."

No. She couldn't marry Marcus. What if the curse was true? What if she conceived and Marcus died?

Panic made her voice slightly breathless. "Tom and Mike like the duke because his horse doesn't bite and his cook bakes good biscuits."

Mrs. Cullen chuckled. "I do have to say dinner was excellent last night, but I think your family is more interested in your happiness than in horses or baked goods."

Enough was enough. If she didn't bring this conversation to a close, she was sure to say something she'd regret. "Mrs. Cullen—"

Marcus's mother put her hands on Cat's. "Please, just listen to me, Miss Hutting. I'm sorry to force myself on you this way, but what I have to say is very important to me, and I think—I hope—to you and Marcus as well." She squeezed Cat's hands gently. "This is my only chance to say it. As soon as we are done here, my husband and I are continuing our journey to Dublin. We've been away too long as it is."

Cat sighed. "Very well. I will listen." It was probably the most efficient way to end this uncomfortable meeting.

"Merrow." Poppy suddenly jumped up onto the table. Fortunately she didn't land on the seedcake plate or knock over a teacup.

"Poppy, where are your manners?" She moved to push Poppy back onto the floor.

"Oh, let Poppy stay, Miss Hutting." Mrs. Cullen stroked Poppy's head and set her to purring again. "I don't mind the wee cat."

There was nothing wee about Poppy, but chances were if Cat tried to push Poppy off the table, Poppy would just jump back up. The creature was very stubborn.

"I believe you had something to tell me, Mrs. Cullen?" She let some impatience show in her voice.

Mrs. Cullen's hand stopped—and Poppy complained. She started stroking again. "I want to tell you about my marriage to Marcus's father."

Cat definitely didn't want to hear that. "Mrs. Barker already shared the story."

Marcus's mother frowned. "Oh? What did Ursula say?"

"Er, not very much." She shouldn't have mentioned it. When would she learn to hold her tongue?

Mrs. Cullen gave her a long look. "Knowing Ursula, she told you Gerald was a womanizer who married me because that was the only way he could get me into his bed."

There was no point in disputing it. "She did say you loved him, though. And that you didn't believe in the curse."

Mrs. Cullen suddenly looked years older. "Yes, that's true."

"Do you believe in the curse now?" If the curse *wasn't* real—

No, she still shouldn't marry Marcus.

Poppy gave an odd little growl and looked up at Mrs. Cullen. Marcus's mother must have stopped petting her.

"I don't know. I suppose in a way I do, though I'm not convinced Isabelle Dorring is to blame for it."

"W-what do you mean?"

Poppy jumped off the table. Mrs. Cullen picked up a seedcake crumb that had escaped and put it on her plate. "The Dukes of Hart do not have happy childhoods, Miss Hutting, though I believe—I hope—Marcus is the exception." She smiled and tapped the table to emphasize her points.

"Think about it. They never know their fathers and, until my husband's generation, never had any siblings. Their mothers—well, the story is their mothers are selfish, cold creatures interested only in wealth and prestige, but since I was painted with that brush, I'm willing to believe that at least some of those duchesses loved their babies. More likely they were pushed out of their sons' lives by the men who became the dukes' guardians."

Cat could certainly agree that that was a distinct possibility. Men, especially men who thought they had important duties, could be very highhanded.

Mrs. Cullen shrugged. "Be that as it may, it can't be disputed that the poor boys are told from the time they can understand that they will die before their own son is born. That rather casts a pall over one's expectations of life, wouldn't you say?"

"Yes. Yes, indeed." *Poor Marcus.*

"I gave Marcus to his aunt to raise for many reasons, but one was that if she took him, Marcus would grow up with his cousin, Nate. I hoped if he had a more normal childhood, he might learn how to love."

Mrs. Cullen leaned forward and touched Cat's hands again. "I do think Marcus cares for you, Miss Hutting. I think you and he might be able to break the curse, which is why I've taken so much of your time today."

Break the curse? "I'm sure you are mistaken."

"I loved Marcus's father when I married him. I thought my love would be enough, but it wasn't."

"Mrs. Cullen, I am not marrying your son."

"I think he will ask you again. He will not give up. He considers himself obligated—"

"I've told him that he is not."

"—but I believe he . . ." Mrs. Cullen sighed and bit her lip. "I'm not certain he loves you yet, but I'm positive he feels *something* for you. If it is only lust, you must remain adamant that you won't have him."

Marcus lusting for her? The thought was rather exciting. . . .

No. No, it wasn't.

"You do not have to worry, Mrs. Cullen. I am a dedicated spinster."

The woman went on as if Cat hadn't spoken.

"But if it *is* love . . ." Her face almost glowed. "If Marcus loves you, Miss Hutting, the curse will be broken. That's the key, the answer to the puzzle—the duke must marry for love. Promise me you won't marry him until he admits that he loves you."

Clearly the woman was a bit unhinged. The best thing—the kindest thing—to do would be to humor her.

"Very well, Mrs. Cullen. I promise not to marry the duke until he says he loves me."

Chapter Fifteen

June 20, 1617—Marcus has gone up to London with his mother again, and Rosaline and Maria are snickering. I hate it. They make certain I hear them say he will not come back. But he will. Soon. And then we'll be together. I don't need anyone else but him.

—from Isabelle Dorring's diary

Cat stood at the front of St. Valentine's, listening to the organ fill the stone church with music. An odd melancholy washed over her. She'd spent so many hours here, playing with her sisters in the pews while Mama worked on the altar flowers, running up and down the steps to the pulpit, watching Papa preach his sermons.

She smiled. And hiding from the first Duke of Hart's tomb monument. It had taken Papa a long time to puzzle out why she refused to go anywhere near that part of the church. Finally he'd realized what the problem was and had explained that the duke and duchess lying side by side, hands folded in prayer, were only marble, that their actual bodies were enclosed in the large stone box underneath.

She glanced down at the floor. The second duke was here, too, under the middle aisle, but the rest were stowed away in the castle's chapel. Cursed men couldn't be buried in St. Valentine's, though that was never said outright, of course. One didn't insult the man who held one's living.

Had Marcus seen his ancestors' resting places? They hadn't toured the church the day he'd posted the Spinster House notice.

She started to turn to see if he—

No. I cannot look at him.

His presence was an invisible force pulling her eyes his way, but she had to resist it. The more sensible villagers had stopped speculating about them, even after Mrs. Greeley had seen him go inside the Spinster House. She didn't want to start the gossip up again.

So she'd been avoiding him. It had taken some doing—Marcus had seemed determined to talk to her—but she'd managed it for the few days since his mother's visit.

She swallowed a nervous giggle. Mama had been quite surprised by her willingness to attend to so many of the last-minute wedding details. And then yesterday the duke's friends had returned to Loves Bridge, and they had kept him busy. Tomorrow—or perhaps today—he'd go back to London for good and the problem would be over.

Her heart felt like a rock in her chest.

Could his mother be correct? Was there hope that he loved her and the curse could be broken?

No. Perhaps if he didn't feel that he'd compromised her, they could find a way to be . . . friends, at least, but now she could never tell if it was love or guilt or, er, lust that was behind his offer.

She heard a muffled cough, a baby babble. The church was full now. Everyone had come to celebrate Mary and Theo's wedding.

She looked at the couple standing next to her. Mary was

so beautiful, so radiantly happy. Theo, earnest and sweet and nervous in his best clothes, drummed his fingers against his leg. And Papa stood before them, cloaked in the vestments of his office.

She stood precisely where she'd stood when Tory and Ruth had married. Likely she'd stand in the same spot when Pru's and Sybbie's turns came. Sister after sister, starting their own families while she—

She lifted her chin. While she lived happily ever after in the Spinster House. She had no desire to wed.

Liar.

Nonsense. She wanted to write. She wanted privacy. She wanted quiet.

She forced herself to concentrate on the music instead of her thoughts. The Marquess of Haywood was an accomplished musician, as good as or perhaps better than Mr. Wattles, the new Duke of Benton. And he'd been very accommodating. He hadn't objected at all when Papa had asked if he might play the organ in church as well as the pianoforte in the hall later. Papa loved to include music in his services. He said it brought people out of their everyday concerns so they could feel the presence of the Lord.

Unfortunately today she was more aware of the presence of a different sort of lord. The duke was sitting in his family's pew next to his other London friend, Lord Evans. She'd observed him out of the corner of her eye when she'd come in. He was devastatingly handsome, dressed formally in his dark coat and white cravat.

Had he admired her green dress? It was one of her favorites. Mama said it matched her eyes—

Silly! It didn't matter what the duke thought about her dress. He was going back to London and would hopefully have a long life before he had to marry . . . someone else.

Oh, God.

Mary says I should hear what Marcus wishes to tell me. Perhaps I—

No. She couldn't listen to the duke. If she did, she might allow herself to be persuaded.

But if Marcus's mother is correct, our marriage might break the curse.

But Mrs. Cullen had admitted she wasn't certain that Marcus loved her. He'd offered for her out of duty. Or worse, out of some odd compulsion.

Or some not-so-odd compulsion—lust.

Some alarmingly lustful feeling snaked through her at that thought.

I do not want to be a widow before I'm a mother.

But what if Marcus does *love me? Then—*

Oh, drat. Her thoughts kept chasing themselves like a dog after its tail.

Papa had closed his prayer book. The wedding must be over. Mary was now Mrs. Theodore Dunly.

By the time Cat signed the parish register and made it over to the hall, the party was well under way. Lord Haywood was as skilled on the pianoforte as the organ and was playing a jig accompanied by Mr. Linden on the fiddle. Some of the adults and most of the children, including Pru and Sybbie and the twins, were dancing—well, in the children's case, jumping and spinning would be a more accurate description.

"We'll be celebrating your wedding next, Cat," Anne said, coming up with Jane.

"We will not." She glared at Anne. "And I do not appreciate your spreading tales, Miss Davenport."

But if Anne hadn't started the rumor, Marcus would not have come to the Spinster House and kissed me.

Something fluttered low in her belly. She was certain that kiss had been a mistake, but it was not one she entirely regretted.

Anne flushed. "I only said I'd seen you go into the trysting bushes with the duke. I didn't say anything about what you might have been doing there. Other people added that to the story."

Of course they had.

"You would have done the same if you were in our position, Cat," Jane said. "You know you'd go to almost any lengths to get the Spinster House."

Well, yes, that was probably true. She could understand the desperation Anne and Jane must be feeling.

Jane's brows slanted down. "And what do you mean yours won't be the next wedding? The duke offered for you, didn't he?"

How did they know that?

Likely, Mama had let something slip. She hadn't been especially happy when Cat told her she would not be the next Duchess of Hart.

"Yes, the duke asked, but I declined."

"You *did?*" Anne and Jane said simultaneously.

"Of course I did. He only offered because of the gossip. He didn't really, er, ruin me." Drat it, now she was blushing. "I don't know why you think I'd accept him. You know I have no wish to marry."

Or *had* no wish. . . .

I still don't wish it. I have exactly what I've always wanted: my independence.

If only she felt happier about that.

Anne and Jane looked at each other as though they couldn't believe what they were hearing.

"You know the duke was staring at you all during the wedding ceremony, don't you?" Jane asked.

Her silly heart leapt. "Don't be ridiculous."

Anne leaned in to keep her voice low. "And don't look, but he's staring at you right now."

Cat couldn't stop herself. She did look—she knew exactly

where Marcus was in the room—and met his eyes. She flushed and quickly glanced away. "I'm sure it doesn't mean a thing."

"I wouldn't be so certain," Jane said. "He's ended his conversation with one of the beautiful Wendley twins and is coming this way."

Oh, God. She couldn't talk to him now. Everyone would be watching them. "I'm going to see if Mama needs any help."

"Coward." Anne grinned. "I wouldn't mind if the handsome Duke of Hart wanted to, er"—she waggled her brows—"talk to me."

"Stop it." Oh, good. Marcus had been waylaid by Lord Evans. She had a few more seconds in which to make her escape. She turned and walked briskly in the opposite direction, hoping it wasn't obvious to everyone in the room that she was fleeing.

Unfortunately she'd been so focused on getting away from Marcus, she'd failed to note where she was going—or, rather, whom she was approaching. She almost bumped into her annoying cousin Juliet and her cousin's obnoxious husband, Viscount Uppleton, who were stationed strategically by one of the food tables.

"Well, if it isn't *Miss* Hutting." Juliet's lips twitched up into her customary small, false smile. "I must tell you how *wonderful* we think it is that you managed to put on such a *brave* face during the service. Isn't that right, Uppie?"

Lord Uppleton's mouth was fully occupied with masticating a large biscuit, so he merely nodded.

"Brave face?" She knew where this was headed. Why couldn't this branch of the family have limited itself to a congratulatory letter as they'd done when Ruth married? At least the heir, Juliet's older brother, was absent. "I don't know what you mean. I'm sincerely happy for Mary. She and Mr. Dunly are very much in love."

Juliet patted her hand. "How *nice* of you to say so. But it must be such a *terrible* burden to find yourself so *firmly* on the shelf while your *younger* sisters wed."

Cat snatched her hand back. She'd like to tell the nasty, stuck-up—

No. While it would be extremely satisfying to let her disagreeable cousin know that she had declined an offer of marriage from none other than the Duke of Hart, who far outranked her husband *and* her father, it would be a big mistake and unworthy of her.

"It's not a burden at all. I do not look to marry."

Juliet gave her husband a speaking look, revealing exactly what she thought of Cat's declaration. Uppleton, however, missed it as he was busy selecting another biscuit from the tray at his elbow.

"I *quite* understand." Juliet let a distinct note of pity creep into her voice. "It is *most* unfortunate that gentlemen prefer younger women, when those of more *mature* years have a far more settled and sensible manner, is it not? I *do* feel for you. But your parents must be *so* pleased you've chosen to dedicate your life to looking after them in their declining years."

I will not lose my temper. I will not lose my temper.

Though she did wish she had a nice, large glass of red punch to spill all over Juliet's pale yellow gown.

"I'm quite certain my parents haven't given a thought to their declining years."

"Catherine, how lovely to see you again."

Cat's back stiffened. Drat! That was her aunt.

When Marcus called her by her full name, she felt warm, pleasant shivers. When her aunt called her Catherine, she felt shivers also—the sort one got when chalk squeaked across slate.

She turned slowly to find not only the countess, but the earl, behind her.

Remember your manners. You don't want to cause a scene at Mary's wedding. "So nice to see you, Aunt, Uncle."

Her aunt was not fooled by her lie. She sniffed. "You are in looks, Catherine. No one would guess you've twenty-six years in your dish."

"I don't, Aunt. I'm twenty-four." Not that twenty-six was elderly, of course, but she might as well insist on accuracy.

The countess smiled thinly. "Oh, yes. That's right."

"Yes, yes, you're looking quite well for a woman your age," the earl said. "Guess you've given up all hope of marriage, eh?" He reached over and plucked a biscuit off the rapidly diminishing pile. "Are these good, then, Uppleton?"

The viscount nodded, having a full mouth again, and brushed a few crumbs off his waistcoat.

"I'm quite content as I am," Cat said to no one in particular. She'd be more content if she could get free of this group.

The countess leaned closer as she looked over Cat's shoulder at something behind her. "I must say I'm very surprised to see the Duke of Hart," she murmured. "Why is he here?"

"He was invited."

The countess frowned. "Don't be pert, Miss."

Remain calm. Hold on to your temper.

"I'm not being pert, Aunt. You must know Papa owes his living to the duke. Since His Grace was in residence, Papa invited him. It would have looked very odd—insulting, really—if he hadn't." She forced herself to smile. "And it was so kind of the duke's friend, Lord Haywood, to provide music for the ceremony and here in the hall. He's quite accomplished, isn't he?"

She might have been speaking Greek. Her aunt and cousin looked at her blankly.

"But why did Hart *come*?" Juliet hissed.

"Because he had no other engagement?"

She was going to get herself slapped by both women if she continued on this way. At least her uncle and Lord Uppleton were no longer part of the conversation. They were competing with each other to see who could grab the last biscuit.

"I'm afraid I really don't know anything else," Cat said. "You will just have to ask His Grace if you require more particulars."

Juliet's eyes lit with unpleasant excitement. "He must have come here because of the scandal, Mama."

Come because of a scandal? She must have misheard. The only scandal she knew of had originated in Loves Bridge courtesy of Miss Anne Davenport. "I assure you, the gossip is groundless. Nothing happened."

Juliet looked at her as if she were daft—but then Juliet often looked at her that way. "How would you know? You haven't been to London."

"No." So she had no idea what Juliet was talking about—that also, was quite common. "What I do know is the duke came to Loves Bridge because the Spinster House was empty. By the terms of the curse, he's required to deal with finding a replacement personally."

She was not going to tell them she was the replacement. They would have to find that out on their own.

Juliet snorted. "You don't believe in that silly curse, do you?"

"Whether I believe in it or not, the duke does."

The countess sighed and shook her head. "Catherine, dear, you mustn't be so naïve. You don't really think a man of the duke's position, with his education, would be so superstitious as to believe in something as unscientific as a curse, do you? Come now. He may have *said* that's why he came to Loves Bridge, but the truth is something else entirely."

Juliet nodded. "He compromised poor Miss Rathbone dreadfully, and then refused to do the right thing and marry her. He had to flee London or find all doors shut firmly in his face."

"Now, Juliet, let's not overstate the matter. No one is going to exclude the Duke of Hart," the countess said. She leaned closer. "I usually wouldn't sully your virginal ears with such a tale, Catherine, but the duke was found rolling around in Lord Palmerson's shrubbery with poor Miss Rathbone."

"Passionately kissing her, her dress pulled down to her waist and her hair all undone!" Juliet added with rather unbecoming enthusiasm.

The countess waved her fan as if to cool her face. "We can only be glad he wasn't doing something of an even more intimate nature with her when Lady Dunlee came upon them."

"Indeed!" Juliet managed to look scandalized and thrilled simultaneously. "And then when Miss Rathbone's father confronted the duke at White's, His Grace not only said he would not marry the girl, he said he couldn't ruin her reputation because she didn't have one."

"Despicable." The countess snapped her fan closed. "But then the Dukes of Hart are well known to be womanizers."

Oh, God! Miss Rathbone. The Boltwood sisters had mentioned her—and bushes—at the fair meeting, the day the duke was hanging the Spinster House notices.

Had Marcus really been on the ground in the shrubbery where anyone might come upon him, kissing a half-naked woman?

Her stomach twisted. *What a fool I've been.*

It was all clear now. The duke might have asked Papa for her hand, but he knew she'd never accept his offer. She was the Spinster House spinster, for God's sake! The kisses that had meant so much to her had been nothing to him. He was bored, perhaps lustful, and hoping to use her to satisfy his animal needs.

Well, he'd very much mistaken the matter!

"What's amiss, Catherine?" the countess asked. "You suddenly look out of curl."

"Surely you didn't form a tendre for the Heartless Duke, did you?" Juliet muffled a giggle.

The countess sighed and shook her head sadly. "That was very foolish of you, Catherine, but I suppose it was to be expected. The duke is a practiced seducer, and you're very green, my dear. No town polish at all, even at your advanced age."

Her aunt was quite correct about that. Thank God she had no experience with men of the duke's ilk.

"As long as there was no harm done—" The countess's brow rose. "There *was* no harm done, at least of an, er, permanent nature, was there?"

Cat felt her face turn red. "Of course not."

The countess didn't look as if she quite believed her, but at least she didn't dispute the matter. "Then mark it down to experience, Catherine. You'll be wiser next time." She tittered. "*If* there is a next time."

There bloody well would *not* be a next time. She was swearing off men for the rest of her life, which had been her intention all along until a certain snake had slithered down from London.

"Don't look now," Juliet whispered, "but the Cursed Duke is headed this way."

She couldn't bear to speak to him now or even stand near him. She would do something she'd regret, like punch him or . . . or break into tears.

"If you'll excuse me, I must go. I find I'm feeling a trifle unwell."

Marcus saw Catherine dart away from the Countess of Penland and Lady Uppleton.

Where the hell was she going? He felt as if he'd been chasing after her ever since the day his mother visited, trying to get her alone for a private word—and perhaps something else he didn't wish anyone else to witness. He'd yet to be successful. She always claimed she was busy with some task for Mary's wedding.

Well, Mary and Dunly were well and truly riveted now. He'd be damned if he was going to let Catherine fob him off any longer.

He changed course, trying to follow her without appearing to do so, though certainly the two harpies she'd been talking to made note of his detour.

"Oh, Your Grace. Yoo-hoo! Over here!"

His stomach sank. Could he pretend he hadn't heard Miss Cordelia Boltwood?

No.

The group of men he was passing stopped their conversation about some sheep ailment to snicker.

"I believe Miss Cordelia is trying to get your attention, Your Grace," Emmett said helpfully. The blackguard's face was perfectly serious, but his damn eyes were laughing.

"Yes. Unfortunately, however, I—"

Miss Gertrude swooped in to grab his arm. He was able to catch a glimpse of Catherine vanishing through the door to the churchyard before he was towed over to see what the other Miss Boltwood wanted.

"You must be the first to taste my gooseberry tart, Your Grace," Miss Cordelia said when Miss Gertrude deposited him at her side. "I'm accounted quite a dab hand at baking, you know. I believe my gooseberry tart is the best in the village. In fact, I'll wager you've never tasted one better, even in London." She cut him a generous slice. "You must try some."

"Miss Cordelia, I'm afraid I—"

Miss Gertrude dug her elbow into his side. "Yes, we

know you'd rather run after Miss Hutting, Your Grace, but show a little discretion, if you please. The gossip about your interlude with her in the bushes—"

"—and your scandalous visit to the Spinster House, which Mrs. Greeley witnessed—" Miss Cordelia interjected.

"—has died down. If you insist on pursuing her so obviously, you will blow the dying embers back into a full-fledged conflagration."

Miss Cordelia shoved a plate with the slice of tart and a fork into his hands. "Yes, indeed. Most people will give Miss Hutting the benefit of the doubt, *if* you leave them any doubt at all. But if you pursue the poor girl so publicly—"

Miss Gertrude giggled. "Oh, I wouldn't say she was a *poor* girl, Cordelia. I think she's quite lucky to have a lusty fellow like the duke here panting over her." She dug her elbow into his side again.

Damnation. He wasn't blushing, was he?

Miss Cordelia smiled. "Indeed. But as I was saying, duke, if you pursue Miss Hutting with that hungry and rather desperate look on your face, anyone with any imagination will be able to guess exactly what you are up to."

"Not that the girl couldn't do with a little bit of fun." Miss Gertrude tried to elbow him again, but he'd learned from his previous encounters and evaded her.

"Yes, indeed." Miss Cordelia leaned a bit closer. "I'll tell you, duke, that one reason the gossip was so very delectable is that it was so unexpected. Miss Hutting is always very stiff and serious. Why, I'm certain more than half the men in the village are afraid of her." She shook her head in amazement. "Everyone was flabbergasted that she could be persuaded to do anything at all untoward."

"Especially with a man," Miss Gertrude added. "We all were half convinced she didn't like the breed"—she raised her brows significantly—"if you know what I mean."

He did, but he wasn't going to say so. And how could they believe Catherine was stiff? She might be a little prickly, but that was only to protect her soft heart.

He had better eat the tart if he wanted to get free to follow her. He took a bite. It *was* very good. "This is delicious, Miss Cordelia."

Cordelia smirked. "I told you it was."

He took another bite. Fortunately he had a large mouth. One more forkful, and he was done. He handed the plate back to Cordelia.

"All right, off with you now," she said, putting his empty plate on the table. "But do try to be a bit more circumspect."

"And give Miss Hutting a kiss for us," Miss Gertrude said, giggling.

He just smiled and headed for the exit. He did stop to congratulate Mr. and Mrs. Hutting, and he paused to shake Dunly's hand and kiss Mary's, wishing them much happiness and reiterating that Dunly should enjoy his honeymoon without a thought to any of his castle duties. And then he was finally through the door and out into the quiet country afternoon.

Where rational thought at last asserted itself. He should not go to the Spinster House. Catherine clearly did not want to speak to him. She would not have found so many excuses to avoid him the last few days nor fled the reception just now when she'd seen him approaching if she was amenable to any sort of discussion.

The Misses Boltwood said that the gossip had died down. Certainly no one had shunned Catherine today. He could go back to London confident that her reputation was intact. He was a free man with a clean conscience.

His feet ignored his thoughts, carrying him down the hill toward the Spinster House.

Dunly had let drop that his mother had stopped to see Catherine before returning to Ireland. He'd like to know what they'd discussed. And he'd brought the third duke's diary with him. Catherine might wish to see it.

And, yes, he'd admit he wanted to kiss her. Just one kiss to say good-bye. She'd looked so beautiful today, so tall and slender and composed. He couldn't take his eyes off her, as everyone in the church must have noticed. Alex certainly had teased him about it enough.

And she'd looked lonely. He'd swear he'd seen that in her eyes. He should recognize the expression. Loneliness was his constant companion.

He could see the Spinster House clearly now, but there was no sign of Catherine. She must already be inside.

He stopped at the road. This was madness. He should go back to the hall. Miss Hutting had everything she wanted—solitude, quiet, time to write. She'd chosen the life of a spinster. He should let her live it as she wished.

Zeus, wasn't that typical of his luck? The one woman he wanted didn't want him. She was completely unswayed by his wealth and power.

But she *had* been swayed by his kisses. A determined spinster would have pushed him away, slapped him, boxed his ears, but Catherine had clung to him and kissed him back. Her hands had slid over his body—his clothed body, unfortunately—and into his hair.

He started across the road. If she was adamant that she wouldn't marry him, he'd leave Loves Bridge in the morning. Alex and Nate were still planning to go walking in the Lake District. He would join them.

He strode up the walk and rapped on the front door.

No answer.

He knocked again, harder. Still no answer. He tried the latch. Locked. Was Catherine not home, then? But where could she be? Everyone in the village was at the party.

She must have gone walking, though he couldn't say he liked that idea. The country was safer than London, true, but even in the country a woman alone was at risk. He needed to find her, but where should he look? She could have taken off in any direction.

He turned to leave and almost tripped over Poppy.

"Blast it, cat, you nearly caused me to measure my length on that very hard walkway behind you."

Poppy sat down, tail twitching, and stared at him.

"You don't happen to know where Miss Hutting is, do you?" And now he was talking to a cat. If Poppy replied, he'd know for certain that he'd become completely unhinged.

Poppy blinked and then started round to the back of the house. When he didn't immediately follow, she stopped and looked at him.

"So you want me to come with you?"

"Merrow!"

He glanced around. Thank God no one was nearby to witness this.

The cat set off again. Marcus hesitated.

Oh, hell, what do I have to lose?

He followed Poppy, who led him past a lean-to that looked like it might once have stabled a single horse and through a gate into the garden—where he nearly pitched headlong into an overgrown bush.

"Bloody ivy." Miss Franklin had allowed the creeping plant to run amok so that it almost completely obscured the path. He made a mental note to have Emmett send someone over to tidy up as he stooped to untangle his feet. Once free, he looked for Poppy—she was sitting by the back door, grooming her paws.

He trod carefully through the rest of the tangled vegetation to join her. "I suppose you think I should knock on this door also?"

Poppy paused long enough to stare at him as though she couldn't believe she was in the presence of such a dunderhead.

"Yes, all right. I expect that's why you brought me here."

The cat sneezed and moved on to grooming her ears.

He knocked. Again, no answer. Just as he'd expected.

"See? This is no better than the front door. Worse actually. I didn't have to risk my neck to reach the front door."

Poppy yawned.

"So do you have any other bright ideas?" Good God, he *was* trying to converse with a cat. What was next? Discoursing with a dog?

Poppy stared up at the door latch.

"No one's home, I tell you."

She meowed and stood on her hind legs, swatting at the latch with her forepaws.

"Zeus, you're a stubborn creature." He put his hand on the latch. "See, it's lock—"

The door swung open.

Chapter Sixteen

June 25, 1617—Marcus is back in Loves Bridge.
He came to me the moment he returned. Poor man.
His dreadful mother is trying to force him to marry
a wealthy duke's daughter, but he wants no part of
the match. I am the one he loves, and—I blush as I
write this—he showed me the extent of his love this
afternoon. I never imagined something that sounded
so unpleasant could be so wonderful. I am married
now in all but name.

—from Isabelle Dorring's diary

The blackguard! The scoundrel! The bloody miscreant!
Cat paced the floor of her bedchamber. She'd come up here to throw herself on the bed and sob her heart out, but by the time she'd reached the top of the stairs, she'd moved beyond tears to fury.

The bloody rake. He'd offered for her when he'd been rolling around in the bushes with some half-naked London girl just days before. Disgusting!

Her bedchamber was too small to contain her rage. She

strode into the room where she'd had Isabelle Dorring's portrait moved.

"You were right to curse the Dukes of Hart," she told the painting. "They *are* despicable."

And to think she'd seriously considered this duke's sham proposal for even a moment. He must have been laughing at her, amused that he'd been able to lure her into misbehavior. It would have served him right if she *had* accepted his offer. Where would he have been then?

More to the point, where would she have been?

She closed her eyes, remembering all too clearly the feel of his lips on hers, the hot wet stroke of his tongue, the weight of his body pressing her against the hard door. . . .

She leaned back against the big cabinet, her legs suddenly weak, her treacherous body heavy with desire. She wanted him here to—

Zeus! What was the matter with her? Had the dastardly duke turned her into such a light-skirt that she could want him even while hating him? Oh, no. If he were here right now, she'd slap him soundly and kick him in the shins. She'd strangle him with his cravat. She'd drag him into her bedchamber, tie him to the bed, and—

Lud! Where had *that* idea come from?

She took a deep breath. If she could get her temper under control, then perhaps this other emotion would subside as well. She forced herself to smile. Calm. She needed to be calm, to think calming thoughts. Thoughts of snowflakes drifting to the ground. Of swans gliding on a lake. Of sunlight filtering through the trees.

She hadn't always been able to manage her anger. When she'd been younger, she'd screamed and thrown things and pulled Tory's hair and ruined one of Ruth's favorite drawings. But she'd worked hard since then. Now she never lost her temper, no matter what the provocation. She was quite proud of her control.

There, that was better. She'd go back downstairs. Maybe she'd even return to the party. Now she'd be able to converse with His Grace without shouting or poking him in the chest or spitting in his eye and scratching his lying face to ribbons.

Bollocks! Control could go bugger itself. She grabbed a porcelain shepherdess from the top of the cabinet and flung it against the wall, shattering it into a thousand pieces.

That felt good. She looked over the selection of other potential missiles and chose an ugly china dog. Ah, it was heavier than it appeared. Good. She heaved it with all her strength toward her room—and almost caught Marcus in the head. He ducked and the dog flew past him to crash against the far wall.

"What the hell was that about, Catherine?"

"You!" She would gouge his eyes out. She would knee him in the groin. She would tear him limb from limb.

She threw herself at him, her hands aiming for his neck. Poppy, who'd come up with the duke, yowled and darted back down the stairs.

He caught her and held her easily while she struggled to punch and kick him.

"You toad! You snake! You—"

He brought her up against him, holding her firmly.

Lud! The moment her body touched his, it betrayed her, softening and molding itself to his hard length. She inhaled his familiar scent and had to fight to keep from resting her head on his broad chest.

He's a rogue, a scoundrel, a blackguard, a womanizer.

Her body wasn't listening.

"Catherine, love, what has put you in such a state?"

His voice was gentle, deep, warm.

Lying.

She pushed against him, and he loosened his hold so she could lean back, but he didn't let go of her completely.

"Don't call me 'love,' you villain. Think to cozen me, did

you? Well, you can take yourself back up to Town and dive into the shrubbery with whomever you like. I don't care."

"What *are* you talking about?" He leaned nearer to sniff her breath. "You don't smell of spirits."

His mouth is so close—

"Of course I don't. What are you thinking?"

Oh, blast. Her anger was slipping away to be replaced by an equally hot and intense emotion.

"That someone laced your punch and you drank it too quickly. If you're not accustomed to alcohol, it will go straight to your head, you know."

"I have *not* been drinking."

He frowned. "Then why did you just attack me?"

"My aunt and cousin told me the real reason you came to Loves Bridge."

He looked puzzled. "The real reason?"

"Yes." Hope bubbled up in her chest. Perhaps the story Juliet and her aunt had told her wasn't true after all. "The scandal."

"The scandal?"

She scowled. "What are you, an echo? They said you'd been caught with a girl in the shrubbery."

"Ah." His cheeks flushed. "Yes. Miss Rathbone."

So it *was* true. Her heart turned to lead. She pushed against him again.

Marcus tightened his arms. "She was trying to trap me into marriage, Catherine."

"Oh? Like I did?"

"No. I wish you *would* try to trap me."

His hands started moving up and down her back, and she suddenly knew how Poppy must feel when someone stroked her. She wanted to purr.

She should insist he let her go. His nearness was stealing her good sense.

"Miss Rathbone hid in the bushes and jumped out at me

as I walked past, Catherine, knocking me down and causing us to get tangled up."

She couldn't help it—she giggled.

"It does sound rather ridiculous, doesn't it?"

"Mmm." The heat of his body seemed to be melting hers. She wanted so badly to put her head on his chest, but she could *not* give in.

Wait. He'd missed a few details.

"You didn't need to"—she flushed, whether with embarrassment or something else, she couldn't say—"pull her dress down."

"But I didn't. She did that herself, as well as take all the pins out of her hair to make the scene she'd staged all the more damning." His voice was tense, and he was holding her very tightly now, but she found she didn't object. "I was not about to sacrifice myself for that scheming jezebel."

"Of course not." An odd feeling of protectiveness formed in her chest. Poor man. It must be horrible to have to watch one's back like that.

"The devil of it is," he said, his voice low and tight, "I'm so lonely sometimes I'm tempted to give in to the jades." He bent his head close to hers, whispering hoarsely, "And it's getting worse, Catherine. The loneliness is eating me alive."

His words tore at her heart and called to something inside her that she hadn't known was there. She wanted to hold him close, to make his loneliness go away, if only for a while.

Perhaps she could.

She turned her head and brushed her lips over his cheek.

"Catherine." His whisper was harsh, pained.

She touched her mouth to his.

He groaned, and his hand came up to hold her head still. His tongue plunged deep, filling her with heat and need, sweeping away any remaining hesitation.

Her hands slid under his coat, roaming over his back and

buttocks. She pressed closer to him, but it was not close enough.

He lifted his head, eyes desperate. "I-I had better go."

Yes, he should go. If he stayed, a line would be crossed that could never be uncrossed. They would end up in bed, and she would give him her virginity.

What did she need it for? She'd never marry. It was a fair price to pay for a memory she would have for the rest of her life.

She would ease his loneliness and her own for a little while, just this once.

She tightened her hold on him. "Don't go."

Marcus froze. "Do you know what will happen if I stay?"

"Yes."

He wet his lips, his body tense as a bowstring. "Be certain, Catherine, because once we start . . ." His jaw flexed. "I'm not quite in control."

"I won't change my mind."

He looked down at her, his eyes searching hers as if trying to read her heart. And then his hands moved to cup her face so she couldn't look away.

"I promise you that I will try to see that you do not conceive, but you must promise me that if we should make a child between us, you shall send me word the moment you know you are increasing."

A child? She hadn't thought of that—

Silly. There was nothing to worry about. The chances that this one encounter would result in a child were very, very small. She'd once overheard Tory telling Ruth, after Ruth had been married for a while, that it often took several months of trying before a husband's seed took root.

"If you won't swear it, I shall find some way to drag myself down those stairs and out of this house right now"— Marcus's laugh was short and shaky—"even though I am certain it will kill me to do so."

Of course he would want to know about an illegitimate child. He thought he'd not live to see a legitimate one. It was very sad. He was so good with the twins. He'd make a wonderful father.

She smiled. "I swear I will write you, Marcus, as soon as I know, if there should be a child." And then she stretched up to touch her mouth to his again.

He stood still as a statue.

She faltered. Could she have misunderstood?

No. All at once his control shattered. His arms swept round her, crushing her against him, and he kissed her back.

At first his mouth was rough and overwhelming and a little frightening. She stiffened. Perhaps she'd made a mistake.

But even as that thought formed, his touch gentled. His lips coaxed instead of demanded. They moved to brush over her eyes, her cheeks. They paused by her ear to whisper, "Shall we go to bed?"

The words sent a shiver of nervous anticipation through her. She didn't trust her voice, so she nodded.

Marcus swung her up into his arms. "Which room?"

"That one." She pointed. She wouldn't call it Isabelle's. Isabelle had no part in what they were about to do.

Marcus carried her into the bedchamber, set her on her feet, and turned her so he could unfasten her dress.

"Damn tiny buttons." His voice was as thick as his fingers. "How did you get into this?"

"My mother helped me." *Mama will wonder how I got out of it.*

No. Mama will never know. The Spinster House is my place, my separate world.

The dress was now pooled at her feet, and Marcus's bare hands were sliding over her shoulders.

"Your skin is like silk," he murmured, bending to kiss her neck.

Oh! The touch of his lips sent waves of heat through her, turning her knees to jelly. Her breasts ached and the place between her legs—

This is wrong. I should stop him. We aren't married.

If we were married, the specter of death would be crowding into the room with us.

What if I am just another woman to him?

It doesn't matter. I love him.

And if I conceive?

I will welcome Marcus's child. I won't be like Isabelle.

He had loosened her stays, and as they fell away, so did her worries. She was here with him now. She was his—and he was hers. She turned to wrap her arms around him.

He shouldn't be here. He shouldn't do this. Catherine was sweet and wonderful and she didn't understand what she was risking. How could she? She was a virgin.

I am taking what is only a husband's right.

But she doesn't plan to marry.

I should *marry her. She should be wearing my ring before I take her to bed.*

But if she wore his ring, he'd not live to see their child.

There wouldn't be a child. He would pull out before he sowed his seed in her. And he would only lie with her this one time. Surely once would be enough to cure him of his obsession with her. It might even blunt the power of the curse for a while. He could go back to London and live for years before necessity forced him to get an heir.

His mouth covered Catherine's, and she opened to him at once. He plunged into her warmth as his hands grabbed the sides of her shift.

He should go slowly. It was her first time.

It felt like *his* first time. He was as eager as he'd been then. But Catherine deserved more than the awkward fumbling of a callow youth. He had years of experience and discipline. He should use them.

He slipped his hands under her shift and raised it slowly, sliding his palms over the firm curve of her bottom and up the lovely arch of her back, his thumbs brushing the sides of her breasts. Her skin was so soft, so smooth.

He broke their kiss so he could pull the cloth up and over her head. And then he looked at her, standing in front of him in only her shoes and stockings, her hair still up.

She blushed and started to cover herself, but he stopped her.

"No, Catherine." He turned her so she faced the window, the afternoon sun bathing with warm light her beautiful, round breasts, her slim waist and belly, the reddish curls between her pale thighs. "Let me see you."

"I'm sure we should pull the curtains," she said, her voice trembling with embarrassment and nerves. She was flushing, all of her.

"No. I want to see every curve, every shadow of your beautiful body."

She tried to twist so she wasn't facing him so directly.

"Don't hide." He touched her breast and watched its nipple pebble.

"You are the one hiding. Why don't you take your clothes off?" Her words were brave, but he still heard the tremor beneath them.

"I will, soon." There were many different ways to play this game, but this time—his only time with her—he wouldn't play any games at all. They should have at least an hour before anyone wondered where they were. He wanted to enjoy every minute. "In a little while."

"Now."

"I am afraid that once my clothes come off, my control will, too, Catherine. Let's wait, please? Just a little longer."

She looked at him suspiciously, but he was telling the truth.

"At least take your coat off."

"All right. I can do that." He *was* rather warm. He struggled out of his coat.

"And your waistcoat."

That was easy enough to shed.

"And your cravat."

He'd never freed himself from a length of linen so quickly.

"And now, your sh-shirt?" She looked at him cautiously, as if shedding his shirt might turn him into a ravening beast.

"Come help me with it."

She stepped cautiously toward him, but when he didn't pounce on her—he forced his hands to stay at his sides—she relaxed and concentrated on freeing the buttons at his throat. He felt her fingers brush his chin; he watched her bite her lower lip as she concentrated. He breathed in the clean, lemony scent of her hair and skin.

She was so different from the London women he knew, as different as Loves Bridge was from Town.

Zeus, he wished he could stay here and have an ordinary marriage like Catherine's sister and Dunly were starting today, but thanks to his weak-willed ancestor and Isabelle Dorring, that wasn't something he could hope for.

Ah, that's right. He'd meant to show Catherine the duke's diary and discuss his mother's visit—

Perhaps some other time.

She'd got the shirt buttons open now and had started to pull his shirt out of his pantaloons.

"Ohh!" Her fingers traced the line of hair over his stomach to his chest. "Your body is so hard, and yet it's soft, too."

"Um." The part that was hardest she hadn't encountered yet, but it was pushing insistently against his pantaloons, eager to be free. He grabbed the hem of his shirt and pulled it over his head.

Catherine ran her hands over the muscles in his arms and shoulders, and then hugged him, pressing her cheek to his chest. "I can hear your heart beating."

It was a wonder she couldn't see and feel it, too, it was thudding so hard. He wanted her more than he'd ever wanted any woman in his life.

Slowly. Go slowly. This is her first time and your only time with her. Savor it.

It was difficult to go slowly, though. He drew in a deep breath and concentrated on the sensation of her palms sliding over his back, her breasts pressed against his skin.

He ran his fingers through her hair, plucking out her pins one by one, until the lovely silken mass, a mix of fire and light, tumbled down her back. He kissed her neck, right under her ear, and whispered, "You still have your shoes and stockings on."

"Oh!" She giggled nervously. "I'll just get them off, shall I?"

"Allow me."

"No, really. I'll—oh!"

He knelt before her and kissed her belly. "Hold on to me, if you need to."

"I won't—*ohh!*"

Her hands grabbed his shoulders as he kissed the top of her thigh, so very close to his ultimate goal. Her warm, musky scent tempted him, but he wouldn't go there yet.

He untied her garter and slowly, slowly slid her stocking down her leg, kissing her inner thigh, her knee, her calf. She was breathing in little pants and moans. Her legs were shaking; the scent of her desire urged him to hurry.

He would not hurry.

"Lift your foot, Catherine."

"Uh." She looked down at him, her face flushed, her eyes not quite focused. "What are you doing to me?"

He smiled and lifted her foot for her—at least she was aware enough to bend her knee. "Removing your shoes and stockings."

That earned him a breathless giggle. "I don't think I'll survive the process."

"You will." Though he might not. He slid the other stocking off more quickly, and then touched her core gently with his index finger. She was wet and slick and very ready for him.

"Ohh!" She jerked her hips back, and then moved them toward him again, so he took a small taste, his tongue just brushing her sensitive nub.

Her hips jerked back again, and she moaned.

It would be so easy to make her come now. One more touch and she'd be there. But if this was his only time with her, he had to make it last as long as he could.

He stood and kissed her slowly. "I love how soft you are." He slid his hands over her arms. "And how you smell and taste." He grazed his lips over her jaw. "And I love how you gasp and moan when I touch you." He rubbed her nipples with his thumbs and smiled—and panted a bit himself—when she drew in her breath, closed her eyes, and arched to press her breasts into his palms.

If he didn't get her on that bed soon, he was going to embarrass himself.

He jerked back the coverlet, put his hands on her waist, and lifted her onto the mattress. Then he scrambled out of the rest of his clothing.

"Oh."

Catherine was staring at his cock. It *was* rather hard to miss.

"May I touch it?"

"Yes." The word came out as a croak.

He grabbed the bedpost to stay upright as she ran one finger carefully over his length and then cupped his bollocks in her hand. This was good. He should give her a few moments to become familiar with him.

"All men hide this in their pantaloons?"

He strangled on a laugh. "Yes."

Her eyes widened, and she looked at his cock again.

"It's usually smaller." He swallowed. "And not so, er, stiff."

If only they had more than this one time. . . .

No. He couldn't turn Catherine into a kept woman. This once could perhaps be forgiven, but it couldn't be repeated.

And once it was over, he might not want more. This time might cure him of her. It would be good if it did. They had no future together.

Unless she conceived—and then he had no future at all.

She wouldn't. He would be careful.

He leaned over to kiss her, pressing her back against the pillows, and then he was on the bed with her. Enough with going slowly. He couldn't wait any longer.

"I want you, Catherine."

"And I w-want you, too, M-Marcus."

He felt an odd twinge of disappointment.

Why? There was nothing to be disappointed about. He had an eager, willing, beautiful woman naked in bed with him, a woman who had just told him she wanted him. No, he had *Catherine* in bed with him, not just any woman.

What more could he wish for?

Oh, God. He wanted her to say she loved him.

Idiot! He knew nothing of love. Desire—wanting, needing—*that* he understood. Pleasure. Passion. He would use all the skills he'd learned over the years to make this . . . whatever this was . . . wonderful for Catherine.

He kissed her eyes, her nose, the corner of her mouth. He

brushed his lips over her throat, her collarbone, down to the lovely swell of her breast.

"Oh." She was panting again. "Oh, Marcus."

He inhaled, trying to memorize her scent. He wanted to memorize all of her—her taste, the sound of her small breathy moans, the feel of her soft body beneath him—and yet his need to bury himself in her warmth was surging, drowning out everything else.

He had never felt this way before. He prided himself on his control, but his control felt very fragile and unreliable now.

He kissed the side of her breast. Her nipple was already a tight nub. He touched it with his tongue.

Catherine moaned and arched. Her hips twisted on the mattress.

"Marcus. Oh, Marcus."

A thread of pride slid through him. He wanted her to remember this, too, to have it imprinted on her soul. To have *him* imprinted there.

He teased her with light kisses and glancing touches before drawing her nipple into his mouth.

"Oh!"

He did the same for her other breast.

She was writhing under him now, her breath coming in short, fast pants, her hands sliding frantically over his back.

"Please, Marcus. Please."

She was wild with passion. He'd known she'd be this way. She felt everything so intensely.

He wanted to make this last for hours. Forever. But his need was growing too insistent to deny. He moved lower, kissing the underside of her breast, her belly. He dipped his tongue into her navel and then pressed a kiss to the lovely curls beneath it. She smelled damp and hot and ready for him.

He held her hips still so he could touch his tongue to the hard, tight nub hidden in her moist folds.

"Ohh." She spread her legs wider. "Marcus."

He circled the nub with his tongue, savoring her taste.

Her hips jerked down into the mattress. "Marcus." Her voice was high and tight. *"Marcus!"*

It was time. He couldn't wait any longer.

He rose up over her and looked down into her face. Usually, he bedded women in the dark, his eyes closed to focus on his own pleasure, but Catherine was different. He wanted to watch her as he slid slowly into her warmth, her tight channel opening for him, welcoming him—

Until the moment he broke through her maidenhead.

"Oh!" She flinched, sucking in her breath.

He froze. "Are you all right, Catherine?"

"Y-yes." She swallowed, and then smiled at him, running her hands down his back, flexing her hips slightly. "Yes."

Some strange, warm feeling flooded his heart, and he leaned down to kiss her before moving again.

Ah. She was so wet and tight and hot. Every stroke was exquisite torture.

"Oh!" She stiffened under him. "Oh!"

She was close. Very close. He thrust again.

She screamed his name and bucked under him, her hands gripping his arse while her inner muscles gripped his cock, pulling him deeper and deeper into her. He breathed in her hot, sweet scent.

And then the pleasure came, wave after wave of intense, consuming pleasure. He couldn't think—he could barely breathe. He wanted it to go on and on and on forever.

It didn't, of course. After the very last ripple subsided, he collapsed onto Catherine, sweaty, exhausted, and more deeply satisfied than he'd ever been.

He turned his head and kissed her neck, savoring the feel of her body under his, of his cock—

Good God! His cock was still buried deep in Catherine's body.

Chapter Seventeen

*July 11, 1617—We are so much in love, but we must
be discreet. Marcus doesn't want his mother to hear
about us until he's convinced her that he is not
going to marry Lady Amanda. He leaves for a house
party tomorrow. I shall not see him again for a
month or more. How shall I bear it?*

—from Isabelle Dorring's diary

Cat ran her hands up and down Marcus's broad,
sweat-slicked back and tried to breathe. He was still inside
her, in the most private part of her, his body heavy on hers,
pushing her into the mattress. She couldn't move.

She didn't want to. She was exactly where she most
wished to be.

Her hands drifted down to his firm arse. What he had
done to her—what they had done together—had been so
very, very carnal and yet oddly spiritual, too. Something in
her soul had shifted.

She closed her eyes and waited for shame to come.

It didn't.

Perhaps it would come later, when she was alone. Now though . . . Mmm. She hugged Marcus closer. Now she was happier than she'd ever been.

She felt Marcus's lips on her neck. She turned her head to kiss him back, but suddenly he stiffened.

"Fuck!"

She gasped at the obscenity, and then gasped again as he jerked free of her and bolted off the bed, leaving her damp, naked flesh exposed. She shivered with sudden cold and anxiety and pulled the coverlet up over her. "W-what's wrong?"

He was so beautiful. The worry twisting in her gut couldn't distract her from that. The afternoon sun, streaming in the window, highlighted his shoulders, the muscles in his arms, his broad chest, flat belly, and narrow hips. Even his flaccid male bit was oddly handsome.

And not so flaccid. It grew longer and thicker as she studied it.

Marcus grabbed his pantaloons off the floor and almost jumped into them.

"I'm sorry," he said, reaching for his shirt.

"About using that word?" Was that the reason he was scrambling into his clothes? "Don't give it another thought." It had been very shocking, but she certainly wasn't going to take umbrage at it. "I forgive you."

She extended her arms, letting the coverlet slip down. The cooler air now felt good—and made her nipples tighten. She wanted his mouth on them again. "Come back to bed."

He shook his head sharply, his eyes tortured. "It's not the word, though I'm sorry about that, too."

"Then what is it?" Worry twisted again, letting embarrassment and the beginnings of shame in. Had he not enjoyed the encounter as much as she had? She'd thought he had, but then what did she know about such matters?

"I was apologizing for spilling my seed in you, Catherine. I had meant to pull out before that happened." His jaw flexed, and he looked away.

She flushed. This was an embarrassing conversation. "That's all right. I didn't mind." Mind? She'd loved having him pulse into her. She'd felt so close to him then.

And now it turned out it had all been a mistake. Oh, God. The beauty of what they'd just done faded, leaving her feeling old and sad and . . . discarded.

He pulled on his stockings and shoes. "You will have to marry me now. As soon as the party is over, I will talk to your father. Then I'll get a special license. We can be wed in just a few days."

She felt sick. "I can't marry you."

"You have no choice." He put on his waistcoat. "If I had pulled out in time—and I assure you I usually do—you would not be at risk—well, not at so much risk—of conceiving. But as it is"—he shook his head. "I am not such a blackguard that I would allow you to suffer the terrible scandal that an unwed pregnancy would bring."

That's right. What had been an earth-shattering experience for her was just one more pleasant tupping for him.

"But what about the curse?"

He paused in tying his cravat. "What about it?"

Was the man being purposely obtuse? "If you marry me and it turns out I'm carrying your heir—" Oh, God! It finally hit her.

I could be pregnant with Marcus's son.

She was elated and horrified at the same time. Her stomach knotted. She was going to be ill.

No, she wasn't. She swallowed determinedly.

"If you marry me and I'm carrying your son, you might d-die."

He shrugged and arranged the linen folds more to his

liking and then struggled into his coat. "That can't be helped."

"It *can* be helped!" She threw off the coverlet and stomped over to him—or stomped as well as she could, naked and barefooted. "I can refuse to marry you."

She still had some control over this situation. She had a choice. He couldn't force her to wed.

"Catherine, be reason—" He turned to find her just inches from him. "Good God, woman, put on some clothes."

"Why? You weren't complaining about my nakedness a few minutes ago."

"I'm not complaining now, I'm just—" He stepped around her to grab her shift and shove it at her. "Here."

She snatched it out of his hands. "What? Do you wish me to go back to the party? Shall I stroll over on your arm and announce to everyone what we've been about?"

"There will be no need for that. If my seed does take root, everyone will know exactly what we've been about in a few months' time."

"They'll know far sooner than that if you insist on marrying me out of hand."

"What does it matter? If you're increasing—"

"But I might not be, isn't that right?"

He scowled at her. "Yes."

"Then let's wait to see which it is."

He was still scowling. "But I've dishonored you."

"I didn't feel dishonored until now." It was true. What had been special and glorious and wonderful now felt sordid and shameful. She pressed her lips together to keep from crying.

Marcus made an odd little noise, something between a growl and a sigh, and put his arms around her. "I'm sorry, Catherine."

"You are used to this sort of activity, but I am not." Oh, drat. She *was* going to cry.

"I know, Catherine." He stroked her hair. "I'm sorry."

She tried to stop the tears. She sniffled and swallowed, but there was no damming them. They surged out on a sob.

She *hated* crying. Her nose got red and stuffy and she always got a headache.

Marcus held her, but there was nothing loverlike about his touch now. He could have been her father. Lud, he could have been a total stranger.

She finally found the strength to push herself away. "I am not going to marry you."

He looked at her, but his eyes were shuttered. She had no idea what he was thinking. "All right. I will not speak to your father now. Let us wait until we know for certain if you are increasing."

"I still won't m-marry you."

Even she could hear the waver in her voice, but Marcus, tactfully, did not mention it.

"I'm going back to London, Catherine. I'll leave in the morning. I think, ah, *things* will be too hard to manage if I stay in Loves Bridge. The Boltwoods have noticed our closeness, and the rumors are likely to start up again. My departure and continued absence should persuade everyone that any suspicions are groundless."

Marcus was going to leave? She felt a bubble of panic rise in her throat. He was going to desert her just as the third duke had deserted Isabelle.

No. She must not allow her imagination to run wild. The two situations were not at all alike.

"Just remember," Marcus was saying, "you swore to write me immediately if you discover you are with child." The shuttered look lifted briefly, and she caught a glimpse of his pain.

"I said I would write. I will—*if* I am enceinte."

He sighed and took her hands, holding them in his large,

warm clasp. She tried to pull away, but he tightened his grip briefly, and she chose not to struggle.

All right, his hold *was* comforting.

"You are not alone, Catherine. Whether you consent to marry me or not, I shall take care of you and any child. Things may not be easy, but they will be all right. I have wealth and power, and I can and will protect you." His grip tightened. "Do not give in to despair as Isabelle did."

She jerked her hands free. "I am not such a coward." Suicide was terrible enough, but she would never kill her baby.

Marcus frowned. "I don't know that Isabelle was a coward, Catherine. I think she must have felt overwhelmed and abandoned and saw only one way out. I don't want you to do the same. Write me. I will come, and we will find a way to deal with the situation."

"So you aren't going to marry someone else immediately like the third duke did?" She tried to laugh. She'd meant it as a joke, but it had come out more like a wail.

"Of course not." His frown deepened. "Though I will have to marry eventually."

He would. He still needed an heir. And when that happened—

Oh, God. She would die.

"I've been meaning to tell you that I came across the third duke's diary," he said, "hidden in a desk's secret compartment. If his scribblings are to be believed, he did love Isabelle and planned to defy his mother to marry her."

Plans were one things. Actions were something else entirely.

"But he didn't marry her."

"No. I don't know why." Marcus shook his head. "I think he didn't know she was increasing. There's no mention of it in his diary, and, from reading the entries, I'd say he was the sort to have written about it in embarrassing detail."

He grimaced. "He seems to have worn his heart on his sleeve."

Something this duke clearly did not approve of.

"However, I do not have to worry about that, do I? You will tell me if you are bearing my child."

His gaze held hers so she couldn't look away. The part of her that had been most involved in their recent encounter suddenly felt heavy and soft. Did she hope she was carrying his child? How very foolish!

"I said I would, and I keep my word."

He studied her for another heartbeat, and then nodded as if he believed her. He pulled out his watch and frowned. "I've been away from the party long enough—maybe too long. I have to go."

"You're really leaving for London in the m-morning?" Drat. Her voice had wavered again.

"Yes"—his brows rose hopefully—"unless you've changed your mind about marrying me?"

She couldn't trust her voice, so she just shook her head.

"Then there's not much more to be said, is there?" He started for the door.

He's going to leave without holding or kissing me again.

Panic clawed at her throat, but stubborn determination kept her rooted where she stood. "Wh-when will you be back?"

He paused, but didn't turn to look at her. "I won't be, unless you send word that you're with child."

His voice was calm, but when she looked more closely— which was hard to do with the silly tears trying to force their way out of her eyes—she saw his fingers were curled into tight fists.

He did look back then. "Or if you write to tell me you've changed your mind about wedding me."

She shook her head again. She couldn't do that.

He nodded. "Very well. As I said, I'm hopeful that by

leaving I'll stop any further speculation about our connection, but I can't guarantee it. If things become unbearable, let me know."

He didn't ask her to swear it, which was good because she wouldn't have done so. She couldn't justify keeping his child from him, but her reputation was her own affair.

He looked at the bed, and she tried to memorize the line of his brow, the sweep of his lashes, the angle of his chin. This was likely the last time she would ever see him.

She bit her lip hard. She would *not* cry anymore.

And then he looked at her. She thought he was about to say something, but instead his jaw hardened. "Good-bye, Catherine."

She nodded to acknowledge she'd heard him. If she tried to speak, she *would* start crying. Or she might throw herself at his feet and beg him not to leave, and she had too much pride for that.

He hesitated, clearly waiting for her to say something. When she didn't, he bowed slightly and left. She listened to his steps echo down the stairs and then heard the back door open and close.

She took a quick step to the window, just in time to catch a glimpse of him before he was hidden by the overgrown vegetation.

Oh, God.

Oh, God.

She'd never see him again.

She stumbled to the bed and sat down heavily as her legs gave out.

The room felt so empty. *She* felt empty. She'd always thought it silly when people talked about hearts breaking, but now she knew it was true. Hearts *did* break, and the pain was too intense for tears.

"Merrow."

"Oh, Poppy. I didn't see you come in."

Poppy leapt up onto the bed and butted her head against Cat's hand. This was odd. Poppy tolerated her with moderately good grace and would allow herself to be petted occasionally, but she'd never sought Cat out.

"Did you realize I needed company, Poppy?"

Poppy blinked at her and then butted her hand again, admitting nothing.

It didn't matter. A calm, quiet, restful companion was exactly what Cat needed at the moment.

She sat on the bed in her shift, stroking Poppy and staring out the window.

How could he not have pulled out in time? He'd never made that mistake before, even as a green boy. He took great pride in his control.

Except just now, at the most important moment, his bloody wonderful control had failed him.

Marcus made his way through the tangled garden and crossed the road toward the church. Sounds of conversation, laughter, and music drifted down from the hall's open windows. The party was still going on, but he wasn't quite ready to rejoin it. He turned toward the graveyard instead.

What the hell am I going to do?

What he'd told Catherine. He'd go back to Town in the morning and try to forget this interlude had ever occurred.

He snorted. And he'd go dancing with fairies on the Thames as well. There weren't enough light-skirts or brandy casks in all of London—no, in all of England—to make him forget Catherine.

I don't want to forget. It was perfect . . . all but my failure to pull out.

All right, that had been perfect, too. Emptying his seed in Catherine's warm, welcoming body had been so much better than pumping into the cold air, spending himself on the sheets. If he had the luxury of living a normal life, he'd even hope that they'd made a child together.

But I don't have that luxury.

Perhaps he should go to the Lake District instead of London, even if Nate and Alex decided against the trip. Walking miles and miles with only sheep for company—and perhaps Nate and Alex—would put this sorry situation in perspective.

But then if Catherine does write to tell me she is—

That is, if Catherine should write, it might take weeks for her letter to find him. That would be disastrous.

A red squirrel darted across his path and scrambled up the wide trunk of an old oak.

Blast it, he should have had her promise to send him word the moment she discovered she wasn't pregnant as well. Now if he didn't hear from her, it might just mean she'd decided to defy him and carry the child without his knowledge.

I can tell Dunly to let me know—

No. What could he say to Dunly without violating Catherine's privacy? Send word if your sister-in-law becomes noticeably stout?

Of course not.

He wandered among the gravestones. How long would it be before Catherine knew whether or not she was increasing? A woman generally had her courses once a month, but some had them less frequently. He could be waiting on tenterhooks for a damnably long time.

Zeus! He slammed his fist down on one of the headstones. *How could I have lost control that way? I wagered my life for a moment of pleasure.*

He was only thirty. He should have years and years ahead of him before he had to marry. But if Catherine had conceived, he couldn't let her bear the child out of wedlock. The entire village would shun her. And what if the child was a boy? Then the babe would become the next Duke of Hart, but only if he and Catherine were married when the infant was born.

And then the poor little mite would be cursed, too. Perhaps it would be better to let him be born a bastard.

No. Bastardy was never a gift.

He took a deep, calming breath. He was getting ahead of himself. With luck, Catherine had not conceived. The interlude in her bedchamber would just become a pleasant memory.

The thought was exceedingly depressing.

And if she wasn't carrying his child, he'd never see her again. How could he bear *that*?

He leaned against the headstone. Perhaps he didn't have to. Emmett had said he should spend more time at Loves Castle. He'd enjoyed becoming involved in the management of the place and getting to know his tenants. If he was at the castle, it would be natural to come into the village from time to time. He could even look in at the Spinster House to be sure all was in order and to see how Catherine went on. . . .

No. Whom was he fooling? If he saw Catherine, he would want to bed her. He'd just proven how weak his control was where she was concerned. If they'd been lucky enough to escape pregnancy this time, he couldn't tempt fate by having relations with her again, even though his damn, mindless cock was insisting vehemently that one time with Catherine was not enough.

It isn't, but it's all I'm going to get.

Unless she *had* conceived. Then he'd have months to live with her and love her and watch her grow round and heavy with their child.

Months, not years. And he'd never see the baby, would he? Unless he was exceedingly lucky and Catherine gave him a daughter. It had happened once before. It could happen again. . . .

No. I can't hope for such luck. And I'll still need a son to carry on the title.

He straightened. He was getting nowhere with this. He might as well go inside, even though the last thing he wanted was to be around people.

He glanced down at the gravestone he'd been leaning against and read the name on it. Of course. Isabelle Dorring. Blast! He'd like to push the damn thing over. It was a lie anyway. Isabelle wasn't buried here.

If only the curse was as much of a lie.

When he entered the hall a few minutes later, the Misses Boltwood pounced on him.

"You've been gone quite a while, duke," Miss Cordelia said, waggling her brows.

Miss Gertrude giggled. "One hour and fourteen minutes." Her brows joined her sister's in jumping up and down. "We timed you."

"You must have had quite a *conversation* with Miss Hutting." Miss Cordelia nudged her sister and they giggled harder.

"Yes. An exchange of many *pleasantries*."

"For an *hour* and fourteen minutes."

"You must have had a lot to *talk* about."

Good God, the ladies had clearly had a few too many glasses of punch. He looked around the room. Would no one come to his aid?

Apparently not. Nate was still playing the pianoforte. He managed to catch Alex's eye, but the scurvy fellow just smiled and continued his conversation with Miss Wilkinson.

Well, Alex could plan to walk back to the castle, then.

"I think the dear vicar will be celebrating another wedding soon, don't you, Gertrude?"

"And maybe a christening nine months later—oh."

The ladies suddenly realized they had strayed into hazardous territory.

"No one believes in that silly old curse," Miss Cordelia said.

Miss Gertrude nodded vigorously. "This is 1817, after all. The previous dukes' deaths were just unfortunate coincidences."

Five unfortunate "coincidences"—every single duke for the last two hundred years.

He'd had practice hiding his emotions. Now he smiled at the women. "Actually, I was visiting Isabelle Dorring's grave. Or, I suppose I should say, her gravestone."

Their jaws dropped in unison.

"Why would you do something daft like that?" Cordelia managed to ask.

Why indeed? "No reason. I was just wandering through the graveyard and happened to stop there."

The ladies were still gawping at him. He couldn't fault them. It *was* a rather preposterous tale, but he was not about to tell them where he'd been before his stroll through the churchyard.

"Good God, she turned you down." Cordelia looked at her sister. "Can you believe it, Gertrude? Cat turned him down! What is the matter with that girl?"

"She has feathers for brains, that's what's the matter," Gertrude said. "Or rocks. I could understand why she would shy away from Harold Barker—who *would* want to get buckled to that man?—but to turn up her nose at this!" She gestured at Marcus. "She must be blind as well as doltish."

He did not wish to confirm their suspicions, but he couldn't stand silent and listen to them malign Catherine.

"Miss Hutting *is* living in the Spinster House, ladies. I believe that makes it quite clear that she is perfectly content with her unmarried state."

Both elderly ladies rolled their eyes.

"Nonsense!" Cordelia said. "No female in her right mind

would choose a life of virginity over a night in your bed, duke."

"With or without a marriage proposal," Gertrude added.

Cordelia snorted. "Except for Cat. I'm sure she'd want a ring on her finger first. She *is* the vicar's daughter."

Dear God, don't let me look as guilty as I feel.

"And as stiff and proper as a nun."

She is not!

Cordelia nodded. "Stiffer. Likely cold, too."

If they only knew . . . which they will if Catherine has conceived, blast it.

"But if anyone can warm her up," Gertrude said, "you can, duke." She winked at him. "I'm sure you know your way around a bed."

Cordelia sighed. "Yes, indeed. If only I was a few years younger."

Good God! A few years? The woman must have at least sixty years in her dish, if not seventy. And she and her sister were both spinsters themselves.

Er, best not wade into *those* waters.

"Yes, well, it's been very pleasant chatting, but I must go speak to my friends, Lord Haywood and Lord Evans. I wish to get an early start tomorrow."

"Early start?" Gertrude looked at her sister and then back at him. "You aren't leaving us, are you, duke?"

"Sadly, I am. I find I must return to Town."

The two elderly sisters stared at him in silence.

Then Cordelia put her hand on his sleeve and shook his arm slightly. "Don't give up, duke. Cat will come around. You'll see. You just need to be persistent."

If only it was that simple.

He gently freed his arm. "Madam, I know you mean well, but I must ask you not to pursue this topic any further."

"Do you want us to speak to her for you?" Gertrude asked.

"No!" That came out a bit too forcefully. He made himself smile. "No, thank you. It is very kind of you to offer, but . . . no. Now I really must take my leave."

"When will you be back?" Gertrude asked.

Cordelia reached for his arm again, but he was able to avoid her without being too obvious about it . . . he hoped. At least it didn't stop her from speaking.

"Perhaps you should stay away for a week or two, duke. Give Cat time to miss you. Then she'll fall into your arms the moment you return."

"Yes. Well, I doubt that I will be returning. Good afternoon, ladies." He bowed and turned—

And almost tripped over the twins. They were staring at him, large eyes dark in their pale faces. Mikey—and even Tom—looked to be on the verge of tears.

"You can't leave, dook," Mikey said, throwing himself at Marcus and wrapping his arms around his legs.

Tom raised his chin and used his sleeve to wipe away his tears. "You're supposed to m-marry Cat."

Oh, blast.

Chapter Eighteen

July 25, 1617—Dear God! My courses are now two weeks late, and my stomach is severely unsettled. The smell and even the look of some foods have me running for the chamber pot. I must be increasing. But what am I to do? I wish Marcus was here to hold me, but he is still away at his house party. I must write to him. He will marry me and all will be well.

—from Isabelle Dorring's diary

Something brushed across Cat's cheek.

"Mmpft." She swatted at it and turned over in bed, settling back to sleep. She'd been in the middle of a wonderful dream. Marcus had just been about to—

The thing swatted back, hitting her nose this time.

"Go away, Poppy. I'm sleeping." Ever since that afternoon with Marcus, Poppy had taken to inviting herself into Cat's bed. It was very odd. Had her scent changed or something?

She blushed, digging deeper into the covers. If something

was different about her, fortunately, only Poppy seemed to have noticed.

"Merrow." Poppy rubbed her face against Cat's.

"It's too early. See, the sun isn't even up." Cat finally opened her eyes. Her room was actually quite bright. Too bright.

She sat up abruptly, sending Poppy leaping to the floor. "Good God, what time *is* it?" She lunged for her watch on the bedside table. "Nine o'clock! I've never slept this late."

Except she'd been sleeping this late rather often recently. She pushed her hair out of her face. What was the matter with her? She was always tired now, and her breasts were tender and achy—

Aching for Marcus's touch.

She buried her face in her hands. She *had* to forget him. She wasn't going to be some silly Miss, languishing for her lover. Marcus wasn't her lover. They had only done . . . *that* once.

She closed her eyes as her body remembered in throbbing detail exactly what they'd done. Marcus had been gone three weeks—three *long* weeks—but she recalled exactly how he had touched her as if it had happened yesterday.

Lud, it had been wonderful. She'd had no idea she could feel such things. She wanted more—

But she couldn't have more. And in any event, her breasts were really too sensitive to be touched.

She climbed reluctantly out of bed. If she hadn't already missed more than one fair planning meeting, she might have stayed under the covers. But she'd promised Jane and Anne she'd be there today.

Ouch! She bumped her breast with her arm as she pulled on her shift. She put her stays on more carefully and then her dress. Odd. Her bodice felt a bit tight. She hadn't thought she'd been putting on weight. Just the opposite. Even the smell of certain foods made her stomach rebel.

She must be sickening. Or perhaps her monthly courses were coming on. It was about time for them to make their appearance. She frowned. When had she had them last? She should pay more attention—

Oh.

Oh, God!

She dove for the chamber pot and emptied the contents of her stomach into it. Eew.

She sat back on her heels and pressed her fingers to her forehead. She couldn't be increasing. A woman didn't conceive the first—and only—time she had sexual congress with a man.

Though Marcus had seemed to think it was possible. He *had* told her to write him.

She eyed the chamber pot again as her stomach twisted.

Nonsense! She was just late, that was all. Her body had been shocked and disordered by the, er, experience with Marcus. Things were sure to right themselves in a few days.

Hopefully.

She opened the window and dumped the chamber pot's disgusting contents over the sill. Then she hurried down the stairs. Unfortunately, there was no time for tea, but she could get a cup and a bit of bread at the inn.

"Cat!" She looked over to see Jane and Anne coming toward her on the walk.

She fell into step with them. "Why aren't you already at the inn, Anne? Didn't you ride there directly?" Poor Anne. Her father had just remarried and moved his new wife and her sons into Davenport Hall.

"I did, but when I arrived and didn't see you or Jane— and did see the Misses Boltwood—I decided to go for a walk. I did not wish to be the only unmarried target for the ladies' dubious advice."

Anne hadn't stopped by the Spinster House on her way to Jane's. That hurt.

No, it was just as well. If Anne had come by, she would have found Cat in bed or, worse, hanging over the chamber pot. "What kept you, Jane?"

"Randolph needed me to find a paper for him." Jane snorted. "Of course it was exactly where I'd told him it was. He just couldn't manage to look under the book he'd put on top of it."

"How annoying." Cat waited for a self-satisfied feeling to bubble up at the thought of her own housing good fortune, but it didn't come. Ever since she'd made the mistake of letting Marcus into her bed, her contentment with the Spinster House had ebbed.

All right, she hadn't been as content as she'd expected even before then. Life in the Spinster House was a little too quiet and a bit lonely. But she was still adjusting. Things would get better soon. The situation with Marcus had . . . confused her.

Once I get used to his absence, I'll be fine.

They were walking past the lending library now. No one had taken it in hand since Miss Franklin left. Perhaps that was something she could do to pass the time when she wasn't writing.

"Why are you late, Cat?" Anne asked.

Good God, how did Anne know her courses were—

Oh. She was talking about being late for the *meeting*. "I overslept."

"No little brothers or sisters to wake you up, eh?" Jane said.

Of course! That must be why she was sleeping so much. "Precisely. And I don't have to share a bed"—drat, she wasn't blushing was she?—"with Mary any longer."

"You wouldn't have to do that now that Mary's wed." Jane raised her brows. "Which I hope you'll be soon. The thought that I'll be able to move into the Spinster House—"

"*You'll* be able to move in?" Anne scowled at Jane. "Don't bet on it."

"Definitely not!" What was the matter with Jane? "Why in the world do you think I'll be getting married?"

I'll have to marry if I'm increasing.

No, I can't. The curse—

"Have you heard from the duke recently?" Jane exchanged a significant—and very annoying—look with Anne.

Cat's stomach heaved. She pressed her fingers to her mouth, but fortunately, it was a false alarm. "Of course not." She swallowed. "There's no reason for the Duke of Hart to write to me."

"But when is he returning?" Anne asked.

"Never. That's what Mama said he told Thomas and Michael, and I don't believe he would lie to children." The twins had been heartbroken.

Anne frowned. "I thought he told them he didn't know, but he was afraid it might not be for a long time."

"That's the same thing. He was just trying to soften the blow for the boys, but they'd heard what he'd said to the Misses Boltwood." Mikey had cried inconsolably that night, Mama had told her, though that might also have been due to Mary's leaving. But even Tom had been teary-eyed.

Oh, lud, Jane and Anne were looking at each other with that annoyingly knowing expression again.

"What *is* it?"

"I was talking to Lord Evans at Mary's wedding," Jane said. "He thought the duke was very, er, interested in you."

Which he had been. *Extremely* interested. He'd explored every interesting inch of her, some of which she'd never explored herself.

"His Grace is very kind. He takes an interest in everyone." Jane rolled her eyes.

"That's not the sort of interest Lord Evans meant," Anne said, "and you know it. He meant a matrimonial interest."

If I'm increasing, Marcus will insist we marry despite the curse.

"We think the duke cares for you, Cat," Jane said.

Did Marcus care for her or was what had happened between them merely a case of a worldly duke taking what a silly country spinster was offering? She hadn't thought so at the time, but she'd been so overwhelmed by all the new sensations, she hadn't been thinking at all. He could have been laughing up his sleeve at her.

With all his experience, he'd probably found what they'd done in her bed sadly flat.

Oh, God, she didn't know what to think. As more time passed, her recollection of what Marcus had said and how he had looked dimmed. The only thing that hadn't faded was her body's desire to do what they had done again.

And again.

No, that wasn't true. What she felt in her heart hadn't faded either.

"Have you forgotten about Isabelle's curse? Marriage for the duke is a death sentence. He has no desire to take up permanent residence in the churchyard anytime soon."

But if I'm increasing . . .

Oh, Lord, if I give birth to a bastard, the scandal will be enormous. Papa is the vicar, for God's sake.

"But if the duke marries you for love," Anne said, "won't that break the curse?"

But Marcus hadn't said anything about love. He'd offered because he'd spilled his seed in her.

"I don't know why we're having this ridiculous conversation. I'm a confirmed spinster. The duke knows that. He's the one who gave me the keys to the Spinster House."

They finally reached Cupid's Inn.

"You're a spinster now," Jane said, "but that doesn't mean you'll be a spinster forever. Look at Miss Franklin."

Yes, Miss Franklin.

"Miss Franklin was an aberration." Cat pulled open the inn door. "Mama says that as far as she can remember, no other spinster has ever wed." Which is exactly what she would do—remain a spinster forever. If she couldn't have Marcus—and she couldn't—then she wouldn't have anyone.

And if I am increasing?

Oh, God. Oh, God. I can't be.

Cat would be the first to admit she wasn't paying much attention during the fair planning meeting. She sipped her tea and willed her courses to start.

"Pining for your duke, are you?" Miss Gertrude said when Cat failed to respond to something she'd asked.

It was going to be hell if every time her attention wandered, someone was going to throw Marcus's title in her face.

"Which duke?"

Every single woman in the room rolled her eyes then, and baby Malcolm farted, though that, of course, had not been intentional.

"*Which* duke?" Miss Cordelia said. "Let's see, how many dukes have wandered into Loves Bridge in the last few years?"

"The Duke of Benton, for one," Cat said.

"Not the Duke of Benton." Miss Cordelia snorted. "The Duke of Hart, of course. The boy who was sniffing around your skirts just a few weeks ago."

"Likely doing more than sniffing," Miss Gertrude said, nudging her sister.

"He did seem very interested in you, Cat," Viola Latham said, having examined Malcolm's bottom and confirmed that noise was the only thing that had emanated from that region. "We all remarked on it."

Helena Simmons nodded. "Even my husband mentioned it, and he never notices anything of that nature." She snorted. "If he can't eat it or drink it or swive it, he doesn't see it."

Helena and her husband did not have a happy union.

"So when is the duke returning to Loves Bridge?" Miss Cordelia asked. "And when will there be a wedding?"

Cat's stomach heaved, but she swallowed it down. "He's not coming back, and there won't be a wedding."

"Oh, there'll be a wedding," Miss Gertrude said, waggling her brows. "He's like his father. He knows he has to marry you to have you, and any fool can tell he wants to have you." Her brows jumped even more. "Desperately."

Oh, God, if I am increasing, everyone will know exactly what I did with the duke.

She took a deep breath.

My courses will come today or tomorrow. They have to.

"Remember the curse," she said. Why didn't anyone else remind people of that damned curse? "The duke must put off marriage as long as he can."

Miss Cordelia flicked her fingers at her. "It will take more than a silly curse to keep that boy from between your legs."

She really was going to cast up her accounts—perhaps she could aim for the Misses Boltwood's shoes.

"Cordelia," Viola said, "remember Cat is a virgin as are Jane and Anne"—her brows rose—"and you and your sister, I presume."

Cordelia blushed slightly and shrugged. "Yes, yes. But we don't have any patience with roundaboutation, do we, Gertrude?"

"No, indeed." Gertrude snorted. "Modern mealy-mouthed ways. In our day we got right to the point, and the point is, Cat, that the duke is as lusty as they come. Lud, his pantaloons were—"

"I really must be going." She did not want to hear what Miss Gertrude thought about Marcus's pantaloons. "I find I'm not feeling quite the thing."

"I know just what will cure you," Miss Cordelia said. "A nice tumble between—"

Cat was out the door before the woman could finish her sentence.

Oh, Lord, how was she going to survive the Boltwood sisters?

She started walking toward the Spinster House. As the proverb said, time was a great healer. Each day without Marcus was a day closer to forgetting him.

No, she'd never forget him, but in time he'd fade to a pleasant memory. Getting her courses would help, too. She was often emotional around the time they arrived. And *surely* the Boltwood sisters would stop teasing her when the weeks went by and Marcus stayed in London.

"Cat!"

She looked up to see her sister Mary waving and walking toward her.

"What are you doing here?" she asked as Mary came up. Mary and Theo had been back from their honeymoon for over a week, but Theo's house was on the castle grounds, so Mary didn't come into the village that often. "You look very happy. Marriage must agree with you."

The pain in her chest was nausea, not jealousy.

"It does." Mary gave a little skip. "I came to see Mama. Oh, Cat, I think I have the most wonderful news, but I need to have Mama confirm my suspicions."

"Really?" Mary looked as if she would burst if she didn't unburden herself immediately. "What is it?"

Mary blushed. "I shouldn't tell you. I forgot. You aren't married."

She would *not* push her sister into that very tempting thorn-bush they were just passing. "I don't see what being married has to say to anything."

"Of course you don't. You're still a virgin."

She should just continue on to the Spinster House in her virginal ignorance, except she wasn't still a virgin, and she was very much afraid she might not be able to hide that fact much longer. "I'm not an idiot, however."

Mary could never keep a thing to herself for long. "No, of course you aren't." She gave another little skip and grabbed Cat's arm. "I think I may be increasing!"

Cat's stomach plummeted. "But it's too early, isn't it? You've been married just a few weeks."

Mary nodded. "Yes, I thought it was too soon, too, but Mama warned me it was possible to conceive quickly, especially when one is young."

At least I'm not young.

"Mama said she's quite certain you were started on her wedding night."

That was rather too much information.

"So when I noticed all the signs, I thought perhaps the same thing had happened to me."

"Er, what signs?"

Mary was too excited to remember she was talking to a supposed virgin. "Well, the first thing, of course, is missing your monthly courses. Mine are almost a week late."

"Ah." Surely a week was not so very late?

"And then there's the tiredness, the sore breasts, the nausea, the sensitivity to smells, that sort of thing." Mary skipped again and clapped her hands. "Oh, won't it be wonderful if I really am enceinte?"

"Yes." *Oh, God; oh, God; oh, God.* "It would be wonderful." *I'm going to vomit.* "Give Mama my best."

Cat started to walk faster. She needed to get to the Spinster House before she disgraced herself.

"Aren't you coming with me to the vicarage?"

"No." Cat swallowed and managed a smile. "You'll want to talk to Mama alone, won't you?"

"Oh, yes. Of course. She'll be so happy." Mary waved and headed across the green.

Cat swallowed again and almost ran past the lending library and up the walk to the Spinster House. She'd never make it inside, but she could manage—just—to make it to the garden where she had some privacy to empty her stomach over an unsuspecting, overgrown, nondescript bush.

She had a letter she needed to write to the Duke of Hart.

Marcus danced in Lord Easthaven's ballroom with Lady, er . . . what was the girl's name? Beatrice? Belinda? Something that began with a "b."

Maybe.

Better be cautious and not refer to her by name at all. Not that the girl would correct him. She was such a toadeater, she'd likely change her name to whatever he called her.

"Are you enjoying the ball?"

"Oh, yes, Your Grace." She stared up at him with a revoltingly worshipful gaze.

He'd asked her to stand up with him because of her hair. It was reddish gold like Catherine's. When he'd seen her from behind, he'd thought for a moment she *was* Catherine, and he'd been so blasted happy, his bloody heart had jumped.

Well, his heart and another organ.

And then he'd seen her face. She was one of the Earl

of Ambleton's daughters. Pretty enough, but she wasn't Catherine.

"It's a beautiful night," he said. Ha! Only if you liked damp and drizzle.

"Oh, yes, Your Grace."

Good God, did the woman have a single original thought in her head? Catherine would have laughed at him and told him—

He could not think about Catherine.

"Are you planning to remove to the country for the summer?"

"Oh, yes, Your Grace."

He had thought he might be required to go to Loves Bridge, but apparently there was no need of that. It had been three weeks, and he hadn't heard from Catherine. She must know by now that she was not increasing.

He should be happy. Overjoyed. Delighted. Ecstatic.

He felt distinctly blue-deviled.

He'd checked the post every day. Every bloody day he'd waited with dread for Finch to present him with his correspondence, and every day he'd felt disappointed instead of elated when he'd flipped through the pile of cards and letters to find there was none from Catherine.

It was just the uncertainty. That was all. Now that he knew his . . . mistake hadn't had consequences, he could feel relief.

Eventually.

It would take time, but he'd started the process. Today he'd made a point of being away from home so he wouldn't spend every moment waiting for the letter that wasn't coming. He needed to keep busy. After a few weeks—or months—this blasted longing would fade.

"Your Grace?"

He looked back down at the girl. Damnation. She must have said something other than "oh, yes."

"I'm sorry. My attention wandered."

She blushed—prettily, he supposed. "I was merely wondering if you were going to the country, too."

"Ah. No." He could go to one of his other estates, of course. He probably should go. But he had no desire to be anywhere but in Loves Bridge, so he would stay in London. There was more to distract him here.

Except none of it was working. Riding in Hyde Park, attending the theater, strolling through the museums— wherever he went, Catherine was there in his thoughts. He wanted to show her all of London and see her reaction. He would even escort her to a literary salon or two if she wanted. He wasn't part of that set, but no one would turn away the Duke of Hart—

But he wasn't going to see Catherine again.

Lady Whatever-her-name-was smiled at him. He smiled back.

That had been the wrong thing to do. Her eyes lit up.

"Then you'll come? Papa will be so delighted."

"Er, come?"

"To our country estate." The girl actually frowned. That was progress. "I just invited you."

"Ah, yes." While he would never be a success on the stage, he had perfected a few acting skills. He didn't usually bother to employ them, relying instead on a pointed set-down, but he was more at fault here than his companion. "I would enjoy—" He paused and then let his shoulders droop slightly while he shook his head. "I'm so sorry. I've just remembered. I must stay in Town."

The girl's frown deepened to a scowl. "Why?"

Perhaps she did merit a set-down. "Private business." He allowed his lips to curl slightly into an expression that was half smile, half sneer. "I'm certain you understand."

Apparently she didn't. She opened her mouth to protest again, but fortunately the dance ended.

"I'll just return you to your chaperone, shall I?" He put her hand on his arm and started to tow her across the room toward Lady Ambleton.

"I thought we might stroll in the gardens." The girl dug in her heels, slowing their progress. "It's such a lovely evening, Your Grace."

Now he remembered. Her father was said to have made some poor investments and was looking to refill the family coffers. Well, it wasn't going to be with *his* coins.

"It's raining."

She batted her eyes at him. "We can take shelter under a tree." She leaned forward slightly, and he suddenly realized the neck of her dress was quite low. He had an excellent view of her breasts.

He might just as well be viewing a pair of apples. No, plums. *Small* plums.

"I'm sure you'll keep me dry, Your Grace."

"Well, you're wrong there." *Idiot!* Hadn't he learned anything from his mistake with Miss Rathbone? He could not let his attention wander. This wasn't Loves Bridge; it was London. Women were hiding behind every bush and potted plant, hoping to trap him into marriage. "You will want to return to your mother before the next set so you can find a more amenable partner."

"Don't you mean amiable?" she said a bit waspishly, finally allowing him to guide her toward Lady Ambleton.

"That, too."

Once he freed himself from Lady Annoying, he retreated to the refreshment room, which is where Alex and Nate found him.

"Enjoy your dance with Lady Barbara?" Alex asked while helping himself to a lobster patty.

At least he now knew the girl's name. "No."

"I didn't think so." Alex popped the entire patty into his mouth.

That would keep him quiet for a while. Unfortunately Nate's mouth wasn't full.

"Why did you come, Marcus? You've been glowering at everyone all night. More than one person has remarked on it to me." Nate frowned. "Some have even noticed that your ill temper dates from your return to London. They've asked me what happened in Loves Bridge."

"I hope you haven't said anything." Good God, he would not have Catherine's name bandied about.

"Of course I haven't. What would there be to say?" Nate frowned. "Nothing did happen in Loves Bridge, did it?" His frown deepened. "That's what you told me."

"Right. Nothing happened." Blast. Now he'd got Nate worried. That was the last thing he needed—Nate going on and on about the bloody curse. He'd likely snap the poor man's head off. And for no reason. Nothing at all had happened in Loves Bridge, as evidenced by the fact Catherine hadn't written him.

Nate grinned. "Good. I'll confess I was worried for a while, especially after you spent that time with Miss Hutting in the bushes and then disappeared after her sister's wedding. But when you were willing to return to London, I realized my concern was groundless. And of course *she's* not interested in marriage. She must be well settled into the Spinster House by now."

"Yes, I'm sure she is." He did not want to discuss Catherine. "I say, isn't that Viscount Motton over by the window? I thought you said you needed a word with him."

"I do. Where is he? Oh, yes, I see. If you'll excuse me?"

"Gladly," Marcus muttered as Nate headed across the room.

"You're a lovesick dunderhead, you know."

"W-what?" He snapped his head around. Alex had finished his lobster patty and was now helping himself to a glass of champagne.

"You heard me. You may have fooled Nate—he was busy playing the organ during the wedding and then the pianoforte afterward—but I saw how you looked at Miss Hutting. And I know the signs of infatuation." He took a large swallow of champagne. "Too well."

Oh, God. Alex never talked about the woman who'd jilted him, but Marcus knew he wasn't completely over the experience yet. "I'm sorry about Lady Charlotte."

Alex waved his concern away. "Go back to Loves Bridge and marry Miss Hutting, will you?"

If only it were that simple. "I can't. You know about the curse."

"I thought if you married for love, you'd break it."

"Yes. But if it's not love I feel for Catherine, I'll likely die within the year." He definitely lusted for Catherine. But did he love her? How the hell was he to tell those emotions apart?

"What does it matter? As far as I can tell you're as close to dead now as you can be without being planted in the churchyard."

God, that was damnably true.

Alex's look was direct, yet not unsympathetic. "Would you rather have a few months of wedded bliss with Miss Hutting or a lifetime of misery knowing you weren't brave enough to risk everything for what you wanted?"

Put that way. . . .

"I think I'll go back to Hart House."

Alex frowned. "Alone?"

"Yes." Marcus laughed. "For God's sake, don't worry—and don't get Nate worrying. I just think it's best if I take my disagreeable self home"—he smiled—"and think about what you said. Tell Nate I'm tired, will you? And I'll see you both tomorrow."

Marcus left the refreshment room without attracting Nate's attention, dodged a number of other acquaintances, and slipped out of Lord Easthaven's town house. The streets were quiet, and the rain had thinned to a drizzle.

Did he love Catherine?

He certainly wanted her. She haunted his dreams and caused him to wake painfully hard.

He'd thought to slake his lust with one of the many accommodating London light-skirts, but when he'd arrived at his favorite brothel, he found he couldn't take another woman to bed. His cock refused to play, dangling between his legs as if dead. He hadn't stayed beyond five minutes and had likely ruined his reputation among the London Cyprians.

Bloody hell! He enjoyed a romp in bed as much as the next man, but now . . .

He kicked a loose stone and sent it clattering over the pavement.

Now something had changed. He'd changed. What he'd done with Catherine had been more than an enjoyable act of copulation. Minds and hearts had been involved.

It *had* been an act of love.

But did that mean he *loved* Catherine?

He crossed the street to Hart House, the glow from the gaslights making the puddles glitter and the cobblestones shine.

It didn't matter. He might not know what love was, but Alex was right. He felt dead now. He'd rather have a handful of months sharing his days—and his bed—with Catherine than years and years of life without her.

He'd go to Loves Bridge and ask her to marry him.

He grinned and took the steps to his door two at a time.

He'd leave in the morning. He'd like to leave now—and might consider it if the moon was full—but such bizarre behavior would shock poor Emmett and Dunly and the others at the castle and would set tongues to wagging. He didn't want that. He hadn't yet persuaded Catherine to have him.

Finch opened the door before Marcus could grasp the latch. Damnation, the butler must have been watching for him. Now what?

"I can let myself in, you know, Finch. No need to hover by the door."

Finch frowned and tugged on his waistcoat. "I have put your correspondence in the study, Your Grace."

Oh, right. The way he'd been waiting for the post every day, Finch must think he'd want to have that news immediately.

"Thank you. I'll look at it in the morning. I'm off to bed now."

Should he tell him he was leaving at dawn? No, better save that for Kimball. His valet was apt to get his nose out of joint if he thought Finch knew something before he did.

Finch cleared his throat. "I believe you would wish to read it tonight, Your Grace."

He froze. "Oh?"

Finch nodded, not meeting his gaze. "Yes, Your Grace."

"Very well. Thank you."

He started for the study, alarm coursing through his veins. Something was wrong.

Finch had left a lamp burning. He saw the post immediately. Most of it was off to the side, but one white rectangle lay by itself in the middle of the desk.

He walked slowly over to it and picked it up. It was from Loves Bridge. From the Spinster House, which could only mean one thing.

He broke the seal. The writing was neat, feminine. There was a splotch in the middle as if a tear had fallen on the ink.

Your Grace,
I am sorry to be required to inform you that I believe I am increasing.

Sincerely,
Miss Catherine Hutting

Chapter Nineteen

August 1, 1617—Marcus has married the duke's daughter. Rosaline showed me the notice in the London paper. Oh, God, what am I to do?

           —from Isabelle Dorring's diary

She was sorry.

He let the letter slip from his fingers and flutter down to the desk.

She was *sorry*.

He'd been so focused on his own feelings, he'd forgotten about Catherine's. She wasn't like the other girls. She didn't want to marry. She certainly didn't care about becoming a duchess. She wanted to live alone in the Spinster House and write. This pregnancy would ruin all her plans.

No, it needn't do that. Yes, she'd have to marry him, but he would hire nursemaids and governesses and tutors. All his properties were large. She could go off by herself to write whenever she wished. He would expect her to warm his bed from time to time for the few months he had with her before the curse sent him to the grave, but surely that wasn't too much to ask? She'd proven herself passionate—

Oh, God, no. That wasn't what he wanted. Even his randy cock wasn't enthusiastic about the notion of Catherine being little more than a live-in mistress.

He dropped into the desk chair and rubbed his face. Did she care for him at all?

She'd never said so. She'd only said she wanted him.

But she'd let him into her bed. Surely she wouldn't have done that if she hadn't felt *something* for him besides lust. Catherine wasn't a light-skirt. He'd been her first lover.

But that doesn't mean she loves you.

Oh, Lord. I want *her to love me. I want it far too much.*

He surged back to his feet and started to pace in front of the fire.

Catherine did seem to care whether he died or not. Hadn't she mentioned the blasted curse when she'd said she wouldn't marry him?

Perfect. The curse that had been such an attraction for the grasping women who'd been past Duchesses of Hart was exactly what was keeping Catherine from accepting his offer.

He paused by the far wall. All right, he would absolve his mother of that sin. But the ladies who'd been vying to become *his* duchess certainly valued the fact that they could look forward to his early demise.

He turned to stride back the other way.

But caring whether he lived or died didn't mean she loved him. She would likely feel that way about anyone, even the detestable Mr. Barker.

I saw the pain in her eyes when I left her. I swear she didn't want me to leave.

But she hadn't stopped him.

Likely it was his own emotions he'd imagined in her expression. Perhaps she'd only been appalled by her behavior, finally realizing the magnitude of what she'd done, how she'd put all her plans in jeopardy.

His gut clenched. Surely she didn't feel the panic and despair Isabelle Dorring had felt?

No. She'd written to him as she'd said she would. She must know she could rely on him to help her.

He turned his back to the fire. And he *would* help her. He would marry her. It might not be what she wanted, but that was immaterial now. Neither of them had a choice any longer—they'd made their choice three weeks ago.

And she *had* made the choice. It hadn't been rape. He'd offered to leave. He'd even warned her there was a risk of conception. Yes, he should have pulled out in time, but what was done was done. He hadn't meant to impregnate her.

Now she was carrying his child, so she had to become his wife. He would not let his son or daughter be born a bastard.

He snatched Catherine's letter off the desk and tossed it into the fire. No need to advertise the fact that they had anticipated their vows. People might wonder, but babies did sometimes come a few weeks early.

He headed for the stairs and his bedchamber. He needed to try to get some sleep. He intended to leave at first light. Tomorrow he would see Catherine. *Zeus!* He'd thought he'd never again have that pleasure, but now . . .

Now he was filled with an unsettling stew of anticipation and dread.

Cat was dreaming of Marcus. He was in her bedroom, and she was naked—

Something brushed over her cheek. She swatted at it, but Poppy was too fast. Cat's hand passed through the air without touching anything.

The light sensation came again.

"Go away, Poppy." She snuggled deeper into her bed. "I'm dreaming."

"About me, I hope."

She'd swear that was Marcus's voice.

Her eyes flew open. Her room was still filled with shadows, but she could see Marcus's face just above hers.

Was she dreaming? She reached out to cup his jaw.

His strong fingers wrapped around her hand and turned it, his lips skimmed her palm. The sensation of his mouth brushing over her skin sent expectation humming through her.

"Your cheek is rough."

"I didn't take the time to shave."

She *must* be dreaming, and this Marcus must be a phantasm called up by her desire. It was too early for the real Marcus to be here. She'd just posted her letter yesterday afternoon.

But he felt very real.

"Is it true? Are you actually here?" she whispered.

"Yes, Catherine. I'm here." His voice was deep and husky and warm—and there was a note of humor in it, too. And desire. Surely desire.

"Show me."

"Show you?" He sounded hesitant.

"That you're really, really here." She pulled back the coverlet to make her invitation plainer. "Please."

She knew she'd missed him, but she hadn't realized how much until now. Her body was on fire, her breasts, the place between her legs, everywhere aching for him to do what they had done before. There was no danger now. She couldn't become pregnant. She already was.

For a moment she thought he was going to refuse. She bit her lip. She wouldn't beg, though the need surging through her urged her to do so.

And it wasn't just her body. Her heart ached, too. She'd been so lonely without him.

It was still too dark to see his expression—his back was to the window—but perhaps there was enough light for him to see hers.

"Shall I get undressed?" His voice wasn't completely steady.

"Yes."

She scrambled out of her nightshift as he removed his coat. Then she watched as he shed his waistcoat, shirt, shoes, stockings and, finally, his pantaloons.

Three weeks ago his body had been so strange. Now it was familiar and precious, a gift she could hardly wait to hold again.

He climbed into bed and stretched out beside her. She put her arm over his chest, buried her face in the angle between his shoulder and neck, and breathed deeply. He smelled so good. He felt good, too, solid and strong. All the fear, the loneliness, the anxiety that had gripped her since he'd left drained away.

She ran her fingers over his chest, down his flat belly all the way to his male bit. It was long and hard and thick.

Desire surged in her again. She was empty, and she needed him to fill her.

"As you can see—or feel—I missed you rather dreadfully," Marcus said with a breathless little laugh. And then he turned and brought his mouth down on hers.

There was nothing gentle or tentative or graceful about this lovemaking. Marcus tried at first to go slowly, but she was having none of it. Her need for him was too raw. Her hands slid down over his muscled back to grab his arse and pull him closer.

"Now, Marcus. Please."

He didn't argue.

She came apart the moment he entered, convulsing around him as he slid deep, deep into her. And then, as if in echo, she felt the warm pulse of his seed.

He collapsed onto her, and she held his damp, relaxed body tightly.

Oh, God, how she loved him.

He lay like that for a few moments, and she savored his solid weight pressing her into the mattress. Then he turned his head and brushed her cheek with his lips.

"That's a splendid way to say good morning." He lifted himself off her and drew her against his side, pulling the coverlet up over them.

"Mmm. I'd love to say good morning that way every morning." She ran her fingers over his chest. She felt wonderful. Relaxed and at peace.

"That sounds like a brilliant idea." He grinned. The room was lighter now so she could see his face clearly. His eyes gleamed, his smile was broader than she'd ever seen it. He looked very, very happy.

"Though I'm not a hundred percent certain I could survive the experience daily." His grin widened even more. "But I would try. I would definitely try."

She grinned back at him. Having him here was heaven, though the Almighty would likely not approve. At least there was no planning meeting to interrupt her today.

Wait a moment. . . .

"How did you get in?"

"The same way I did last time—the back door." He kissed her nose. "You really should lock it if you don't want riffraff showing up in your bed."

"Oh." She started to sit up. If Marcus got in, then someone else could, too. Not that she expected anyone to try, but it would be terribly, er, *awkward* to be found naked in bed with the Duke of Hart.

Marcus wrapped his fingers gently around her arm to stop her. "Don't worry. I locked the door behind me."

He tugged, and she let him pull her back down so she rested her head on his chest, her arm draped over his muscled stomach. She listened to the steady beat of his heart as his hand stroked up and down her back. Mmm. She felt so warm and relaxed and happy. She could stay here forever.

"I'd lecture you on the need to be more careful if you weren't going to be moving to the castle so soon."

Her contented, lazy peacefulness evaporated in an instant, and she jerked up to frown down at him. "What do you mean? I'm not moving to the castle."

"Yes, you are."

Marcus's body was finally content, but, more importantly, so was his mind and his spirit. He'd been so miserable these last few weeks, but that was over now. Now he would have Catherine with him for as long as he was given to live.

God, how I love her.

He looked up at her lovely breasts dangling above him, at the delicate line of her collar bone—and the deep furrow that had appeared between her brows. He reached up to trace the line, but she pulled her head back.

"No, I'm not."

He was too sated to be alarmed. "Yes, you are." He smiled and traced the line of something he could reach. He watched her nipple pebble before she moved back farther. She was almost off the bed.

He leaned up on one elbow. "Well, after we marry, of course. We don't want to scandalize people more than we have already. I'll go for a special license today, and your father can marry us as soon as may be." His smile widened. "But I'm not waiting for Mrs. Greeley to make you a gown—unless you insist."

Her frown hadn't gone away. If anything, it had deepened. "Marcus, I am not marrying you."

Good God, she sounded serious.

He sat up. "But you have to, Catherine. I got your letter. I know you're increasing."

He rested his hand on her belly, excitement and wonder

coursing through him. His child—a new life that included some spark of him—was there.

She put her hand over his. "No, Marcus. Don't you see? If we aren't married when the baby is born, he can't be your heir. The curse won't apply." She smiled at him finally and cupped his cheek. "You'll get to hold your son and watch him grow. And we can have more children. We can have a family."

A family. Zeus, I'd give anything to—

"No."

"No?" Her brows slammed down. "Why not? It's the perfect solution."

He didn't want Catherine to be his mistress. The thought was obscene. He wanted her to be his wife.

"No, it's not. Remember how everyone shunned you over our interlude in the bushes? This time there will be no doubt what we've been doing."

She flushed. "It doesn't matter."

"Of course it matters. Your family would be put in a terrible position. Think of Mary as Dunly's wife. Or your father. He's the vicar, for God's sake."

Catherine picked at the coverlet. "Perhaps I could live somewhere else. You have other estates, don't you?"

"I do, but people are the same everywhere. And never think word of our situation wouldn't get out. The *ton* loves to gossip, and your cousin Lady Uppleton and your aunt Lady Penland most of all."

Her face was now very pale. "I don't care."

She was brave and independent, but she'd lived her entire life in a village where everyone knew her and accepted her. Yes, she was an original, but she'd not strayed far from propriety's path—or, at least not that anyone knew. When her activities with him came to light—which they would in a few months—she would learn that being a true social outcast could be very, very painful.

"And what about our children, Catherine? They would be gossiped about and pointed out as examples of the evils of lust. None of the other children would be allowed to play with them." He brushed a strand of silky hair off her face. "Bastards have a very hard life. Even a duke's bastards."

She shook her head and looked down at the bed.

"And there's this as well. If you *are* carrying a boy, as my firstborn son he should be the next Duke of Hart."

Her chin came up then, and she met his gaze. "Yes, and have to suffer from the curse."

Sadly that was true.

"I grant you the title comes at a great price, but it also comes with great wealth and privilege." He'd considered letting the title revert to the Crown, but now that he'd started to manage his land and know his people, that option held no appeal. "And when I marry, as I'll have to do, and have a son, how do you think our son will feel when that younger half-brother inherits all that should have been his?"

"He won't care about such things."

"Only a saint could not care." He clasped her hand, stilling her fingers from their nervous picking at the bedclothes. "I want *your* son to be the next duke, Catherine. I want you to be the one to guide him when I cannot and see that he treats his people well, that he grows up to be an honorable man."

She slipped her hand free and got out of bed, picking her nightshift off the floor and putting it on. She stood by the window, looking out over the tangled garden. "There must be another way." She glanced back at him. "Our children can go to the United States. Title and birth mean nothing there."

He went to stand next to her. He wanted to wrap his arms around her, but she was so straight and stiff, she might as well have lettered DO NOT TOUCH across her back.

"I wouldn't be so certain of that, Catherine. People are people. Americans might not have lords and ladies, but I suspect most of them are quite aware of a man's—or a woman's—birth. Illegitimacy is a burden anywhere."

She scowled down at the innocent vegetation.

"And would you want your children to move so far from you? You would never see them if they sailed to the States."

She bit her lip. "I-I could go as well."

"And leave your parents and brothers and sisters here?"

"Y-yes."

That was far too high a price for her to pay. Catherine might wish to live in the Spinster House so she could have quiet and solitude in which to write, but only a fool would think she'd want to be separated from her family by an ocean.

"And would you also leave me? I cannot abandon my lands."

She glanced up at him, and then looked out the window again.

"Our son can go into trade here, then, and make his own way. The world is changing, Marcus."

"Not that quickly." He brushed her cheek with his thumb and felt dampness. He so wished he hadn't put her in this position, and yet he could not bring himself to regret what they had done together in her bed. "And our daughters? What will become of them?"

"Oh!" She jerked away from his touch. "You may be right about everything, but I still will not marry you. I will not be responsible for your death."

"You won't be. I knew exactly what I was risking when I took you to bed."

She sniffed, whether in disdain or to hold back tears, he couldn't tell. "You made a mistake. You shouldn't have to pay with your life."

That was too much. He grabbed her shoulders and turned her to face him. "I did *not* make a mistake. My time with you has been the happiest of my misbegotten life. I love you, Catherine. I'd rather have a few months with you than years of bloody soulless living without you." He couldn't stop the words from pouring out. He was reduced to begging. "Please marry me, Catherine. I cannot bear it if you won't have me."

She was gawping up at him, so he did the only thing he could think to do—he kissed her.

Chapter Twenty

August 3, 1617—I have seen Mr. Wilkinson and arranged things as I wish them without him guessing my plans. Everything is done; all that is left is to finish it.

—from Isabelle Dorring's diary

Marcus loved her.

Cat smiled, her cheek resting on Marcus's chest. They had ended up back in bed, of course. Saying yes she would marry him and love him for as long as they both should live—and she hoped that was far longer than a few months—could not be said only in words. It had to be said in actions, too. This time, every kiss, every touch was a celebration of their love, and their final union was far more than a simple joining of bodies. It was a marriage of hearts and souls as well.

Marcus tipped her head up so he could look into her eyes. "You're wonderful, Catherine."

She felt wonderful.

"Thank you for agreeing to have me."

She grinned. "I should like to have you again."

He chuckled. "Witch! The spirit is willing, but the flesh is weak."

He looked so relaxed and happy, it made her that much happier. "I'm not certain you should be quoting from the Bible in this situation, Marcus."

"On the contrary. I assure you this has been a deeply religious experience for me." He traced the side of her face with a finger. "An experience I feel certain your dear father would wish to have legitimized in church as soon as possible." He kissed her quickly on the mouth and sat up, swinging his legs over the side of the bed. "And that is why we must, unfortunately, get dressed. We need to tell your parents our good news, and then I need to procure a special license. I would like to be married as soon as possible. The longer we wait, the more obvious it becomes that we anticipated our vows."

"All right." She'd rather stay in bed with him all day, but she could see his point. And, in any event, he was already pulling on his pantaloons. She watched until his lovely muscled arse was covered and then climbed out of bed and reached for her shift. "Mama will be delighted that I'll finally be someone's wife. She had run out of men to throw at my head."

Marcus put on his shirt and then helped her lace up her stays. "I suppose she will have to put aside her match-making efforts for a while. Henry is rather too young for marriage."

Cat laughed. "I can't imagine Henry or Walter being at all amenable to Mama's marital machinations even when they are old enough to wed." She slipped on her dress. "You know, Jane and Anne will be delighted to hear we are getting married."

He lifted a brow as he buttoned his waistcoat. "Why is that?"

"Because they are the other two spinsters, of course, and now one of them will get to take my place here."

"Oh, Lord, that's right." He stepped over to look in the mirror as he tied his cravat. "Do you suppose they will insist I blindfold myself again when they draw lots?"

"I doubt it. They know you won't play favorites." She combed her hair and put it up. She could do it all by feel, but she should check to see how it looked. Rather than trying to peer around Marcus, she'd use the mirror in Miss Franklin's old room. "I don't know which of them I hope gets the house. Jane has to put up with Randolph, but Anne has a new stepmother to contend with."

She took a step toward the door—and almost stepped on Poppy.

"Ack!" She did a quick shuffle to reclaim her balance. "What are you doing?"

Actually it was clear what Poppy was doing—she was peering under the low cabinet just outside the bedroom door. The question was why.

An unpleasant thought struck. "I hope you're not playing with a mouse."

Marcus came over to watch Poppy bat at something with her paw. "Do you have a mouse problem?"

"Not that I know of, but I assumed that was because Poppy took care of things. Oh, look." Poppy had fished the thing—or, rather, things—out from under the furniture. Thankfully neither was a rodent.

"Here, let's see what you've got there," Marcus said. Poppy sat down and started licking her paws, letting him pick up her finds. "It's a bit of pottery and a key."

Cat examined the pottery shard. "That looks like a piece of the china dog I threw at you after Mary's wedding."

"You almost hit me in the head with that, you know."

"Yes. I'm sorry. I was angry about your interlude in the bushes with that London girl."

"Miss Rathbone? Good God!" Marcus shook his head. "Not that I'll ever consort with another woman, but if you ever suspect I am doing so, please just ask."

"Don't worry. I don't usually lose my temper like that." She kissed his cheek as she took the key from him and turned it over. "Hmm. I *thought* that knickknack felt heavier than it should have. This must have been inside. What do you suppose it unlocks?"

"I have no idea." From the tone of Marcus's voice, it was clear he also had no interest in finding out. "Let's go see your parents. The key has been here for years. It'll still be here when you get back."

"Don't you have even a shred of curiosity?"

"Not when I'm eager to make arrangements for my wedding." He grinned. "I'm going to try to be noble and not visit your bed again until you have my ring on your finger, but I know my limitations. The fewer days I have to test my willpower, the better."

She grinned back at him. "You don't have to wait. You can sneak in the back door."

"I am not sneaking into your bedchamber again, Catherine."

"But—"

"No." Marcus's jaw hardened. "I have to think of your reputation. Loves Bridge is a very small village with a very long memory. I don't wish to give the Misses Boltwood and their ilk anything more to gabble about."

"Oh, very well." She was beyond caring what the gossips said, but she knew a losing battle when she saw one. She started to put the key down.

Poppy hissed.

She looked down at the cat. The animal was staring at the key, tail twitching. "I think Poppy wants us to attend to this immediately."

"It certainly does look that way." Marcus drummed his

fingers against his leg and then shrugged. "I suppose I can't object. I *am* indebted to her."

"Why in the world are you indebted to Poppy?"

"The day of Mary's wedding, I was going to give up when I found your front door locked and go back to the party, but Poppy insisted I try the back door. She wouldn't take *no* for an answer, which I suspect is the case here as well." Marcus shook his head. "She's almost as unsettling as the curse. No offense meant, of course," he said, bowing slightly to Poppy.

Poppy stared at him and then turned and walked toward the storage room. She paused on the threshold to look back at them before disappearing inside.

"I'll wager that if we don't follow her, she'll hunt us down and bite our ankles," Marcus said. He stepped aside and swept his hand in the direction Poppy had taken. "After you, Miss Hutting."

"Coward."

He chuckled. "Guilty as charged."

When they entered the room, they found Poppy stretched out on top of the big cabinet.

"So, Poppy, do you want us to look inside that piece of furniture?" Cat asked.

"Merrow."

"Good heavens!" Cat looked at Marcus. "It's as if she understood what I said."

Marcus was staring at Isabelle's portrait where it was propped against the wall, but snorted at Cat's words and turned his attention to her. "Let's not get carried away. I know the concept of a curse is bizarre"—he glanced at the portrait again—"but the notion of an intelligent cat is—"

Poppy hissed, showing her teeth.

"Pardon me, you are quite correct. A gentleman never criticizes a lady." Marcus raised his brows and looked down at Cat. "It does seem that Poppy wants us to examine the cabinet."

"Yes." Whether Poppy was giving them a message or not, Cat was quite eager, now that she had a key in hand, to poke around that particular piece of furniture. She opened the cabinet door to reveal its many small drawers, each decorated with a different, intricate carving.

"Which one do you want to try first?" Marcus asked.

"This one, of course." Cat reached for the drawer adorned with the picture of a cat sitting on what looked very much like a windowsill.

Marcus laughed. "Poppy would approve."

Poppy sneezed and licked her hind leg.

The key slid easily into the keyhole, but turning it was rather more difficult.

"Oh, drat. I can't open it."

Poppy growled.

"Shall I try?" Marcus asked. "We don't want Poppy losing patience and pouncing on your head."

She laughed. "Very true."

Marcus's fingers were stronger, but it still took him a bit of effort before they heard the scrape of the lock opening.

Cat reached for the drawer—and stopped. Isabelle's curse had affected Marcus's life far more than hers. She glanced up at him. "You look inside."

He gazed back, his eyes suddenly guarded. Then he nodded and pulled the drawer open.

"There *is* something here." He reached in and lifted out an oilcloth packet. Inside were a small book and a letter.

"The letter is addressed to Isabelle." He turned it over. "The seal is unbroken." He glanced up at the portrait. "She must never have read it."

Cat looked up at the painting, too. For some odd reason, she felt Isabelle wanted them to find these things.

"And the book?" Cat laced her fingers together to keep from snatching it out of Marcus's hands.

He put the letter on top of the cabinet next to Poppy and opened the book. Cat crowded up against him so she could see, too.

"Oh! It's Isabelle's diary," she said.

"Yes, it does appear to be." Marcus started to close it.

She grabbed his arm. "We have to read what she wrote." She would go mad wondering about it if they didn't. "I think Isabelle wants us to." She inclined her head toward the portrait. "She looks happy about it, don't you think?"

Marcus frowned at her. "Don't let your imagination run away with you, Catherine. Besides, we don't have time. I wish to see your father and get that license today."

"Yes, of course." How could Marcus not be as curious as she was? "Let's just read the last entry, then. That should only take a minute." She shook his arm a little. "Please? It will eat at me until we do."

Marcus stared down at her. For a moment she was afraid he would refuse, but then he shrugged. "Very well."

He glanced up at Isabelle as if he was waiting for her to forbid this invasion, but then carefully turned the pages.

Isabelle had had rather large and flowing handwriting, ornamented with far too many flourishes until the last few entries. Then her writing became smaller and more cramped as if her spirit had shrunk as well.

"Here it is," Marcus said. "Well, it's not an entry, really. It's addressed to the third duke."

He read:

August 4, 1617

To the Duke of Hart:

"I shall never forgive you for promising me marriage and then wedding another. You have taken my heart, so I am taking your firstborn, the child who should be your heir.

Cat looked up at Marcus. "She couldn't have known the baby was a boy."

He shrugged. "Perhaps she really was a witch."

"Don't be ridiculous."

"Look, do you want me to read this or not?"

"Read it, of course. I promise to hold my tongue."

He raised his brows, but when she kept her lips pressed tightly together, he went back to the book.

> *You shall never see him. I hope no Duke of Hart ever sees his heir until one of them has the courage to marry for love and not for profit or influence or to please his bloody mama. You are a craven scoundrel, sirrah. May you suffer even one-tenth the pain you have caused me."*
>
> *Isabelle Dorring*

Marcus looked up at Isabelle as he finished and bowed. "I must agree with you, madam. My sincere apologies for my ancestor's behavior."

Cat tugged on Marcus's arm. "You know, Isabelle never says she's going to drown herself. She doesn't even curse anyone. Not really."

"Perhaps that's in the papers Wilkinson has."

"Perhaps." Cat felt a flicker of hope. "Or perhaps there isn't a curse."

Marcus frowned. "Explain that to my ancestors."

"Their deaths *could* be coincidences."

His right brow winged up in skepticism. "That's a lot of coincidences."

She wasn't going to waste precious time arguing with him now. "What does the letter say?"

"Let's see if Poppy will let us read it."

Poppy had put her paws on the paper, but she sat up when Marcus reached for it and graciously allowed him to take it. She watched as he broke the seal and opened the single sheet.

He gave a low whistle.

"What is it?" Cat pressed close to him again, and Marcus put his arm around her.

"It's from the third duke, and it's also dated August 4."

"What does it say?" Marcus was holding the paper too high for her to see. "Read it—or give it to me to read myself."

"Impatient, are you?"

"Yes!" How could the man joke at such a moment? They might be on the verge of learning something important. "Don't tease me."

"But it's so amusing to do so."

Cat actually stamped her foot.

Marcus laughed and looked back at the letter. "Gah! I can't imagine what Isabelle saw in my popinjay ancestor. The fellow's prose is so florid and full of hyperbole, it's painful."

"Then just give me the gist of it." This was not the time for Marcus to turn into a literary critic.

"Very well." His eyes scanned the lines and his brows shot up. "Apparently the duke's mother found Isabelle's letter about the baby—it had come to London while the duke was still away at a house party. His mother read it and, being very much against that match, decided to put a false notice in the papers. The duke hadn't married Lady Amanda at all. They weren't even betrothed." He looked up at Isabelle's portrait, sounding a bit dazed. "And the poor girl must never have known."

"Good heavens!" The effrontery of the duchess was breathtaking. "Can you do that—publish a lie?"

Marcus shrugged. "Some would say everything in the newspapers is a lie. However, in this case the duchess was apparently bosom friends with the publisher's wife so could print whatever she wanted." He looked back at the letter. "Good God, the duke writes that he is coming to Loves Bridge the next day to marry Isabelle."

"And when he arrived, everyone told him she'd drowned herself." Cat looked at the painting. Did Isabelle look surprised? Happy?

I really am losing my mind if I think a two hundred-year-old painting can hear what we're saying.

Marcus nodded. "He must have found this, realized Isabelle hadn't read it, and locked it and her diary away here." He folded the letter back up.

"So everything was his mother's fault." Cat wished she could travel back in time and offer the duchess a piece of her mind. "Well, and Isabelle's, too. If Isabelle had only waited to talk to the duke directly, none of this—the supposed curse, the Spinster House—would have happened. Isabelle would have married her duke and become the next duchess."

"Yes, but the duke does bear some responsibility. He should have been far more decisive from the beginning." Marcus shook his head, putting the letter and the diary back in the drawer. "This does change things. It will take me a while to fully comprehend what it means."

"I know what it means! It means you don't have to worry about the silly curse any longer. You'll live a long, wonderful life, and we'll have a family together. Oh, Marcus, aren't you happy?" She wanted to throw her arms around him and dance for joy.

But she didn't. Marcus did not look convinced. "Perhaps."

She tried to tamp down her enthusiasm. "And even if there is a curse, your mother thought you'd be the one to break it."

"Yes, she said as much to me."

What was the matter with him? "You're marrying me for love, aren't you?"

"Yes." He smiled then and touched her stomach above

the place their child was growing. "I suppose we'll know for certain about the curse in nine months' time, won't we?"

"Not in nine months' time—now." She did wrap her arms around him then. "You *must* decide to live as if the curse is broken. Don't let it shadow your happiness another moment."

"I'll try." He cupped her face. "Having you by my side"—he grinned—"and in my bed will certainly help."

He kissed her, and she tightened her hold on him. She would do anything she could to keep him from worrying about the future.

Kissing seemed to be working. His hands were beginning to wander in a very interesting direction—

"Merrow!"

Cat jerked back as Poppy yowled and sprang down from her perch on the cabinet.

"Oh, Poppy! You startled me."

"Yes. Rather poor timing, madam," Marcus said. "Miss Hutting and I were in the midst of a very interesting, er, discussion."

Poppy, looking not at all contrite, blinked at them and then ran out of the room and down the stairs.

Marcus laughed. "I guess it's just as well we were interrupted. We still need to seek out your parents so I can make an honest woman of you."

Cat laughed back at him. "And I an honest man of you."

"Yes, indeed." He offered her his arm. "I am very much looking forward to that."

She put her hand on his sleeve, and they followed Poppy down the stairs and out of the Spinster House.

Curious about the curse?
Keep reading for an excerpt from

HOW TO MANAGE A MARQUESS,

the next book in the
Spinster House Series.

And don't miss

IN THE SPINSTER'S BED

to learn all about the exploits of
Miss Franklin and Mr. Wattles.
Available now from Zebra eBooks!

Nathaniel, Marquess of Haywood, strode across the road from Cupid's Inn, where he'd left his horse, to the Loves Bridge village green, all the while arguing with himself.

Slow down. You don't want to attract attention.

But Marcus is in danger.

You don't know that. And you can't burst into the vicarage in a panic. Think of how odd it would look and how angry Marcus would be.

Oh, hell.

He stopped and took a deep breath. He was overreacting. This was Loves Bridge, not London. Miss Hutting, the woman who he feared wished to trap Marcus into marriage, was a vicar's daughter, not a conniving Society chit. Marcus had said she wanted to be the next Spinster House spinster, not the next Duchess of Hart.

But apparently everyone thought Miss Hutting would make a splendid duchess. Worse, they seemed to think Marcus was attracted to the girl.

He started walking again.

He'd just finished an excellent meal—he and Alex, the Earl of Evans, had been congratulating each other on avoiding the dinner at the vicarage—when he'd happened to hear Marcus's steward talking to Mr. Dunly, the steward's assistant and Miss Hutting's sister's betrothed. That's how he'd learned of the gossip.

And when he'd shared it with Alex, Alex hadn't been surprised. He'd known about it and hadn't told him, blast it. But then, Alex didn't think Marcus's life was in danger. He didn't believe in the curse.

Bloody hell! He should have been more suspicious when Marcus was willing to accept that dinner invitation. He'd just assumed his cousin—well, really far more like his brother as they'd grown up together—was safe here. Loves Bridge was the curse's birthplace. Surely the villagers would realize the Duke of Hart had to avoid marriage as long as he could.

Yet it appeared that none of the villagers believed in the curse either.

Why the hell didn't they? They and their ancestors had seen it play out. Marriage was a death sentence for a Duke of Hart. For two hundred years, none had lived to see his heir born.

And now that Marcus had passed his thirtieth birthday, it was getting harder and harder to keep him safe. Good God, he'd never expected Marcus to go out in Palmerson's gardens and end up in the bushes with that Miss Rathbone. He'd been so relieved when they'd left London for Loves Bridge. Stupidly, he'd let his guard down.

I hope I'm overreacting.

He should have made it a point to find out more about the vicar and his family. He—

"Good evening, Lord Haywood."

Damnation. He'd been so lost in thought, he hadn't noticed the two old ladies strolling toward him. They must be the Boltwood sisters. What wretched luck. Alex had told him—Alex always knew these things somehow—that they were the leading gossips of this little village.

He forced his lips into a smile and bowed slightly. "Good evening, ladies."

"Looking for some company, my lord?" The shorter woman batted her eyelashes at him.

Nate repressed a shudder. "No. My thoughts are company enough, madam."

The other old woman clicked her tongue. "A handsome young lord like you alone with your thoughts? That will never do."

Her sister nodded and then waggled her thin white eyebrows suggestively. "We saw Miss Davenport loitering around the Spinster House, looking very lonely."

Miss Davenport.

A very inappropriate part of him stirred at the name.

Miss Davenport had arrived at the inn the other day just as he and Alex were coming to have a pint while waiting for Marcus to finish posting the Spinster House vacancy notices—with Miss Hutting, as he later discovered.

But Miss Davenport—Zeus! She'd looked like an angel, the sun touching her smooth, honey-blonde hair, making it glow. Her eyes were as blue as a lake on a cloudless summer day. He'd looked down into them as he'd opened the door for her and felt himself being pulled deeper and deeper . . .

He frowned. He'd seen dark currents swirling below her polite expression and had a sudden, bizarre urge to ask what was troubling her. It was quite unlike him. He'd even inhaled to speak, but her clean, sweet scent had gone straight to his, er, head and caused all rational thought to evaporate.

Thank God Alex had spoken. She'd looked away, and the odd connection he'd felt with her had broken.

And it would stay broken. I am not in the market for a wife.

Oh, blast. He'd let his mind wander a bit too long. The Misses Boltwood were now snickering and nudging each other.

He sniffed in his best marquess manner and looked down his nose at them. "I'm quite certain Miss Davenport would not welcome my intrusion into her solitude, ladies. If you saw her by the Spinster House, she might well be entertaining hopes of being the next Spinster House spinster." Marcus had told him the woman was one of the three ladies—along with Miss Hutting and a Miss Wilkinson—vying for that position, though Miss Davenport might not care for him sharing that detail with the queens of the local gossips.

Miss Davenport a spinster? What a waste of—

The woman's matrimonial plans—or lack thereof—were none of his concern.

"The Spinster House!" The shorter of the Misses Boltwood curled her lip and snorted. "I can't imagine what Isabelle Dorring was thinking when she established that place. Spinsterhood is an unnatural state."

The other Miss Boltwood nodded. "A woman needs a man to protect her and give her children."

Her sister elbowed her, waggling her eyebrows again. "And keep her warm at night."

Since both ladies looked to have reached their sixth or seventh decade without nabbing a husband for themselves, their enthusiasm for the activities of the marriage bed was more than a little alarming.

"As you must know," Nate said, "Miss Dorring had good reason to distrust men. It's not surprising she would wish to offer other women a way to live comfortably without the need to marry." Miss Dorring had been very badly served by the third Duke of Hart. The man had got her with child and then wed another. And so the woman had cursed Marcus's line.

Familiar worry knotted Nate's gut again. Was Marcus

safe? Surely nothing terrible could happen at the vicar's dinner table.

The taller Miss Boltwood shrugged and flicked her fingers at him. "Bah. From all accounts, Isabelle knew what she was about. Her mistake was letting the duke into her bed before she'd got him to the altar."

"Though you must admit, Gertrude, that if that duke looked anything like this duke, poor Isabelle can be forgiven for getting her priorities confused." The shorter Miss Boltwood's lips curved in what could only be considered a lascivious fashion. "Have you seen the man's calves? His shoulders?"

These elderly ladies can't *be lusting after Marcus.*

The thought was too horrifying to contemplate.

"I'm not blind, am I, Cordelia? And what about his—"

"I'm afraid I must continue on my way, ladies." It might be rude to interrupt the women, but some things could never be unheard.

"Oh, yes, of course." Miss Gertrude winked. "Here we are, keeping you cooling your heels when you must be anxious to meet Miss Davenport."

"I am not meeting Miss Davenport."

Unfortunately.

No! Where the hell had that thought come from? There was nothing unfortunate about it. He had no time for nor interest in a marriageable woman.

Why not?

Because I have to keep Marcus safe. There would be time enough to marry later, after Marcus—

No. I can't think about that.

"You aren't the duke, my lord," Miss Cordelia said. "You don't have to worry about the silly curse."

Miss Gertrude nodded. "And Miss Davenport is a comely armful in need of a husband."

Very *comely* . . .

She could be the most beautiful woman in the world, but she was not for him.

"And I'm certain some estimable man will realize that." He bowed again. "If you will excuse me?"

He didn't wait for their permission. He wanted to get out of earshot as quickly as possible.

He wasn't quick enough.

"The marquess has an impressive set of shoulders, too, Gertrude."

"Yes, indeed. Miss Davenport is a very lucky woman."

He resisted the urge to turn and shout back at them that he had no interest in Miss Davenport.

Which would be a lie.

But he could have no interest in the girl. What he had— must have—was an immediate interest in Marcus's safety.

He strode—

No. Slow down. Don't be obvious. Marcus will be angry if he thinks I'm spying on him.

And he wasn't spying, precisely. He was merely keeping a watchful eye out.

He strolled toward the vicarage, which just happened to be directly across from the Spinster House. Was Miss Davenport still there? He didn't wish to encourage any gossip, but surely it wouldn't be remarkable to engage the woman in conversation if he encountered her. Actually, it would be an excellent thing to do. That way he could watch for Marcus without being obvious about it.

Ah, Miss Davenport *was* still there, dressed in a blue gown that he'd wager was the same shade as her eyes. A matching blue bonnet covered her lovely blonde hair. She was slender, though not too slender, and just the right height. If he held her in his arms, her head would come up to his—

Bloody hell! I'm not holding the girl in my arms.

He jerked his eyes away from her—an action that was far

harder than it should have been—to look toward the vicarage. What luck! Marcus was just leaving. Miss Hutting was with him, but in a moment the girl would—

Good God!

He stopped and blinked to clear his vision. No, his eyes had not deceived him. Miss Hutting had just pulled Marcus into a concealing clump of bushes.

Hadn't Marcus learned *anything* from the disaster with Miss Rathbone?

It was the blasted curse. Marcus wouldn't do anything so cabbage-headed if he was in his right mind. But what could Nate do to save him? He couldn't very well "accidently" barge into those bushes.

He glanced back at Miss Davenport. Oh hell, she was staring, too. If she told anyone what she saw—

His blood ran cold. If those gossipy Boltwood sisters got wind of this, Marcus would be hard-pressed to avoid parson's mousetrap, particularly as Miss Hutting's father was the parson.

Well, this was something he *could* attend to. He'd have a word with Miss Davenport. Surely he could persuade her to keep mum.

He strode quickly toward the woman.

Miss Anne Davenport, baron's daughter, looked at the Spinster House. It wasn't a remarkable edifice. In fact, the place looked like all the other village houses—two stories, thatched roof, of average size. It was much smaller than Davenport Hall, the comfortable house she shared with her father.

And would all too soon share with a stepmother and stepbrothers.

Oh, God!

She forced herself to breathe deeply and finally the suffocating feeling passed.

The Spinster House would be spacious for a woman living alone.

She'd not given the place much thought before. She'd been only six when Miss Franklin, the current—no, the *former*—spinster had moved in twenty years ago. Miss Franklin had been very young at the time. Everyone expected her to be the Spinster House spinster for forty or fifty or even sixty years, if she enjoyed good health. So when Papa had taken up with Mrs. Eaton, Anne hadn't thought the house was a solution to her impending problem.

But then just days ago, to the surprise and shock of the entire village, Miss Franklin had run off with Mr. Wattles, the music teacher, who turned out to be the son of the Duke of Benton and was now, with his father's passing, the duke himself. Even the Boltwood sisters hadn't sniffed out *that* story, and they were almost as accomplished at ferreting out secrets as Lady Dunlee, London's premier gabble grinder.

And then the Duke of Hart had come to Loves Bridge, as he was required to do whenever the Spinster House fell vacant. Anne had had to pinch herself to prove she wasn't dreaming when he'd interrupted their village fair meeting to post the notice announcing the Spinster House opening. The Almighty—or possibly Isabelle Dorring—had answered her prayers.

But her friends Jane Wilkinson and Catherine Hutting wanted to live in the Spinster House, too.

Yes, but her need was greater.

Melancholy washed over Anne. She bit her lip hard. Her mother had died almost ten years ago. She should be over her loss by now. And she was. The searing pain and the emptiness she'd thought would swallow her from the inside out were gone, at least most of the time. But there were still moments when she missed her mother dreadfully. Times she wanted to share something that had happened or ask her advice.

Like now.

How can Papa wish to marry Mrs. Eaton? She's a year younger than I am.

But Mrs. Eaton was also a widow with two young sons. She could give her father an heir.

Her stomach twisted. The notion was disgusting. Obscene.

It was the way of the *ton*.

But it wasn't the way of Loves Bridge. Surely the vicar would never behave in such a manner if he were widowed.

Of course, he already had a number of sons.

Anne glanced over at the vicarage—

Good God!

She shook her head and blinked, but she hadn't imagined the scene. Cat was darting into the trysting bushes and hauling the Duke of Hart in after her.

What should I do? Run for the vicar? No. Cat could be ravaged before he arrived. I'll have to save her myself. Surely together we can subdue the man. He might be stronger, but Cat and I are strong, too. The odds would be in our favor. I'll just—

Wait a moment.

Cat had pulled the *duke* into the bushes, not the other way round.

Perhaps it was the duke who was in need of rescue.

But Cat wants to be the next Spinster House spinster. Why would she go into the trysting bushes with a man?

Anne stared at the bushes. It had been several minutes, and neither Cat nor the duke had emerged. The branches weren't thrashing about. Clearly no one was struggling to get free.

Which could only mean they were doing something other than fighting in there.

Heavens! There was only one reason a couple went into the trysting bushes, and it wasn't to discuss the weather.

If word gets out, Cat's reputation will be ruined. The duke will have to marry her.

Anne chewed on her lip.

If the duke marries Cat, she can't be the next Spinster House spinster. The choice will be between just Jane and me.

Excitement bubbled up in her chest.

She tried to push it back down. Cat and Jane were her closest friends. She'd known them for as long as she could remember. They'd shared confidences, cried on each other's shoulders. Hadn't Cat and Jane comforted her just the other day when she'd told them the sorry tale of Papa and Mrs. Eaton?

But Cat had definitely been the one forcing the duke into the shrubbery. She must have changed her mind about a life of spinsterhood.

Of course she had. The Duke of Hart was nothing like Mr. Barker, the stodgy farmer Cat's mother had been throwing at her head these last few years. His Grace was handsome and wealthy. *And* he didn't have an annoying mother living with him. If Cat married him, she'd have time and room to write the novels she'd always wanted to write. And if there really was a curse hanging over his head, she'd be a wealthy widow before long.

I'd be doing her a favor in spreading the tale.

It wouldn't take much. Just a word in one of the Bolt-wood sisters' ears and the story—likely a much embroidered version of the story—would be all over the village in an hour or two.

The Spinster House should go to a true spinster, not a fallen woman. . . .

"Miss Davenport."

"Ack!" She jumped several inches above the walkway. Dear God, the Marquess of Haywood was at her elbow.

Her heart gave an odd little jump as well.

She'd met many men of the *ton*—she'd had a Season and been dragged to endless house parties—but she'd never met a gentleman like Lord Haywood. With the strong planes of his face, his straight nose and thin, sculpted lips, he could be a Greek statue come to life. And his warm, hazel eyes seemed to look straight into her soul. When he'd opened the door for her at the inn the other day, she'd had to curl her fingers into fists to keep from brushing back the lock of brown hair that fell over his brow.

He'd been so serious, so unlike his friend, Lord Evans. Lord Evans had laughed and flirted, but when Lord Haywood had spoken—just a few polite words—odd tendrils of warmth had curled low in her belly. Even now, though his tone had been rather harsh, his voice sent excitement fluttering through her.

"I didn't see you approach, my lord." *My voice doesn't sound as breathless as I think, does it?*

If it did, the man didn't notice. Or maybe he did and it annoyed him. His brows slanted down farther.

"You didn't see me because your attention was elsewhere."

He sounded disapproving. *She* wasn't the one engaged in scandalous behavior. In fact, now that she thought more about it, she remembered hearing the Boltwoods gossiping about the duke at the fair planning meeting.

"Indeed, it was. I was quite surprised—shocked, really—to see His Grace bringing his London tricks to Loves Bridge, exploring the vegetation with a marriageable female."

I should definitely spread the story. The man can't be allowed to continue to prey on young women.

Lord Haywood's mouth flattened into a hard, thin line and his aristocratic nostrils flared. "Miss—"

"*Merrow.*"

His frown moved from her to the large black, white, and orange cat who'd appeared at their feet. "What the—" He pressed his lips together, clearly swallowing some less-than-polite comment. "Go along, cat."

The cat sat down on the walk and stared at him.

"That's Poppy," Anne said to fill the oddly strained silence. "She lives in the Spinster House."

The marquess glared at her.

What would Mama make of him?

A thread of sadness tightened round her heart. She would never know.

The marquess turned his glare back to Poppy. "Now what's the matter with the animal?"

"What do you-oh." Poppy *was* behaving rather strangely. Her back was arched, hair standing on end, and she was hissing. But it wasn't Cat's scandalous behavior in the bushes that she was objecting to. No, Poppy was looking down the walk toward the inn.

"I think the Misses Boltwood are coming this way," Anne said.

Poppy must agree. She yowled and darted toward the Spinster House.

"Blo—" Lord Haywood caught himself. "Blast. I just encountered them headed in the other direction."

"Well, I *suppose* it might be another set of elderly ladies. They are still too far off for me to see clearly. In a—what are you doing?"

The marquess had grabbed her hand and was tugging on it, trying to get her to go off in the direction Poppy had taken.

"I'm hauling you out of harm's way. Perhaps they haven't noticed us yet."

Sadly a part of her wanted to go with him, but the more sensible part urged her to dig in her heels. Vanishing into the bushes with a man was bad, but going inside an empty house—with bedrooms and beds!—was far worse. "Lord Haywood, the Spinster House is locked."

"I know that. I'm following the cat into the garden."

She'd just come from the garden. It made the trysting bushes look like a few small shrubs. "The garden is completely overgrown."

"Precisely. The vegetation should hide us nicely." He pulled on her hand again. "Hurry along, will you? Do you *want* those gossips to find us together?"

An unmarried man and woman conversing in public on a village road wasn't at all remarkable, but with this man it suddenly seemed scandalous. And it was true the Boltwood sisters could weave a tale that made sitting in Sunday services sound sinful.

All right. If she were being completely honest with herself, the thought of going into the wild Spinster House garden with Lord Haywood was surprisingly thrilling. Silly. He looked like he was more likely to throttle her than kiss her. . . .

He won't really throttle me, will he?

Of course not. She stopped resisting and let him pull her into the shadowy leafage. She would have heard if the *ton* considered the marquess dangerous. All anyone ever said of him was that he'd dedicated himself to keeping his cousin single and thus safe from Isabelle Dorring's curse.

Oh.

Perhaps she shouldn't mention she was hoping to force the duke to marry Cat.